Heart of STEELE

Successful Chicago corporate lawyer Steeleman Krueger returns to his small-town roots in central Illinois with one objective – to crash his half-brother Conn's wedding and spoil his snooty mother's grand plans. But when Steele meets his brother's intended bride, he finds the opposite of what he expects. Instead of a shallow gold-digger, Rebecca Sedder is a shy and quiet young lady, totally unsuited for his slob of a brother. Now Steele's got a new goal, to find out why sweet and hard-working Becca would agree on such short notice to marry his brother. The more she refuses to tell him, the more curious he gets, and the more attracted to her he becomes. He knows his conniving mother is behind everything, and he's as eager to find out why as he is to find out the truth of his past his mother has deliberately withheld from him his whole life.

Rebecca Sedder is between a rock and a hard place. Forced to wed a man she despises to save the reputation of one she cares deeply for, she can't breathe a word of the truth to anyone, or the deal is off. Conner Morse's older half-brother Steeleman Krueger shows up in town in the nick of time and promises to help Becca out of her predicament. She wants to jump at his offer and tell him the truth about everything, but she can't, or someone dear to her will suffer the consequences. She doesn't want to get involved in the family feud involving Steele and his mother, but she's already smack-dab in the middle and can't escape. No matter what Steele says, she knows she has to go through with marrying his brother. But Steele has another idea. The wedding can go on as planned, with one little change – he'll replace his brother as the groom!

Heart of
STEELE

by

Kessa Stranberg

Licensed and Produced through
Penumbra Publishing
www.PenumbraPublishing.com

PRINT EDITION
Printed in USA

ISBN/EAN-13: 978-1-935563-15-0
Copyright 2009 by Kessa Stranberg

Also available in ebook ISBN/EAN-13: 978-1-935563-14-3

~AUTHOR FOREWORD~

In my estimation, one of the hardest things a person must do is forgive someone else for a perceived wrong. Reconciliation, especially after terrible events or an unhappy past, is difficult and sometimes impossible to accomplish. But a heart hardened by hatred or soured with regret cannot fully love, and forgiveness must clear the way before love can take residence.

On the surface, this story, the first I ever completed, may seem like a typical romance, but it is also about forgiveness and how it affects one's ability to love. I hope you enjoy it and always find a way to forgive others, even when they seem not to deserve it.

Our greatest gift as human beings is the ability to love ... and to forgive.

Kessa Stranberg

Heart

of

STEELE

by

Kessa Stranberg

CHAPTER 1

"*W*ell, I'll be damned."

Propping his elbows on the arms of his burgundy leather chair, Steeleman Krueger rested his fingertips in a spire and studied the phone. He had fielded quite a few awkward calls from women who were more than acquaintances and not exactly friends, but none of those exchanges could compare in shock value to the unsettling conversation he'd just had with his mother.

"I'll be damned!" he said again, chuckling as he spun his chair and glanced out the window of his thirty-fifth floor Chicago office. "She actually asked for my help." He chuckled wickedly. "Today must be that proverbial 'cold day in hell.'"

He turned back to his desk and eyed the phone again. He hadn't spoken to Queen Lila since Aunt Sybil's funeral nearly four years ago, and their brief meeting then had been anything but amicable. Now, out of the blue, she'd invited him 'home,' as if he traveled from Chicago to Fenton to see her and the rest of 'the family' on a regular basis.

For a change, she'd been almost chatty, despite her ingrained arctic tone. She glossed over details of the dairy accident, then made a lot of noise about profit projections for the family's newly combined enterprise corporation. He saw the pitch coming but was still surprised when she encouraged him to invest in it. This was the first time he could remember her wanting him to participate in anything involving the rest of her family. The key was his trust fund. Of course he'd have to voluntarily revoke his controlling interest in the trust to access the money.

He leaned back in his chair and smirked, thinking what favorite clichés Uncle Charlie would likely offer up if the sweet old man were around to witness this odd development. He could almost hear the crusty sage saying, "Your slitherin' momma must think you just fell off the turnip truck, son. I tell ya, something fishy's goin' on. She's up to no good. Any fool knows a she-leopard don't change her spots. She'll always be a bad apple. I wouldn't trust her any further than I could throw her."

Uncle Charlie was no longer around to guide him, but Steele still relied on the elderly man's country-simple axioms. Nevertheless, he couldn't help being intrigued when his mother mentioned the special affair planned for next weekend. When he prodded for more details, she ended the conversation, repeating that she'd like him to attend.

Steele ran a hand over his mouth. If his mother had any hope of luring him back to Fenton after all this time, she'd succeeded. His little brother was getting married, and Steele couldn't help wondering what poor woman he'd managed to knock up. He wouldn't miss this show for anything.

He glanced past the open blinds on his glass door, to the central office beyond. Irene leaned over one of the lateral cherry file cabinets, busily rifling through the middle drawer. He hit the intercom button on his phone. "Has Nate come back to the office yet?"

Irene looked around, then marched into his office and closed the door. "What's going on, Steele?"

He shrugged. "Why would you assume something's going on, just because I want to talk to one of the senior partners?"

She rested her manicured hands on her narrow, nearly nonexistent hips clad in a teal silk suit. "You're making a big fuss about not telling me why. So what's this about – the phone call from that woman who wouldn't give her name?"

He sighed. He couldn't pull anything over on Irene Levinstraud, Hastings, Fehrnman & Reinhold's fifty-something office Nazi and mother superior. She seemed to think it was part of her job description to screen all his calls and find out his secrets before he did. Whenever an unidentified women demanded to speak with him, Irene was right there, insisting on knowing which client's wife wanted his attention. She'd quickly figured out how he spent much if his after-hours time, and she never skimped on advice about it. Right now was no different. "I'm telling you, Steele," she warned, shaking a finger at him. "if you don't put a stop to 'entertaining' those women, it's going to catch up to you in a bad way."

He grimaced. "I told you, I simply escort them when their husbands are unavailable. So far, no one has objected. Anyway, I haven't 'entertained' anyone since Thanksgiving, so it's no longer a problem."

"Fine," she grumbled, adjusting the half-lens glasses perched on her thin nose. "I just don't want you jeopardizing the firm's reputation, not to mention your career, all for–"

"Relax. It's not a big deal and never was."

She elevated her head of perfectly coiffed short brown dyed hair. "Then why aren't you looking for a suitable, marriageable, young lady to occupy your free time? You've been here six years, and it's high time you settled down."

Steele leaned back in his chair and sighed. "Would it do me any good to tell you to mind your own business?"

"Of course not."

He laughed and leaned forward. He couldn't fault Irene. In her own way, she meant well. She kept him on track and made his work run smoothly. It had taken him quite a while to warm up to her, but when he finally realized what a marshmallow she was on the inside, their relationship blossomed into a surrogate mother-son thing. Irene might have everyone else at the firm toeing the line, but Steele knew deep down she was a softy, a good woman who loved her family and doted on her grandchildren.

She was one of the few people he trusted enough to confide the full story about his unsavory past. She understood what a conniver his mother was, and had warned him to stay away from her and her little fiefdom back in Fenton. But he needed no warnings. He already knew better than to tangle with his mother. Except ... this time he couldn't resist. This time he might have a chance of finally getting what he wanted.

He glanced down at some papers on his desk and jogged

them in an officious manner. "I need to clear my schedule for the next couple weeks, and I want to get Nate's approval before I leave."

"And where do you think you're rushing off to on such short notice?"

He didn't face Irene. "My mother's invited me home for a family event scheduled for next weekend. I want to arrive earlier than she expects, to check out a few things."

When Irene failed to respond, Steele looked up and found her frowning at him. "So," she snarled. "It was your mother on the phone. Tell me why, after the low-down, dirty way that so-called family of yours has treated you, would you even consider going back to Fenton to attend some fancy occasion she's planned? And if it's so important, why would she wait until now to invite you? Obviously that was an afterthought."

Steele rose to his full six-foot-three-inch height and towered over Irene, but she didn't back down as she insisted, "Well? What possible reason would you have for wanting to see any of them again?"

"To find out if—" He pressed his lips together and turned to look out the window behind him. Chicago's glass, steel, and concrete skyline looked just as bleak in early summer as it did in mid-winter. The view reflected how he felt when anticipating another meeting with his family. "My mother's cooking up some kind of deal. She wants something from me, or she wouldn't have bothered to contact me. For the first time in my life, I might actually have some bargaining leverage with her. I don't want to pass up the opportunity to ... to get information from her."

"Steele," Irene said softly behind him, "if your mother were ever going to reveal the identity of your real father, she would have done it a long time ago."

He turned and gripped the back of his chair. "Tell Nate I had a family emergency. I'll call him when I get to Fenton. I need to pack, arrange for lodging, and try to get out of here before rush hour."

"Don't even think of leaving before you finish the changes

to the Carson-Dunlevey contract." Irene skewered him with a sympathetic scowl.

Steele pushed his chair against his desk. "Right. I'll have it to you within the hour." At the moment, the Carson-Dunlevey contract was the least of his worries.

He circled around his desk. Grabbing his charcoal jacket from the cherry coat rack, he slipped it on and straightened it with military precision. When he reached for the door, Irene touched his sleeve. "Be careful, Steele. You've been away from them for a long time, and you've done well without them. I'd hate to see them hurt you again."

He managed a smile. "Don't worry. I'm a big boy now, and I can take care of myself. The Ogre wouldn't dare try to knock me around anymore, and I don't give a damn about anyone in that grungy little one-horse town, so there's nothing they can do to me. I'm going back to take one last look, and then I'm out of there, for good."

CHAPTER 2

*B*ecca took a deep breath and leaned over the bathroom sink to peer at her reflection in the medicine cabinet mirror. Her hand shook so much she had trouble holding her tube of concealer to smooth a layer over the greenish tinge on her left cheek.

She didn't want to get ready and go with him. She didn't want to have dinner with Conner Morse and his parents. She didn't want to look at his beady eyes or hear his nasty, cackling laughter ever again. But she had no choice.

Her parents knew something was wrong. In the few weeks since she'd begun seeing Conn, they had each expressed their disapproval. Her mother had taken it as a personal insult and called her stupid and irresponsible. Her father had tried to reason with her and show her the error in her judgment. But she'd dismissed their arguments. She couldn't allow them to interfere. They didn't understand the situation, and she wasn't at liberty to explain. She *had* to do this.

She touched a fingertip to her cheekbone and winced. The spot where Conn had backhanded her three nights ago still ached. She was lucky all he'd done was hit her and spout some curses. She could have suffered a lot more than a few bruises. It galled her to play the silent victim, but speaking out would only make things worse – for everyone, not just her.

When Lila Morse had seen what her son had done to her face, she made no apology, but extracted a vague assurance from him that it wouldn't happen again. Becca knew better than to think Mrs. Morse would keep Conn under control. And she knew better than to trust Conn to treat her right.

Biting her lower lip to fight off tears, she sucked in a deep breath and applied a coat of mauve color to her mouth. As she eyed her handiwork in the mirror, she didn't recognize the startled, angry stranger staring at her. Golden-brown eyes dulled with despair showed dark circles underneath and seemed to have sunk into her head. Her slender, heart-shaped face appeared pale and haggard. It was easy to visualize a ghost's skull framed by shoulder-length sable hair once thick and luxurious but now limp and lackluster. This was a preview of the horror in store for her, now that Conn Morse had entered her life.

In less than two weeks she would cease to be Rebecca Jean Sedder, an individual with free will. Once she became Mrs. Conner Lee Morse, she would be just another of the many acquisitions of the Morse family. She would be Conn's personal property to abuse as he pleased. And she could do nothing to prevent it – not if she wanted to keep her father out of jail. With that fate facing her, she knew she was better off dead.

"Hurry up, Reba Jean!" Conn's voice boomed as he banged on the bathroom door. Startled, Becca dropped her tube of lipstick in the sink. She hated being called Reba Jean, and Conn knew it. No one ever called her that. No one but him.

"We're having dinner with Mom and Dad, not going to some beauty contest. So stop worrying how you look, like anybody really gives a damn." She heard him pop a beer tab and snicker.

"Becca's not going anywhere with you." Becca froze at the sound of her father's voice near the door. "I want you out of my house right now, and take that alcohol with you."

"Back off, old man. You're just a washed up boozehound. Where to you get off preaching to me about drinking?"

Becca heard Conn's nasty chuckle and knew her father, a recovering alcoholic, wouldn't handle the insult well. She couldn't have her father trying to go up against a bully like Conn, especially while wearing a back brace after the accident at the dairy.

She grabbed her makeup from the sink counter and stuffed it in her patchwork denim handbag. "I'm ready," she blurted as

7

she swung the door open and wedged herself between Conn and her father in the narrow hallway. "I just need to get something from by bedroom. Conn, why don't you wait for me in the car?" *And leave my dad alone! Your family's done enough harm to mine!*

"I'm ain't waiting outside, Reba Jean!" Conn roared loud enough for the whole neighborhood to hear. "And whatever you were gonna get in your room, forget it. My Mom's expecting you, and you damn well better get your butt in gear, if you know what's good for you." The bathroom door shuddered under the impact of his fist. "Now come on!"

"You lay another hand on my daughter, you stupid son-of-a-b—"

"Dad," Becca cautioned.

"Becca, I know you didn't run into a door. He hit you. If he doesn't leave right now, I'll call the police and—"

"Dad, don't. Conn is—"

"Go ahead," Conn snarled. "Call the cops on me, old man, and see what happens." He flicked Becca a warning glare, and she shut her mouth. For the sake of her family, she couldn't afford to anger his mother by involving the authorities.

She eyed Conn and felt sick at the sight of his puffy gray eyes, thin, scraggly dark brown hair, and splotched, clammy complexion. His uni-brow and coarse features gave him a permanent ill-tempered frown. His beer belly stuck out over too-tight tan trousers, and his pale yellow shirt stretched across his middle like a blister. At twenty-seven, he was as mean as a grizzly and grossly out of shape, presenting a depressing picture of what too much booze and too little responsibility could do to a man. Considering the money his mother threw around to establish her social standing, Becca wondered why she didn't insist Conn take more pride in his appearance.

"Becca," her father said, "this is killing your mother and me. We can't understand what you—"

"It's all right, Dad. I know what I'm doing. Just ... you have to trust me." Unable to look her father in the eyes, she stared

8

down at the faded powder blue carpet. "Please, stay out of it. Okay? Please."

"Yeah, old man. Butt out." Conn grabbed Becca by the arm. "What I do with your daughter ain't none of your business. And if you don't keep your nose out of it, you'll never see your little Reba Jean again. 'Cause I won't let her step foot in this dump once we're married." He squeezed her arm harder when he snarled the word 'married.' She winced and jerked away from him.

"Married! Becca! What—"

"Please, Dad. We'll talk about it later. *Please.*"

"Becca!"

Her father looked so frail, bent over with a cane in his hand as he tried to support his weight without straining his back. In the last month, his dark hair seemed to have turned almost totally gray. Tears clouded her eyes, and she hurried over to him. She knew what she had to do, but she blocked the situation from her mind as she gave him a quick kiss on the cheek. "Everything will be okay. Tell Mom not to wait up."

Her father narrowed his dark eyes. "Your mother gets off work at eleven. It won't take you that long to eat dinner." He sighed and raked a hand through his hair. "I know I can't keep you from doing what you're bound to do, but I'm begging you not to even consider marriage to that ... that—"

Conn belched and pushed Becca aside. "Mommy Dearest said we're getting married, so that's what we're gonna do, old man. Nobody argues with her once she's got her mind made up."

Tossing his beer can at the bathroom wastebasket, he missed by a wide margin and turned away as the can bounced off the stool and rolled to the tub. "What are you looking at?" he growled, scowling at Becca.

"Nothing." She cast her gaze down and skirted around her father. "Can we go now? I wouldn't want to keep your mother's catered dinner waiting."

When she glanced back at her father, he shook his head and averted his eyes, as if ashamed to look at her. She swallowed back her tears. She wanted to tell him what was going on, but she knew she couldn't. He'd do something to interfere, and for his own good she couldn't let him jeopardize the situation. "I know I owe you and Mom an explanation, but I can't right now. Just trust me, Dad. Please."

"Come on!" Conn yelled, grabbing her arm with painful force and dragging her behind him.

She lurched and stumbled backward. Righting herself, she yanked her arm from his grasp. "Keep your hands off me!"

"Only till after next Saturday." He leered, flashing his large yellowish teeth. "Then you're all mine."

"Becca!" her father called after her.

She glanced over her shoulder as his thin, drawn face turned livid. "I've got everything under control," she lied. "There's nothing to worry about. I promise."

Conn grunted and shoved her toward the front door. "Yeah, and I promise to take real good care of your little girl, Mr. Sedder. And next weekend, when I'm your son-in-law, you and me will have a good ol' time guzzling brewskies and trading BS on the front porch." He waved a hand in the air. "Later, old man."

* * * * *

Seated in Conn's red Mustang convertible, Becca kept silent until he pulled away from her house. Touching her bruised cheek, she rasped, "I asked you not to say anything about ... about the wedding until I had a chance to tell–"

"Well, when were you going to let everybody know? After we were already married a year or two? We're tying the knot next Saturday. Mom's already applied for the license and got the church reserved, but hardly anybody in town knows what's going on. You ain't told your family or anybody you work with." Conn smacked his steering wheel and glared at the road. "I ain't some hairball you're gonna sweep under a rug, Reba Jean. You're gonna be my wife, and you darn well better get used to the idea. Cuz that's what Mom wants."

10

Fuming, Becca crossed her arms and looked away. As Conn haphazardly guided the car down the street, a damp breeze whipped her hair about her face. Strands slapped and raked at her eyes, making them sting and tear up. She wiped her eyes, knowing her tears were due to more than just the turbulence from the top being down. She hated the idea of marrying Conn Morse. She hated *him*, a carbon-copy of his father, James Morse, in his early fifties, big and burly and vulture-ugly. He kept a fifth of whiskey tucked in his bottom desk drawer at the family's Ford and Chevy automall dealership. Willing to sleep with any woman but his own wife, he was the scourge of the town. And he had the embarrassing habit of patting his privates whenever he talked to customers in the dealership showroom. Becca looked at Conn and shook her head. *Like father, like son.*

The Morses were one of the wealthiest families in Fenton and owned several major sources of commerce in the area besides the dealership, including Greenvalley Dairy, one of the largest milk processing plants in the state. Counting the dealership, the dairy plant, the dairy farm Greenvalley Acres, and the trucking firm Greenvalley Transport, the Morses employed over two thousand rural workers. But Conn didn't care about any of that. Like his father, he pretended to sell cars at the dealership while devoting most of his energy to drinking and carousing. Rumors circulated about him taking advantage of underage girls, but he'd never been held accountable, probably due to his mother's formidable influence in Fenton and the county.

Slamming his car into a telephone pole when he was a junior in high school left him with glass cuts permanently riddling his acne-scarred face. He might have had passable looks before that senseless accident, but now he was just as ugly on the outside as he was on the inside. Considering his sketchy backseat reputation and the crowd he ran with, Becca could see why his mother decided it was time to secure him a wife and force him to settle down. Left on his own, all he'd come up with would be some gold-digging tramp hunting a meal ticket – someone unworthy of Lila Morse's stringent approval.

11

Massaging her brow, she tried once more to think of a way out of this mess, but couldn't. Lila Morse would see that their wedding took place as scheduled. Mrs. Morse always got her way, and with that 'evidence' hanging over her father, there wasn't a damn thing Becca could do to stop it.

Conn reached over and clenched her thigh with his big rough paw. He rubbed her leg with embarrassing familiarity until she knocked his hand aside and jerked her knee away. "Your mother told you to keep your hands to yourself. If you—"

"Only till after the wedding," he snarled. "Once we're married, I'll do whatever I want with you. And I only have to wait one more weekend."

Scowling, she smoothed her flowered cotton skirt to erase the disgusting sensation of his touch.

He eyed her and smirked. "If you weren't such a damn priss, Reba Jean, maybe we could have a little fun before the wedding. And you owe me, since you're the one that got us roped into this mess in the first place."

She glared at him. "I didn't get us into anything. It was you and your antics that made your mother intervene and force you to settle down."

"Yeah, but *you* made the deal with her." His face twisted with anger. "I was doing just fine before you came along. Now everything is all screwed up!" He hit his steering wheel again. "I don't *want* to get married!"

Becca stiffened. "Neither do I. At least, not to you."

"Then why'd you let the old hag talk you into it?"

"You know exactly why. Your mother made it clear what would happen if I didn't go through with this farce of a wedding."

He snorted. "Your old man's just a stumbling drunk. Always has been, and always will be. Anybody else would've let him take the blame whether he deserved it or not. He's—"

"I'm not just anybody else. I happened to believe him when he said he wasn't drinking on the job. And I'm not going to let him pay the penalty for something he didn't do. He was *not* responsible for Larry Carter's death. You know that, I know that, and your mother knows it most of all."

Eyeing the road ahead, Conn shook his head and smiled. "You sure are a piece of work, Reba Jean. You even got yourself believing your excuses. But we both know this ain't about your daddy. It's the money. How much was it dear old Mom offered to pay you to play housewife and mommy? Thirty-thousand?"

Becca bristled. "No amount of money in the world would convince me to marry you."

"Yeah? Well, you're doing it, ain't you? Thirty-thousand dollars is a tidy wad. How about I pay you a little on the side to give me a sample before we say 'I do?'" He reached behind as if he were about to pull his wallet out of his hip pocket. "Would twenty bucks loosen you up some?"

She turned away. "I wouldn't have to endure your gutless insults if you were man enough to stand up to your mother."

He grabbed her wrist and wrenched her arm painfully. "I'll show you I'm man enough!"

She jerked away from him. "All you have to do is say 'no,' Conn. That's all it takes. Tell your mother you're not going to marry me." Eyeing him with sudden eagerness, she urged, "There's still time. You could–"

He stomped on the accelerator and the tires screeched, sending the car fishtailing wildly down the street. As he approached a stop sign, he slammed on the brakes, and Becca's seat belt clenched her chest hard.

"You know the great Lila Morse," Conn bellowed, gripping his steering wheel as if he were trying to strangle it. "She doesn't let nobody say 'no' to her. And she doesn't give up on an idea once she gets it in her head. She picked you to be her daughter-in-law, and she ain't gonna accept nobody else. She already told me that." He stewed in silence as he guided the car out of the modest residential area toward downtown Fenton.

The setting sun grazed the tops of trees behind aged brick buildings lining the rain-dampened thoroughfare. In the fading pink light of the cloudy evening, Conn lit a cigarette and puffed in distraction. With his gaze riveted on the road, he frowned and

13

murmured, "You better not nag me after we're married, Reba Jean. I don't need no griping old lady. And, no matter what my Mom says about grandkids, I don't want no bunch of squalling brats making my life hell. You better not hatch any little monsters, or I swear I'll make you sorry you're alive."

"Believe me, you've already done that." Becca stared at Conn's sagging, bloated profile and paled at the possibility of their impending marriage producing a brood of youngsters in his image. The idea nauseated her. She gulped and turned away.

After a moment she made herself look back at the cigarette dangled from his slack lips. He didn't want to marry her any more than she wanted to marry him. Her only real hope of avoiding the nightmare of living with him was to ensure he wouldn't go along with the deal his mother had forced on her. "Isn't there any girl you know that you really like, Conn? Haven't you ever been in love? Surely there's someone you'd rather marry besides me."

He blew smoke at her. She coughed and turned away as he said, "How come *you* ain't never been in love, Reba Jean? You're twenty-six years old. Most girls your age already got an old man and a couple rug-rats running around. And not many of them are as good-looking as you. So how come you're still single? Huh?" He settled back in his seat with a self-satisfied grin. "Been waiting for 'Mr. Right,' ain't ya? Well, lucky for you, I just happened along with a big wad of money to light your fire."

Becca sneered. "For your information, Conn, thirty-thousand dollars is not a big wad of money. It's chicken feed compared to what you're used to spending on yourself in a year's time."

"Don't forget about my trust fund." His beady gray eyes glittered as he looked her up and down and added, "You ain't forgot. You probably can't think of anything else." He laughed and flicked ashes over the side of the car as he pulled away from downtown Fenton's one and only traffic light. "So, what are we gonna do, baby? Race to see who can spend it all first?"

Becca swiped a hand over her face. There was no reasoning with him. From the things his mother had said, she knew he couldn't discipline himself to stay within a budget. His quarterly trust fund distributions amounted to about fifteen thousand a year. Living rent-free at home with his parents, with careful spending habits, he should have been able to live comfortably. But he still depended on his mother's handouts disguised as paychecks from the dealership to supplement his very expensive hobby – wrecking cars.

When they married, he would be able to fully access his trust fund. But the way he blew money, in no time the trust would be gone, and then they'd be living on whatever Becca managed to bring home working at the bank, which wasn't much. Evidently he hadn't thought things through that far.

She sighed. There had to be a way to talk sense to him. Surely he wasn't that stupid. Well, maybe he was, but she wouldn't give up. "If you want what's coming to you, Conn, you'll have to do exactly what your mother tells you. You'll have to get married and settle down and behave yourself. And," she chided carefully, "your mother wants grandchildren. You'll have to do everything just the way she wants. Otherwise, your portion of the profit shares from your family's farm, the dealership, the dairy, and the trucking firm will stay locked away in trusteeship, and you'll have to make do with the quarterly distributions you're getting now. You won't be able to get your hot little hands on one additional red cent until you turn thirty. If your mother cuts off your allowance before then, you'll have to watch your spending. You won't have any other money to blow in the meantime."

He smacked his steering wheel again. "I show up at the dealership every day and do whatever the old bag wants. I *earn* that money! But every time I piss her off, she threatens to cut off my pay. She's been holding that over my head for years." He went quiet for a second then ended, "But no matter what she says, she can't make me turn into a card-carrying family man if I don't want to. Even after we're married, I ain't gonna let some dumb broad lead me around by the nose like *she* does my dad. I can wait her out. I only have two-and-a-half more years to go, then I'll be old enough to get my money. And to hell with her!"

Becca perked her brows. There was a chink in his armor and she aimed straight for it. *"Think*, Conn. Since your mother has threatened to cut off your allowance, you don't have the luxury of time on your side. You can either do as she says, or get a real job and work like the rest of us."

He huffed and blustered like a two-year-old throwing a tantrum. "I don't give a damn about the dealership, the dairy, or the money. She can shove it all where the sun don't shine!"

Becca glared at the overgrown child sitting beside her. No matter how cleverly Conn's mother schemed, she would never make him into a respectable adult. He would always be a selfish, evil little boy trapped inside an ugly man's body. And left on his own, he would never do what was right. Someone else would have to push him.

"It seems to me your mother is making you do exactly what she wants, regardless of what *you* want," Becca taunted. "The only way you're going to stop her is tell her you won't marry me. Find someone else totally unsuitable, that you know she'll despise, and elope right away. Then she won't have any reason to hold me to our deal, and maybe she'll let my father off the hook. That's the only way, Conn. You have to stand up to her."

He gave her a murderous look. "Yeah, that's just what you want, ain't it? I take the heat and you get away free. Well, I ain't gonna make it that easy for you to get rid of me." He looked her over from head to toe. "Maybe having you for my little wifey ain't gonna be as bad as I thought." Abruptly he turned the car and headed toward the edge of town.

Becca stiffened. "What are you doing?"

"Taking a detour." Conn grinned and flicked his burning cigarette out of the car.

Her heart seized as she glared at him. He seemed more than angry, almost sinister. She didn't know the cause – either the liquor he'd consumed, or his building resentment over the deal she'd been forced to accept from his mother. The last time he exercised his brute superiority and expressed his displeasure over their impending marriage, he hadn't bothered to find a secluded

16

place. He had simply slapped her right where she sat in the seat next to him as he drove to his mother's house. As she glared warily at him, she got a gut feeling this time he wasn't planning a repeat of his boorish display three nights ago, but something far more despicable.

The deserted blacktop led to Fenton's small airfield a few miles out of town, and connected to a state route further north. Becca wasn't sure what Conn had in mind and didn't want to find out. Attempting to remain calm, she hugged her purse and sweater in her lap and warned, "We're supposed to be at your parents' house in fifteen minutes, Conn. You know how your mother despises tardiness. We should–"

"Trust me," he growled, gunning the accelerator and whipping the car around an oncoming curve, "this ain't gonna take long. They don't call me 'The Minute-Man' for nothing."

She gripped the armrest and careened against the door. *What the hell is he planning?* "Conn–"

"Shut up, Reba Jean! Just shut the hell up! This is all your fault – yours and your daddy's. And I ain't gonna sit around anymore and let you treat me like crap. If I have to get married because of you, then I'm gonna enjoy myself. And you ain't gonna talk me out of it or scare me with threats. I don't care what my mother says, I ain't marrying no little piece I ain't taken for a test drive first."

He maneuvered around another curve, then slammed his foot on the brakes. The car skidded to a halt on the wet pavement near the soft dirt shoulder. Low-hanging trees dripped dew from the hard shower earlier that afternoon.

He turned on her. "You been prancing around with your nose stuck up in the air long enough. Now I'm gonna do what I shoulda done from the start. I'm gonna show you who's boss. And you ain't gonna say a word about it to nobody. You hear? You're gonna shut up and take it. Now, come here!"

CHAPTER 3

*C*onn reached for Becca, but with her seat belt already unfastened and her hand on the door latch, she eluded his grasp. By the time he realized what she was doing, she had already scrambled out of the car. Cursing, he flung his door open and charged after her.

She was frightened, but he was out of shape, and her fear gave her an edge. Unable to catch her, he yelled some choice vulgarities, then loped awkwardly back to his car. When she heard the engine roar and the tires squeal, she turned to see the car barreling straight for her. At the last instant she jumped out of the way. Conn plowed past her, hitting a small tree and putting a nasty crinkle in the right front fender. Spouting more profanity, he put the car in reverse and stomped on the accelerator. Mud sprayed everywhere, and the car spun sideways, its rear tires digging deep ruts in the soft wet shoulder.

Shaking from an adrenaline high, Becca gasped for air as she eyed the car. With its back tires buried almost to the top of the wheel wells, it was definitely stuck. Keeping watch on Conn, she scurried sideways up the road.

He climbed out of the car, slipped, and went down in the wet grass and mud. Lumbering to his feet, he called her a few ugly names, swung around to kick the car door shut, and fell backward again. Yelling obscenities, he hoisted himself up and hung onto the car for support. When he steadied his footing, he bellowed, "That's it, Reba Jean! Put out or get out! You can have it your way till we're married. But after that, you won't have a choice!"

Hugging her purse and sweater, she turned and trotted away

from him.

* * * * *

Becca's cornflower blue flats, caked with mud, rubbed her heels as soon as she started her trek, but she kept walking. As darkness encroached, the damp summer evening turned cool. Glad she'd had the sense to keep hold of her purse and sweater while vacating Conn's car, she bundled up. She glanced at her watch, then looked back over her shoulder again. She'd been walking ten minutes, but it seemed much longer.

Instead of heading back toward town, she had run toward the airport. She thought Conn had driven down the road far enough that she'd be closer to the airport than to town, but now she doubted her judgment. She hadn't considered the fact that she might not find assistance at the air center. It was late and no one was liable to be at the airport office or hangars. She doubted a commuter flight would arrive in the middle of the week. Regardless, she wasn't going to turn around and backtrack. Conn might still be waiting for her, mad enough to do her real harm. She had no choice but to follow the path she'd chosen.

Tears formed in her eyes. She didn't bother to wipe them away, but neither did she indulge herself and let more tears come. Swallowing back the urge to cry, she quickened her pace. She knew she had every right to be unhappy about her situation, but wallowing in self-pity wouldn't make things better. Through no fault of her own, her life was in a mess. She had assumed the burden for her father's misfortune and knew she could do nothing else. She might have temporarily escaped Conn, but sooner or later she'd have to go back to him and accept her fate. Her father's future depended on that.

Once she and Conn were legally married, she wouldn't be able to refuse what he'd obviously wanted this evening. She had dreamed of the day she would marry and live happily with a loving husband. But when she thought of Conn touching her, that dream became a sickening nightmare and nauseated her. She couldn't imagine closing her eyes and lying still for it.

The glow of headlights rounding the curve ahead of her sent a jolt of terror through her whole body. Her first instinct was to dart for cover until she remembered Conn's car was stranded back in the opposite direction. In the unlikely event he'd managed to free it from the mud, he would drive up behind her. She assumed he would abandon the car and head toward town for help rather than try to hitch a ride and pick her up, or exhaust himself by running after her.

She stepped to the side of the road and waved her arms to flag down the oncoming vehicle. It drove past but instantly came to a halt. The back-up lights flashed on, and the car smoothly approached her in reverse.

As she scurried toward the black BMW sedan, she saw a Fornelli Imports license plate frame. Lou Fornelli owned a fleet of dealerships in Chicago and various towns dotting the state. His ads ran all the time on the local TV stations but didn't offer serious competition for the Morses in the three surrounding counties. Not many farmers bought expensive luxury sports cars. She stopped a short distance from the car, feeling fortunate to be rescued by a passerby who didn't patronize the Morse family car business.

As the car sat idling, the driver's door flew open and a huge silhouette in a business suit emerged. A lump of raw fear lodged in Becca's throat when she realized she was about to ask a stranger – a tall, brawny man – for help. She might be running across someone worse than Conner Morse, if that were possible. Before she could second-guess her decision, a baritone male voice edged with concern called out, "Are you all right, miss? May I give you a ride into town?"

Trapped between apprehension and desperation, she stammered, "I ... uh ... I don't know. I–"

With a few rapid steps he stood before her, towering over her. Her heart pounded, and she shivered. "I'm Steeleman Krueger," he declared. "I just drove down from Chicago. Did your car break down? Do you need a ride into town? It's really not a good idea for you to be out here alone."

In the fading evening light, she managed to make out his features. With raven hair and eyes that shone like sapphires against tanned skin, he was a dream-man coming to her rescue. He wore an obviously expensive, well-tailored suit that fit his trim, muscular body to perfection. His face was shadowed with concern as he extended a hand and offered, "Let me help you. You look as if you're about to collapse. What happened?"

The tears she'd refused to let flow earlier suddenly flooded her eyes. Either her tense emotional state, or the compassion in his voice, or a combination of both made her fall apart. As her sobs racked her, she tried to gulp them back, but it was no use. She hid her face in her hands.

She stiffened when he cradled her shoulders with his arm and escorted her toward his car. "You'll be all right," he assured. The irony of his words made her cry harder, and her stomach clenched. She knew she definitely wouldn't be all right. He pressed her close, and she caved in to him, giving free rein to her pent-up anger and fear.

Accepting the white linen handkerchief he took from his inner jacket pocket, she caught a faint whiff of crisp, clean cologne. When her tears subsided, she felt hot and weak. Pulling away from him, she wiped her face and murmured, "I'm sorry. I'm such a blubbering idiot."

"Don't apologize," he said with a smile. "If it makes you feel better, then it's what you need to do."

He opened the passenger door, helped her into the soft gray leather seat, then closed the door for her. During the moment she was alone, she sucked in a calming breath. Overdosing on the addictive new-car smell, she watched him circle around the front of the car. She tensed as he opened the door and slid into the driver's seat. When he turned to face her and gave her a quick once-over, she lowered her gaze.

"Are you ... do you need to go to the hospital?" he murmured. "Or the police?"

She felt her face glow with embarrassment when she

realized what he must be thinking. "No. I just ... I had a little trouble. *Car* trouble. That's all."

In the dim light of the instrument panel, she saw the tension in his face relax. He eyed the road and put his car in gear. "Where did you break down?"

She huddled in the seat. She didn't want him to take her back to Conn. "A couple miles down the road. The car's stuck. I think it will need to be pulled out. Could you just ... um ... take me into town so I can call my sister and get a ride home?"

"I have a cell phone you're welcome to use. And I'll be glad to drive you wherever you want to go."

Becca nodded, then averted her eyes from his probing stare. He drove on in silence. The few moments it took to reach Conn's Mustang made her walk of escape seem like an arduous exercise in futility. She gulped when her escort slowed to a stop, his headlights shining on Conn's car parked askew off the side of the road. Frantically she looked for Conn. She didn't see him anywhere, but she wasn't taking any chances. "Could you ... would you mind locking your doors?"

Her gentleman driver turned in surprise but quickly obliged her by hitting the power lock control. He eyed her for a long moment, then looked back at Conn's abandoned car. "You really got stuck, didn't you?"

She cleared her throat. "Yeah, I, uh..." She couldn't come up with a quick lie to conveniently explain away the truth, so she fell silent.

Still eyeing the Mustang, he observed, "Those are dealer plates." He turned on her as if he were expecting an explanation. His expression was peculiar, almost accusing.

She felt herself blushing again. "It's not my car. I was riding with someone else, and..."

"And that's why you wanted me to lock the doors? Because you thought he might still be around somewhere?" She looked shamefully down at her lap when he prodded, "Perhaps you should tell me what happened, Miss..."

"Sedder. Rebecca – Becca – Sedder." She swallowed hard

and sucked in a rasping breath. "I'd appreciate a ride back into town, Mr...." Swiping at her eyes, she sighed miserably. "I'm sorry. I know you told me your name, but–"

"Krueger. Steeleman Krueger."

"Steeleman?" She glanced at him. "That's an unusual name."

He shrugged. "A family surname. Please, just call me Steele."

She frowned. Mr. Krueger wasn't the only man with a family surname for a given name. Conn was dubbed Conner Lee Morse in honor of the maiden names of his grandmother and great-grandmother on his father's side of the family. Perhaps the naming convention was more common than she had imagined.

"You're having more than just car trouble, aren't you, Becca?"

The sound of her name spoken in this man's soft, deep, compelling voice made her feel warm and safe. Her eyes stung with new tears, and she longed to confess her problems to him. But he wasn't here to rescue her from her fate – he was merely someone who'd happened along. It wasn't fair for her to burden him with her situation. She looked away from his penetrating eyes and mumbled, "I appreciate your concern, Mr. Krueger, but I really don't want to talk about it right now. Could you just drop me off in town? I'll call my sister to come and get me."

"Let me take you home. Where do you live?"

The thought of her father seeing her in her present condition – teary-eyed, with her makeup smeared and mud on her shoes – made her want to avoid going home. "I wouldn't want to put you out. Really, Mr. Kru–"

"Steele. Please."

She gulped. "Steele. I just–"

"I insist. You look as though you could use some help. It won't be any trouble at all for me to take you home."

She bit her lower lip. "I really need to get cleaned up first. I don't want to have to explain to my father..."

He perked his black razor brows and looked her over.

"Understood." As he drove away, leaving Conn's abused car behind like a discarded carcass, he offered, "If you want to freshen up, you're more than welcome to use the facilities at my hotel room. I have a reservation at the Standish Inn."

"The Standish! Oh, no, I couldn't possibly—"

"It won't be a problem."

"But the Standish is a really classy place and—"

"I know." He glanced at her, then looked back at the road. "You'll be my guest. No questions asked."

Becca gasped and slid down in her seat the moment Steele's headlights illuminated the form lumbering along the road.

"Is that the man you were riding with?" Steele asked as he slowed to a rolling coast and looked in his rearview mirror.

Becca whirled around in her seat, cowering as she watched Conn lope toward them. Obviously he thought they were going to pick him up. She turned on Steele in terror. He took one look at her and urged the car away. She heard Conn cursing behind them. With a deep breath of relief she sank back in her seat.

Mercifully, Steele didn't ask for an explanation as he drove into Fenton. In the silence that descended on them, Becca fumbled with her face and hair. She knew she must look a fright after riding in Conn's convertible with the top down and then bawling like a lost calf. As they approached Fenton's downtown square, she became more anxious. "I don't want anyone to see me like this. Please, could you pull over somewhere and let me call my sister?"

Steele sighed and pulled the car into a parking space on the deserted square, not far from the Standish Inn. Becca eyed the courthouse and the regal Standish sitting one block off the square. She'd never been in the hotel but knew it was frequented by the social upper crust of Fenton – if there was such a thing. A favorite dining spot for well-to-do locals, out-of-county residents, as well as tourists, the historic inn had become a haven for weekend getaways. With its wraparound porch supported by stately white columns, the old brick three-story building was an area landmark.

When Becca dared to look at her escort, she found him frowning as his gaze danced over her face. Impulsively he reached out and took her chin in his hand. "Did he do this to you?" he growled.

She blinked in astonishment. Steele Krueger sounded as if he knew Conn Morse and harbored a strong dislike of him.

"The bruise on your cheek. Did he hit you?" Steele skimmed his thumb lightly over her injured cheek, and his touch made her skin heat. Unable to admit the truth, she shied from him.

He put the car in reverse and pulled onto the street. "You're coming with me right now, Becca."

"But–"

"No argument." He drove into the back parking lot reserved for Standish Inn guests, then turned off the car and faced her. "That's the last time he'll lay a hand on you. I promise."

Becca scowled at the man beside her. He seemed to take personal offense at the abuse she'd suffered. She didn't know what his interest was, but she was determined to phone her sister and get home as soon as possible. She'd had enough of men for a while, and she knew she had no business putting her trust in a stranger, no matter how attractive and compelling he was.

CHAPTER 4

$\mathcal{A}$s Steeleman Krueger checked in at the lobby front counter, Becca surreptitiously eyed her surroundings, wondering why he chose to stay at the Standish Inn. From the looks of it, the landmark was getting on in years and beginning to sag here and there, with extra wear around the edges. It was a tradition in the area, but plenty of modern motels were conveniently located near the interstate only five miles away.

She took a closer visual sweep. The dark English walnut paneling and stately décor lent an air of rich regality. The carpet with its old-fashioned vine design was a bit worn but still cushiony underfoot. Translucent tulip-shaped lights mounted on the walls gave the lobby a warm, soft glow that whispered, 'welcome home.'

The staid ambiance of the aged hotel made Becca feel out of place as she looked down at her dirt-caked shoes and casual summer skirt spattered with dried mud. She hugged her denim purse and scurried behind Steele as he followed the uniformed porter to the elevator.

Her only consolation for her embarrassment was that, so far, she hadn't come across anyone who recognized her. She couldn't afford to be seen going up to a hotel room with a man when she was scheduled to marry Lila Morse's son in less than two weeks. There would be talk, and Lila would not be pleased.

* * * * *

"Feel free to freshen up," Steele called out as he tipped the porter and closed the door. He turned to find his new companion eyeing his quarters with open awe.

The suite, a large combination bedroom-lounge, contained an array of coordinated cherry furniture. A matching chest, dresser, and nightstand complemented the richly draped king-size four-poster bed. Facing the bed, a wall-sized entertainment center sported a compact stereo and large-screen TV with a DVD player, refrigerator, and wet bar. Floral prints and English country scenes framed in a tastefully ornate style added to the suite's air of old money. Two maroon silk upholstered wingback chairs sat on either side of a round lamp table near open French doors leading to a courtyard balcony. Lined brocade drapes swayed in the cool damp breeze ripe with the heady scent of honeysuckle.

Steele watched Becca tour the room, her golden eyes wide with childlike appreciation. She moved with the grace of a young, innocent swan ignorant of her own beauty. He focused on her slightly parted lips, remembering the delicious sensation of holding her in his arms. He wanted to kiss her with reverent tenderness and take away all the hurt and worry he'd seen in her eyes – but he knew better than to get anything like that started. She was already having man-trouble, and he had no business adding to it.

"This room is fabulous! I had no idea ... I mean ... I've never been inside the Standish before."

As she grinned sheepishly, he struggled to hide the unexpected desire that gripped him. She seemed so innocent compared to his usual brand of female companionship, and he found her refreshing. He admitted he was drawn to her but quickly reined himself in. Considering what he suspected about her, he knew he couldn't allow himself any real interest in her. To lust after her would create an impossible situation. Forcing a calm smile, he suggested, "Why don't you have a seat and let me see if I can clean your shoes?"

She looked down at her feet. "Oh. I guess ... yes, I guess I'd better get out of here and let you get settled in." She looked at her watch and darted toward the phone on the nightstand. "I'll just call my sister and–"

"Relax, Becca. You don't have to rush off. No one is

expecting me until this weekend, so I'm at your disposal."

He smiled to alleviate her nervousness, but she wrung her hands and stared wide-eyed at him, seeming more anxious as she stammered, "Um ... you were very nice to help me out and give me a ride into town, Mr. Krueger–"

"Steele."

"Steele," she repeated, sucking in a deep breath. "But I really should go. It ... it isn't right for me to be here."

He perked his brows, surprised at her streak of moral fortitude after having just been with Conn. "I hope you're not worried that I'll try something–"

"Oh, no, that's not what I meant. I..." She flailed her hands then turned away.

She didn't make a sound, but he knew she was crying again. He walked over and ducked around to face her. When he saw the tears streaming down her cheeks, he pulled her into his arms. She hesitated then curled against him as if she were hanging onto a life preserver in the middle of the raging ocean. He knew she was in some kind of trouble and in desperate need of help, but she seemed too ashamed or afraid to ask for assistance.

She was so soft and warm against him. He felt things stirring inside that he knew he shouldn't allow. When he looked down at her huddled in his arms like a trembling kitten, a wave of protectiveness washed over him. He wanted her, this sweet young thing. He knew almost nothing about her, except that she was off-limits to him. Still, he wanted her like he'd never wanted a woman before. What the hell was the matter with him?

Gently he stroked her face bruised from recent abuse, and suffered an odd mixture of emotion. Despite what he suspected, when he looked her, he saw innocence stamped all over her. The very thought of Conn putting his hands on her brought him to an immediate boil. He vowed to make that gutless slob pay for it.

Closing his arms around her, he kissed the top of her head. The faint flowery scent emanating from her hair soothed him. His inner rage subsided, allowing him to marvel at his jealousy. He had no right to Becca, but he also knew she was no match for Conn. She deserved better.

Mastering his desire, he held her at arm's length and grinned. "You can't make a habit of crying on my shoulder. All my clothes will be soaked and I'll have nothing to wear."

Wiping her eyes with her fingertips, she turned away from him. "I'm sorry. I don't usually fall apart like this. I don't know what's wrong with me."

He placed a hand on her shoulder. "Obviously you're distraught and exhausted. Why don't you lie down for a few minutes and try to relax while I see if I can clean your shoes?"

When she gave him a hesitant look, he smiled with winning charm – at least that's what he hoped it looked like. "I promise you'll be perfectly safe with me. How about some soothing music?" He went to the entertainment center and turned on the stereo. Soft instrumental music floated through the room. Lowering the volume, he faced her. "There. How's that?"

She fidgeted and clutched her purse to her chest. He sighed, not wanting her to be afraid of him like she was afraid of Conn. He didn't know exactly what Conn had done to her, but he could guess. He wanted her to understand that she had nothing to fear from now on. "Give me your shoes, Becca, and lie down for a little while. I promise no one will bother you. When you feel up to it, I'll take you to dinner, then home."

"You really don't have to do that. It's late and I–"

"I'm here in town all alone, and I can't think of a better deal than the one I just offered. Anyway, I haven't got much else to bargain with. Say yes. I promise you won't regret it."

She eyed him as if she were trying to see through him, into his soul. Finally she said, "May I use your restroom?"

He nodded and watched her close the bathroom door behind her. At least she didn't bolt and run from him.

He heard the water running and figured she was tidying up. Trying not to think about her, he glanced around the room, then settled his gaze on the bed. Quickly he looked away from it, just as he heard her emerge from the bathroom.

"Sorry to take so long. I was trying to fix my face, but finally realized it was hopeless."

"You look wonderful," he assured. And she did. To him she appeared radiant, despite her rumpled, mud-spattered clothing and her thick dark hair slightly mussed. *Maybe not despite it, but because of it.* Lord, why was he feeling so lustful? She needed a friend, a protector – not another predator.

She flashed a smile and eyed the floor. "You're too kind."

"No, I'm telling the truth. You're beautiful." As she blushed, he knew beautiful didn't come close to describing how she looked to him. All adjectives fell short of conveying what he felt about her at that moment, standing in his hotel room. Her golden brown doe eyes furtively searched his face, managing to unearth in him something he didn't know he had – the capacity to feel yearning and tenderness for a woman he'd just met. He feared it was more than just sympathy and compassion that flooded his body, and he wanted to squelch it before it turned into full-blown desire.

She fidgeted, and he realized he was staring at her. "Give me your shoes, Becca, and try to relax for a few minutes."

With a nervous swipe of her hand across her chest, she finally looked down and toed off her flats. He zeroed in on her slender, naked feet. Barefoot, she seemed even more vulnerable. His neck tightened with urgency, and he swallowed hard.

Reaching down, she picked up her shoes and handed them to him. "You're a hard man to say 'no' to, Mr. Krueger."

He grinned as the intensity inside him eased. With an odd lightness in his chest, he carried her shoes to the bathroom.

* * * * *

Standing barefoot, Becca felt helpless. She didn't know what difference her shoes made, except that she couldn't run as well on outdoor terrain without them. She'd already had to run from one man tonight, and she was beginning to worry she might have to run from another.

30

As she stared at the open bathroom door, she heard water streaming and wondered about her sanity, thinking of horror stories about naïve women trusting strangers. Steele Krueger seemed nice, but she didn't know him. All the while he lulled her with reassurances, he could be planning something very bad.

She frowned, certain that wasn't the case. If he intended to harm her, he would have done so when he'd had her alone in his car on the deserted airport road. And when she'd cried, he comforted her. That wasn't the action of a calculating predator. She was sure he was a kind man trying to lend a helping hand.

When she remembered the feel of him close to her as he held her tenderly in his arms, the memory of it sent soothing warmth through her tense, aching body. He didn't hesitate to offer what she needed, and the intimacy embarrassed yet thrilled her. She realized she missed the bodily contact and cringed with shame as she glanced at the open bathroom door. She couldn't afford to indulge in useless fantasies. By Saturday after next, she'd have more bodily contact with Conn than she could stomach.

She squelched that thought, then looked at the bed, recalling Steele's suggestion to lie down and rest. Her feet hurt, and her arms and legs felt like lead. Exhausted from stress and worry and lack of sleep for the past several weeks since her father's accident and Lila Morse's proposal, she'd had trouble concentrating at work and jumped at every little noise. A few stolen moments of relaxation seemed harmless enough. She certainly could use some quiet time, and elevating her feet might ease the soreness gripping her legs.

She shook her head. No, I shouldn't even be here!

But the bed looked so inviting. She couldn't resist walking closer. What harm will it do to lie down for a minute while he's in the bathroom? As soon as I hear him come out, I'll get up.

Skating a hand over the plump, silken tapestry comforter, she sat down on the edge of the bed. As the luxurious softness cushioned her, the resident tension eased out of her body, and her eyes grew heavy.

She glanced at the phone sitting on the nightstand, knowing she should call her father, but wondering what she could tell him that wouldn't make him upset. Even if she called Meg and stayed overnight at her house, she'd still have to explain to Dad in the morning why Conn hadn't brought her home. How could she justify running from Conn into the arms of a stranger, and keep Dad from jeopardizing everything? He already disliked Conn, and one more incident of violence would push him too far. He'd make trouble, then Lila Morse would exact revenge.

Massaging her brow, she sighed. Her head felt like an overloaded washing machine stuck in the spin cycle.

As she heard the water running again, she glanced at the bathroom, then down at her nude feet resting on the floral carpet. Steele really was scrubbing her shoes, just as he'd promised. She rubbed one foot over the other, realizing those silly flats had truly hurt her feet. But what else could she expect? They were casual dress shoes not meant for running.

She chewed her lower lip. The idea of a man handling her shoes made her feel strange. It was an intimate gesture perhaps not entirely proper. But she didn't care. Instinct told her to trust Steele – and she did. Despite his size and the fact that she barely knew him, she felt safe with him. He seemed gentle and caring, and he treated her like a rare and wonderful flower. She wasn't used to that. Somehow he'd won her confidence. She couldn't explain it, and she didn't want to. She just wanted to take advantage of the calm security for as long as it lasted.

With another peek at the bathroom, she lifted one foot onto the bed, then the other. The effort exhausted her, but the reward was instantaneous. The inviting plushness cradled her as she sank down, and the comforter closed around her like welcoming arms – like Steele's arms. She eased on her side, feeling so good. The soft music lulled her as a warm blanket of calmness enveloped her. With a sigh, she let her eyes slide shut. *I'll just lie here for a minute. No harm in that...*

* * * * *

When Steele came out of the bathroom with Becca's shoes, he found her lying on his bed. The sight of her resting innocently without a care in the world made his desire for her surge.

He turned off the stereo, then walked over to the bed and looked down on her. Long dark lashes brushed her pale, delicate, face, and her full lips seemed to beckon him. His mouth watered at the thought of kissing her. She was beautiful and he wanted her, but he knew better than to try to make her his, even for a little while.

Bending down, he set her cleaned shoes on the floor beside the bed, then straightened and eyed her again. The prudent thing would be to wake her and take her home. Instead, he stood there, looking down on her, imagining that she was his – until he became hard with the need to have her. He knew next to nothing about her but let himself want her until the yearning hurt. It had been months since he'd been with a woman, and he hadn't realized until that moment just how lonely he was. If only–

No, this isn't right!

Raking his fingers through his hair, he groaned and turned away. He'd promised Becca she'd have no reason to worry about him taking advantage of her, and he intended to keep his word. Her situation was bad enough without him intruding and complicating things with his unexpected lust. He had to stop torturing himself.

He walked from the bed to the French doors and stopped, looking outside to distract and calm himself. The yellow glow of the town square streetlights softened the darkness, and the cool night air wafting across the balcony had lost some of its humidity. But the sound of leaves rustling in the breeze invigorated him, and the sweet scent of honeysuckle reminded him of Becca. Rather than taming his desire, he managed to make it worse. Exhaling, he turned from the balcony and stole another glimpse at the forbidden fruit lying on his bed.

Stop it! Just stop thinking about her!

He groaned again and dragged his hands over his face, then

glanced at the chairs nearby. The thought of sitting down sent a wave of exhaustion over him. The drive from the city had been hectic, and by the time he'd reached the outskirts of Fenton, it was nearly dark. Unexpectedly finding Becca wandering along the airport road sent a jolt through him he'd had a hard time overcoming. He wondered what would have happened if he hadn't found her. But he *had* found her, and that was all that mattered.

He glanced over his shoulder at her again. He was tired and lonely, and she was in need of help. He let his eyes travel over the soft seductive curves of her body. She was quiet as a mouse, so vulnerable, so close. With her back to him, he had plenty of room to lie on the bed next to her. He told himself that sleep was all he was after. He knew he'd rest a lot better lying in bed rather than slouching in a chair. Surely she wouldn't begrudge him a short catnap. He'd get up in twenty minutes or so, and she'd never know he'd been lying beside her.

She made a little moaning sound in her sleep that gave his heart a lustful twinge. He swore under his breath. Let her sleep – let *him* sleep. Things would be clearer, after a short nap.

He kicked off his shoes, then shed his jacket and draped it over the back of the nearest chair. Jerking the tails of his shirt from his trousers, he undid the buttons half way down and rolled up his sleeves. Relieved of the stringent neatness of his business attire, he glanced uninterested at the chair awaiting him and eyed Becca on the bed.

It would feel so good to lie next to her and relax ... take a load off.

He almost convinced himself that lying down and pretending to sleep next to this woman he'd just met would be a perfectly acceptable thing to do, but his nagging hardness made him rethink it. Without further debate, he plopped down in the chair nearest the French doors.

The drapes billowing in the breeze reminded him of entwined bodies undulating in the rhythm of lovemaking. With a huff he ignored the teasing image and closed his eyes. Sprawled out, he rested his hands across his stomach tight with tension and forced himself to ignore his swollen crotch. In a few moments he was dreaming of Becca and making delicious love with her.

CHAPTER 5

*B*ecca floated adrift, not alone, but in the arms of a man. He held her secure but not too tight. She knew him. He whispered his name ... *Steele.* He said he would help. He promised she could trust him. *Steele...*

She rolled on her back and opened her eyes, then bolted upright. In the dim light from across the room, she didn't recognize her surroundings. Everything was different, strange, *wrong.* This wasn't her bedroom. Where was she?

Her innards twisted as her bare feet touched the carpeted floor. Then she remembered. The Standish. Steeleman Krueger. She scanned the room and caught sight of him sprawled in the chair near the open balcony doors. She squirmed with a peculiar mix of attraction and fear, noticing he'd taken off his jacket and unbuttoned his shirt. Why?

To relax, of course. Apparently, when he'd come out of the bathroom and found her napping, he'd decided to let her rest. He'd taken off his jacket and set it aside to avoid wrinkling it while he waited for her to wake up. Quietly guarding his post like a valiant prince watching over his Sleeping Beauty, he'd fallen asleep and still snoozed in the chair instead of the big fine bed she guessed he'd paid a pretty penny to sleep in. She skated a hand over the cushy comforter. The bed offered more than enough room for two, but he'd opted for propriety over comfort. She melted with a warm feeling of gratitude when she thought of his self-imposed inconvenience to ensure she rested undisturbed.

She eyed the suite door and stood, knowing it was time for her to go. As she started forward, her foot nudged something. She looked down and saw her shoes devoid of the mud that had plagued them earlier. Grabbing her purse from the bed, she stepped into her shoes, admiring Steele's job of cleaning them.

She glanced sidelong at Steele stretched out in the nearby chair and fought the urge to take a closer look. This would be her only chance to examine a gorgeous man without being caught blatantly staring. Letting her curiosity get the better of her, she tiptoed around the bed and stood just a foot or so away from him. With a fleeting smile, she assessed her slumbering prince.

In the oblique light from the partly open bathroom door, he looked relaxed with his head resting to the side. She admired his thick, sleek, jet-black hair framing his wide brow. Long black lashes fringed high cheekbones, and his straight, aristocratic nose balanced sensuous full lips and a strong jaw line. His corded neck led to a massive chest and richly toned skin. She wanted to see more, but his tee shirt stopped her.

Sleeping innocently, he looked harmless until she caught sight of the veins lacing his sinewy forearms exposed by his rolled up sleeves. Obviously he worked out, and his shoulders seemed broad enough to make two of her. She sucked in a shaky breath. With that kind of brawn, she knew he was more powerful and potentially dangerous than his retiring pose suggested.

She looked toward the suite door again, reminding herself she should leave, but felt her gaze drawn back to the man dozing only a few feet from her. She focused on his arm resting across his stomach and saw his watch – expensive and classy, unlike Conn's cheap black sports watch. She eyed his naked ring finger. If he was married, he didn't advertise it with a wedding band.

With a deep sigh, she reminded herself of her impending obligation that rendered him out of her reach. But that didn't mean she couldn't look. Smiling, she let her gaze slip downward, then flinched with embarrassment. *What in the world could he be dreaming about, to get his ... to put him in the physical state he was in? Or was that normal for a sleeping man?* She gulped and blushed, realizing she ought not be staring.

Exhaling with shaky resolve, she decided to leave and avoid any mortifying confrontations or explanations. She'd never see him again, and he wouldn't come looking for her. Their brief time together would be the one bright memory she savored in her dreary future with Conn Morse.

Before she could stop wallowing in her private martyrdom, Steele awoke and looked up at her standing over him. He seemed confused, surprised. As he ran a hand through his hair, he glanced down at himself, then lunged from his chair. Startled, Becca dropped her purse on the floor with a thump.

"I'm sorry," Steele said, turning to grab his jacket. "You were sleeping so soundly, and I was really tired–"

"I'm the one who should apologize," she blurted. As she bent down to retrieve her purse, she tried to calm her embarrassment and purge from her mind the image of his glorious body and engorged maleness. "I had no business falling asleep on your bed." She eyed her feet, then looked at him. "Thank you for cleaning my shoes. You did a great job." She sighed and smoothed her skirt. "I really should go." She glanced at her watch and felt a stab of horror. "Oh, no! It's so late!"

"It's 3:17 a.m.," Steele confirmed, frowning at his watch as he rolled down and buttoned his shirt sleeves.

"I was supposed to be home by nine. My parents probably have the police out looking for me." Of course her mother and father would be worried, but that's not why she felt so jittery. If Lila Morse got wind of her night spent with a stranger, she'd have hell to pay. It didn't matter that nothing happened. What else could the woman think when Becca had slept with a man in his hotel room half the night? She couldn't let this jeopardize her deal with Mrs. Morse to protect her father.

She pulled her sweater tight across her thin cotton blouse and clutched her purse to her chest. "I've got to get home right now. I have to be at work by eight o'clock." Putting a hand to her head, she groaned. "How could I be so stupid?"

"I'm sorry. It's my fault. I should have woken you. And I definitely shouldn't have fallen asleep myself."

As Becca watched Steele button his shirt and step into his shoes, she noticed he avoided looking her in the eyes. Maybe he was more embarrassed than she was, and she began to wonder why. What had he been thinking when he'd settled down in that chair for a nap? Obviously his thoughts weren't entirely pure, or he wouldn't be suffering now from that very self-evident erection. When she considered the possibilities, she blushed hotly.

"I'll drive you home," he offered, pulling on his jacket.

"No. I'll call home then call a cab." She really didn't want to call home, but she also didn't want to spend more time alone with this man who stirred feelings in her she had no right to experience.

"By all means, call home, but don't call a cab. If your staying in my room has done real harm, my driving you home won't make things worse." He turned away long enough to modestly tuck his shirt into his trousers. When he buttoned his jacket and turned around, his telltale hardness was hidden.

He caught her staring, and she looked away. "Um ... maybe I'll skip the phone call and just go home." Glancing at him, she hedged, "I hope my being here won't cause problems for you."

He smiled and placed a hand at her back to urge her to the door. "I have no one to answer to."

"No wife?" she prodded, immediately regretting blurting out that bold question. She knew she must sound like a desperate idiot, but she couldn't believe this attractive and apparently well-to-do man didn't have a nice little family waiting at home.

"No parents, no wife, no kids, no steady, nobody," he reassured, still smiling as he escorted her to the elevator. When the elevator closed, he turned on her with a penetrating look. "What about you? I assume you're not married."

She massaged her left hand still free of the brand of marriage to Conn. "No – at least, not yet."

He perked his brows, obviously waiting for an explanation.

She bit her lip. She didn't want to tell him. She didn't want to tell anyone. But she figured she owed him the truth. "I ... I'm supposed to get married Saturday after next." With that admission, she couldn't look him in the eyes.

"You don't sound happy about it."

She glanced up to find him eyeing her carefully. Unable to

endure his scrutiny, she looked away. "I'm not. Definitely not."

He started to say something else, but the elevator opened and saved her from further discussion. She hurried beside him through the lobby and outside to the dimly lit parking lot.

"How about breakfast?" he offered, opening her door.

"I don't think so, Mr. Krueger." She slid into the passenger seat. At that inopportune moment, her stomach growled.

Grinning, he bent down and said, "I think that bear in your belly has a different opinion, Miss Sedder. Do you know of an all-night café nearby?"

Wilting with embarrassment, she offered, "There's a truck stop just outside of town. It's the only place open at this hour – but I'd prefer someplace with a drive-through." She squelched the thought of Mrs. Morse finding out she was spending time with a man other than her son. The sick feeling in her gut told her it was already too late to worry about that. Swiping a hand over her hair, she added, "I imagine I look a mess."

He closed her door, then circled around and got in on the driver's side. Shutting his door, he fastened his seat belt and started the car. Eyeing her in the glow of the instrument lights, he murmured, "To me, you look fabulous. But ... you might want to touch up that place on your cheek."

She fumbled in her purse for her compact and groaned when she saw her face in the tiny mirror. Hastily she began dabbing on concealer and powder. "I can't tell much in the dark, but I think I look like I lost a boxing match."

He touched a hand to her knee as he pulled out of the parking lot. "You're beautiful, Becca. Don't sell yourself short. And don't settle for less than you deserve."

She looked up at him. "What do you mean by that?" His tone hinted that he knew more about her than she'd told him.

"I mean," he said, eyeing her, "I don't know exactly what the situation is with you and Conn, but you definitely shouldn't marry him."

She glared at him in amazement. "How did you know..."

"I came to Fenton to attend my brother's hastily arranged

wedding. Since you were with him last night, I assumed you were the designated bride."

Becca felt a wave of nausea roll through her. Brother? He was Conn's *brother*? She wished she'd heard wrong but knew she hadn't. For a long while she couldn't speak. In the dark silence she watched the man beside her maneuver smoothly through the flashing yellow traffic light as he headed for the restaurant she'd mentioned. What kind of sneaky bastard was he to keep that critical truth from her and pretend he didn't know what was going on? How long had he known she was Conn's fiancée? What in the hell had she gotten herself into?

She stared at him in shock, having no idea what to say. Gradually the import of the situation hit her. When she recalled his reaction after picking her up, she heated with anger and embarrassment. "You knew the score the moment you saw Conn walking down the road."

He shrugged. "I figured things out before that – when I recognized the dealer plates on his car."

"Yet you said nothing and let me go on believing you were genuinely interested in helping me."

"I was – *am* – interested in helping you, Becca."

"Oh, right. I suppose you find this all very entertaining."

He eyed her sternly. "Not in the least, I assure you."

Her lower lip trembled. "And to think I slept with my future brother-in-law! How could you–"

"Becca..." He grabbed her nearest hand. She tried to jerk free of his grasp, but he wouldn't let go. "Listen to me. It's not what you think. I wasn't trying to pull something over on you. Please have something to eat and let me explain."

With her thoughts scurrying like frightened mice and her stomach churning with the hard, grinding noise of a millstone, she glanced out the side window, wondering if she could unfasten her seatbelt and roll safely out the door to escape this nightmare. Now she knew exactly what was meant by the cliché, 'out of the frying pan, into the fire.'

When they pulled into the gravel parking lot, she felt close to hyperventilating. This whole situation was insane – it had to be a mistake. Could he be playing some cruel joke? Why would he do that? She looked beyond the windshield to the restaurant's plate-glass windows and saw only a cook, a waitress, and two truck drivers. Finally she found her voice and turned on him, managing to squeak, "You're Conn's brother? He said he had a baby brother that died a long time ago, but never mentioned any other brother. I had no idea..."

"You're not alone. I'm one of Lila Morse's best-kept secrets." Steele smiled with arctic calm and shot her a wry look. "I'm the older brother nobody wants to talk about."

Becca surveyed him in disbelief. He betrayed no resemblance to Conn, except for his dark hair color and general body size. No one would guess by looking at him that he was related to Conn. But now that she was aware of it, she noticed he bore some similarity to Lila Morse. His facial features were regal and well defined, and his eyes were the same cold steel gray. "I thought you said your last name was Krueger."

He shut off the car. "It is, and has been since my adoption."

Becca frowned. "Adoption? But how?"

"Have breakfast with me and I'll explain." His smile disappeared as he added, "Now that you know the awful truth about me, I hope you won't hold it against me."

She glared at him with a new sense of mistrust. If he was a Morse, she didn't want to have anything to do with him – but, for the moment, she had little choice. She needed to find out what was going on and where she stood with the Morses. Steeleman Krueger appeared to be her best source of information, and she would have to deal with him. Unhappily, she realized having no choice had become a familiar refrain in her life.

CHAPTER 6

$\mathcal{S}$teele selected a booth by a window, and the sleepy, overweight waitress in her fifties perked up. Immediately Becca excused herself and went to the restroom, then called home on the nearby pay phone. Her mother answered on the first ring. "Becca, are you all right? My God, we thought–"

"I'm fine, Mom," Becca mumbled, glancing over her shoulder at Steele watching her from the table and apparently able to hear what she said. She turned her attention back to her mother's voice blaring over the receiver.

"–father's worried half out of his mind after that Morse bastard stormed over here, looking for you, and said someone in a black BMW had picked you up. What the hell happened? What did that bastard do to you?"

"I'll explain later. I–"

"You explain it to me right now, little girl, and get yourself home. We have some talking to do. Your father said you were planning to–"

"I've got to go now, Mom. I'll be home in a little while." Before her mother could say more, Becca hung up the phone and returned to the booth where Steele sat watching her.

"Everything all right?"

She slid onto the red vinyl bench seat opposite him and eyed the two cups of coffee sitting on the marbleized gray Formica tabletop. "With my mother, it's hard to tell sometimes."

Grabbing the sugar dispenser sitting by the napkin holder, she shook a teaspoonful into her cup. As she stirred her coffee, the waitress ambled over to take their order. When she left, Becca eyed Steele and prodded, "So, what made you decide to finally 'fess up about being Conn's brother?"

"Half-brother," he clarified. His eyes were cool, but she thought she saw strong emotion seething beneath his deceptively calm exterior. "I didn't want to tell you at all, but I figured you'd find out sooner or later, and I wanted you to hear the truth straight from me." He looked down at the table and gripped his coffee cup. Holding it close to his mouth, he sipped in silence, avoiding looking directly at her.

He seemed embarrassed by his affiliation with the Morse clan. Considering what she knew of them, she couldn't blame him. Lila Morse was a highfalutin schemer trying to keep a tight rein on her philandering husband and her rowdy, lowbrow son. She put on airs of the rich and classy, but with James and Conn failing to live up to her social expectations, she surely found them to be a major source of disappointment. Apparently she'd written off her husband long ago, but hadn't yet given up hope of reshaping Conn into the kind of man she wanted him to be. To accomplish the makeover, she'd extorted Becca's unwilling assistance.

Stirring her coffee, Becca murmured, "You said something about being adopted." When Steele failed to say anything, she looked up and found him staring at an indefinite spot on the table. His face seemed full of pain. Impulsively she reached out and touched his hand.

Glancing at her, he set his cup down and sighed. "It's not a pleasant story. Suffice it to say that I wasn't a welcome first addition to the Morse household. About eighteen years ago, my mother's aunt Sybil and her husband Charlie took me to live with them at their farm outside of Edgarsville. They never had any children, so I assumed their last name when they adopted me and made me their legal heir. I was almost fourteen."

Becca scowled and did some quick figuring. He had to be about thirty-one, maybe thirty-two – five or six years older than she was. "How could your great aunt and uncle adopt you? Wouldn't your parents–"

"My mother signed away all rights to me. She was glad to be rid of me. And so was James Morse."

44

Becca watched in silence as Steele finished his coffee. When he said Conn was his half-brother and mentioned James Morse by name rather than addressing him as his father, she understood. Obviously Mr. Morse was not his biological parent. The revelation stunned her. She wanted to prod for details but could tell by his sullen look that he was in no mood to volunteer more information.

Just as the waitress brought their food and refilled their coffee, the bell above the café door jingled. When Becca glanced over and recognized the stocky, black-uniformed policeman scanning the restaurant, she cringed.

In high school Mike Beckman ran with a wild crowd that included Conn Morse. Now he was a local cop who performed his job with a heavy dose of self-importance. He had a reputation around town for being a hard-nose, but he also played favorites. While he flaunted his official power and intimidating certain people, Becca suspected he looked the other way when it came to his friends. Conn was one of the few in Fenton who enjoyed privileges above the law while Mike Beckman was on duty.

To complicate matters, when Becca had quit college and returned home to work at the bank to help her parents financially, Mike, newly divorced, had asked her out a couple times. He seemed nice enough, but Becca wasn't interested, although her mother tried to push her to date him. Now he was married again and had a son, but she imagined he still harbored resentment over her repeated refusals to date him. When he locked his stern but inquisitive gaze on her and walked toward the booth she shared with Steele, she knew she was in trouble.

"Becca," he accorded with a flicker of a smile, once he reached their table. "You doing okay this morning?"

She fumbled with her silverware. "Uh ... yes. You?"

"Yeah. Just fine." He gave Steele a scathing survey, then eyed her again. "I hear Conn had some car trouble last night."

She eyed her plate. "I guess he did."

"He said you were with him and headed toward the airport to get help. But you never came back, and you never showed up

45

at your house. He thought somebody in a black BMW picked you up."

Mike turned his attention to Steele and prodded, "I guess the black 760Li parked out front is yours."

Steele cut up his eggs and mixed them with his hash browns. Clipping off a bite of bacon, he eyed Mike and admitted, "That's right. Is there a problem?"

Mike cleared his throat. "How about you tell me," he ordered in an official businesslike tone, "who you are and what you're doing here in Fenton."

"Name's Krueger," Steele obliged, sliding a forkful of food into his mouth. He closed his lips over his fork with sensual smoothness and savored the mouthful, eyeing Becca with a teasing sultry look as he did so. Swallowing, he turned on Mike. "I drove down from Chicago last night. I have personal business here in Fenton."

Mike stood his ground. "What exactly do you do in the Windy City, Mr. Krueger?"

Glaring up at Mike, Steele announced, "I'm a corporate attorney with Hastings, Fehrnman & Reinhold. I review business contracts, sign my name to threatening letters, and occasionally litigate liability suits."

"I see." Mike perked his brows.

The moment Steele mentioned litigation of liability suits, Becca froze. She feared that was why he had come to Fenton – to offer professional expertise to his mother in the case involving her father and Greenvalley Dairy. She felt sick.

Turning on her, Mike chided, "You've made a lot of people awfully worried, Becca. I'm surprised at you, staying out all night with a man you just met. Considering the fact that you and Conn are supposed to be getting married–"

"I assure you," Steele cut in, "that Becca's integrity has not been compromised. I wouldn't dream of taking advantage of my little brother's intended bride."

Mike scowled. "You're Conn's–"

"Yes."

46

Mike scowled, his face dawning with a glimmer of recognition. "Oh yeah. I remember you. You moved away several–"

"Yes. Now, if there are no further questions, we'd like to get back to our meal, Officer..." Steele eyed Mike's name badge and flicked him a cold glare. "Officer Beckman."

Having been abruptly dismissed, Mike pinched the visor of his hat in a mock gesture of farewell and murmured, "Sorry to have bothered you." He turned and walked out.

Steele returned his attention to his food, as if Mike Beckman's interruption was but a minor annoyance. A lesser man would have been shaking in his shoes under Beckman's challenge, but not Steele. He didn't seem to be afraid of anything or anyone. Becca found his self-confidence reassuring until she remembered her father's predicament. She eyed Steele warily. "So ... you're a lawyer."

He looked at her and shrugged, as if he didn't know there was potential trouble brewing between her family and his. She was afraid to prod, but she had to know. "Is that why you came to Fenton, to handle your family's legal needs at the inquest?"

"I assume you mean the inquest involving the liability case and a possible wrongful death suit against Greenvalley Dairy."

She nodded, feeling queasy.

"No." He ran his napkin over his mouth and gulped his coffee. "My mother mentioned something about the accident, but that's not why I came. She has her own lawyers. I'm here to see about some personal business that will probably involve quite a bit of time and research." He gave her an odd, penetrating look and added, "Of course, I have to admit that I was more than just a little curious. When I heard the startling news of my brother's impending marriage, I immediately put in for vacation and high-tailed it down here. I couldn't wait until the weekend to see for myself what kind of woman was about to marry him."

Becca felt her face heat and knew her cheeks were a brilliant pink. "Believe me, I'm not doing it by choice."

"I know. But why would a bright and beautiful young lady

like you agree to marry a low-life scumbag like Little Connie?"

"Little Connie?" Becca snickered as she chased the bulk of her breakfast around her plate with her fork.

"I imagine I'm the only one alive who dares to call him that. He hates it."

She giggled again, then graced Steele with a furtive gaze, watching him take one bite after another, entranced by his every movement and facial expression. His performance of eating gave her a rare visual feast. She had never seen anyone take in sustenance with such inviting, sexy ease. She caught herself imagining he would make love to her with equally engaging sensuality.

With that thought, she heated and looked down at her plate, figuring she must be more tired than she realized. Despite knowing that he was from the enemy camp, she found herself attracted to him. He appeared to be everything a woman could want in a man, but her delight faded when she reminded herself he was not the man she was slated to marry. Instead it was his disgusting half-brother. Trying to cleanse her mind of her impending doom, she focused on finishing her breakfast. After a few bites, she lost her appetite. Sighing, she cradled her coffee cup neglected on the table. When Steele put a hand over hers, she eyed him in surprise.

"You never did explain exactly why you agreed to go along with this farce of a marriage, Becca. I have to assume it's something my mother engineered."

Scowling, she withdrew her hand from his and picked up her fork to toy with her food again. She was not at liberty to discuss the arrangement she'd made with his mother. To do so would violate their agreement and jeopardize the deal to protect her father. "I really can't say."

"Why? Because you don't know why you agreed, or you aren't able to divulge your reasons?"

"Yes."

He set his coffee cup down. "Yes to which – the former or the latter?"

"The latter." Sighing again, she crumpled the paper napkin lying in her lap and stared at the table. "Could we change the subject, please?"

He looked at his watch. "It's nearly five. How long does it take you to get ready for work?"

Becca eyed her watch and did some back figuring. By the time she arrived home, showered, and strategically dodged a face-to-face run-in with her mother, it would be time for her to head to work. She gulped the last of her cooling coffee and murmured, "I guess I'd better get going. I may work at a bank, but I don't get to keep banker's hours – whatever those are."

* * * * *

"I haven't been in Fenton for years," Steele declared as he drove through the dark, sleeping town. Dawn would not come for another fifteen minutes. A big, scraggly dog trotting down the sidewalk and a few darting moths were the only living creatures to brave the yellow glow of the streetlights. "In some ways it's changed. In other ways it hasn't. The bakery's still there, under a different name. Sellars' Drugstore is gone. It used to be on the corner where that video store is now."

Becca nodded. "Mr. Sellars sold out and retired five years ago. He died last year."

Steele frowned. "I can still remember that old man like I'd seen him yesterday. He used to make me ice cream sodas for free while he told the wildest, most unbelievable stories about his trick terrier, Blinky, who supposedly could howl 'Hello,' bark out 'Jingle Bells,' and climb trees. I sneaked over to his house one time and tried to catch old Blinky in action. The dog nearly flew over a six-foot fence trying to get at me."

Becca chuckled, but her humor faded when she saw the dark look on Steele's face. Obviously not all his childhood memories were amusing like those involving the late Mr. Sellars and his clever dog Blinky. "I guess Fenton isn't home to you anymore."

He eyed her, then looked back at the road. "It never was."

Becca ached to ask him about the bad blood between him and his family, but she held her tongue. If he wanted to tell her, he would do so in his own good time.

"Uh, turn here," she blurted almost too late. He responded quickly and executed the turn onto her street without putting them into a careening slide. She grimaced. "Sorry. I should have been paying attention."

He smiled as if he knew why she couldn't keep her mind on the road. She couldn't keep her mind and her eyes off him, and she supposed it was obvious. She fished for conversation to fill the silence between them. "So, how long did you say you expected to stay in Fenton?"

He shrugged. "As long as it takes. With my brother finally getting married..." He shot her a dark look. "...I need to settle some personal issues. I can't put it off any longer."

Becca cringed at the mention of the wedding, missing the import of the rest of his statement.

"Becca," he said with sudden urgency, looking at her again, "I wish you'd tell me what's going on with you and Conn and my mother."

She bit her lower lip and glanced out her side window. "I would if I could, Steele. But I can't. Please don't ask me."

"You know you don't have to go through with this."

Tears clouded her eyes as she repeated sternly, "I told you, I *have* to. I don't have a choice."

He huffed. Her determination seemed to irritate him. "What could my wicked, black-hearted mother possibly have on you that would force you to walk into something like this with your eyes wide open?"

"I can't explain it. Please, just drop it, okay? I don't want to think about it or worry about it. I just want to forget the whole mess!"

Steele gripped his steering wheel. "Don't bury your head in the sand and hope this problem will go away. Weekend after next, you'll be saying 'I do.' Then what are you going to do?"

When he looked over at her, she felt her heart sink into her stomach. He might think he was helping by butting in, but he was only making things more difficult for her. Up until yesterday evening, she had nearly convinced herself she could close her eyes and block out the reality of life with Conn and actually survive it as she suffered it. But not now. Not after being with a real man who grabbed her heart and soul and imagination with such thorough intensity. She gulped back her tears and looked out the side window again. "I'll just have to ... to learn to live with it. That's all I can do."

"Becca, listen to me. No matter what my mother has told you, no matter what you think the situation is, you do not have to marry Conn. There has to be another alternative. Please don't do something that will ruin your life. And marrying Conn *will* ruin your life. He's an unconscionable slug. He—"

"You don't have to tell me what I'm letting myself in for," she croaked as tears streamed down her cheeks. She swiped at her face and looked out the side window again.

Steele pulled the car to a halt at the side of the street. She glared at him in surprise. "Why are you stopping here? My house is several blocks down the—"

He grabbed her by the shoulders and pulled her toward him. "I'm not going to let you do this. Do you hear me? I don't care what you think is at stake, nothing is so important that you have to make a sacrifice like this."

"What do you know about it?" She tried to wrench free of his grasp, but his hands were like vices. "You have no idea what's at stake!"

"No, I don't. But you're going to tell me. Now."

More tears clouded her eyes. She wanted to tell him, but she couldn't. She suspected that he, like her father, would do something foolish to interfere if he knew the truth. And then Lila Morse would strike a deadly blow against her father as punishment. "I can't, Steele. Please..."

She saw real anger in his eyes. Impulsively he drew her to him. She tried to free herself, but he wouldn't release her. When he clamped his mouth over hers in violent desperation, she moaned and pushed at his chest. He was solid as a rock, and she couldn't budge him. She knew she should distance herself from him and put a stop to their intimacy, but struggling against him was useless. He was too strong and determined. And when he held her tight and mauled her lips with his, she found the sensation too shocking and enticing to resist.

As his lips softened and caressed hers more gently, she felt her last bit of opposition slip away. He parted his mouth from hers long enough to draw a ragged breath. When he looked her in the eyes, she saw his desire and need and compassion. She couldn't refuse him. As he kissed her again, he caressed her arms, massaging vitality back into her. When he cradled her neck and face in his hands, she moaned and melted against him. Her chest throbbed with a painful mixture of remorse and excitement. Her whole body hummed with anticipation – of what, she wasn't sure, but she knew she had never felt anything quite like this before, and it was sensation she didn't want to give up. Tears filled her eyes. "Oh, Steele. I ... I don't know what to do!"

"Do exactly what I tell you," he murmured huskily. "Stay away from Conn and my mother. Don't see them, don't talk to them, don't have anything to do with them. Let me handle everything from now on."

When he let go of her, she felt weak enough to collapse. She eyed him fearfully. "But–"

"No 'buts,' Becca. You've got to trust me."

He touched a hand to her face, and she curled into his caress like a kitten starved for affection. He kissed her again, then put the car in gear. Daylight eased through the trees just as he pulled in front of her house. With a parting soft kiss, he reached over and flung her door open. "I'll be in touch. Promise me you'll stay away from my mother and my brother."

As the car dinged a warning that her door was open, she gave him a fearful glance, then fumbled with her seat belt.

"Promise me, Becca."

Finally she nodded her head in silent agreement. After

climbing out of the car, she closed the door and trudged to her house. She looked over her shoulder to see Steele leaning over, catching her with his gaze. His strength and intensity almost convinced her there was a way out of this mess after all.

When he pulled away, she turned and stumbled on a crack in the sidewalk. Her amazing encounter with him left her drained and physically weak. She wiped lingering tears from her eyes, hoping, wishing she could depend on her new champion to rescue her, but the specter of Lila Morse loomed too dark and large in her mind to let her dream she could escape that woman's evil clutches. At this point she knew she'd never be blessed with love and happiness, and she felt too confused and disheartened to face the reality awaiting her in less than two weeks.

CHAPTER 7

"*W*here have you been all night, Rebecca Jean? And who was that man that dropped you off?" Puffing vigorously on the burning stub of her current cigarette, Becca's mother Emily glared at her while fishing through the pockets of her frayed chartreuse velour robe for her pack and lighter. "I haven't had a wink of sleep since I got off work last night."

"Sorry. I know I should have called earlier, but–"

"Your father is so tied up in knots with worry, he's in too much pain to walk," her mother countered, getting right in her face. "After that Morse creep came charging over here and said you'd left his car to go for help, then didn't call or come home, we were scared to death, thinking you'd been kidnapped or something. I called the police, but they wouldn't do anything once they found out the Morses were involved. And all this time, you were out catting around, doing who knows what with who knows–"

"I said I was sorry." When Becca tried to slip past her mother, she blocked the doorway. Becca slumped into her father's old vinyl recliner and felt the worn, faded pink chenille bedspread covering it shift under her weight. It did little to keep her sister Meg's kids from pulling more stuffing out of the splits in the chair's seat and back. "I lost track of time."

"And I'm supposed to just shrug it off? You've got a watch. Did the battery stop, or were you too busy doing other things to check the time?"

Sighing, Becca looked up, surprised to see tears brimming in her mother's reddened eyes. She cringed with guilt. "A lot of stuff was going on. I'm really sorry." She rested her numb head against the recliner, feeling the weight of her exhaustion and her mother's anger bearing down like an elephant sitting on her. "I need to get ready for work, and I don't have time for another one of your lectures."

"Another one of my lectures? So, now I'm a nag?"

"I didn't mean it that way."

"But you said it." Her mother swiped the back of her hand across her eyes and turned away. "I know I haven't been the greatest mother in the world. I made mistakes, but I did the best I could with you girls. When you were growing up, I was under a lot of stress and didn't have anybody to turn to for help, with my mother being sick. Your dad's family was just a bunch of worthless drunks, and for years he was like the rest of them, always getting into trouble and losing jobs. I couldn't depend on him for anything."

Oh, here we go again. "Mom, would you stop with the martyr routine? I know you had a crappy life, but–"

"Maybe to you I sound like I'm whining about nothing, but you don't know what it was like, trying to raise you and your sister. You were too busy having fun being kids while I worried and worked myself to death, trying to keep this family together and put food on the table. And this is the thanks I get."

With trembling hands she grabbed a nearby swirled black plastic ashtray and crushed the smoldering butt of her cigarette. Flicking her lighter repeatedly, she ignited a new cigarette and pointed it at Becca like a smoking gun. "You're a twenty-six-year-old adult, so act like one. Next time you decide to go off and do something harebrained, think first how it might affect other people."

"I never meant to hurt you and Dad," Becca said with a sigh, knowing it was hopeless trying to appease her mother.

"Yeah, well, we all do stuff and never mean to hurt anyone, but it happens anyway." Blowing smoke at the yellowed ceiling, her mother shook her head, then leveled Becca with a glare that could peel wallpaper. "I was hoping you'd learn by Meg's mistakes and not hop from one guy to another. It's bad enough she got pregnant when she was only sixteen and didn't even know who the father was. We've had to raise her *and* her kids. But you're old enough to know better. If you're going to sleep around, for Heaven's sake, do it with one man at a time."

Becca lurched forward in her father's chair. "I am *not* sleeping around, Mother."

"Well, where have you been all night? With a man, right? And it wasn't Conn Morse."

Becca looked away. She couldn't deny that.

"And to think I used to worry about you not wanting to date." Her mother snorted, blowing smoke from her nostrils like a diminutive dragon.

Becca massaged her forehead. How could she be interested in dating when she spent all her time and energy enduring her mother's unpredictable ranting and raving, while watching her father silently battle the bottle? She'd learned to focus on appeasing everyone to smooth things over while Meg did just the opposite – slipping away to play at the neighbors, then later sneaking out to party and get drunk to escape the tension at home.

But Becca couldn't just walk away and leave everything in a mess. She was a fixer, always trying to make things better. Like the time she spent days painstakingly gluing together the grocery store china her mother had collected for months, then shattered in a fit of rage over some issue Becca couldn't even remember. Did the repaired china make her mother happy? No. It only made her face the guilt of her lost temper. She dumped the patched set into the trash without so much as a 'thank you' for Becca's wasted effort.

Becca crossed her arms defiantly. "Face it, Mom. You never were one to give constructive criticism when it came to dealing with the opposite sex. You just waited until somebody messed up and then pointed out their mistakes. Growing up, all I ever heard from you was how boys were after only one thing."

Her mother waved a hand in the air. "So now it's my fault you're messing with the wrong men – because I gave you lousy advice when you were a kid?"

"No, that's not what I meant." She shook her head as her

mother puffed madly on her current cigarette. She knew her mother cared about her family, although she had a strange way of showing it. *Just stop apologizing. Whatever you say or do won't be right.* She gripped the chair arms and glared up at her mother. "When you said boys were bad news, I assumed you knew what you were talking about. Then I saw all the trouble Meg was having, and decided I was better off leaving men alone."

"Well," her mother snarled, "that doesn't seem to be your attitude anymore." Pacing in front of the recliner, she took a couple ragged, shaky draws on her cigarette and flipped ashes into the plastic ashtray cupped in her hand. "I swear, I don't know what's gotten into you, Becca. It was bad enough when you quit college. That nearly killed your father. He was so proud of you. You had everything going for you – unlike the rest of us. I've been working my butt off, sewing bras and girdles in the garment factory for the last fifteen years, while your father's done everything from working construction to driving a truck. And poor Meg was never book-smart like you. Most of the time she doesn't have the sense to tie her own shoelaces. She's been boy-crazy ever since she got out of diapers and can't even manage to take her birth-control pills right. But you had a chance to make something of yourself. You could have been a CPA, but threw away your scholarship to work full-time as a bank receptionist." She rolled her eyes, then shook her head. "You really blew it."

Becca clenched handfuls of her skirt, then smoothed her palms over her knees. "It's been seven years. Why do you keep throwing that up to me?"

"Because you're still wasting time at a nowhere job and doing absolutely nothing with your life! In the last seven years you could have finished school and gotten a decent job earning a respectable living. Instead you're greeting the same customers and balancing checkbooks for little old ladies who hobble into the bank and can't even remember how they got there."

Staring at her mother's fuzzy tan house slippers spattered with coffee and the remains of a hundred breakfast spills, Becca began to regret all over again her decision not to continue with school, but she refused to feel guilty. With a state scholarship paying tuition only, she'd managed to get her associate's degree by living at home with her parents and driving back and forth to attend the junior college extension classes in Marion, while working part-time at the bank in Fenton. If she'd moved away to attend a four-year school, she would have had to work full-time to pay for living expenses, and wouldn't have been able to send money home to help her parents catch up on their delinquent house payments.

She looked up at her agitated mother, realizing now was not the time to hash over the reasons. Her mother was in no mood to listen – and never was. As she pushed up from her father's chair, it groaned in agony. "If the bank hadn't let me switch to full-time after I finished school in Marion, you and Dad would have lost the house and been out on the street. And with two kids and no husband and no job, Meg certainly couldn't have helped. At the time it seemed like the right thing to do."

"It might've seemed right to you, but it was plain stupid."

Becca ran her fingers through her tangled hair and headed down the hall toward her bedroom. Maybe she should have walked away from everything and let everyone she cared about suffer the consequences of their choices. But she couldn't. Despite the problems her family faced, and her mother's dour attitude, she knew they all loved each other and had some good times together. She could still remember sitting around the table, her dad laughing and telling wild, improbable tales to entertain his two girls, 'the prettiest little ladies in the whole town,' he always said.

But even as a child, she could tell her father hurt inside despite his laughter. She sensed something in him all twisted and wrong – something he couldn't reach and smooth out. And the more he suffered, the more he'd screw up, going on uncontrollable drinking binges, only to sober and realize he'd lost yet another job and made things even more difficult for his family.

The more he drank, the angrier her mother became, until

58

anger was a way of life for her. As Meg got older, she became more daring in her flights of escapism, until reality – pregnancy – caught up with her. Her kids only added to the fracas of the Sedder household. They always needed looking after, as did Meg herself. Becca couldn't take the easy way out and walk away from them. She had to stay and help. Dealing with them took nearly all her energy and time, with too little left to nurture her own interests and needs.

Her own interests? What were they? Maybe she'd used her family's ongoing tribulations to avoid pursuing a life of her own. She shook her head and charged into her bedroom, refusing to accept that. No, they needed her, and she had to help them. Her family deserved to be happy, despite their troubles. And they'd been doing better until the accident at the dairy.

"What's done is done," she said, facing her closet door as her mother scurried up behind her. "I can't change that. But as soon as I save up enough money, I'll finish my degree."

Squashing the life out of her cigarette, her mother immediately lit up another. "How are you planning on doing that, now that Conn Morse is hanging around and making everybody's life hell? You think he's going to let keep your money and go off to class everyday? I don't think so."

Becca folded her arms protectively across her stomach and turned away. She didn't want to think about Conn.

"Meg's made her share of mistakes," her mother said. "And she seems to be doing better, now that she's married to Pete. But what you put us through in the last couple weeks tops anything stupid your sister ever did. I swear, Becca, I don't understand how you can be so book-smart, yet so dumb about men. Conn Morse is the worst person you could possibly mess with, and you can't even be faithful to him. What's wrong with you?"

Becca glanced at her watch without facing her mother. "I have to shower and get ready for work."

Her mother grabbed her by the arm, her seemingly frail body possessing surprising strength. "Your father said last night you and Conn are planning to get married. Tell me it's not true.

You'll ruin your life. Can't you see that?"

Becca wrenched free of her grasp and whirled on her. "It's something I have to do. I can't explain it – I just have to do it. The wedding's scheduled for six o'clock the Saturday after this coming weekend." She turned away and opened her closet door before her mother could see her tears.

"That's two days before the inquest on the dairy accident. What's going on? Does this have something to do with your father? If there's some kind of problem, and you know something the rest of us don't–"

"There's no problem. Don't worry about it." Rifling through her clothes, Becca swiped at her eyes. "I don't have time to talk right now. I'm going to be late for work."

She pretended to concentrate on gathering her ensemble then finally heard her mother say, "Okay, we'll talk about it tonight, after I get home from work. But I don't want you having anything to do with that Morse scum until you tell me and your dad exactly what's going on. Do you hear?"

Becca let out a ragged sigh. She had already promised Steele the same thing, although she knew Lila Morse wouldn't let her keep either promise. "Fine. Now, will you let me get ready?"

She turned to find her mother staring oddly at her as she demanded, "Who were you out with all night, Becca? Who was that man who brought you home in that fancy black car?"

"Nobody." Becca swallowed hard, in no mood to discuss Conn's brother with her mother. "Just someone kind enough to give me a ride. That's all."

Her mother ground the remains of her latest cigarette in her handheld ashtray. "From what I could tell, he was giving you more than just a ride when he let you off in front of the house. I saw him kiss you, and it wasn't a just a peck on the cheek."

Becca glanced at the window of her tiny bedroom. The sky had grown lighter, and she was running out of time.

"What's with you, Becca? For the longest time you didn't seem interested in anybody, then all of a sudden two weeks ago you started seeing Conn Morse. He treats you like pond scum, one minute smacking you in the face, and the next claiming he's going to marry you. When he came storming over here last night, looking for you, he was madder than a rattlesnake tied up in a gunnysack. I knew he must have done something awful bad to make you jump out of the car, straight into the arms of another man."

Staring at the window, Becca ignored the clouding of her eyes. No matter how much she cried, she always seemed to have a fresh supply of tears, especially when she didn't want them.

"Becca, honey..." Her mother touched her arm, and the tears rolled down her cheeks. "Whatever that Morse slug did—"

Becca wiped her eyes and plowed past her mother. "Nothing happened. Don't worry about it." She darted into the bathroom.

"How can I not worry?" her mother murmured from the bathroom doorway. "You know you have no business marrying that creep, yet you're determined to go through with it, despite what everyone else says. And I can see you don't want to marry him. Is that why you were out all night with that other man – to take your mind off the stupid mistake you're about to make?"

Hastily Becca stripped off her clothes. "I really have to get ready for work." She reached for the shower controls and turned on the water. Stepping behind the pink flowered curtain, she avoided the spray until the water warmed up. When it reached the right temperature, she drenched herself in the blast and tried to ignore her mother's presence.

"Who were you out with, Becca? Why won't you tell me? Good grief, he's not married, is he?"

Becca closed her eyes to the watery onslaught hitting her face. Finally she turned and blinked her eyes. She knew her mother wouldn't leave until she found out what she wanted to know. "He's not married, and he was a perfect gentleman. We just talked. That's all."

"So, tell me who this mystery man is!"

Becca sighed. "His name is Steeleman Krueger."

"Steeleman..." Her mother fell silent for a long time. Just

when Becca thought she'd left the room, she heard her mumble, "Good Lord Almighty, Becca! He's Conn Morse's *brother*. Do you have any idea what kind of mess you've gotten yourself into? You are really playing with fire!"

Swiping a hand over her wet face, Becca barked, "I know, Mom. Now, will you please get out and let me shower in peace?"

CHAPTER 8

*R*eturning to his hotel room after he'd run a brisk three miles along the streets he used to haunt as a kid, Steele peeled off his sweat-soaked running clothes. The old neighborhoods seemed different somehow. The trees were scraggly, less full, many replaced with new saplings. The houses looked older, less impressive than he'd remembered. He had jogged within a block of his mother's ostentatious white southern plantation-style house, but didn't get close enough to actually see it. After nearly eighteen years away, he still wasn't ready for that yet.

By the time he showered, dressed, and called his office for messages, it was nearly eight-thirty, and he was ready for breakfast. He opened his briefcase, powered up his laptop, then emailed the changes on the Carson-Dunlevey contract. Irene had demanded he finish the contract before he left yesterday. He smirked, feeling clever to have sneaked out with the promise he'd send it from home before he left town.

Once he got transmission confirmation, he unhooked his Blackberry connector. As he called room service, he reached for the phonebook to see just how many banks there were in town. It only took him two phone calls to find the bank where Becca worked. She seemed a bit startled and embarrassed to hear from him, but he detected an underlying happy tone in her voice. Promising not to keep her tied up long, he asked how she was doing and invited her to have lunch with him. When she hedged, he quickly bulldozed over her doubt and informed her he would pick her up at eleven, her designated lunch hour. She seemed unable or unwilling to object further. Satisfied, he hung up with a smile, but that faded when he eyed the phone and realized he had one more call to make.

* * * * *

"You said you wouldn't be arriving until Saturday. But I wasn't a bit surprised to learn this morning that you'd been here since last night."

From the other end of the phone line, the painfully icy voice of Lila Morse made Steele cringe, as if he were still a child enduring her disapproval. He forced a smile. "I didn't upset your plans by coming early, did I?"

"As usual, Steele, you've managed to create difficulty just by being here. You always were bent on making trouble. I had hoped you'd grow out of that, but obviously you haven't changed a bit."

He squelched the urge to justify himself – he didn't have to explain anything to her anymore. "I didn't want to leave your preconceived expectations of me unfulfilled."

"Your interference has caused some unflattering speculation about your brother and his fiancée," she said in a slightly elevated tone. "I've already received calls from a few of the women in the garden club. Soon there will be talk all over town about the mysterious man who swooped in and snatched Rebecca Sedder from Conn's grasp. I can't help but think you sneaked into Fenton ahead of schedule just to stir things up."

"Believe me, if I had known it would be that easy to cause Little Connie trouble, I would have returned long before now." Steele grinned.

He heard his mother huff irritably. "Are you ready to talk business? I assume that's why you called."

He perked his brows. The grand old dame had never been one to mince words. "Shall I drop by the dealership in about half an hour to–"

"No. It would be better if we met privately, somewhere other than the dealership. I wouldn't want you to run into James or Conn. The mere sight of you would instigate more trouble."

He smiled again. "I see." Obviously she didn't want him talking to Conn, and he suspected the reason was Becca Sedder. "Nevertheless," he declared brightly, "I think I *will* stop by the dealership. You'll be there, won't you?"

"Steele–"

"I'll see you in about thirty minutes, Mother." Before she could object further, he hung up.

His stomach churned in anticipation of their meeting. He rarely felt this energized, even when walking into a courtroom with doubts about the strength of a case. Turning to his bland breakfast of toast and oatmeal and juice, he suddenly lost his appetite. The desire to fight had completely overtaken his desire to eat, but he filled his stomach anyway. He wanted to be well fueled for this first confrontation with his mother after years of silence. His success – or failure – would dictate how everything else would go.

* * * * *

Although the repair shop appeared busy, Steele found the newly built, impressive dealership showroom completely devoid of customers. Four salesmen hulked like vultures inside one of the glass-partitioned offices and observed him as he walked in. Immediately a tall, gawky fellow broke from the group to greet him with a toothy smile and an extended hand. "I'm George La–"

"Save it, pal," he snapped. "I'm not here to buy a car. Lila Morse – where is she?"

After stuttering around a little, George looked over his shoulder and pointed. "Down that hall, last door on the right."

Steele nodded curtly, then breezed past him. Glancing at each of the glassed-in offices as he traversed the hallway, he noticed The Ogre and Little Connie weren't anywhere to be seen. Knowing he was coming, his mother probably created excuses to get them out of the way.

He tapped on the glass door and saw her standing behind her sleek cherry desk, eyeing him like a cobra ready to strike. He hadn't seen her since Aunt Sybil's funeral four years ago, but she looked pretty much the same – older, of course, with a few more lines around the eyes and mouth. She still maintained her slender figure and signature board-stiff posture. Her black hair, cropped short and styled in a slight bouffant, seemed dull, probably from repeated coloring. Her natural golden complexion appeared pale and washed out – no tan for her. Dressed impeccably in a jade-green silk dress with a sharp Mandarin collar, she seemed more suited to a glittering banquet hall than a car dealership back office. Sporting that familiar hard, uncompromising frown indelibly imprinted in his memory, she lifted a hand and signaled him to enter, as if she were the Queen of Spades gracing a lowly deuce with audience.

Scowling, he opened the door and stepped inside. "You're looking well," he offered.

"Let's skip the polite chit-chat, Steele. We have business to take care of." She eyed her diamond-encrusted bracelet watch then glared at him. "I hope you'll make this easy for both of us and agree to the terms I've–"

He put up a hand to silence her, refusing to let her take control of the conversation. She wanted something from him, and he would make her pay dearly to get it. "*You* contacted *me*, remember? I'm in no hurry to sign the revocation of the profit-sharing trust. I don't need the money. In fact, to receive a distribution of that amount right now would be financially awkward for me. My tax liability would be outrageous."

His mother betrayed no outward sign of anger or impatience, except for a nearly imperceptible hardening of her mouth. "I told you on the phone yesterday that my financial advisor suggested you roll over a portion of your distribution from the trust fund into another type of account, along with James and Conn and me. And joining with us to reinvest the largest portion of your distribution back into the family's umbrella corporation would offset any large capital gains for several years."

Steele shrugged. "In that case, I don't see any advantage in

66

revoking the trust. The money will still be tied up under someone else's management, with even more restrictions."

"The corporation's management will be more financially sound. Under Southern Illinois Bank & Trust, the profit-sharing account has suffered consistently low performance for the past several years. And the interference of Judge Forrester as co-administrator of the trust is awkward. He has to authorize every proposed expenditure from the combined funds. But by reinvesting your share of the profits, you would have more say in the fund's management, and you would see tremendous potential gain. I've had my accountant prepare a projection report. It looks excellent."

Steele smirked. "I'm sure it does – on paper."

His mother hardened her already disagreeable scowl. "According to the trust stipulations, since you have already reached your thirtieth birthday and Conn is getting married, both of you have the option to voluntarily close out the trust and move the money elsewhere."

"But I don't have to put my money where you put yours."

"No, you don't," his mother snapped. "I simply wanted to offer you the opportunity to join with the rest of us in pooling the total funds for the best possible return. Our umbrella corporation is doing exceptionally well, considering the area's sluggish economy. You'll make a much faster return on your money than you would investing in junk bonds or stocks with another management firm that would lump you along with thousands of other investors you don't even know."

He perked his brows. "Maybe I'd like to devise my own investment strategies independently ... play the stock market."

She huffed. "You have better sense than to risk that much money when you know absolutely nothing about–"

"I've been investing a portion of my personal earnings for several years now, and I've done quite well for myself – without your advice and criticism."

Her gray eyes, heavily rimmed with mascara and black eyeliner, flashed like blown fuses. "I hoped you'd be reasonable about this, considering your brother is about to be married. He'll need extra money to set up housekeeping and maintain his new wife. Obviously you can't think of anyone but yourself. I'm guessing you'll keep the trust in effect out of pure spite."

He eyed her, sensing she wasn't telling him everything. "Why are you desperate to close the trust account? When Conn marries, he'll get access to his money, regardless of what I do."

"But knowing how Southern Illinois Bank and Trust operates, and how domineering Judge Forrester is, I'm afraid it could take months after Conn's married for the account to be properly audited and closed out. Conn needs access to all his money now. If you agree to close your part of the trust, the bank trustees and Judge Forrester are less likely to drag their feet. My only concern is that Conn gets his money as soon as possible, since he's getting married in less than two weeks."

Steele shrugged. "Marriage is considered a valid lifestyle change. He could petition the trustee for a special dispensation like I did when I used part of mine to help pay for law school. That should tide him over until he can get the final distribution when his portion of the trust is closed."

He could see his mother seething as she reiterated calmly, "It would be much simpler and faster to close the trust and convert the funds to another account temporarily. I'm willing to put everything in writing to ensure that your portion remains unattached during the transfer. The–"

"You're damn right everything will be in writing." He glared at her. "Including the name of my real father."

He didn't think anything could shake his mother's cold demeanor, but that demand visibly startled her. She took a moment to recover. "That has nothing to do with the trust money, Steele. I fail to see–"

"You've failed to see a lot of things over the years, Mother, dear. Deliberately." He sat on the corner of her desk and crossed his arms over his chest. "If you want me to cooperate with you, you're going to have to give me an incentive. I want to know who my real father is."

She turned away from him. "I'm sorry. I can't give you that information. I told you a long time ago that I didn't know–"

"Oh, come on." He looked her up and down and smirked. "I can't believe there was ever a time in your life when you were careless or ignorantly trusting. You always know exactly what you're doing, always measure the risk of consequence before making any decision. You're too calculating to have ever made a mistake, even in the throes of passion – if, indeed, you ever had the capability to experience that emotional state."

She whirled on him with a jagged snarl. "You–"

Before she could lambaste him, he turned to see what she was suddenly staring at. Conn stood outside her office, glowering like the jealous sibling that he was. Wrenching the doorknob, he flew into the office and flung a set of keys across his mother's desk. Steele leapt to his feet to avoid being struck by them.

"I couldn't find that truck anywhere on the lot," Conn growled, eyeing Steele but refusing to verbally acknowledge him.

Steele looked to his mother and found her blushing like a young girl caught flirting. "Wait in your father's office for me, Conn. In a few minutes I'll help you look for it."

Conn glared at Steele. "What's *he* doing here?"

Lila stiffened. "Steele and I have business to discuss. Now, go to your father's office and wait for me, please."

Conn walked up to Steele and looked him in the eyes. Towering over Conn by several inches, Steele smiled down on him and teased, "You've put on a bit more weight since the last time I saw you, Little Connie."

Instantly enraged, Conn swung at him, but Steele caught his fist in the palm of his hand. Conn jerked away and bellowed, "You were with my woman! She's *mine*, and you took her!"

Still smiling, Steele perked his brows. "I didn't see your name on her anywhere. And believe me, I took my time looking."

Conn started to swing at him again, but Lila pulled him back. "Go to your father's office *now*."

Turning on her, Conn wailed like a spoiled child, "But he was out with her all night, and I never even got any from her!"

"Conn, that's *enough!*"

In stunned fascination, Steele turned on his half-brother. He had assumed the worst about Becca's relationship with Conn, but Conn's slip suddenly put everything in a different light. No doubt he had verbally degraded Becca, and obviously he had hit her. But he had never been sexually intimate with her. The realization did something strange to Steele, deep inside. Now, more than ever, it was supremely important to him to keep Becca away from this toad masquerading as a man ... this thing he'd been forced to accept as his brother.

He glanced at his mother. She was in control of her emotions as always, but he could tell that, underneath that titanium-alloy exterior, she was close to a meltdown. Conn had opened his big, stupid mouth and had embarrassed himself – and her – yet again.

He gave Conn a smile of superiority. "You never were one to share things graciously. And now that Becca's spent some quality time with me, I doubt she'll be interested in becoming your wife." Knowing Conn would take the insult as intended, he waited for the fireworks. By experience he had learned when everyone yelled and screamed, the truth eventually came out. And that's what he was after – the truth.

Conn lunged at him. "You thieving pig!" Steele pushed him aside and tensed for a physical fight. Conn skidded erratically along his mother's desk, flailing his arms to keep from falling backward. Once he regained his balance, he gave Steele a murderous look but didn't try to attack him again. "You always wanted everything I got, 'cause you were jealous. You knew nobody wanted you, and you hated me because of it. You–"

"Conn!" his mother barked. "Be quiet! I'm sure no harm has been done. The wedding will go on as planned. Now go to your father's office."

Slinking under her glare, Conn gave her a tail-between-his-legs glance and grumbled, "I'm not marrying some little slut that *he's* had first."

Steele eyed his mother as she clenched her fists at her side and stared Conn down. She looked cool, but her jaw muscles twitched erratically, and he knew she was hot under her pristine Mandarin collar. "You *will* marry her, just as planned."

"No, I won't!" Conn shouted with childish insolence. "Not after she's been with *him*!"

"I don't blame you, Connie," Steele taunted, pretending to examine his fingernails. "I'm a hard act to follow."

Conn made some unintelligible blustering noises before finally blurting, "Stupid jerk!"

Smiling, Steele looked up, expecting his mother to order him away. To his amazement, she grabbed Conn by the arm and shoved him out of her office. "Wait for me in your father's office. Do not step foot out of there until I come for you. Do you understand?"

When Conn left, she turned to face Steele, her face livid. He grinned. "My, my, my! What a mess your happy little family is in, Mrs. Morse. A son whose future bride despises him, a trust fund you seem desperate to get money out of, and a pending wrongful death suit. There's a lot going on here that needs looking into."

She bristled. "You keep your nose out of things and mind your own business, Steele. I have attorneys to handle the situation with the dairy, and I don't need or want your legal advice. As for Conn and his fiancée, there won't be any more trouble as long as you stay clear of her."

Still grinning, he shrugged and eyed his fingernails again. "Maybe I don't want to stay clear. Maybe I liked what I saw last night and–"

"I'm warning you, Steeleman Delbridge Krueger, you stay away from Conn's fiancée, or–"

"Or what?" He glared at her. "You can't threaten me. You have nothing to hold over me. *You're* the one who wants something from *me*, so you ought to try being a bit nicer to me, *Mother*."

She gave him a nasty glare, then sat in her desk chair with regal dignity and opened a lower drawer to her right. Pulling out a burgundy leather portfolio, she handed it to him. "Here's the complete written agreement concerning the dispensation of the trust and reinvestment into Greenvalley Enterprises. Look it over. When you've made a decision, call me. But don't take too long. I want everything finalized before your brother's wedding Saturday after next."

Smirking, he accepted the packet. "Why do I get the feeling your rush to dissolve the trust has nothing to do with Conn getting married? Are you perhaps having a bit of money trouble?" He noted with satisfaction that her face darkened.

"The complete financial statements for all the subsidiaries, including the dealership, are enclosed, along with profit projections for the next two years. I'm sure you'll find everything in order and to your satisfaction."

He eyed the folder then locked glares with her. "I'll look over what you have drawn up here, but before I agree to anything I'll insist on examining all the corporate books personally. I want to see for myself just what kind of financial mess you want me to sink my money into."

His mother's jaw muscles twitched violently before she managed a smile. "Fine. Whenever you're ready, I'll make them available to you. Just let me know."

Nodding once, he turned toward the door of her office. Before exiting, he made one last stab. "Oh, I was just wondering. What exactly is it you have on Rebecca Sedder that is making her so determined to marry Conn when she would rather squash him like the nasty cockroach that he is?"

His mother grabbed a pen and clenched it hard in her hand. "Rebecca Sedder is none of your business, Steele. I'm warning you, don't interfere."

"And ... what's liable to happen if I do?"

She sighed irritably. "Don't be selfish, Steele. You have everything going for you – good looks, intelligence, a high-paying job. Don't ruin what few joys Conn can look forward to."

"Wait. Let me get a violin and make this a real tear-jerking moment."

"Steele, please. For Conn's sake, leave the girl alone."

"For Conn's sake? What about _her_ sake? I saw what he did to her face. Nobody should have to put up with that. Believe me, I speak from experience."

His mother stiffened. "You speak from experience that happened a very long time ago. And you have to admit you were a difficult boy to handle."

He snorted. "Only after I got big enough to hit back." He suddenly wished that James Morse were in the dealership right now. He'd like to give him a real taste of abuse, now that he was a grown man and capable of defending himself.

Obviously realizing she was getting nowhere with him, his mother changed her tack and pleaded, "Steele, if you have any compassion for the girl at all, you'll leave her alone. Sticking your nose where it's not wanted will only make things worse for her. If you want to toy with someone while you're here in Fenton, I'm sure there are plenty of other women who are available and willing. And with your assumed male prowess, I have no doubt you will find several with ease."

He bristled. "My alleged 'male prowess' is none of your damned business."

She smiled then. It was not a pleasant thing to see. "You may not realize it, Son, but I've maintained an interest in you over the years. I've kept tabs on your ... accomplishments."

"You have no right to call me 'Son.' You signed that away with my adoption papers. And you don't have any right to tell me whom I can see and whom I cannot."

His mother flashed him a warning glare. "I'm telling you, Steele. Rebecca Sedder is absolutely off-limits to you. I don't want you to see her or talk to her or try to contact her in any manner whatsoever. Do I make myself clear?"

He smiled. "Crystal." Glancing at his watch, he eyed her daringly. "So, I guess you're not going to be too happy about the fact that I'm picking her up for lunch right now."

She shot to her feet. "Steele!"

He was on his way down the hall before she could make

more admonishments or threats. It pleased him to know he'd unsettled his mother, but he needed more information before he could assemble the proper ammunition to go up against her. And he was hoping Becca could supply some of what he needed.

CHAPTER 9

*A*s Becca greeted customers from her receptionist desk in the lobby of Southern Illinois Bank & Trust, she kept busy stuffing envelopes. Facing the main double doors, opposite the teller counter, she sat in the open like a lone duck swimming in a huge pond. She grabbed another flyer announcing the bank's newly expanded drive-up hours, then stilled, imagining stares focused on her back. With a sigh she looked down at the stack of envelopes she'd finished, and her 'Hi, I'm happy to assist you' smile slipped from her lips. Was she just being paranoid, or did everyone in town already know about the latest development in her nonexistent love life? Gossip about her spending the night with her fiancé's brother could only be bad for her father.

She glanced around furtively, knowing no one she worked with would say anything to her face. The furtive looks, overly pleasant smiles, and whispers that stopped whenever she entered the break room confirmed it. These were good people who wouldn't butt into someone's business without invitation. They'd been sympathetic and supportive after her father's accident at the dairy but never mentioned her sudden association with Conn Morse or commented on her cheek after he'd hit her. Apparently they thought she knew what she was doing. They were wrong.

She folded another flyer. *Just keep your mind on work. You'll get through this – one minute after another, hour by hour, a day at a time. You have to.*

"Hey, Becca. How are you doing?"

Becca looked up with a start, then remembered to smile. She waved to Laura Browning with her curly-headed toddler in tow, heading for the next available teller. *Laura's so lucky to have such a cute, sweet child.* She frowned. *Conn's children won't be cute or sweet. They'll be disruptive monsters just like him. Conn's children ... my children.*

She clamped her lips together, then shook her head, refusing to harbor negative thoughts. She had to survive this but wouldn't if she allowed her dislike of Conn to get in the way.

"Got any extra check ledgers?"

Becca snapped to attention with another ready smile and faced hollow-chested Ned Larrison. He wore a loud plaid short-sleeve shirt and stiff new overalls. "You're looking sharp today, Mr. Larrison," she said, handing him a ledger from the stockpile in her drawer.

"So are you, Missy. If I was fifty years younger..." he mumbled with a grin as he hobbled off. She suppressed a chuckle. The old dear was an incurable flirt, but she didn't mind.

Getting back to her task, she stuffed the last three envelopes, then jogged the stack and secured it with a rubber band. Squirming from the sudden crawling sensation in her stomach, she swallowed and checked her watch, deciding to wait until after lunch to take the envelopes to the mailroom. Steele was supposed to pick her up in about fifteen minutes. She hoped to spot him through the double glass doors, before he came inside the bank to get her. She needed to make sure nobody saw her leaving the bank with him, to avoid more talk getting back to Mrs. Morse. She already had enough to explain.

She rubbed her forehead irritably. She'd tried to refuse Steele's lunch invitation, but he bulldozed over her objections, unaware of the jeopardy he put her father in. She'd just have to tell him when he arrived that she couldn't go with him. Maybe she could still save the situation without incurring Mrs. Morse's wrath. Why hadn't she just said 'no' up front? *Because I want to be with him. Oh, God, what am I going to do?*

Becca heard the lobby doors swoosh and looked up, fearing Steele had come early. Relief washed over her as she watched Mrs. Ida Kiefferson amble over, clicking her dentures as she folded her wispy wheat-shaft body into the chair facing the desk. When the elderly woman handed her the envelope containing notices of renewal for her certificates of deposit, Becca managed a smile. "Good morning, Mrs. Keifferson. I'll be happy to look up the new APR for you before I renew these CDs for you."

"No, that's okay. Just go ahead and renew them."

As Becca turned to her keyboard, Mrs. Kiefferson leaned forward and said, "You're such a pretty thing." She patted Becca's arm with a shaky, gnarled hand. "Glad you finally smartened up and got yourself a *real* man." She winked behind soda-bottle glasses that magnified her eyes in a dizzying blur.

Becca tried to laugh off Mrs. Kiefferson's comment, then looked around and caught several of her coworkers glancing at her. With a few deft keystrokes, she renewed the CDs and sent the confirmation to her printer. "Is there anything else I can help you with today?"

"I wonder if he still likes butter-crunch cookies," the old woman muttered to herself.

"Who?"

"Why, your young man, of course."

Becca blinked in confusion. "Conner Morse?"

"Oh, Heavens, no!" When Becca gave her a puzzled look, Mrs. Kiefferson smiled conspiratorially and whispered, "Steeleman Krueger, the man you stayed with last night at the Standish."

Becca felt her face blaze. "How ... what makes you think I spent the night at the Standish Inn – with anybody?"

Mrs. Kiefferson winked again. "Harlan Busby, my nephew, works the reservation desk. He reserved Steele's room over the phone. Got him a nice suite with one of those big king-size beds. And he was there when you two came sneaking into the hotel, like you thought nobody would notice." She giggled. "I couldn't wait to come in here and get the scoop."

Becca looked around again, then rasped, "I'd appreciate it if you wouldn't mention anything about that to anyone. I'm in a bit of a tight spot right now and–"

"Oh, I don't have to say a thing," Mrs. Kiefferson mumbled, waving a hand. "Everybody knows by now."

Becca gulped down the roiling sensation in her stomach. *Everybody, including Mrs. Morse.*

"Harlan said Steele's grown up to be quite a looker," the elderly lady mused in her tinny voice as she rested her curved back against the chair. "Course I always knew he would. He was such a handsome boy. Nothing like that nasty little brother of his ... what's his name? Condor, or something. I can't ever remember. Now what kind of woman would name her kid that, I ask you? And to kick her firstborn son out of the house and let somebody else raise him ... now that's got to be a one mean-hearted witch."

Becca looked around, then muttered, "Do you know what happened to Steele? I mean, why his mother adopted him out?"

Mrs. Kiefferson steadied herself with her thick rubber-tipped cane and leaned in close. "That son-of-a-biscuit-eater, Jim Morse! That's what happened. He hated that poor boy, and everybody old enough to remember knows why. He beat on him something fierce till Steele got big enough to fight back. Oh, Miss Lila pretended everything was hunky-dory. But Steele was to the point where he really acted up, getting into all kinds of mischief and making scenes. After a couple of rows in public, Judge Forrester finally put his foot down."

Reaching for the printed CD renewal confirmations, Becca scowled. "What do you mean?"

"The judge told Lila and that worthless no-good varmint she married that Steele was going to get taken away from them in a big nasty legal mess if they didn't all straighten up. The judge made Steele get a job after school and during the summer, so he'd stay out of trouble and out of the house, away from ol' Jim. My Lowell, rest his soul, was still managing Peck's A&P back then, before DollarMax moved in and put us out of business. Lowell didn't really need the help, but he took Steele on to stock and make deliveries, just to keep him busy."

Becca handed Mrs. Kiefferson her renewals. "For how long?"

Mrs. Kiefferson ran a gnarled finger across her shriveled

chin. "About two-and-a-half years. Steele was eleven, I think, when Lowell hired him on. He was a good worker, and Lowell really took a liking to him. We would've adopted him ourselves," she said with a crooked smile, "if we hadn't already had five kids of our own, and several grandkids to boot. I got to know Steele better when Lowell had him bring a sack or two of groceries to Judge Forrester's house a couple times a week."

Becca perked her brows as Mrs. Kiefferson explained, "The judge's wife was pretty much an invalid, confined to a wheelchair by then. MS, you know. I agreed to stay with her during the day, to lend a hand and cook meals and such. Course the judge paid me, but I would've done it for free if me and Lowell hadn't needed the money. I really liked Miriam Forrester. She was a good-hearted woman, the kindest, most caring person you'd ever in your life meet. It really weighed on me when she passed. But I guess it was for the best. At the end there, she was really in a mess. I don't know how the judge kept going. It must have torn him up inside to see her go downhill like that. But you could tell he loved her. Oh, my." Mrs. Kiefferson paused to slide a fingertip under her glasses and dab her moist eyes. Becca handed her a tissue from the box sitting on her desk.

"Thanks, deary. Anyway, I'd keep a batch of fresh-baked cookies just for Steele, and he'd stay for a while to visit with me and Miriam, whenever he came to deliver groceries. Miriam would always give him advice and ask him how he was doing in school, if he had a girlfriend, that sort of thing. She liked talking with him. And Lowell didn't mind, even when we'd keep Steele for an hour or two. Lowell knew Miriam couldn't get out, and she really enjoyed Steele's visits. Plus I think it made Steele feel good to know somebody actually did care about him."

Mrs. Kiefferson's scowl returned when she added, "But we knew Steele was still having trouble with that pond scum, Morse. The poor boy always had some lame excuse for his bruises, but we knew better. That man ... a terrible daddy for any boy, but especially for Steele. Didn't want him around, didn't believe he was his to begin with."

Becca sat back, shocked by the old woman's candor. Giggling, Mrs. Kiefferson whispered, "Oh, there was plenty of gossip about that, let me tell you, when ol' Lila hurried herself up and married the son of the local car dealer. Course, Morse Ford wasn't nearly as big back then, before Lila got her mitts into it. What a step down for the Delbridges! Lila's snooty momma Bianca never quite recovered. Figured her prissy daughter could do better. But I don't think ol' Lila had much of a choice, seeing as how she didn't have time to take her pick of eligible bachelors, if you know what I mean. And when Steele came along about six months later – weighing over nine pounds and healthy as a little horse – well, everybody knew he wasn't premature like Lila claimed. I guess it was a while before ol' Jim realized she'd pulled one over on him. But once he caught on, it was Steele who paid the price."

Becca felt heaviness in her chest as Mrs. Kiefferson continued, "Everything came to a head when Steele was about thirteen and finally decided he'd had enough of ol' Jim. They got into fight bad enough that the neighbors called the law. That's when Judge Forrester finally stepped in and made Lila and Jim find somebody willing to take Steele and raise him right. Bad publicity was the last thing Lila wanted, since she thought she was Queen of Fenton. Her momma wasn't having anything to do with it, so she went to her Aunt Sybil and her husband Charlie for help.

"Sybil and I go way back, you know. Went to school together. She was a Steeleman back then, her and her prissy sister Bianca. That's how ol' Lila ended up hanging that name on Steele. Anyway, Sybil and Charlie took Steele to their farm outside Edgarsville. He turned out to be a big help to them. Charlie had heart problems, you know, and it was hard for him to keep up with the cultivating and planting and everything else around the place. But Steele pitched right in. He was a real trooper. Sybil and Charlie ended up adopting him and raising him as their own. And then he took the Krueger name."

Mrs. Kiefferson sighed, and her bony chest seemed to

deflate like a leaky balloon. "Sybil and Charlie, they were good people. Nothing like Lila and her mother. I never did like Bianca. She always thought she was better than everybody else 'cause her daddy owned the biggest farm in the county and started up the dairy and that milk-trucking outfit. But Sybil wasn't like that. She didn't put on airs. Now that Bianca's dead and gone, ol' Lila acts like she's gonna take her place. And I don't like her any better than I did her momma. Whatever rock she crawled out from under, I sure wish she'd crawl back!"

Mrs. Kiefferson reached over and patted Becca's hand again. "I'm so glad you're not going through with that silly marriage that prissy cow Lila arranged. She's a conniver, and nobody in their right mind would marry an awful, nasty coyote like her youngest – unless they were in trouble with her. And that's a tight spot for anybody to be in. But now that Steele's back in town, he won't let his momma do anything bad to you."

"Really, Mrs. Kieff–"

"Everybody's hoping you and Steele tie the knot and leave old what's-his-name standing at the altar all by himself!" Mrs. Kiefferson giggled again, then smiled sympathetically. "Steele's a good man. You couldn't do any better."

Looking around as if she'd lost her train of thought, Mrs. Kiefferson eyed the main entrance then brightened visibly. "Speaking of the handsome devil..."

Becca glared as Steele approached her desk with a self-satisfied air. "Sorry," he murmured as he smiled down on her. "I'm a little early."

Mrs. Kiefferson grabbed her cane and pushed herself up. Looking Steele over appreciatively, she announced, "Well, Harlan didn't exaggerate a bit!" She reached out to him. "Come give an old woman a hug. How many years has it been, Steele?"

"Too many." Steele chuckled as he dwarfed Mrs. Kiefferson in his massive arms. "How are you doing, Mrs. K?"

"Feisty and forgetful. Can't complain. Looks to me like *you're* doing pretty darn good!"

"I planned to stop by and see you while I was here."

With a sidelong glance at Becca, Mrs. Kiefferson smiled. "That'd be nice. Right now, though, I have some errands to run, and I think you have more important business to take care of."

"Is there something I can do for you? Would you like me to walk you to your car?"

"No, no," Mrs. Kiefferson admonished. "I can see you've got something else on your mind." Eyeing Becca again, she winked. "Take this young lady out to lunch and dazzle her. You can always visit with an old woman later, when you haven't got anything better to do."

Steele laughed and reached out to steady Mrs. Kiefferson as she toddled toward the main doors. When it was obvious she could make it on her own, he turned to Becca. "Ready to be dazzled?"

Blushing, Becca refused to look at anyone. She got her purse out of her bottom desk drawer and let Steele escort her out the double doors.

* * * * *

As Steele walked with Becca to his car, he realized he couldn't have asked for a more perfect day. Everywhere he looked, the world bloomed with color and new life, as if he'd awakened from a long dark sleep, finally seeing the light of day. He sucked in a deep, rejuvenating breath. The balmy air, filled with the twitter of birds above dull traffic noises, carried the cloying sweet scent of bushes with white flower clusters, planted in brick islands in the parking lot. Thanks to his mother Lila's fastidious gardening, he knew the bushes were a hybrid variety of viburnum.

Ignoring the memories associated with the Morse house, he looked down at Becca walking beside him and suffered a rush of excitement. It seemed silly for him to have such giddy feelings, but he understood why. The simple touch of his hand on her back put thoughts in his head he hadn't had in a long time – thoughts he knew he shouldn't be having about her. "It's so nice outside, would you mind having lunch outdoors?"

She managed a smile. "At the park by St. Mark's? A lot of people will be—"

"No. I was thinking someplace more secluded. I know the perfect spot on the edge of the country club grounds. We can pick up something at a drive-through."

"Don't you have to be a member of the country club to access their grounds?"

He shrugged as he opened the car door for her. "My mother's a member. I doubt they'll refuse me entry."

* * * * *

The park-like setting of rolling hills and softly rustling trees – and the nearness of Becca – made Steele feel like a new spring colt kicking up his heels. He tried to rein himself in, but it was no use. Carrying their bagged lunches and drinks, he accompanied her down a winding flowered path leading to a white gazebo for two nestled in the privacy of bushes with arching branches bursting with pink blossoms. *Weigela.* He stifled the intrusion of his mother's influence and smiled at Becca.

"It's so beautiful and peaceful here," she murmured, sitting down beside him in the enclosure.

As he watched Becca take in her surroundings with childlike appreciation, he had to look away. He didn't feel peaceful at all. Seeking out Becca was the worst thing he could possibly have done – for himself and for her. The timing was wrong. He'd made a good life for himself in Chicago, and the task he needed to take care of required all his concentration. He simply wasn't ready to make a commitment to anyone right now. But something inside him wouldn't let Becca go. Glancing at her profile, he followed the line of her delicate nose, lush lips, and long slender neck, all begging to be caressed with artful patience. Becca was a sweet, beautiful girl who deserved to be cherished by a man who understood love and knew how to give and accept it reverently. He doubted he was that man, but for the first time in his life he *wanted* to be that man. A hot flush washed over him when he envisioned her dark hair falling about her face as she moaned his name in ecstasy.

"Thank you for rescuing me from the sack lunch sitting in the refrigerator at work," she said, smiling innocently up at him.

Caught in the middle of his private fantasy, he glanced down and ripped open the wrapper of his chicken sandwich.

"It's amazing what a little fresh air and sunshine can do for a person," she continued. "I haven't felt this good since ... I don't know when."

Without taking a bite of his sandwich, he set it aside and took her hand in his. "Neither have I."

She stared up into his eyes, then blushed and pulled her hand away. "It must be the weather," she said with a chuckle. "Spring fever."

This isn't right. Don't lead her on if you can't deliver. Concentrating on his sandwich, he tore off a bite and stared in the distance to keep from looking at the object of his desire.

"You mentioned you had personal business to take care of, but you never said exactly what it was."

Swallowing down his food, he shrugged, still not daring to look at her. "An old score to settle with my mother. I'm trying to get information from her."

"And when you're finished, you'll be going back to Chicago."

She said it as an accepted fact, no hint of question. He put his sandwich aside and turned to face her. "Look, Becca. I know this is awkward for you. It's awkward for me. But I really like you, and I think you like me. I want to spend time with you – as much as I can while I'm here. But I can't promise anything long-term. Right now, that's the best I can offer."

She put a hand on his arm. "I'm not asking you to make any kind of commitment. We've known each other for less than a day. I enjoy your company, and I don't want you to worry about feeling obligated beyond that."

He looked into her golden brown eyes, soft and trusting

84

like those of a fawn. He knew he should be relieved by her off-the-hook disclaimer, but he wasn't. Foolishly he'd hoped to hear something more from her. He sighed. "I know my mother has her claws dug into you somehow, and I'm determined to rectify that. But I can't do it without your help. If nothing else comes of our being together, I want you to be safe from her machinations. I can't stand the thought of my little brother putting his filthy hands on you."

She looked away from him. "I'm grateful for your help, but I don't want you or anyone else sticking their neck out for me. I've made my choice, and I have to live with it."

"No, you don't." He grabbed her by the shoulders and turned her to face him. "You can choose instead to tell me what my mother's holding over you, and trust me to help deal with it."

She eyed him, and for a moment he thought she was going to open up to him, but she turned away. In desperation he reached out and pulled her close, brushing a feathery, lingering kiss across her lips. She tasted like grilled chicken and smelled soft and flowery like the Carolina jasmine he remembered his mother nurturing on her patio so many years ago. The intrusion of that memory startled him, and he wondered why he kept thinking of flowers every time he was close to Becca. *Because she's like a rare and beautiful flower – someone who needs protection from those who would trample her.*

As Becca quivered with uncertainty in his arms, he ignored the interference of his mother's influence and concentrated instead on Becca. He relished her nearness, savoring the sensation of touching her lips with his. He wanted to kiss her again, with more intensity, but he drew back. Locking gazes with her, he grazed the back of his fingers across her cheek, waiting for further encouragement. She blushed and stared down at her lap. "We shouldn't be doing this."

"Why not?"

"Because ... because," she choked, "in little over one week, I'm going to be your sister-in-law."

He shot up from the bench and turned away. Leaning

against the gazebo frame, he glared across the rolling greens. He couldn't understand why she was so determined to stick with that lame plan, and why she absolutely refused to explain her position to him. The only thing left to do was try to pry the information out of her by guessing. "You're not marrying my brother for love. That much is clear. Is it money?" He turned on her, waiting for her reaction.

She glared up at him. "No."

"Then the only other reason you could possibly have to go through with this farce cooked up by my mother is that you're trying to protect someone."

When she looked away, he knew he was getting close. "You're not trying to protect yourself, but somebody important to you. Somebody you care about." She squirmed. "A family member."

"I told you," she objected, putting up a hand, "I can't divulge the details."

"Because my mother threatened to cancel the deal if you did." He looked to her for confirmation, but she refused to face him. "Just nod if I'm right." She glanced up, then nodded. He breathed a sigh of relief. "Finally, we're getting somewhere." He sat down beside her. "Let's see. You've got ... what? A sister, and your parents. And some grandparents, aunts and uncles, and cousins. That's it, right?" She looked at him again and nodded begrudgingly. "Tell me a little about your sister."

She let out a long sigh. "Meg. Megan. She's a couple years older than me. She's married for the second time and has four kids, with another one on the way."

He could tell by the way Becca talked about Meg, there was no connection to his mother. "What about your mom?"

Becca shrugged. "She works nights at the garment factory. And," she added with a grimace, "she chain smokes. I've been trying for years to convince her to quit."

Steele smirked. "That leaves your dad." When he saw her recoil with a skittish glance, he knew. "At the diner this morning, after I said I was a lawyer, you brought up the accident at my mother's dairy." When she glared at him with a stricken look, he made the connection. "Was your dad involved in the accident?"

"I told you, I can't discuss any of this!"

He rubbed his chin as his mind leapt to the obvious conclusion. "Then let me speculate. My mother told you she's holding some kind of evidence that will implicate your father and point blame for the accident. Evidence she promises will conveniently disappear the day you marry Conn."

Becca gave him a bug-eyed look of surprise, and he shook his head, laughing bitterly. "Don't you know how the blackmail game works? The person holding the goods holds all the power and always asks for more in return than it's worth – over and over and over again. You never come out ahead in blackmail when you're the victim."

Tears misted her eyes as she closed them and tilted her head back. "I don't have any other choice!"

Steele gripped her shoulders, wanting to shake some sense into her. "Yes you do. What's the worst thing that can happen if you don't cooperate with my mother?"

She sighed miserably and faced him. "My father could be sued for negligence and wrongful death and possibly go to jail."

Scowling, he maintained his grip on her shoulders. "Okay. And what's the worst thing that can happen if you *do* cooperate with my mother?"

Becca squirmed, trying to turn away from him. He could see she didn't want to make herself say the awful things she was trying to push out of her thoughts, but he would say them for her because they needed to be said. She needed to face her alternatives without any reservations, to make the right choice. "You'll end up married to my weaseling half-brother, a drunken abusive bully who will beat you and molest you and maybe end up killing you."

Wincing, she drew her arms to her chest, trying to hold back her sobs. He knew she was about to break, but he couldn't stop now. "Neither alternative looks good, but you've got to be fair and realistic with yourself, Becca. I know you must love your father very much to be willing to take the brunt of punishment for something he did. But that's not playing fair. It's not your place to protect him in a way that makes you suffer and become vulnerable to danger."

"But he *didn't* do it!" she wailed. "He's not responsible, and he doesn't deserve to be punished. He wasn't drunk. He filed the safety report on that maintenance scaffolding several weeks before the accident, saying the welds were weak and cracked. The scaffolding was supposed to have been replaced. But it wasn't."

"It was your father's job to inspect the maintenance equipment?"

Becca nodded. "He was the safety officer for his shift, and he filled out another report on the scaffolding a couple months before, when one of the milk tanks needed repairs. He was mad because the scaffolding hadn't been replaced then. The night of the accident, one of the tanks started having some kind of pressure build-up, and the maintenance crew had to do an emergency repair. They were going to use that old scaffolding to get to the top of the tank, but my dad told them not to, because it was unsafe. Then the shift supervisor said they couldn't afford to let the tank pressure blow and cause more damage, so the men climbed the scaffolding, and it collapsed. That's how my dad and the others got hurt."

Becca wiped her eyes, murmuring, "My dad may be permanently disabled, another man could be paralyzed, and the third man is dead. And your mother is withholding evidence that would prove my father wasn't to blame. She threatened to replace it with false evidence to implicate him if I don't do what she wants!"

"What kind of false evidence?"

Becca bit her lip as tears streamed down her face. Steele handed her a clean handkerchief from his pocket. She dabbed her eyes and nose, then said, "Blood work from the hospital. Your mother told me she could persuade the doctor who was on duty at the emergency room to testify and produce a report showing my dad's blood-alcohol level was well beyond the legal limit of intoxication at the time of the accident. If that evidence is mentioned at the inquest, he won't ever receive disability compensation. And he'll face criminal charges."

Steele shook his head. "If the evidence existed at the time of your father's examination, real or fake, the blood test results would have to be processed and reported to the proper authorities right away. In cases of suspected negligence, that's the law. Introduced later at the inquest, the report on your father would be highly suspect. Who was the doctor?"

She shrugged. "Farnsworth or something like that. I'm not sure. He's new in town."

Steele let go of her shoulders. "And my mother's on the hospital board that okays new staff hires. Now I have something to work with."

Becca gripped his arm. "Steele, don't. If your mother finds out I told you–"

He kissed away her objection. "Trust me, Becca. I can handle my mother." Becca didn't seem reassured. He stroked her hair, wishing suddenly they were in a more private place. "The important thing is for you to stay clear of Conn. He's already hit you, and he'll hurt you again if you give him the chance. I don't want any more harm to come to you."

"But what if he comes over to the house and–"

"You won't be there. You're going to spend all your free time with me. Meanwhile I'll be looking for proof of the safety report my mother's withholding." He smiled and kissed her again, then glanced at his watch. "I'd better get you back to work."

"What about your mother?" she asked, following him to the car. "What am I supposed to tell her while you're off playing detective?"

"Stay out of her way. If she presses you, pretend you're still going along with her wedding plan."

"Steele, if she starts suspecting we're up to something–"

"Just let me handle everything. Trust me on this, Becca." He tossed the remains of their lunch in a garbage can near the parking area. Preoccupied with plans to deal with his mother, he said very little as he drove Becca back to the bank. When she opened the door to exit the car, he suffered another wave of passion. Holding her close, he kissed her deeply before letting her go. "I'll pick you up for dinner tonight around seven."

She frowned. "If I'm supposed to pretend to go along with your mother's arrangement..."

"That doesn't mean you can't have fun. You're not a nun."

She gave him a startled look and asked, "Where are you taking me?"

"Someplace we can enjoy ourselves. Nice, classy."

She nodded. "I'll try to dress appropriately."

He caught her arm as she turned to leave. "Don't worry, Becca. Everything will turn out okay. Trust me."

CHAPTER 10

*S*haken by Steele's perceptiveness and the speed and ease with which he'd managed to extract the truth from her about her arrangement with his mother, Becca returned to her desk in a daze. She wanted to believe him when he said everything would be okay, but she knew it was too soon to tell. If he didn't have his hands on the original safety report filed by her father, his mother's alternate evidence would stand at the inquest. Despite Steele's reassurances, Becca knew that for now she had to continue operating under the assumption that Mrs. Morse still controlled the situation.

Spotting elderly, bowlegged Lewis Finklemeyer pushing the mail cart loaded with afternoon deliveries, Becca grabbed the envelopes she'd stuffed and labeled. Lewis smoothed a stubby hand over his balding pate, then adjusted his green silk bowtie and straightened his matching vest as she approached. She smiled and handed him the envelope packet. "Could you save me a trip to the mail room, Lewis?"

"Sure thing, Miss Becca." He grinned as he took the packet and placed it in the outgoing section of his wheeled cart. "Did you have a nice lunch?"

Her smile slipped for a second, but she quickly put it back in place. "Yes, thanks. You?"

He shrugged. "The usual. Ham sandwich and chips."

Becca suffered a twinge of sadness as she looked into Lewis Finklemeyer's slightly rheumy eyes. He'd been a widower for as long as she'd known him. "Make sure you get outside and enjoy the day," she said, touching his shoulder as she turned away.

When she walked back to her desk, she saw the very last

person she expected or wanted to see, sitting in the same chair Ida Kiefferson had occupied before lunch. Lila Morse turned and smiled. "I trust you and Steele enjoyed your outing at the country club."

Trying to give herself time to overcome her surprise, Becca said nothing as she circled around behind her desk and sat down. Facing Lila, she finally managed in an even tone, "Is there some banking business I can assist you with, Mrs. Morse?"

Lila leaned forward with aristocratic stiffness and murmured, "There is nothing you can do that I won't find out about. The country club called me to confirm that Steele was an authorized guest on my membership."

"And that would concern me how?" Becca snipped politely as she busied herself going through a small pile of papers awaiting her attention.

Lila sat back with a disgusted sigh and stared at her in silence. Becca tried to ignore her until she said, "You're overdue for your last dress fitting at Bertov's. Today's Friday. With the wedding next Saturday, you aren't giving the seamstress much time to make the needed alterations."

Becca met Mrs. Morse's even stare. "I'd just as soon show up in a gunnysack for Conn's wedding."

Lila sneered as if she were going to spout something savage, then forced a smile and soothed, "Last-minute jitters are normal. You'll get through them as long as you don't let anyone put contrary ideas in your head."

"You mean contrary to *your* ideas?"

"Whatever Steele might have told you makes no difference in our arrangement. He is in no position to help you. In fact, if I know my eldest son, he's merely stringing you along so that you'll play into his hands."

When Becca refused to acknowledge that statement, she went further. "He wants you because Conn has you. That's the *only* reason. As soon as he ruins you for Conn, his interest in you will disappear."

Remembering Steele's advice to continue playing along

92

with his mother, Becca took a deep breath to fortify her courage. Glancing around to make sure no one else heard, she responded, "First of all, Conn doesn't *have* me – at least not yet. And second, Steele isn't interested in me. He's merely enjoying my *platonic* company during his stay in Fenton."

Lila surveyed her with a stony glare. "There's nothing going on between you two?"

"That's right." Becca returned her attention to her papers, hoping Lila would get the hint and leave.

"Then that kiss he gave you when he brought you back from lunch was just an innocent gesture between new friends?"

Becca frowned at Lila, fearing the evil bat had been sitting in the parking lot spying on them. "I don't know what you're talking about," she bluffed. "Obviously you've been misinformed."

"I see. Well, that's reassuring to hear, after Steele visited me at the dealership earlier this morning, hinting at a situation I found quite disturbing."

Becca glared at her, awaiting her explanation.

"To spite Conn, he made it clear he intended to *deflower* you before your wedding."

A mix of undecipherable emotion zapped Becca. "You *told* him I was–"

"*Inexperienced?*" Lila smiled with satisfaction. "No. I didn't have to. Even without the benefit of viewing my copy of your medical records, he already seemed aware of your situation. Of course, that doesn't surprise me." She folded her hands in her lap over her gold clutch purse. "Considering the number of women whose company he has enjoyed, he would be able to pick up on that right away, from your skittish behavior."

Becca let out a ragged breath and felt tremors building in the center of her chest. She knew better than to believe anything this woman told her, but she also had serious doubts about Steele. As suave and handsome as he was, she assumed he had indeed bedded many women. And if he were aware of her lack of sexual experience, why would he even bother with her? Was she a casual challenge or just a dalliance? Was the objective merely to steal her innocence? Considering that he planned to stay in Fenton only for a week or two, that might be true. Even if he did manage to rescue her from the clutches of his mother and his brother, he wouldn't be around to enjoy the spoils of his victory. She sighed miserably. She'd be loved then left alone – but that was still preferable to being Mrs. Conner Morse. "I have work to do, Mrs. Morse. Why are you here?"

Lila's smile didn't reach her eyes. "I took the liberty of arranging with your supervisor for you to take the rest of the afternoon off. You'll accompany me to Bertov's to complete the fitting for your wedding gown. Also, we'll select a few suitable outfits for you. I can't have you being seen with the family, dressed in your usual ready-wear rags."

Becca looked down at her trim cotton dress. It fit her well, flattering her figure, but didn't bedazzle. It wasn't tacky or unstylish, just economical. Some of the bank's female employees wore expensive suits, but she didn't have the luxury of splurging all her meager income on her wardrobe. "I'll go to Bertov's if you insist, but I can't allow any of the activities associated with our *agreement* to interfere with my work schedule. The fitting can wait until tomorrow."

"The seamstress doesn't work after five, or on Saturdays."

Becca shrugged. "Then I guess the dress is done."

Lila scowled like an angry thundercloud. "Your supervisor already agreed you could leave early. Come with me now to my car, and we'll get this errand taken care of." Her mascara-enshrouded eyes flashed a warning as she added, "I'd hate to have to go to further lengths to convince you."

Becca surveyed her adversary, deciding it would be prudent to concede. She shut down her computer, reached for her purse in her desk drawer, and got her keys. As she stood to leave, she asked, "Conn won't be coming along, will he?"

Lila's mouth became a hard line. "No, of course not. It wouldn't be proper for him to see the gown before the wedding."

"Good. I don't want to set eyes on him till next Saturday."

Glaring, Lila snarled, "As you wish."

Quickly Becca said her goodbyes, then followed Lila out to the parking lot. "I'll meet you at Bertov's," she said.

"No, you'll ride with me."

"But my car—"

"Leave the door unlocked with the key in the ignition. I'll call and arrange to have someone at the dealership drop it off at your parents' house."

"I don't think—"

"Trust me," Lila reassured as she gave Becca's nine-year-old compact a scathing once-over. "No one's going to bother stealing that piece of junk."

* * * * *

Standing on the fitting platform beside Becca, Lila pinched the pinned side seams of the wedding gown's bodice and nodded. "Yes, Mrs. Scovall, I think this will do – as long as my future daughter-in-law doesn't lose any more weight between now and next Saturday."

Eyeing herself in the dressing mirror, Becca felt like a horse at a sale barn. Under different circumstances, she would be ecstatic to be fitted for her impending wedding. But considering that Conn would be the recipient of the prize delivered in this gift-wrapping, her heart went numb with grief.

With her approaching doom weighing on her mind, she appraised the sleeveless white silk moiré gown. The straight fitted skirt flowed into a long train to accentuate the extra long veil secured with a crown of small white silk flowers. With very little beading or lace, the gown could double as a formal. It wasn't Becca's first choice, but Lila insisted it made her look very elegant. She was right, of course. Becca guessed she didn't really care for the dress because Lila had selected it over her own preferences.

Middle-aged, grandmotherly Mrs. Scovall made no comments or suggestions that would contradict Lila Morse. She did as she was told and collected the gown to make the designated alterations.

"Now," Lila ordered, "let's find you a suitable dinner dress and some lingerie." Checking her watch, Becca donned her clothes, then followed Mrs. Morse back the sales floor. She doubted Steele's mother was aware of her dinner date with him at seven, and she needed to make sure she arrived home in time to get ready. She had no idea what she would wear.

"You have lovely shoulders," Lila announced as she lifted a sleeveless teal taffeta dress with matching shawl from a nearby rack. "I'm sure this will be very flattering on you."

Without comment Becca accepted the dress and went back to the fitting room to try it on. Emerging a few moments later, she waited for approval. "Oh, yes. Very nice." Lila flicked a hand in the air at the attending saleswoman. "We'll take it."

Crooking her finger, she motioned Becca toward the lingerie section. "You'll need a strapless bra. These black lace ones are quite pretty. Find one in your size and pick a pair of matching black lace bikini panties. Yes, over there."

She moved on. "Men love garter belts. This one in black lace will complement your other pieces. You know of course," she said, without turning to face Becca, "that, for personal convenience, you should wear the panties *over* the garter belt." Becca nodded with bland disinterest.

"You'll need some stockings. I like the elegant feel of this silk blend." Lila smiled, strolling toward the cash register with her selections. "Once you're wearing all this, you'll be amazed how your mood improves."

Becca was tempted to point out that her mood would be greatly improved if Lila would call off her marriage to Conn. But she knew that would accomplish nothing except to anger her future mother-in-law. Eager to get out of the store and away from Lila Morse's control, Becca hurried to change her clothes so Lila could complete the purchase. With bags in hand, Becca followed her to her silver Lincoln Continental.

"I expected you for dinner at the house this evening," Lila

mentioned for the fourth time as she started her car.

"Sorry to inconvenience you, Mrs. Morse, but I promised my father I'd make him dinner." She tried not to cringe as she told that lie.

"I hope our little discussion about Steele earlier didn't upset you too much. The truth may be hard for you to accept, but a young woman as inexperienced as you are has no business associating with the likes of my oldest son."

Becca wanted to challenge her and ask why she was so negative about Steele, but she didn't want to give away her position by trying to defend him. Obviously she couldn't say anything that would change his mother's opinion of him.

Lila turned off Main Street and headed for Becca's neighborhood on the east end of town. "Steele prefers older married women," she said, as if she assumed Becca would want to know all the details. "Particularly the wives of his firm's wealthiest clients. They're safe and usually grateful fodder for a sexually active man who doesn't want to be tied down. That's why I'm certain his interest in you stems from sibling rivalry, and nothing more."

"I might agree with you," Becca said carefully, "if Steele were actually interested in me. But he's not."

Lila forced a smile. "Oh, he's interested – but not for any reasons that might occur to you. And despite his polished exterior, Steele's not a gentleman. Don't delude yourself into thinking you can make a family man of him. That's something he will never be."

"I'm not surprised, considering he didn't have much of a family life, growing up in Fenton."

Lila shot Becca a mean glare and remained silent as she pulled her car in front of Becca's parents' house. Clutching the shopping bags containing the alluring new clothing intended to entice Conn, Becca swore silently that she'd be damned before she'd wear any of it for his benefit. She opened the car door.

"I'll call you tomorrow," Lila said as Becca stepped out of the car.

"Don't bother." Becca slammed the door hard, then trudged up the front steps. Glancing at her watch, she saw she had little time to get ready before Steele arrived to pick her up. She heard Lila's car roar away from the curb, but didn't look back.

* * * * *

At 6:15 Becca walked into the house and found her older sister sitting in her father's recliner, watching a rerun of *Gilligan's Island.* Meg wore a pink-and-white striped tent shirt over gray sweat pants. With her bleach-blonde hair pulled atop her head in an unruly mess, she managed to be pretty despite her vacant-eyed attention on the TV.

"Where's Dad?" Becca asked.

"In bed. Those pain-killers really knock him on his butt." As Meg turned off the TV and labored up from the recliner, Becca winced. Meg's stomach was huge. She doubted her sister would make it to her August due date – or else she was going to pop another set of twins.

Looking around the small, dark-paneled living room, Becca scanned for signs of Meg's monsters. She didn't hear any juvenile carnage – screaming and breakage – coming from the kitchen or the basement. "Where are the kids?"

"Pete's got 'em." Meg stretched and rubbed her lower back. "He's taking them to BurgerBarn. He dropped me off so I could fix supper for Dad tonight."

Becca rolled her eyes, wishing Pete luck. He was a brave man. She glanced at her watch and grimaced. She was running out of time. "Dad likes to eat before seven. You should get him up."

"I thought maybe you and I could talk a little first. You know ... about that *thing* you've got planned for next Saturday at the Methodist church."

"Sorry, I'm kind of in a rush." Becca headed for her bedroom.

"Hot date?" Meg asked, following her. "Can't be that hot,

98

with a scumbag like Conn Morse."

Becca tossed the Bertov's bags on her twin bed and darted to her closet. "I'm not going with Conn." She looked over her shoulder as Meg eased herself down on the bed and eyed the bags.

"Then it must be that new guy you stayed with last night. Conn's brother. Geez, Bec. Mom's fit to be tied."

Becca turned on her. "His name is Steele Krueger, and he's Conn's *half*-brother."

"Steele ... ohhh," Meg cooed. "I always thought he had such a sexy name. Too bad he moved away before I got out of grade school." She laughed. "By the way you're blushing, I take it he's still a whole lot better looking than Conn."

"Meg, stop, will you? I don't know what Mom told you, but there's nothing going on. Steele's in town only for a few weeks. I'm just spending a little time with him. That's all."

"Right before you walk down the aisle with Conn. Yeah, Bec, there's nothing wrong with *that* picture."

Becca turned and aimlessly ransacked her closet. She couldn't think straight. "He's picking me up for dinner at seven, and I don't have any idea what to wear. Either help me find something or get out."

"Holy cow!" Meg exclaimed. "Why don't you wear *this*?"

Frowning, Becca turned to find her sister fondling the luxurious taffeta dress she'd pulled out of the Bertov's bag. "Lila Morse bought that."

"So? If you're going to cheat on Conn right before your wedding, you might as well do it in style. All the better if his wicked momma pays for it."

Tilting her head, Becca considered the suggestion and smiled at the irony. "You're right." She hurried over to examine the haul laid out on her bed. The dress had very few wrinkles in it, but Becca wanted to look perfect this evening. It might be her only chance to impress a man who would appreciate the effort. "There's a steamer in the top drawer of my dresser. Could you–"

"Sure." Meg lumbered off the bed. "If you're going to

shower, you'd better get to it."

Becca darted for the door, then turned and grabbed the new bikini undies. "I want to wash these out before I wear them, but I'm afraid they won't be dry by the time–"

"Microwave them. It always works for me."

"Won't they melt?"

"Not if you keep an eye on them. Rinse them out while you're in the shower and I'll take care of it while you finish getting ready."

"Thanks." Becca pecked Meg on the cheek and dashed toward the bathroom, grateful her sister was being supportive rather than critical like their mother.

* * * * *

Wearing only her strapless black lace bra and matching skimpy garter belt, Becca finished fastening the silky stockings. She had to admit Mrs. Morse was right. Once she put on those alluring undergarments, she did feel different – more feminine, more attractive. When Meg returned and tossed her the microwave-toasted underwear, she giggled. "Holy crap, Bec! He's gonna be all over you like flies on honey. You are in for some kinda trouble! I hope you're ready for it."

Blushing, Becca stepped into the barely-nothing underwear. As she pulled the satin-lined taffeta dress over her head and shimmied into it, she worried about Meg's warning. Judging by Steele's reaction to her last night when he'd slept only a few feet away from her, she knew her sister was right. She was in for a whole lot more trouble than she could handle. She sighed nervously as Meg zipped up the dress for her.

"Um, Meggie ... when you ... um ... you know. The first time you–"

"Went on a date?"

Becca stepped away and turned to her dresser. She avoided looking at Meg in the mirror as she brushed her hair. She and Meg had talked about a lot of things over the years, but amazingly Becca's lack of sexual experience had never been a topic of discussion. Becca knew she needed advice in handling Steele, and Meg was the only source available at the moment. "The first time you were ... with a guy."

Meg laughed and rubbed her distended belly. "That was four and a half kids ago. I wasn't even sixteen then. I hope you're not asking for details, because I was drunk on my ass at some stupid party, and I don't remember much about it."

Realizing Meg's experience wouldn't be a good example to emulate, Becca decided not to pursue the topic further. She'd just have to deal with Steele on her own. Fiddling with her hair, she pulled it up over her head.

"You should definitely wear it up," Meg confirmed. "Soft and kind of loose, with a clip in the back – you know, that rhinestone one I got you for your birthday. Here. Sit down and let me fix it for you."

As Meg stood at the foot of the bed and styled Becca's hair, she mused, "Mom never was very good at giving motherly advice about sex and stuff. She explained personal hygiene and where babies come from when I was like ... still a kid. I learned about guys and all that crap at school, mostly under the bleachers or in the janitor closet." She snickered. "I guess Mom didn't do much better when it was your turn for the lecture." Picking and pulling at strands of Becca's hair, she put the finishing touches on her creation. "So, I guess your first time with a guy wasn't all that great, huh?"

Becca laughed nervously and got up from the bed to admire the job Meg had done on her hair. "Looks terrific!"

"When *was* your first time?" Meg pursued.

Becca glanced at Meg in the mirror, then went to her closet to find appropriate shoes and a handbag. She pulled out a pair of black leather sandals with three-inch heels and a matching clutch purse. Glancing at her watch, she saw it was almost seven. She managed a smile. "Thanks for your help, Meg."

Meg stared open-mouthed while Becca put on her shoes and slipped a few essentials into her purse. Finally she said,

"Jiminy Cricket, Becca! Don't tell me you're still a *virgin!*"

Adjusting the taffeta shawl across her shoulders, Becca scowled. "Try broadcasting it again, a little louder this time. I don't think everybody in Williamson County heard you."

"You're twenty-six years old. You're a knockout. You spent almost three years in college. How could you not–"

"Junior college, driving back and forth every day. And I've been working since I was sixteen. I just didn't have time for dating. Mom and Dad were going to lose the house, and I was–"

"Come on, Bec!" Meg raised her eyebrows. "Guys had to be coming on to you all the time."

Getting a little miffed, Becca finally spouted, "I knew how to say 'no.'"

"Yeah, until Mrs. Morse came along, looking for a wife for her scumbag son. How could you agree to marry that creep and not even ... I mean ... not even once?" Meg swung a hand in the air and slapped her thigh. "When I was your age, I already had two kids and was on my second husband."

Becca jerked on the taffeta shawl and grabbed her purse. "When you were my age? You're only a couple years older than me, Meggie Lou. And believe me, I didn't agree to marry Conn Morse out of misplaced attraction or girlish ignorance."

"So then, Mom was right. There *is* something going on with Dad's inquest. What is it, Bec?"

Becca glared at her watch. "I've got to go. Steele's going to be here any minute."

"Wait. You're not quite ready yet."

"What?"

"Just hold on. You need one more thing."

Meg rushed out, leaving Becca waiting nervously in her bedroom. A minute later she returned, dangling their mother's small antique onyx pendant on its slender gold chain. "Mom won't mind if you borrow it," she assured with a smile. "It's for a good cause."

Before Becca could object, Meg whipped it around her neck and fastened it. "And you'd better take these." She pulled something from the kangaroo pocket of her shirt and offered the surprise in her closed fist.

Becca held out her hand, then yipped when Meg dropped two packets into her open palm – condoms individually encase in silver foil wrappers. "Where'd you get these?"

"Mom keeps them in her nightstand drawer. She's always giving me some, hoping I'll use them. Fat chance now." Meg laughed as she patted her stomach. "Dad was snoozing, so he didn't see me grab them. Anyway he won't miss them till his back's better."

Becca blushed. "I don't–"

"Better safe than sorry," Meg advised, patting her swollen belly again.

Becca jumped when she heard knocking at the front door.

"Enjoy yourself this evening," Meg urged with a wink, and pushed her into the hallway.

CHAPTER 11

*W*hen Steele arrived to pick up Becca, his stomach churned with dread and excitement. He couldn't wait to see her, but didn't want to admit he'd made little progress that afternoon.

He went back to the dealership after lunch to review the books, but his mother had disappeared. James Morse had been almost civil when he told him to turn around and leave. The dairy plant records had been confiscated by court order, but he had no luck accessing them because he wasn't an official legal representative in the pending inquest. Last, he'd gone to Judge Forrester's office, learning that he was out of town for a few days and wouldn't be back until the middle of next week.

Besides being the judicial officer for the upcoming inquest, Judge Forrester had been involved in Steele's removal from the Morse home and subsequent placement with his great aunt and uncle eighteen years ago. The judge had handled the adoption proceedings, and Steele always suspected he knew more about his background than he let on. He was hoping to talk to him and convince him to reveal at least some small truth to enlighten him about his paternal origin. But now that meeting would have to wait until later in the week.

With just a week before Becca's scheduled marriage to Conn, Steele didn't know whether he'd be able to deliver on his promise to rescue her. In that foul state of mind he stood at her front door, wondering how to salvage the evening – and her future. The moment she opened the front door and stepped outside to greet him, his mood improved.

"You look stunning," he lavished. She blushed under his praise. He reached out, almost afraid to touch her. Feeling a surge in his loins, he wanted to skip dinner and take her straight to his hotel, but squelched the idea. Clearing his throat, he brushed a hand over the front of his charcoal jacket, hoping she wouldn't notice his private indiscretion.

"It's not too much, is it?" she asked, looking down at herself.

He raised his brows as he eyed her breasts bulging above the bodice of her dress, accented by the simple black pendant nestled in her cleavage. Wanting to maul her with his hands and mouth and every other part of his body, he felt himself salivating at the prospect. Surveying her once more, he murmured, "I am unworthy."

She giggled. "So, where are you taking me for dinner?"

He took her by the elbow and escorted her down the chipped concrete steps of her front porch. "Mr. Busby at the Standish suggested Delmarco's Steak House outside Marion. He said it's elegant and private, and the food is excellent. It will be about a thirty-minute drive if we hop on the interstate."

He opened the car door for her and helped her inside. From his vantage he got an excessive view down her dress and spied something black and lacy. Gulping, he closed the door and turned away. *I am so in trouble!*

* * * * *

As Steele drove to Marion, Becca caught herself stealing glances at him, not really listening to what he was saying. When he vowed to keep trying to help her, she mumbled, "Don't worry about it."

"But I *am* worried about it. No matter what happens, I want you to promise me one thing, Becca." He gave her a hard, quick glance, then turned his attention back to the road.

"I know what you're going to say, and–"

"Just promise me you won't marry Conn."

She sighed and looked out the side window. She knew she had to protect her father, but for this one night she didn't want to think about her troubles. She wanted to relax and enjoy herself with the gorgeous man beside her. She looked back at his frowning profile and managed a smile. "All right, I promise." She hoped that would appease his guilt over having failed her so far. "Now, can we change the subject?"

He swept a quick gaze over her and grinned. "Where'd you get that fabulous dress?"

"Your mother bought it for me this afternoon."

"So, that's why she wasn't at the dealership." He laughed. "She was out spending money to make you look good for Little Connie. Too bad he won't get to enjoy it. You're a sly one."

Becca chuckled until she recalled the conversation she'd had earlier with Steele's mother. If what Lila Morse said about her oldest son was true, Steele was a thinly disguised wolf intent on ravaging her innocence. When she looked him over, she conceded he could indeed be dangerous. But she recoiled with revulsion when she thought of Conn providing her first sexual experience. In comparison to Conn, Steele was a welcome alternative, despite the unflattering things his mother had revealed about him. The fact that Becca had known him for just a day made no difference. If she were going to be deflowered within a week, Steele was her man.

Having made that decision, she should have been relieved, but wasn't. Ignorant in the ways of lovemaking and unable to adopt Meg's nonchalant attitude toward sex, she dreaded the idea of being intimate – naked – with any man, especially the hot-blooded virile specimen sitting next to her. The thought of putting herself at Steele's physical and emotional mercy overwhelmed her, and she touched a hand to her feverish cheeks.

"You okay?" Steele asked, glancing at her as he guided his car into the packed parking lot of Delmarco's Steak House.

"Yeah, just a little tired." Becca forced a quick smile, then looked aside, doubting her sanity in agreeing to go off alone with him. As he exited the car and circled around to help her out, she gripped her purse containing the two tiny packages Meg had given her, wishing they – and her impending sexual denouement – would just go away.

Frank Sinatra crooned from the speakers mounted outside the low-slung rustic restaurant, and the heady aroma of cooking meat wafted over couples standing alongside the building, waiting for admittance. Steele breezed past them with Becca in tow and found a hostess to seat them at the private booth he'd reserved.

The booth, a floor-to-ceiling paneled half-circle enclosure, surrounded a small round table draped in hunter green linen. Tall palm fronds looming on either side increased the feeling of concealment. Becca scooted in on one side of the circular bench seat covered in burgundy leather and remained near the edge, expecting Steele to sit at the other end. But he motioned her to keep moving inward, then sandwiched himself right beside her. She couldn't very well shimmy away from him without letting him know she was afraid to sit within arm's reach.

She caught him staring at her again, and her heart skittered when she saw the look in his eyes – something akin to rapaciousness. Squirming in the seat, she glanced down and fiddled with her purse. She jerked with a start when he touched her arm. "Calm down," he whispered. "I'm not going to eat you."

She ran a hand over her brow and tried to smile. "Sorry. It's just that your mother showed up at the bank right after lunch and said something about the country club, like she was having us watched. I'm still a little spooked."

He frowned. "And what did my mother say about *me*, to make you so jittery?"

She opened her mouth, then snapped it shut, realizing she couldn't just blurt out that his mother had called him a promiscuous womanizer and destroyer of innocence. "Nothing much," she lied, adding, "And I'm not nervous because of you. It's this whole mess with your mother I'm worried about."

He nodded. "Well, tonight you're having fun. No worrying allowed." Gesturing at a passing waitress, he said, "Could we get something to drink, please?"

The thin, harried woman zipped to their table with a bright smile. "Of course, sir. What would you like?"

"I'll have Chivas on the rocks, and a glass of water." He turned to Becca, awaiting her request.

"I'll take a glass of water too. And ... and something with alcohol in it." Steele raised his brows and stared at her as she clarified, "Something that doesn't taste too ... alcoholish."

"Something that tastes more like soda pop?" the waitress suggested with a grin.

Becca shrugged. "Yeah."

"Are you sure you want to do that?" Steele murmured with a concerned look on his face.

Breathing fast to quiet her racing heart, Becca blustered, "Yes, I'm sure." She turned to the waitress. "Make it something really strong, please."

Steele scowled at Becca for a moment, then met the waitress's quizzical smirk and ordered with calm authority, "If she wants something strong, bring her a Long Island iced tea."

Perking her over-plucked brows, the waitress gave Becca a knowing look, then smiled at Steele. "Yes, sir. One Long Island iced tea for the lady, coming right up."

As soon as the waitress left, Steele turned to Becca. "Have you ever drunk liquor in your life?"

"No," she admitted. "Not so much as a beer. With my dad a recovering alcoholic..."

"That's what I thought. What the hell's gotten into you?"

She fumbled with her purse sitting on the table. Unable to meet his scrutinizing gaze, she stared at her purse, snapping and unsnapping the top. He sat in silence for a moment watching her, then put a hand on her bare arm. Flinching at his touch, she slid her purse off the table and put it on the seat beside her, as if hiding it and the salacious items inside would somehow make her decision easier. But when she glanced at Steele looming so close, her heart skipped a beat. She was afraid of the unknown, afraid of rejection, afraid of not measuring up, afraid of being hurt, of being left behind.

Afraid. She was tired of being afraid. When the waitress returned with their drinks, all the fear bottled up inside made her grab for that ominous glass of courage, and she gained new insight into her father's daily battle to stay sober.

"I'll be back for your order in just a minute," the waitress promised. "We're awful busy tonight."

"Take your time." Steele reached for his drink. As soon as the waitress departed, he faced Becca.

Avoiding his eyes, Becca gripped the Long Island iced tea he'd ordered for her, took a big swallow, then waited for the consequences. It didn't have the nasty burning lighter-fluid kick she'd expected. It tasted no worse than a strong soft drink. She took another big gulp.

"You'd better slow down on that," Steele warned.

She mustered the courage to look at him. "Why? Think I can't handle it because I've never *done* it before?"

He cocked his head and frowned. "That concoction contains several different kinds of alcohol. Drinking it on an empty stomach will knock you flat on your pretty little fanny."

She took another gulp that warmed her tummy. "Maybe I want to know what it's like to be drunk, just once."

"Okay, but don't say I didn't warn you. You're going to be awfully sorry in the morning."

"I hope not," she murmured under her breath, taking another sip. She wished he would pick up on her double meaning and make things easier for her, but he said nothing as he watched her drink. Having reduced the liquid in her glass to three-fourths empty, she felt a little lightheaded. She giggled without knowing why and was about to take another gulp when Steele grabbed the glass from her. She frowned at him.

"Maybe you ought to save the rest for dinner." He set the glass in the middle of the table, just out of her reach.

Fuming at him, she sniped, "Losing interest already?"

"What?"

She waved a hand in the air, trying to sort out her odd feelings. She was angry with herself, but somehow she wanted to be angry with him. "You're bored wasting your time with a ... a ... an ingénue."

"Ingénue?" He gawked at her, then smiled.

"Your mother told me you prefer married women because they're safe."

His smile became a scowl.

"She said the only reason you were interested in me was because you wanted to spoil things for Conn."

He placed a hand over hers. "That's not true, Becca. I'm interested in you because I *like* you. You're a sweet, beautiful, caring person I want to know better."

"But suppose I wasn't ... you know ... *experienced.* Would you still be interested?"

He withdrew his hand. "What are you talking about?"

She leaned over and grabbed her drink, pulling it close so he couldn't take it away from her again. "You know what I mean. I'm not the kind of girl you normally go out with. If I wasn't supposed to be marrying your brother next weekend, you wouldn't give me a second look, would you?"

He eyed her, running a hand over his mouth to hide his smirk. Before he could answer, the waitress arrived to take their order.

"How's the drink, miss?" the waitress asked. "Would you like another?"

"No, she would not." Steele chuckled as he looked Becca up and down. "She's had quite enough alcohol for one evening."

Grinning, the waitress took their order. Steele requested a big T-bone cooked medium rare. Becca was too flustered to figure out what she wanted, and he ordered a grilled chicken breast for her. When the waitress left again, Becca stared down at her hands clasped around her glass and cleared her throat. "I'm sorry. I shouldn't have repeated those awful things your mother said about you." She rubbed her forehead. "I'm sleepy."

He grimaced. "I shouldn't have ordered *that* drink for you. If your dad ever finds out I got you drunk, he'll kill me."

The picture of her injured father threatening big, strong Steele made Becca giggle. "He'd be even madder if he knew what I was going to ask you to do tonight."

When he failed to say anything, she looked up at him. His brows were arched quizzically as he asked, "Would it have anything to do with the term 'ingénue?'"

She faced him with woozy abandon, trying to maintain her dignity despite the embarrassing subject and her increasing inebriation. With his elbow propped on the table and his chin resting on his fist, he waited for her answer. She looked away from him. Even with a strong dose of alcohol, she couldn't seem to muster the courage to go through with the decision she'd almost talked herself into.

Her head started to spin, and she found herself encircled by Steele's arm as he pulled her close to lean on him. Too numb to resist, she curled against him and closed her eyes.

"Don't pass out on me," he whispered. "I think our salads are coming."

"I'm not hungry." She snuggled closer, feeling safe in his embrace as her fears faded like a forgotten dream.

"Now come on, Becca," he urged, forcing her to sit up. "You need to get a little food in you to sop up all that booze swimming in your bloodstream."

She opened her eyes and stared at the salad sitting in front of her. Steele picked up her fork, took hold of her hand, and placed the fork in her limp fingers. "Try to eat something."

To appease him, she made a valiant attempt to load her fork with salad and hit her open mouth. She enjoyed only partial success. As she made herself chew, Steele reached over and dabbed her chin with his napkin. Ignoring his salad, he smiled and prodded, "Let's get back to this *thing* you were going to ask me to do tonight."

"You should eat," she ordered brazenly as she waved her fork in the air. "You're going to need your strength."

He laughed and straightened in his seat. Placing his napkin in his lap, he directed his attention to his salad and didn't look at her again until it was gone.

Bored with eating and emboldened by her drink, Becca turned on Steele, intending to blurt out the request she'd

111

rehearsed in her mind. *I want you to make love to me.* But the waitress's delivery of their entrees precluded her revelation, and she sighed with mixed relief and disappointment.

As she and Steele ate, she concentrated on eye-hand-mouth coordination and asked him about his work and leisure activities. He had his pilot's license, enjoyed sailing, and played racquetball with his investment counselor, Rick, every Tuesday. He was one of the biggest moneymakers at his law firm, bringing in more word-of-mouth business through his successful handling of clients already assigned to him. The senior partners saw him as their fair-haired boy, apparently thinking he could do no wrong. The more information she pried out of him, the more she decided he was too ambitious, self-confident, and extravagant for her down-home taste. She knew he was out of her league but could see why rich, older, married women found him irresistible.

"So," she said, "you've told me everything about yourself, except who you've been seeing lately." Surprised by her candor, she stabbed a piece of chicken with predatory force and grinned.

He moved his plate aside and leaned back. "I haven't *been* with anyone since before Christmas."

She gawked at him, finding his confession hard to believe, after what his mother had said about him. "Why not?"

He shrugged. "Lost interest, I guess. I don't know. Maybe I was in a rut."

"*Was?* You mean you're not anymore?"

His eyes danced as he looked her over and admitted, "Apparently not."

She wasn't yet ready to explore that open-ended comment. As the wooziness in her head wavered, she eased her Long Island iced tea in front of her. Sipping the remains of the drink diluted with melting ice, she glanced at the bloody carnage on Steele's plate and frowned. "With all the women you've 'dated,' how have you managed to stay single?"

"It's easy to go through the motions, then leave when you don't care."

She scowled through her mental fuzziness. "How can you

make love with someone you don't care about?"

His cheeks darkened, and she found that reassuring until he clarified, "I never confuse casual sex with making love." He leaned forward and sipped his water.

She studied his profile, wondering how they'd managed to wade into these dangerous conversational waters. She'd dropped heavy hints, hoping he'd broach the subject of making love with her and save her the awkwardness of bringing it up herself. He'd played along until somewhere along the way his demeanor changed. He seemed reticent now, guarded. Was he ashamed of his promiscuity, or just confused like she was about the whole love-versus-sex issue? "I'm sorry. I had no business asking you such personal questions. I didn't mean to make you uncomfortable."

He turned on her with a tight smile. "If you want the truth, Becca, go ahead and ask. Just be ready for answers you might not like. I'll be honest, but I won't sugarcoat it."

She glanced away from his penetrating gaze and studied his large, almost graceful hand resting near his water glass. How many women had he touched with those wonderful hands, in ways she'd probably never come to know? She rubbed her forehead and mumbled, "I'm not sure what I want right now."

* * * * *

Steele eyed Becca, regretting they'd moved into this area of discussion. He didn't want to confess his sins to her. When he was with her, he wanted to be a better man in her eyes. But considering what he assumed had been on her mind after listening to his mother vilify him, he figured he'd better explain. He leaned close enough to smell the soft flowery scent of her hair. "If you're considering getting involved with me, you have a right to know what you'd be letting yourself in for."

She reared back and gave him a wary look. "I didn't say I wanted ... I mean, I just..."

He straightened and managed a smile. Regardless of her

113

faltering objections, he knew exactly what she'd been hinting at all evening, and he wasn't about to let her ruin her life by falling for a guy like him. "It's okay. We're both adults. We can discuss this rationally without getting defensive."

"Steele–"

"I imagine my mother told you all kinds of horrible things about my 'extracurricular activities.' And most of what she said is probably true."

Becca shook her head and stared at the table. "You don't have to tell me anyth–"

"I admit I've had sex with a lot of women. But it's always been 'safe' sex – that I can guarantee."

She glanced at him, then lowered her head. Even if she didn't want to hear any of this, he felt she needed to know. Why, exactly, he wasn't sure. But he wanted her to know him, the real him, not the unflattering picture he was sure his mother had painted of him. Not that it would make any difference after next weekend. Once he stopped the wedding, he'd go back to Chicago, alone. "I've always had an aversion to commitment. To commit, you have to give something of yourself, open yourself to someone else. Become vulnerable. And I've never been willing to do that. So it was easy to gravitate toward the kind of casual relationships I happened into."

When she looked at him with those big golden-brown eyes so sad, his confidence withered. He didn't want to admit any more bad things about his character and behavior. But the honesty in her face demanded honesty from him. He couldn't refuse. Taking a big breath, he admitted, "The more I was with partners I didn't love – perhaps didn't even like – the easier it became. Like a habit. It didn't take long for me to get a reputation. Soon I found myself playing escort for nearly every wife of the firm's top clients." He glanced aside. "It's not something I planned, or that I'm proud of. It just turned out that way. And I did nothing to avoid it."

"Steele, I don't care about any of that. I know you're not a bad person." She placed a hand on his resting on the table.

114

He faced her with a scowl of determination. "How can you be so sure I'm not?" He felt especially bad right now, wanting her as much as he did and knowing he didn't deserve to have her.

She shrank back and withdrew her hand. As he leaned against the booth seat and draped an arm across the top edge, she seemed to regain control of her conviction. Staring him straight in the eyes, she said, "Because I can tell. I know."

He studied her face still aglow with the liquor she'd imbibed. She was letting herself become a product of her own wishful thinking. She deserved someone better than him. No matter how much he wanted her, he felt obligated to make her understand and accept that. "The key," he said in a gentle didactic tone, "is to detach yourself from expectations and guilt. Focus on pure, simple, physical gratification, and never let emotions get involved. Once emotions come into play, all bets are off. Things can get complicated in a hurry."

"Steele, please..." She squirmed and shot him a wounded look. He felt like he was telling a trusting child about Santa Klaus's sexual escapades. Santa Klaus, the dear old sweet myth of a man, had to be an adult who participated in the act, especially if there was a Mrs. Klaus. But nobody wanted to hear those sordid details.

"I don't have relationships," he said. "I have 'mutually beneficial arrangements.'" He grabbed his water glass and took another gulp, then set it back on the table. With an arm still resting on the back of the booth seat, he tried to appear relaxed and at ease discussing his loveless sex life. But he was anything but relaxed. "I've been very careful choosing the women with whom I associate – only those I know won't pose problems."

"You mean ones who can't afford to become emotionally attached, because they're married."

He shrugged in acquiescence.

"Because you don't want your life to get complicated."

He sighed, realizing things had suddenly become very complicated since he'd met her. "I detect a note of disapproval in your tone, Miss Sedder."

* * * * *

Disapproval? Disappointment, maybe. Becca eyed Steele's cold, calculating smirk, and the steadiness of his gaze unnerved her. Glancing away, she studied her glass in distraction, almost losing her concentration as she tried to sort out the details of her fingerprint smudges. If Steele chose to have sex with women who wouldn't create emotional entanglements, why was he wasting his time with her? He said he didn't care about those other women. Did that mean he also didn't care about her? Or did it mean he wouldn't consider having sex with her?

She shook her head in confusion. Earlier she might have thought sleeping him would be simple, but now she realized it was much more complicated than a one-night stand. After being with him just a short time, she'd already developed feelings for him that weren't casual or easy to dismiss. Now she felt betrayed somehow, as if he'd let her down or misled her. Had his mother been right about him after all? Her chest ached and she shook herself free of regret over the loss. She'd never had this man to begin with, so how could she be sorry to lose him?

Raking a strand of hair from her face, she mumbled, "If physical gratification is all you're after, why bother involving anyone else? You could just..." She waved a hand in the air. "...do what guys do when they're alone."

In the middle of taking another sip of water, Steele coughed and set his glass on the table with care. When she saw his wide-eyed stare, she realized she'd managed to embarrass him. *Good.* She let a grim smile creep across her mouth, then stared at her lap as a tiny voice of hope whispered in her ear. *He wasn't the unfeeling predator his mother had made him out to be – he just couldn't be.* She wanted her instincts about him to be right so she could believe that underneath the slick veneer of sexual sophistication beat the heart of a real, caring man who, given the chance, could love the right woman. *Her.*

She squinted through her lingering inebriation, trying to see past his troubled frown, deep down into that secret place where he hid his darkest, innermost truth. She wanted to be able to trust him if she was going to let him make love to her. But would that matter after next Saturday? He'd be gone, and she'd be with Conn. She wilted in despair. How had her life become so confusing, so complicated?

Not sure she wanted to ask the question, she hesitated, then said, "So, if I'm understanding you right, you've never really made love with anybody – just had sex. Is there anyone you ever cared about enough to want to make love with, Steele?" Cringing under his predatory serenity, she waited for his answer.

* * * * *

"No."

Steele felt a twinge of regret when Becca blinked and turned away. Had she been hoping he'd give her some small sign they could share a real bond? He'd never given that hope to any other women, and he wasn't about to start now, no matter how sweet and vulnerable and delicious Becca was.

His feelings for her confused him. He didn't want to decide whether it was just lust rearing its ugly head, or something more. He couldn't afford to let it be anything more – not while the truth of his past was still up in the air, making him hold back on his personal life. He was close to emotional ruin, and that wouldn't improve until he settled things with his mother. Whatever the outcome, once that was over, maybe ... maybe he could let go of his shell of protection and allow himself to be vulnerable enough to care. Then again, maybe it was too late for him to make that kind of change.

"You must be a very lonely man," Becca muttered, refusing to face him.

He felt a painful twinge and knew it was truth stabbing him in the chest. She was right. Not wanting 'a very lonely man' to be his epithet, he added on impulse, "I'm willing to explore other options."

117

The moment she looked up at him, her beautiful face aglow with innocent trust, he wanted to kick himself. She looked ready and willing to give herself to him, but he couldn't let her do that. He had no right to lead her on. He was a short-term man and she was a long-term woman. He knew what would happen if the two of them got together, and it wouldn't be good for either of them. They'd have fabulous sex, and she'd start thinking it was love. Then he'd be gone before she could figure out what went wrong. None of it would be her fault, but she'd blame herself and feel unworthy the rest of her life. He couldn't do that to her. He had to stop it before anything serious happened.

Winking, he leaned close and whispered, "Things are looking up. The night's still young, and you're still very, very drunk." He held out a hand to her. "Ready to go?"

Her mouth dropped open and she snapped it shut. She probably wanted to call him every awful name she could think of, but she said nothing, just stared at him aghast.

She thinks I'm disgusting. Mission accomplished. Feeling like a heel, he laughed to cover his uneasiness. "Just kidding. Come on. I think I'd better get you home so you can sleep off your wild night of excess, Miss Party Animal."

CHAPTER 12

*B*ecca didn't recall much after leaving Delmarco's. Her legs almost gave out when she tried to get up from the table, and Steele had to keep an arm around her waist to get her out to the car. He hadn't admitted it, but she knew he'd guessed her plan for him this evening and had just been toying with her, making those ugly, suggestive remarks. She didn't want to be alone in the car with him, much preferring to slap him and walk away, but she hadn't regained enough coordination to execute those maneuvers without assistance.

The ride to Fenton was a blur, and the motion of the car made her sleepy. When at last she became aware of her surroundings, she found herself slouched in one of the wingback chairs in Steele's hotel room at the Standish. Her head no longer swam with nauseating instability, but she still struggled to stay awake until Steele knelt before her, mumbling, "You'd better lie down and sleep this off. I'm betting your dad would be more pissed if I brought you home drunk than if I brought you home in the morning."

She felt his hands on her legs, lifting one and then the other to relieve her of her high-heels, which had, more than once, almost caused her downfall. The intimacy of his touch helped her regain some awareness of herself and her situation. She wanted him to continue touching her but, then again, she didn't. As she watched him set her shoes aside, she saw the concern on his face and assumed he, like she, was having second thoughts about their interlude.

"So ... you've chickened out?" she baited, surprising herself with her insolence. Ever since she'd gotten drunk, she'd said bold and stupid things, unable to keep from blurting out whatever came to the tip of her tongue. After a second, she admitted she was hoping to push him until he backed down and refused to go through with the intimate encounter she'd tried to convince herself was necessary.

Still crouched down, he faced her and frowned. "No. I haven't chickened out."

Her heart seized. "You mean you're still going to–"

"No, I am not – at least not while you're in this condition." He looked her straight in the eyes. "I wouldn't want to be accused of taking unfair advantage of you."

She felt confused. She wanted him, but uncertainty still nagged her. "In the restaurant you said–"

"Relax, Becca. I told you I was just joking. After you baited me, I couldn't resist pulling your chain just a little." He patted her knee and smiled. "I'm going to put you to bed so you can sleep it off, then take you home in the morning. I don't think you want your dad to see you like this. Then all you'll have to worry about is surviving that whopping hangover you're going to have."

"But–"

He put his fingertips to her lips. "No argument. If I decided you could handle us being together, I'd want you to be awake and aware enough to enjoy and remember it – but only when you were ready. Something tells me you're not."

Blushing, she realized he'd called her bluff. She leaned forward, intending to reassure him she was in control of her faculties and knew what she was doing, but ended up falling into his arms. He rescued her from tumbling face-first to the floor, but her purse resting in her lap slid off and bounced on end, its contents scattering at her feet. He pushed her back in the chair and knelt to gather her things.

Standing up, he laid her purse in her lap. She looked up and found him staring down on her with a peculiar smirk. Then she remembered the condoms. Mortified, she opened her purse and saw the two silver packets were missing. When she shot him a questioning glare, he thrust out his palm to confront her with them. She grabbed for them, but with tiger quickness he closed his hand and eyed her with raised brows. Shriveling with embarrassment, she glanced away and mumbled, "My sister gave them to me. She thought I'd need them."

"You might as well put them away." She gawked at him when he tossed them in her lap and added, "They're not going to do you any good this evening."

Wilting under the rejection, she stuffed them in her purse. "I guess you think I'm pretty naïve and pathetic. No wonder you don't want to waste your time with me."

Still towering over her, he smiled. "I don't think you're pathetic. Naïve, yes. But not pathetic."

"Then why won't you—" With a huff she looked away from his penetrating gaze of superiority. She refused to beg. "Just take me home. I'm done making a fool of myself."

"I use the large size."

"What?" She gulped, and her face roared with heat as she stared at him in disbelief. "They come in different sizes?"

Maintaining a straight face, he nodded.

She flailed a hand in the air then squeaked like an agitated bird. He turned his head to hide his laughter. When her eyes darted at his crotch, she put her hand up to shield her face, but not in time to prevent him from catching her staring. Concentrating on her purse lying in her lap, she cleared her throat. "You're joking, just trying to scare me."

"The last thing I want is to scare you, Becca."

She exhaled, and a whimper escaped. She couldn't face him and couldn't stop wondering about the big secret he kept hidden behind his buttoned jacket.

"Let me help you to bed," he offered.

Still unable to look him in the eyes, she put her hands in his and let him guide her from the chair. With a hand on her shoulder to steady her, he stood behind her. Removing her wrap, he set it aside in the chair with her purse. When she felt the zipper of her dress opening down her back, she suffered a wave of emotion hard to identify. Maybe it was inebriation more than lust, but the closer he stood, the more she wanted him. Her breathing came fast and shallow, and when her dress slid down in a pool of taffeta around her feet, she gasped.

"Lord help me," Steele rasped, squeezing her arms. She felt his hot breath on her neck and leaned against him as he massaged her shoulders. She heard him swallow hard and whisper, "If you weren't drunk, I'd take you to bed so fast–" He let go of her and stepped back. "You'd better get under the covers right now, before I do something we'll both regret in the morning."

She craned her neck to look over her shoulder at him. When she saw his flushed, heady look, she sobered. He was the wolf, the savage, starved predator she had envisioned earlier. His eyes glinted like polished steel as they danced over her, begging for permission. She knew the prudent thing would be to grab her dress and run, but the yearning growing inside her denied prudence. She turned and faced him. He looked torn, hungry. She feared if she didn't do this now, tonight, she might never get another chance. And who knew what would happen in the next week? She managed a smile, hoping to encourage him.

His gaze skittered over her, and he gulped. "Becca, I'm having a devil of a time trying to do the right thing. Please tell me to leave you alone."

She sucked in a deep breath, trying to clear her mind of worry and guilt and consequence. Sex or love – it didn't matter. Tonight would be her night, *their* night. Another chance might never come. "I don't want you to leave me alone."

He turned away. "I know you're not ready, and I promised I wouldn't touch you. But right now, all I can think about is–" He groaned and raked his fingers through his hair.

The anticipation made her feel warm and alive. A sense of rightness permeated her body. She wanted his arms around her, his lips on hers, his hands touching her in places she'd never let herself imagine. She wanted his body pressed so tight to hers that nothing could separate them. She suffered a deep ache in her gut and lower – an ache that demanded relief. She knew he could fulfill her need like no one else. "I'm ready, Steele."

He spun around and faced her. Maintaining eye contact with him, she reached up and removed the rhinestone clip from her coiffure, letting her hair unfurl over her shoulders. When he stifled another groan, she knew he wouldn't – couldn't – say no. She closed the distance between them and stood just a few inches from him. He looked at her with undisguised lust but didn't move a muscle. He waited for her to initiate contact. That gesture chased away whatever vestige of doubt she harbored. "Steele," she murmured, pressing her black-lace-clad body against him, "Make love with me. Now." With her breasts mashed against his chest, she offered herself to him.

Bowing his neck, he took her mouth with ravishing speed and delivered soft, hungry kisses as he caressed her shoulders, whispering, "You won't be sorry, Becca. I promise."

* * * * *

Steele swept Becca into his arms and carried her to the bed. She was soft and light and yielding, looking up at him with pools of liquid trust. With her dark hair splayed over the pillows and her breasts rising and falling in fluttering breaths, she made him feel like he'd never felt before, as if he had the strength of ten men and could do no wrong.

As he eyed the bits of black lace daring him to rip them from her slender body, he felt hot tremors building inside him. But he was determined to hold his eagerness in check. He wanted to introduce her to the joys of love with slow, patient reverence. She needed that. She deserved it. For the first time in his life he wanted to be a man who could give that kind of love without holding back.

Managing a moment of clear thought, he bent down and kissed her. "I'll be right back." He darted into the bathroom and returned, bearing a towel. She frowned, but he diverted her attention with a roving kiss and set it aside on the bed.

Dropping his watch on the nightstand, he stepped out of his shoes. As he removed his jacket, he remembered a very important detail. He slipped his wallet from the inner breast pocket then draped his jacket on the floor. Extracting a foil package from an inner sleeve of his wallet, he opened it and placed the rolled sheath on the nightstand, within easy reach when needed.

He sat on the bed next to her and smiled, hoping to reassure her as he unbuttoned his shirt. The methodical details of undressing forced him to be patient despite the maddening urge flooding his chest and loins. She watched his every move as if she were expecting him to rush at her. The tinge of uncertainty clouding her face made him worry her resolve had weakened. He leaned over and nuzzled her neck and shoulders. She curled around him and stroked his hair. Her touch inflamed him, and he had to fight his impatience. He was so anxious about this encounter, it seemed like his first time too.

He shrugged out of his shirt, then pulled off of his undershirt in one fluid motion, dropping the garments atop his jacket on the floor. When he unbuckled his belt, her gaze flew to his hands. He unzipped his trousers and stepped out of them, then bent to remove his socks. When he straightened, he found her staring wide-eyed at his protuberance indiscreetly masked by his navy microfiber briefs. He ran a hand over her stocking-clad legs, giving her plenty of opportunity to look him over and get used to the idea before he went further.

* * * * *

Becca gawked at Steele's muscular, tanned, almost naked body rippling with power and virility. He'd said just a few words since they'd begun this journey into intimacy, but his eyes spoke volumes. His look of needful passion laced with reverence made her feel cherished and respected. Her eagerness mixed with fear was so intense, she suffered a flash of nausea and wondered if that was part of the hangover he'd warned her about. Overwhelmed with emotion, she ignored the hard pounding of her heart as she admired him.

Despite the discomforting conversation about sex they'd

had in the restaurant, she knew this wasn't some casual interlude or power play to best his brother. He wanted to celebrate their union, and so did she. He was magnificent, and she wanted to touch him everywhere, to worship him in ways she couldn't imagine. But she didn't know how, didn't know what to do, or what to expect. Unfamiliar urges raged inside her like wildfire, but she hesitated to act on them. As she glanced again at the prominence looming at his crotch, her ignorance turned to dread. *What if I'm not good enough?*

Her heart pounded harder, about to explode, and when he lay down on the bed beside her, she almost cried out from the strain of conflicting feelings. She didn't want to shy from him and deny what she'd asked for, but deep down she wished she'd never started this odyssey. In desperation, she turned her back to him.

Lying behind her, he placed a hand on her nearest shoulder, cupping himself to her as he smoothed his palm over her arm. She tried to remain still, but her innards trembled. When he nestled his face in her hair and kissed her in the crook of her neck, she almost leapt off the bed. The things happening inside her terrified her, and his touch, his nearness, intensified it. She stiffened when put his arm around her and drew closer. She knew he was working up to a more intimate merging of their bodies, and the details of how he would proceed made her heart race and her head spin worse than any mixed drink ever could.

He moved his hand across her fluttering bare belly, letting it rest motionless there. A minute passed, and then another, but he made no further advances. She wondered if he'd fallen asleep, but she was too embarrassed to turn and face him. After a while, she grew accustomed to the feel of him lying next to her. Her breathing slowed and she relaxed enough to convince herself he wouldn't harm her. He was letting her be in control – whatever that entailed.

Turning toward him, she found a serene expression on his face. With his pupils enlarged, his eyes looked almost black. When she glanced down, she saw he was still enlarged there too. He hadn't lost interest; he'd just been waiting for her to come to terms with what he planned. Her unnamed worries reared up again, and she gulped. "Steele, I–"

"Shh..." With gentleness he pushed her on her back, then covered her mouth with his. His lips roved over her face and neck. When he eased her bra down past her nipples and planted his mouth on one breast then the other, her breath caught. As he mauled and sucked, the sensation surprised her, but not in an unpleasant way. His ministrations brought new meaning to the urges nagging within her, and she reached up, running her fingers through his hair, grabbing thick handfuls. When he paused, she pulled him down and buried his face in her cleavage, writhing under his enthusiastic homage. Her response amazed her, but she didn't worry about it. Another preoccupation held her attention...

* * * * *

Steele reached beneath Becca and unclasped her bra with practiced ease. Pulling it from her, he let it drop to the floor as he surveyed her glorious body, naked down to her hips. He laid gentle kissed down her stomach, reassured when she no longer flinched at his touch. As he approached the last barrier of propriety – her panties – she tensed. He kissed her just below her bellybutton and felt her muscles flutter in rebellion.

Stretching himself alongside her, he cuddled her in his arms and whispered, "Trust me, Becca. I'll take care of everything." He pressed his lips to hers, and in moaning acquiescence she wilted under him. He slid a hand downward, weaving under her garter belt and panties. Feeling the tight curls of her pubic hair, he ravaged her mouth and slipped his fingers into her wet parting. She gripped his shoulders and bucked under him. Kissing her all over her face and neck, he massaged between her legs. She was hot and wet, and he was hard as a boulder, but he vowed not to enter her until she begged.

She moaned and undulated her hips in synchronization with his strokes, groping at his briefs. He grabbed her garter belt, and she lifted her hips, helping him push her lingerie restraints downward. When he cleared her toes, he tossed the tangled mess over the foot of the bed. She ran her hands over his clenched abs, then struggled with his briefs, slipping her fingers under the waistband. Her touch set him on fire. He shimmied out of his underwear and pitched it off to the side, then lay down again beside her.

She looked at his nakedness with a wide, feverish stare. He took her nearest hand and urged her to touch him there. When she curled her fingers around him, he shuddered with pleasure and felt a jolt, fearing he'd go off like a rocket before he had a chance to gratify her. His worry burned into solid lust as she massaged him with inquisitive exploration.

He arched with a moan, closing his eyes. When he felt her move beside him, he looked up just as she straddled him. Her slick spot hit the mark, and he groaned, wondering how he could hold out long enough to bring them both to culmination. He didn't want to flub her first time, but wanted it to be special, memorable, wonderful. In distraction he glanced at the condom within arm's reach, thinking now would be the proper time to don protection. He lifted his hand, but she pressed down on him and rode him, sliding back and forth with excruciating slowness. He grabbed her hips, rocking her faster as he craned his neck to devour her lips and breasts and anything else he could reach.

With his patience destroyed and his body slick with sweat, all he could think about was plunging inside her and submerging himself in her welcoming wet warmth. He pushed her back down against the bed and mashed his mouth on hers. Parting her legs with his, he maneuvered into position. As he stroked her opening with his full length, he felt his self-control slip. Trembling, he rasped, "Becca, honey, I don't know how long I can hold out."

Just as he turned to grab the condom, she gripped his hips and pulled him forward. Caught off-guard and off-kilter, he collapsed, plunging inside her with one great thrust driven by his full weight. They both cried out, he in ecstasy and she in painful surprise as she dug her nails deep into his shoulders. He shuddered, barely able to control himself. "Sorry, sorry," he groaned, smoothing his hands over her face.

Still inside her, he grabbed the towel nearby and tucked it under her thighs. Catching her breath, she buried her face in his chest and wrapped her arms around him. With his heart pounding and his body screaming to keep going, he gasped, trying to restrain himself.

Damn it! It wasn't supposed to be like this! He felt like a tree that had fallen on her, and he knew he'd hurt her. Stroking her hair and kissing the top of her head, he murmured, "I didn't mean to be so rough. We can stop if you want."

She shook her head, still hiding her face against his chest. He moved his hips, and she winced. He'd been a boar, but his body didn't care. It wanted more. He pushed her hair from her face and forced her to look him in the eyes. "I don't want to hurt you."

She touched a hand to his face. He kissed her, ready to pull away, thinking he'd blown it. But she returned his kiss and nibbled his lower lip, giving him a rush of passion that outstripped everything that had come before.

Struggling with caution, he moved inside her with torturing slowness until she uncoiled beneath him. He felt her moving with him, and the trance of instinct overtook him. His hips undulated of their own accord, making it almost impossible to maintain the gentle pace he'd set. As sweat beaded on his neck, he worried this dance demanded more than he'd anticipated, maybe more than he could give.

He quickened and she matched his rhythm. He thrust harder and she mewed again and again under his sweet punishment. Burying his face next to hers, he sucked in the warm scent of her hair and faint perfume. The earthy aroma of sex drove him, and with his chest about to explode, his throat tightened as forbidden words formed in his mind and traveled to his mouth. He wanted to tell her how much he loved her, and he suffered real pain holding back the urge. In the throes of passion, saying "I love you" would be easy, but after the moment passed, it would be impossible to take back those three magical, terrifying words. He clenched his mouth and closed his eyes as emotion robbed him of logic and forced his body to behave and feel what he never had before.

She lurched and cried out, and he felt her clench him with viselike strength. As she moaned over and over, he tried to pull back but knew it was too late. His self-control broke, and he released inside her with a powerful groan of pleasure and regret. He slowed to a sweaty, exhausted halt, breathing hard as he collapsed on her. Moving off center to keep from crushing her, he tried to calm his heart pounding in his ears.

After a long moment, he opened his eyes to slits and glanced at the unused condom still lying on the nightstand. His carelessness, and the ease with which it could have been avoided, made his blunder all the more difficult to face. *Idiot! You really screwed up.* He looked away, unable to consider the possible long-range consequences of what he'd just done.

After his breathing slowed and his heart quieted, he caressed her face. Kissing her neck, he dared to look into her eyes, expecting to see scorn and fear. Instead he saw tears of joy and gratitude. Her complete trust after his negligent abuse made him sorry to the core of his being. He pulled away and sat on the edge of the bed, with his back to her. When she touched his arm, he looked over his shoulder.

"What's wrong?"

He let out a ragged breath. Didn't she realize what he'd done? Maybe she had no idea yet what this meant to her, to him, to the new life they might be responsible for creating. But he knew. He'd lived the nightmare of his mother's mistake and her refusal to accept him, and he'd be damned if he'd let that happen to a child of his.

Forcing a smile, he leaned toward her and kissed her, skimming her face with his fingertips. "Nothing. Nothing's wrong." His eyes danced over her as she looked up at him and returned his smile. "You're beautiful, Becca." He kissed her again, and she blushed. "I want to take a quick shower. Join me?"

"Go ahead. I'll just rest for a little while."

"Are you okay?"

Still smiling, she blushed again. "I'm fine." Reaching out to him, she grazed her palm down his chest. Her touch charged him with renewed desire to have her, but he kept it in check. He wanted to savor this first experience, as bungled as it was.

"Steele?"

He squeezed her hand in his. "Yes?"

"I..." She withdrew her hand and looked aside.

"What, Becca?"

She shook her head. "Nothing."

He leaned over her, planting an arm on either side of her. "Tell me."

Trapped under him, she averted her eyes. "I don't want to upset you."

Fearing the worst, he forced a grim smile. "Say it."

"I think..." Clamping her mouth shut, she shook her head again.

"What?"

She flicked him a quick glance then blurted, "I think I love you."

His heart skipped a beat. He felt giddy, lightheaded. Grinning despite the import of her statement, he bent down and planted a soft lingering kiss on her mouth. Before he could stop himself, he whispered, "I think I'm glad."

She looked at him with what had to be surprised relief.

"Give me a few minutes to shower. When I come back, we'll talk." *Talk about how I royally screwed up, and how I'm going to make it right.*

Kissing her one last time, he got up from the bed and walked naked to the bathroom. As he turned on the shower and waited for the hot water, he realized that, despite what he'd done, he was wild with glee. He hadn't screwed up, not really. Making love with Becca wasn't a mistake by any measure. His one error had been failing to protect her as he'd promised. It was all his fault, but he'd make it up to her somehow. He'd make her see that everything was okay. Whatever came of this night, whatever happened between them, it would be right. Maybe she wasn't ready for what their future together would bring, but he was. All of it. Being with her, planning his life with her, having children, all the untidy surprises of life. He wanted it because, finally, it felt right.

Drenched in hot water, he laughed at his sudden urge to burst into a song-and-dance routine like Gene Kelly, singing in the rain.

CHAPTER 13

*T*oweling off and running a comb through his damp hair, Steele returned to the bedroom, intent on hashing out his feelings and his intentions with Becca. He'd made a grave error in failing to provide protection for their first experience together, but he was prepared to deal with the consequences. He *wanted* to deal with the consequences. The idea of raising their children together in a peaceful, loving home gave him a new perspective on his life he'd never before envisioned, nor even wanted to consider. Now things were different, better, *wonderful*. He felt love for the first time, and he wanted to shout the news to the world – but to Becca first.

When he walked over to the bed and found her sleeping on her side, tenderness coursed through him. Her beauty robbed him of his senses. He couldn't imagine enduring another moment of his life without the assurance that she would be his, always with him. In that moment he knew what he had to do. If nothing else went right in his plan to thwart his mother's machinations, he would marry Becca and protect her from further harm. Once she was his, the conniving Lila Morse could do nothing about it. And the truth about Becca's father would work itself out during the inquest – he'd do his best to ensure that. But first he had to secure Becca for himself, leaving nothing to chance.

With that decision made, he straightened the rumpled covers and pulled them over her shoulders. Then he slid into bed beside her and welded himself to her tender warmth.

* * * * *

Groggy, Becca opened her eyes to darkness. She couldn't

focus on any one object and couldn't seem to get her bearings. Feeling weak and nauseated, and needing to go to the bathroom, she realized she lay in an unfamiliar bed, naked, with someone next to her. *Steele.* Relieved, she retraced the evening's events leading up to their tempestuous interlude. The memory made her heat with shameful pleasure.

Behind her, Steele tightened his arm around her as if dreaming of their experience at the same moment she recalled it. Her heart pounded when she considered what she'd done – opening herself to this practiced womanizer she barely knew, and letting him ravage her innocence. Then like a naïve schoolgirl, she'd confessed her love for him. But he hadn't shrugged her off or walked away; he slept beside her as if the situation pleased him. Maybe making love with him and confessing her feelings hadn't been a mistake, but the best decision of her life.

Still confused, she let out a miserable sigh, then felt a rush of passion when she remembered the joy she couldn't have imagined before that moment. He was incredible – loving, caring, handsome, intelligent, with all the attributes a woman would want in a man. How could she not fall for him? Time would tell whether what they'd shared would last, but for now she had to relieve her bladder.

Carefully lifting Steele's arm off her, she scooted out of bed, then noticed the towel between her legs. Clutching it, she rushed to the bathroom and fumbled for the light switch. Pushing the door shut, she squinted in the light and pulled the towel away. She blanched when she saw the remnants of their lovemaking. Then she knew what he'd done. All that talk about using large size condoms was just that – talk. He hadn't used anything!

Stifling a cry, she stood barefoot on the cool tile floor and glanced around the well-appointed bathroom with its antique replica gold faucets and cultured marble sink. A stylish jacquard shower curtain with a pouf valance in the same pattern matching the bedspread concealed the tile tub surround. All this finery might have impressed her earlier, but now it seemed insignificant as she contemplated her mortifying, uncertain future. She might end up like Meg had – pregnant and unwed, with no prospects for a suitable mate to help raise her child. The one difference was, she would know who had fathered her baby. Knowing didn't matter if he refused to take responsibility and participate in their new family, and she had no way of predicting how he would react if she were indeed to become pregnant from this evening's wild indiscretion. Considering his childhood in an abusive home where he wasn't wanted, and his later noncommittal sexual escapades, she couldn't be sure he would be interested in becoming a family man.

She tried to think what to do, but her mind raced out of control. Should she stay and wait to see how he reacted to this development of which he had to be aware? Her heart screamed *run, run away!* She wanted to escape to a safe place to think things through, and deal with Steele later.

Grabbing a clean towel, she dashed to the tub and turned on the water for a quick rinse-off, hoping the activity wouldn't wake him. She wasn't prepared to face him now. She needed to think, and she couldn't do that under his watchful guidance and sweet manipulation. She had to figure things out, consider her options, and come to a decision that was hers alone.

She turned off the water and stepped out of the tub, listening for signs of him stirring in the bedroom. She heard nothing. Drying off and patting the wet ends of her hair, she slinked to the door and turned off the light to let her eyes adjust to the darkness. Peeking out, she saw his large form under the rumpled covers as he snored softly.

She tiptoed to the foot of the bed and scooped up her undergarments lying in scattered disarray on the floor. Sneaking to the chair where her dress sat nearby in a discarded pile, she fumbled with her stockings, trying to untangle them from her garter belt. Slipping everything on as fast as she could, she contorted her arms and managed to coax the zipper of her dress up her back. With her hair clasp and necklace stowed in her purse, she grabbed her shawl and shoes, then crept toward the door. She froze when she heard Steele moving in bed. Glancing back at him, she waited until she was sure he was just changing positions, then scurried to the door and turned the doorknob, releasing the inner security latch.

Once in the hall, she stepped into her shoes and raced to the elevator, pressing the call button as she looked back at the door to Steele's room. The elevator delivered her to the lobby where she hid in the pay phone station nestled in an alcove. Searching her purse for change, she cursed her inability to afford a cell phone and dropped the coins into the pay phone. She punched Meg's number. The phone rang and rang and rang. Finally Pete answered in a grumpy tone.

"It's me, Becca," she said, deciding not to mince words. "I need Meg to pick me up. Can she get on the phone for a second?"

"Are you in some kind of trouble?" Pete insisted with surprising chivalry.

"No. Just let me talk to Meg, please." Becca looked over her shoulder to make sure Steele hadn't discovered her escape and tracked her down. The older, heavyset woman working the reservation desk appeared to be asleep.

Becca heard Meg mumble something to Pete, then she hollered into the phone, "Becca, what the hell is going on? Where are you? What's wrong?"

"Just come and get me. I'm at the Standish."

"It's five-fifteen in the morning! What–"

"I don't have time to talk right now. I'm okay and nothing's wrong. I just need a ride home."

"But–"

"I'll explain later. Are you coming to get me or not?"

"Uh, yeah, sure. I'll be there in ten minutes."

"I'll be outside on the porch. Thanks, Meg."

Becca hung up, then glanced back at the woman snoozing behind the walnut reservation counter. Slipping out the front door, she shivered in the cool morning air and adjusted her taffeta wrap to cover more of her back and shoulders. Eyeing the door, she perched on the edge of a white wicker settee and waited for Meg's battered blue Cavalier to arrive.

135

* * * * *

"So where's Mr. Wonderful?" Meg sniped as she leaned over and swung the passenger door open for Becca.

Looking over her shoulder, Becca got into the car and slammed the door. "I assume he's still upstairs in bed, sleeping." Meg stared at her, waiting for an explanation until Becca ordered, "Will you drive, please?"

Meg urged her shuddering car forward. "What did he do to make you run away?"

"I'm not running away. I just need time alone to think."

"Think?" Meg looked her over as she putted through town. "The introductions are over. You two did the wild thing – right? Now you're officially a woman. What's to think about?"

Buckling with sudden tears, Becca turned away and glanced out the car window smeared with tiny handprints. She surveyed the drab Main Street buildings hulking in oncoming dawn like survivors of a ghost town. Sighing, she confessed, "There's a possibility I might be ... pregnant."

"What?"

Becca huffed and looked at her watch. "Can you step on it? I'd like to sneak into the house before Mom and Dad get up."

"Becca, how could you think you're pregnant? What happened to those party favors I gave you? You knew how to use them, didn't you? They weren't meant for water balloons."

"Yes, I know how they're supposed to work, but–"

"But you got busy with Steele and forgot about them until it was too late?"

"No! I mean yes. But Steele had his own. I mean, he couldn't use the ones you gave me. They were ... too small."

"What?" Meg guffawed with hysterical glee.

"I'm not joking. It's true. He–"

"Oh, I believe you," Meg assured, still chuckling. "That's not what I'm laughing about."

"Then what's so funny?"

136

"You. This whole situation. What are the chances of a twenty-six-year-old virgin running across a hunk like Steele Krueger – an extra-large hunk – and *maybe* getting pregnant the first time out of the gate?"

Becca scowled. "Well, didn't you get pregnant the first time you–"

"Yeah, but I was a stupid kid, and I was drunk."

"So was I!" Becca blurted, then realized how that sounded. "I mean..."

Meg started laughing again.

"Just hurry up and get me to the house, will you?"

Turning onto their parents' street, Meg quieted. "Seriously, Becca, what are you going to do?"

Becca rubbed her head that ached from confusion and something else she suspected was that hangover Steele had warned her about. "I don't know."

Pulling up in front of the house, Meg put the car in park and turned to her. "Well, why don't you try *talking* to him about it before you go tearing off in a panic?"

"And what's he going to do? Marry me out of pity?"

Meg snorted. "Men don't make stupid mistakes like that unless there are unusual circumstances, or they're inexperienced, or they're just plain careless jerks. I doubt Steele is inexperienced. And if you're so taken with him, he can't be that much of a jerk."

"He's not a jerk," Becca confirmed. "But why would he–"

"Hey, just because he's a big-shot Chicago lawyer, that doesn't mean he can't be as confused as you are about personal stuff. Maybe, since he figured out you hadn't ever been with anybody, maybe he just wanted to ... you know ... *feel* things a little better. Guys don't really enjoy taking a shower in a raincoat, if you know what I mean. And maybe he just messed up the timing. That happens sometimes. Trust me, I know." She rubbed her belly and grinned. "But I'm betting subconsciously he *wanted* to mess up."

Becca glared at her. "Why would you say that?"

137

"Think about it. He's a handsome guy in his thirties. He meets you, a beautiful young innocent about to marry his slug of a brother. What's the fastest, easiest way he can screw things up so Conn won't want to have anything to do with you?"

Becca scowled and shook her head. "I can't believe he'd do that just to get the best of Conn."

"I'm not saying that's what he had in mind. In fact, I'm not saying that he even did it on purpose. But if he cares about you, he's going to find a way to keep you for himself, even if he doesn't want to admit to himself that what he did might not have been a real honest-to-goodness accident."

Becca tried to reason out what Meg said, but her head hurt.

"Talk to him, Bec, before you go jumping to wild conclusions and do something dumb. Give him a chance to work things out with you." She rubbed her belly again. "You never know. You two might be pretty good at parenting and actually enjoy it."

Sighing with exhaustion and confusion, Becca opened the car door and stepped out. "Thanks for coming to my rescue, Meg."

"Anytime. What are sisters for? I'll be over with the kids later, to check on you. Try to get some rest. You look bushed."

* * * * *

By the time Becca changed out of her rumpled evening clothes and crawled into bed, dawn had come. She felt exhausted but not sleepy, yet sleep seemed to be the only plausible escape from the worries that hounded her. She knew she had to rest so she could think things through and come to some kind of decision about her situation with Steele, but her mind kept racing around like a hyper dog trapped in a tiny pen.

Lying in bed, she forced herself to take deep, calming breaths, hoping sleep would overtake her. But instead of relaxing, she focused on the pleasant ache of her recent introduction to love. When she recalled the intimate details of her interlude with

Steele, their bodies merging as one, her heart pounded and sent fiery surges of secret joy pulsing through her.

Steele. Never was a man truer to his name, yet also a paradox. Strong yet gentle, powerful and patient, exciting and understanding. He was everything she could want in a mate, but did he want to be *her* mate? He had acknowledged her admission of love without hesitation, but he hadn't told her he loved her. Perhaps he took for granted that what they'd shared last night was just as good as saying, "I love you." Then again, maybe to him it was just another fine session of sex rather than real love. Was she assuming too much?

And how could he be so savoir-faire after that intimate faux pas – when he *knew* what he had done? He had cuddled her and smiled with satisfaction, but never mentioned the forgotten condom. She was somewhat ignorant of such things, but his previous experience must have taught him better than that. Was it an honest mistake, or was Meg right, that he did it on purpose? The evidence against him looked bad, but she wasn't sure what to think. She knew she couldn't blame him for the error until she discovered his true intentions, if that were possible.

Becca cringed under the covers, squeezing her eyes shut, trying to block out the growing light in her room, as if that would also block out the growing problems in her life. Every time she thought about the possibility that she could become – be – pregnant, her mind stalled. And she didn't want to think what Lila Morse would do when she found out her future daughter-in-law had been intimate with the wrong son.

She glanced at her alarm clock and made herself uncoil and relax. Her mother and father would be getting up soon. With her mother working until eleven at night, she expected her to sleep in, but she was often up by seven. And since her father had begun taking medication for his back injury, he didn't sleep well and preferred to sit in his well-worn recliner rather than lie in bed for extended periods. He would be up before her mother. Delaying her confrontation with them was another reason for her to sleep late. She closed her eyes. Before her mind had a chance to run more troubling thoughts through her head and rob her of tranquility, she drifted off.

* * * * *

Steele turned in bed, dragging the covers over his head to muffle the noise until he realized it was the phone ringing. Fumbling across the nightstand, he heard something hit the floor with a soft thump as he dragged the receiver to his ear and rasped, "Yes?"

"You're still sleeping? It's after eight o'clock. I expected you'd be up long before now."

Recognizing his mother's cold voice, Steele sat up straight in bed, noting he was naked. In a flash he recalled the night before and scoured the room for Becca. All the lights were off, and the room was quiet. Her dress was not in the floor by the chair, and her purse had disappeared. His heart clenched. He knew she'd left, but he had no time to consider the situation as his mother said, "I called to invite you to the house for lunch with the family at noon."

He raked a hand through his disheveled hair and tried to make himself concentrate on the trap he knew his mother was setting for him. But all he could think about was Becca – where she'd gone and why she'd vacated his bed without a word. With sick dread he convinced himself he knew why she'd sneaked away. She was probably worried sick over the stupid thing he'd done last night, and she had every right to be angry with him for his carelessness. He had no idea how he would regain her trust and earn her forgiveness – and elicit her acceptance of what needed to be done to rectify the situation he'd created.

"Steele, are you there?" his mother demanded.

He sighed. "Yes."

"You seem distracted. Trouble sleeping?"

He glanced down at his watch and wallet that he'd knocked to the floor near his discarded clothes. The unpackaged condom he'd neglected to use still lay on the nightstand where he'd left it.

He scowled. "I slept very well, thank you – not that I believe for a moment you're concerned."

"Concerned? No. I assumed your conscience was bothering you, after your eventful activities last night."

"You don't know a damned thing about my activities," he challenged, deciding he should pay closer attention to what his mother was saying. Obviously she was working toward something.

"You'd be surprised what I know, Steele. I got a call this morning from Patsy Ferguson. You remember her? The mayor's wife? It's been several years, but–"

Steele exhaled hard. "I'm happy for you that you still have friends, but I've got to shower and dress. I have a lot of things to take care of today, and I don't think I'll be able to make it for lunch with 'the family.'"

"I suggest you reconsider," his mother growled.

"And why is that?"

"We have a very important matter to discuss."

Steele frowned. "Why don't you save us both the time and trouble and get it over with right now?"

"Fine." She took a deep breath. "Mrs. Ferguson – bless her gossiping black heart – mentioned she and the mayor had dinner at Delmarco's Steak House in Marion last night. She said she saw a young lady she swore was 'that sweet little Sedder girl that's marrying Conn next Saturday' leaving Delmarco's in the company of a man that matched your description. Mrs. Ferguson said the poor Becca-look-alike appeared to have had too much to drink and almost had to be carried out by her date."

"That's a very touching story. What's your point?"

"I'm guessing *you* were the man in question, and it was indeed Becca whom Mrs. Ferguson spied in your company."

Steele decided admitting nothing was the best tack.

"She ended up back at your hotel room with you, didn't she? And presumably she provided you with an entertaining diversion which kept you up and exhausted your resources, causing you to sleep much later than usual."

Steele exhaled with tired disinterest. "Presume all you want. I don't give a damn what you and your gossiping spies suspect."

"Just tell me if it's true." His mother's voice sounded too calm. "Did you take advantage of Becca last night?"

He wanted to blurt the truth and get everything out in the open. *Yes*, he and Becca had made love, and *yes*, he had screwed up, possibly getting her pregnant. But something made him wary about giving away his position, and so he said nothing again.

"Very well," his mother snarled. "I'll get the truth out of Becca when she comes to the house for lunch."

"She's not having lunch with you." That was an order, not an objection.

"Yes, she is. I spoke with her on the phone just before I called you. I suggest you be here at noon. You won't want to miss the discussion."

Steel slammed the phone back on the cradle, smashing the smile lilting in his mother's retort. With a huff he lunged out of bed. He was tired of letting his mother have her way, and he intended to do something about it.

* * * * *

Cutting short his usual morning run, Steele shaved, showered, and opted for breakfast downstairs in the Standish's restaurant adjacent to the hotel lobby. The Standish was indeed a stately old icon, but to him it was just another reminder of his miserable childhood spent with the Morses. His mother and The Ogre had dined at the Standish almost every Saturday night, dragging him along to show the world what a happy family they were. His mother wasn't so concerned about his well-being as she was that he sit still and be quiet and act like a little gentleman in public. Dulling that mental barb had been Steele's overriding purpose in choosing to stay at the Standish on his return to Fenton.

Wearing light gray slacks and a navy polo shirt, he strolled

142

into the restaurant, feeling rejuvenated and relaxed, despite the reminder of his past and the many tasks that lay ahead of him. He was surprised to see several business people populating the restaurant on a sunny Saturday morning, along with a few tourists and the small local crowd. All eyes seemed to zero in on him as he took a secluded table at the rear. He didn't recognize anyone, but he was afraid most of them knew who he was – and what he'd done. As he pretended to examine the contents of the restaurant's maroon leather hardbound menu with its silky gold tassel, he felt like he had 'Ravisher of Innocence' branded on his forehead.

By the time the grim beanpole waitress came to take his order, he'd almost convinced himself a quick cup of coffee would suffice. He wasn't up to enduring the whispered gossip and impolite stares he imagined were directed at him. But when his stomach growled, he gave in to his physical needs and ordered a large breakfast platter with eggs and biscuits and gravy and bacon. The waitress left him with a carafe of coffee, and he guzzled the caffeine juice, hoping to charge up his adrenaline and his courage for the upcoming challenge of meeting his mother on her own turf. Before he subjected himself to that torture, he had a few errands to take care of.

* * * * *

"Irene!" Steele greeted with a hearty gush. "Sorry to call you at home on Saturday, but–"

"What's going on, Steele?" his executive assistant demanded. "Are you in some kind of trouble with your mother?"

What made him think he could fool Irene? "I need you to do me a favor. Can you reach Chuck Lapinski and ask him to call me on my cell phone as soon as possible?"

Steele could picture Irene's familiar scowl as she said, "What do you need with the firm's investigator? What's going on down there, Steele?"

"Nothing I can't handle."

"Steele..."

"I don't have time to explain right now."

She sighed with audible exasperation. "Give me the short version."

"I just need Chuck to run a few background checks and do a little snooping around for me. That's all."

Irene made a little humming, growling noise over the phone. "Do you need me to come down there?"

Steele laughed at that. The fur would fly if Irene tangled with his mother – something he decided he might like to see. He squelched a smile and chuckled again. "No, I don't think so. At least not yet. But thanks for the offer. Just ask Chuck to call me. If I don't answer, tell him to leave a number on my voicemail where I can reach him when I'm free."

"Anything else?"

"No, that's it for now. Thanks, Irene. You're a real sweetheart."

"Um-hm. I get the feeling you've said the same thing to some other woman recently – in a different context. Is that what all this mysterious business is about? Have you gotten yourself snagged in a romantic mess of some sort?"

"Something like that."

"Steele, what *is* going on down there?"

"It's too soon to tell. When I figure it out, I'll let you know."

"You'd better keep me posted."

"I promise." As an afterthought he asked, "Say, what are you doing next weekend?"

"Why?"

"Would you like to come to a wedding?"

"Whose?"

"Mine."

"What? Steele–"

"Gotta run, Irene. I'll tell you all about it later." He hung up before she could grill him. He really did have a lot to do before he met with his mother at noon – and one important stop to make before heading to Becca's house.

CHAPTER 14

*S*tanding under the shade of the lone oak in her parents' tiny back yard, Becca watched Meg and her kids run the crabgrass to bare dirt.

Three-year-old Joshua sat in the nearby sandbox while his twin Jeremy manned a plastic bucket and dumped sand on his head. Ignoring the brotherly indignity, Meg whooped and swayed back and forth on the same ancient swing set she and Becca had played on as children. The rickety, lackluster pink and green framework bowed and groaned under her weight. In the seat next to her, eight-year-old Sean squealed as his eleven-year-old brother Michael pushed him ever higher.

Instead of cautioning the boys about the aged swing set and getting sand in their eyes, Meg played alongside them, swinging much too high for an expectant mother seven months along. Becca scowled and swiped her clammy palms over her crinkled gauze skirt. "Meg, you shouldn't be on that swing set. The chains are rusty and liable to–"

Meg skidded her feet in the dirt ditch under the swing. With lumbering effort, she hoisted herself up from the cracked and faded plastic seat. "Oh, quit being a worrywart, Bec. Life's short – have fun while you can."

"Yeah, right. I followed your advice last night, and look where that landed me!"

Meg faced her and sobered. "Calm down, will you? Everything will work out. Mom will get over her little hissy-fit about you catting around – just as soon as Steele makes an honest woman of you." She grinned.

Becca turned away as new tears welled up in her eyes. She had no hope of that happening, even if Steele were to offer. She was already pledged to marry Conn, and Mrs. Morse would see that she carried through, or their dad would pay for her failure.

As if to rub salt in that open wound, Becca's mother had been waiting for her when she got up this morning. Right away she launched into one of her worst yelling tirades ever, accusing Becca of 'whoring around.' Becca wasn't used to being talked to that way, but she couldn't deny it. What she and Steele had done last night felt so right, even though she knew it was wrong. The consequences of her actions would mean uncertainty in her future – and certain danger for her father if Lila Morse found out. And the way things had been going, Lila probably already knew all about her tryst with Steele. Why else would she have called this morning, demanding she show up at the Morse house for lunch?

"Have you talked to Steele yet?" Meg prodded, placing a hand on her shoulder. Becca shook her head, unable to answer. "But you're going to, right?"

With a sigh, Becca sucked up her dread and faced her sister. "I don't know what to say to him."

"How about 'I love you' for starters?" Meg eyed her. "You *do* love him, don't you?"

Becca glanced down at the ground and nodded.

"Then what's the big deal? You love him, he loves you, and baby makes three. You all live happily ever after. End of story."

"Not quite." Becca swiped a hand across her tear-streaked cheeks.

"Oh, yeah. I forgot. There's still the evil queen and her son the retarded troll."

Becca almost laughed at that. "Right. The queen and the troll."

Meg circled an arm around Becca's shoulders and squeezed. "If I were you, I'd leave them to your knight in shining armor. I'll bet he's working on a magic sword or something right now that'll take care of them."

Becca sighed, wishing that were true. But she knew better. The evil queen had hinted at a dark spell against the knight coming to Becca's rescue. And Becca couldn't chance her champion falling in her service. She would have to endure Queen Lila's sinister scheme and see it through to the end, despite Steele's objections. She felt sick at the very thought of it, but didn't see a way around it.

* * * * *

When the young bleach-blond woman answered the door, Steele was taken aback by the size of her protruding belly. It reminded him of slip with Becca last night, and the possibility that in a few months she would exhibit a similar profile. Assuming this was Becca's sister Meg, Steele noted the smirk on her pretty face and realized too late she'd caught him staring at her ... condition. He straightened. "Uh, hi. I'm–"

"Yeah, Steele. I'm Meg, Becca's sister. Come on in. It's about time you showed up. It's after eleven-thirty. What have you been doing all morning? She hasn't heard a peep from you, and she's a friggin' basket case. She was about to go over and face the Morses – *your family* – all by herself."

"Well, I–"

"I'll handle this," a short, spindly, forty-something woman admonished as she darted in front of Meg. With no smile to soften her hard lined face, she held the door and looked Steele over from head to toe. "I'm Emily Sedder, Becca's mother. You and me need to have a little talk right now, Mr. Hotshot Chicago Attorney."

Mrs. Sedder grabbed Steele by the arm and pulled him into the small dark paneled living room. With a quick look over her shoulder – he assumed to make sure no one else was within earshot – she turned on him, then took time out to light a cigarette. Steele guessed her hands trembled from anger rather than trepidation, because she betrayed no fear as she glared up at him and growled, "Listen up, Lawyer Boy. The crap ends here and now."

She narrowed her eyes and pointed her burning cigarette at him like a nun with a ruler about to smack his knuckles. "I've had enough of your family messing with Becca. She's a good daughter and a sweet girl with a level head on her shoulders. But in the last couple weeks since your creepy brother's been hanging around, she's turned into a nervous wreck and done some of the stupidest things I've ever seen. Agreeing to marry him tops them all! Now there's gossip all over town about her late-night shenanigans with *you*. I got plenty of calls from concerned and just plain nosy folks, and I won't have you sullying her reputation like that. You hear me? You snooty rich people think money lets you do anything you want to everybody else, but you're wrong. I–"

"Mrs. Sedder, I assure you–"

"Shut your fancy Rembrandt-white, hundred-dollar-an-hour yap, and let me finish!"

Steele blinked in astonishment. He started to object, but Mrs. Sedder pointed the glowing tip of her cigarette at him again, and he did as she ordered, shutting his mouth.

"Yeah, you just stand there and try listening to somebody else for a change. You might learn something." She puffed enthusiastically on her cigarette, then flicked the ashes into a small black swirled plastic ashtray clutched in her palm.

Blowing smoke from her nostrils, she gave him another scathing top-to-bottom survey. "I can see why Becca fell for you so quick. You're quite a package, Pretty Boy, with your slick salon haircut, designer clothes, spiffy Rolex, and pricey cologne. Having gobs of money sure sweetens the deal. You're real charmer, aren't you? Bet you know just the right things to say to a woman, to get what you want from her."

"Mrs. Sedder, if you'd just let me explain–"

Her nasty glare silenced him. He wasn't a betting man, but he was ready to wager this scrappy little woman could hold her own if pitted against his mother. Lila Morse commanded a catty turn of phrase, but Emily Sedder wouldn't let her opponent get a word in edgewise.

"Now, I don't know quite what you've been doing with my daughter, Mr. Steeleman Krueger, but I have a pretty damn good idea. By the way Becca was trying her best to defend you this morning, I'm betting you've already gotten into her panties."

Steele felt his face burning. He couldn't dispute that on-target accusation.

"You may have her bowled over, but I'm not going to stand by and let you and your family take advantage of her – or the rest of us. Her father's had his share of bad luck and bad choices through the years, but he's an honest man, a good man, and a hard worker. He loves his family, and it's killing him to see Becca in such a mess. And I sure as hell don't appreciate your snooty momma and her fancy limo-lawyers trying to railroad him for what happened at the dairy. He's suffering right now, and he needs medical care and therapy. But until this deal with the inquest is settled, we're on our own, and we just can't afford the medical bills to get him fixed up. That's what workmen's comp is for, but it looks to me like your momma's trying to sidestep all that and save her precious dairy from having to shell out the money."

"I agree with you," Steele blurted when Mrs. Sedder stopped to take another draw on her cigarette.

She scowled at him. "What kind of idiot do you take me for? You think you can sidle up to me and sweet-talk your way out of this? You're not getting off the hook that easy."

"I'm not trying to get out of anything, Mrs. Sedder. Believe me. I'm here to help Becca – and the rest of you. I don't like what my mother's been doing any better than you do."

Mrs. Sedder's scanned him with her dark, uncompromising eyes. "Well, you sure have a funny way of showing it, breezing in here and using Becca the way you have."

Steele felt himself getting hotter with embarrassment. Becca's mother wasn't about to cut him any slack. "You're right, Mrs. Sedder," he admitted. "I had no business imposing my personal wants on her, considering her situation was already complicated and unworkable. I know Becca's confused and distressed, but believe me when I tell you it was never my intention to take advantage of her – especially not under those

149

circumstances."

"Then what the hell *are* your intentions toward my daughter?" Mrs. Sedder stubbed out her cigarette and eyed Steele as if he were an impossibly complex Chinese puzzle.

Steele glanced at Becca's sister Meg standing some distance away, watching the proceedings as if waiting for some sign of weakness or untruth. He sighed and looked back at Becca's mother, then reached into his trouser pocket and pulled out a small black velvet box. When he opened it to show Mrs. Sedder its contents, he decided the look of shock on her face was worth all the nasty barbs she'd leveled at him. "May I see Becca now?"

Meg walked over, and her eyes bugged when she spied the stunning marquis engagement ring. "Good golly, Miss Molly! That must have cost a fortune!"

He smirked. "Where's Becca?"

Meg dragged her eyes from the ring box as he snapped it shut. "She's in the back yard with the boys."

Steele followed her gaze and breezed through the dowdy kitchen made unpleasantly cheery with a blazing bright yellow sunflower motif on the dishtowels, curtains, and vinyl tablecloth. As he reached the back door, he heard Meg and her mother scuttling behind him. Knowing they'd be gawking out the kitchen window at him, he proceeded across the small fenced yard toward Becca sitting with her back to him in a dilapidated swing set.

* * * * *

Becca jumped with a start when she felt the strong male hands on her shoulders. Knowing it was Steele, she catapulted from the swing and turned to confront him. When she saw his handsome face serene with confidence, all the delicate personal questions she had rehearsed flew out of her head. She staggered back and looked aside.

"Becca, I'm sorry," he said, taking a step toward her. She turned away. She knew she needed to resolve things with him, but

150

she couldn't face him.

"I know there's nothing I can do or say to make up for what I've done, but I–"

"Hey, are you gonna marry my Aunt Bec?" eight-year-old Sean blurted. Becca turned in horror as Meg's two older sons shuffled from the fence and approached Steele. "My mom says you ought to, after what you did."

Michael, the oldest, elbowed his younger brother. "Shut up, dummy!"

"Sean, Mikey" Becca said, rushing over to hush her nephews. "Mind your manners. Mr. Krueger is a guest, and we don't talk that way to our elders. Michael, say hello to Mr. Krueger."

"Hi," Michael mumbled.

When Becca looked back at Steele in embarrassment, she found him smiling as he reached to shake Michael's hand. "Nice to meet you, Michael. And you too, Sean."

She let out a sigh. He was too much of a gentleman to let a couple mouthy kids put him off.

"What did your mom say I did?" Steele prodded, still smiling as sandy-haired Sean and dark-haired Michael eyed him.

Michael shrugged with youthful sullenness. "Oh, Sean, he don't know what he's talking about. Mom never said nothing much of anything, except that you and Aunt Bec ought to get married right away."

Steele leaned forward and rested his hands on his thighs to meet the boys at their eye level. "So, do you two think I ought to marry your Aunt Bec?" He glanced up at Becca and winked.

Michael shrugged again. "I guess, if you like her. It would be better than her marrying that Conn guy. He's a jerk. I don't like him."

"Yeah, a jerk," Sean confirmed, kicking up dirt with the toe of his scruffy sneaker.

"I agree." Steele straightened, then faced Becca. "Sounds like the decision's been made for us."

Becca opened her mouth to object, but was distracted by

151

Meg's twins, Joshua and Jeremy, as they raced toward Steele and latched onto his legs. "Boys, boys!" she cautioned as she reached for them. "Don't get Mr. Krueger's pants dirty."

"I'm washable," Steele reassured, laughing as he bent down and scooped up a child in each of his arms. Beneath the stretchy fabric of his shirtsleeves, Becca saw his biceps bulge like cantaloupes. She gulped in awe.

"And what are your names?" he prodded with a grin, as if he were a giant who'd captured two interlopers in his territory. "Flopsy and Mopsy?"

The boys giggled and mumbled their names as they gawked wide-eyed at Steele. They seemed just as amazed as Becca. Getting a grip on the situation, Becca said, "You boys go in the house and let your mother clean you up. You're both covered with sand." She gave Steele a reproving look, and he knelt down to release them. They ran off, giggling all the way to the back door.

"Cute kids," he said, glancing back at them. "Almost makes you want to have a couple of your own." He turned on her, obviously gauging her reaction to that suggestion.

Her head swam with surprise and anger. "I don't know what kind of game you're playing, but–"

"It's not a game, Becca."

He took her hands in his, and reluctantly she allowed it. She tried to look up into his eyes, to see what truth they held, but couldn't make herself maintain contact.

"We need to talk," he said with a note of urgency in his voice. She scowled at that understatement. Before she could confront him, Meg poked her head out the back door and hollered for Michael and Sean to get in the house. After she repeated the order with a veiled threat of punishment, they trudged away, giving Steele a parting once-over as they left. When Sean waved with a sheepish smile, Steele grinned and gave him a nice parade wave. Sean laughed and scampered to the house after his older brother.

Steele turned back to face Becca, and she crossed her arms,

examining him under a critical new light. "You seem to have a way with kids. I wouldn't have expected that of you."

"There are a lot of things you don't know about me, but I intend to rectify that." His grin faded when she failed to soften her stance "My executive assistant, Irene, has two grandsons that I see once in a while. They're pretty lively, but good-natured. They're great teachers of patience. I enjoy being around them. Your nephews remind me of them."

Becca gave a nod of acceptance, but she wasn't letting him off the hook just yet. He had a lot more explaining to do. "What the hell were you thinking last night?"

Caught off guard, he blushed. "I *wasn't* thinking. That's when things got ... messed up. I'm sorry."

With that look in his eyes, he seemed to be begging for her forgiveness, but still she wasn't ready to concede. "I trusted you. Now ... now–" She threw up her hands and turned away from him. Nothing was coming out the way she wanted. She sounded hurt and petulant, when all she wanted was reassurance from him. She was so confused, she didn't know what to say.

He came up behind her and placed his hands on her shoulders. "I want to make things right, Becca."

Tears sprang from her eyes. She wanted to hear him say that, but not just because he felt it was his duty to do the right thing. She wanted him to *want* her as much as she wanted him. But she wouldn't beg him to say it.

He sighed. "I know I went too far, too fast with you. I wish I'd taken the time to be more patient. But considering our situation, you and I both know we don't have the luxury of time."

She turned to face him. "So ... you rushed to get me in bed, just so Conn wouldn't be first?"

"No! I mean, yes. Sort of. But that wasn't the only reason." His expression seemed pained as he whispered, "I *wanted* to make love with you. I know I should have waited, but I couldn't. And I'm not sorry at all for what we did. Except for the ... except for screwing it up. I *am* sorry about that. But not because I didn't want it to happen. I mean, I did, but only if you were ready for that. And I knew you weren't – not with everything going on with my mother. I just ... lost it. For that – for not giving you a choice in the matter – I am sorry."

Well, that bumbling apology pretty much covered everything, Becca decided. Everything except how they were going to handle the situation. She sucked in a deep breath. "So, what now? When your mother finds out–"

"I think she already knows. Somebody called her and told her they saw us at Delmarco's last night."

Becca swiped a hand over her mouth, holding in the groan threatening to seep out. She figured as much. "So that's why she wants me over there for lunch. She's going to lower the boom on me." Tears flooded her eyes, and she turned away. "I was thinking of myself, of what *I* wanted, and now my dad is going to pay."

"No, he's not." Steele grabbed her shoulders and spun her around to face him. "Listen to me, Becca. My mother is not going to get away with anything. The situation might get a little rough for everyone for a while, but we're going to fight her, and we're going to win. Do you hear me?"

Becca wilted in his arms. She wanted to believe him. She wanted to believe he could make all her problems go away. But she didn't see how he could. "Steele, I–"

"You've got to trust me on this. I'm doing everything I can to get some counteractive evidence against my mother. I've got a private investigator working on it right now. And even if I'm not able to come up with anything before the inquest next Monday, I'm confident something will turn up before it gets to the trial stage. Don't even for a second let my mother fool you into thinking you have to throw your life away by marrying my stupid-ass brother. I won't allow it."

He pulled something from his pants pocket. The moment she saw the black velvet box, she froze. He flipped it open, but she turned aside, refusing to look at it. She couldn't allow herself to be tempted further and chance letting her father suffer. She had to be strong. "Steele, don't."

154

"Damn it, Becca! I want to marry you. At least give me the courtesy of listening to my proposal before you refuse."

Swiping tears from her eyes, she turned on him. "I don't want you proposing to me because you think that's the only way to save me from your brother. And I don't want you proposing because you feel obligated in case ... in case..."

"In case we've made a baby?"

She blushed when he said it out loud. Voicing the possibility elevated it from a fearful uncertainty to a real probability.

"And to save you from marrying my brother? You're damned right I'm going to propose – on both counts."

"But if you don't love me, it means nothing!" She shot him a wounded glare, then looked aside again. He didn't say anything, and that moment of silence spoke volumes to her. Her heart sank.

"What makes you think I don't love you?" he murmured.

"Because ... because you never *said* you did." She eyed him. "We barely know each other, and everything has happened so fast. We haven't had time to think about anything! I'm not naïve enough to believe in happily ever after, and I don't expect you to wave a magic wand and make it happen. But I also don't want you marrying me for the wrong reason. You may think it's the right thing to do, but if you don't love me, it's all wrong, and I won't agree to a mercy marriage, just to find out six months or a year down the road that it's not what you want anymore. I can't say 'I do' when you're not sure you want to."

"I'm sure, Becca." He gripped her shoulders. "I've never been more sure of anything in my life. I *do* love you. After last night, I thought you understood that."

As if to prove what he said, he drew her to him and kissed her with soft thoroughness. The contact of his mouth on hers sent a charge through her, and she felt shaky when he pulled away.

"I know you have doubts, and I can't blame you. I have doubts too. I'm scared, if you want the truth. This is a first for me – I've never felt like this before in my life, and I'm not sure what to do, or how to do it. I'm sorry if I haven't done everything just right. I know I've rushed you and messed things up, but please don't mistake my bungling for insensitivity. I care about you, and I love you. I'm just not accustomed to saying those words." He massaged her shoulders as if he were trying to rub away her insecurity. "I wish I had more time to reassure you and prove to you that my feelings are genuine. But for the sake of your father and our child – and us – I'm asking you to trust me. Please."

Becca stared at him through the kaleidoscope of her tears, trying to see the truth, the earnestness in his heart. This was all happening too fast. She could understand how she, an inexperienced and lonesome young woman, could fall in love almost instantly with a man like Steele, especially after the intimacy they'd shared. But why would he feel the same about her? What did she have to offer him that no one else had?

Before she could puzzle out that question, Steele grabbed her left hand and forced the exquisite diamond ring onto her finger. The band was slightly too large, but that could be fixed. What couldn't be fixed was the fact that she was overdue at his mother's house for lunch, and the ring on her finger would be a dead giveaway that would damn her father to ruin. She started to slide the ring off, but Steele clenched her hand in his and stopped her. "Don't say 'no.' Don't say 'maybe.' I won't take any answer but 'yes.'"

"Steele, you know I can't wear this in front of your mother. She'll–"

"Yes you can, and you will. Now come on." He put an arm around her and urged her toward the house. "We need to go. We don't want to be more than fashionably late for lunch. My mother will be upset enough as it is when she realizes you're not going along with her master plan."

"But my dad–"

"He'll be okay. We've got a week to fix things. Trust me, Becca."

Cradled in Steele's strong arm, Becca trudged alongside him and glanced down at the ring he'd forced on her finger. It was stunning, sparkling in the sunlight like the proud and showy

156

adornment that it was. He must have spent a small fortune on it. And for what? Unless some amazing miracle came along to absolve her father and deliver him from the ruin Steele's mother was plotting, in seven days Becca would walk down the aisle and marry Steele's brother.

As Steele ushered her through her mother's small kitchen, Becca heard her nephews yelling and making explosion noises downstairs in the basement. All hell was breaking loose in their childhood fantasy war games. She and Steele came to a halt when they reached the living room.

Meg and her mom and her dad were all lined up waiting for them. Meg smiled, her face blooming with relief when she saw Becca wearing Steele's ring. As far as she was concerned, all was right with the world.

Her mother's expression was a little harder to figure out. She wore her usual crabby scowl, but there was an uncharacteristic softness in her eyes as she looked at the two of them.

Her dad, trying very hard to stand up straight without depending on his cane, gave Steele a critical visual appraisal. When his eyes had traveled up and down the length of him, he glanced at Becca, giving her a questioning look. Becca managed a reassuring smile, and he smiled back. Turning to Steele, he said, "You take good care of my little girl."

"You can count on it, Mr. Sedder," Steele promised.

CHAPTER 15

*A*s Steele parked his car in the middle of the concrete circle drive, the huge portico of his mother's two-story white clapboard house loomed to his right. He glanced at the clock on his dashboard – seventeen minutes after twelve, just late enough to piss off the old broad. He smiled at Becca, then noticed her hands clasped in her lap. The diamond on her finger stood out against her white knuckles, and she looked pale as she whispered, "Do we really have to go in?"

He gave her knee a gentle squeeze. "Don't worry. Everything will be fine. I can handle my mother." She let out a small sigh, and he stepped out of the car to open her door for her.

As he escorted her up the grandiose steps, he swept his gaze over the majestic matching weeping willows on either side. They helped balance the overblown nouveau plantation architecture. Years had passed since he'd laid eyes on the place, but he still bristled at the sight of it. Despite his uneasiness, he refused to be intimidated by the overbearing stateliness of his mother's home.

As he and Becca approached the entrance, the heavy carved wooden doors parted to reveal a middle-aged woman wearing a droll maid's uniform – black dress with starched white apron, complete with a ridiculous white cap. Steele didn't recognize the maid, and she refused eye contact as she allowed them entry. He smirked as he placed a guiding hand at Becca's back. Of course his mother wouldn't stoop to welcoming visitors at the door herself, even if they were family. Let the hired help do that, with a strong measure of servility.

The tantalizing aroma of cooked chicken made Steele's mouth water as he led Becca past the winding staircase into the dining room. He glanced at the three Morses seated at the table, then surveyed the room that had been the stage for many cold and formal meals lacking the friendly family chatter he imagined took place in other households ruled by love, not hatred.

Under the sparkling chandelier, the table setting looked elegant and perfect, just as he remembered. The pale rose cutwork tablecloth matched the napkins intricately folded and secured with flowered porcelain rings. The creamer and sugar bowl, part of his mother's treasured heirloom china, still looked brand new without a chip or flaw from many years of use. The leaded glass hutch displayed more of her prized dishes.

His shoes sank down in the luxuriously thick rug underfoot, with its ornate pattern of trailing roses complimenting the tiny mauve roses in the wallpaper. The antique solid cherry Queen Anne dining ensemble filled the room with splendor befitting royalty. Silk upholstered chairs cushioned guests while forcing them to sit upright at attention in his mother's presence.

"You're late," she snapped. "Sit down so Patricia can serve the first course."

At the sound of his mother's strident voice, Becca jerked beside him. He stiffened as he eyed his mother sitting at the end of the large oval table opposite The Ogre. Conn sat glowering at the far side, in front of the lace-covered casement windows. An empty chair sat to his left. The only other vacant seat stood directly in front of Steele. Obviously it was meant for him, while Becca was to sit by Conn.

Steele gave Becca's hand a reassuring squeeze, then circled around behind his mother. She watched in prickling silence as he gathered up the table setting next to Conn. "Leave it alone!" Conn growled. When he started to get up from his chair, his mother cleared her throat. He looked at her disapproving glare, then sank back down in his seat.

Steele relocated his place setting and quickly arranged the silverware, glasses, and napkins for Becca to dine beside him. His mother still said nothing as he retrieved the chair by Conn and placed it next to his own. He held it out for Becca and smiled at her, encouraging her to sit. She gave him a wary look, then obliged.

Once seated, Steele shot Conn a goading look but refused to acknowledge The Ogre, who apparently intended to honor the code of silence for now. Both Conn and his father seemed on surprising good behavior. His mother must have laid down the rules of engagement before he and Becca arrived. Flashing a broad grin at his mother, Steele rubbed his hands together. "So, what's for lunch? I'm starved."

Lila raised a hand to signal the maid. Patricia entered the dining room, rolling a cherry serving cart laden with pitchers of ice water and iced tea, and a china soup tureen with matching bowls to complement the rest of the antique service. Patricia filled the crystal goblets with water and tea for Becca and Steele, then dished out bowls of soup, setting them on plates in front of everyone at the table. Lila dismissed her with a nod.

Steele took a drink of water and sampled the chicken bisque that was smooth and satisfying with a rich, delicate flavor. "Excellent cuisine, as always. Too bad your family can't meet the same exacting standards you expect."

His mother elevated her chin, giving him a murderous glare. He smiled, winking at Becca when she shot him a horrified look and admonished under her breath, "Steele!"

He wasn't worried. No matter how badly his mother might want to see him shipped off to Timbuktu, he knew she would maintain decorum. As a member of Fenton's thin upper crust, she entertained the mayor and other influential personages, taking great pains to ensure that every detail of her social accouterments was perfect. For the sake of appearances, she demanded propriety. No matter how much screaming and yelling took place in the rest of her house, she would never allow raised fists, black eyes and bruises, or busted lips and bloody noses to intrude on her prized dining room. Mealtime was truce time, yet Steele detested it, wincing inwardly as the painful memories of his miserable childhood came roaring back with rending speed. His mother's calm demeanor was just a flimsy cover-up for the unrelenting hatred in this house. So many years he'd lived with it, knowing he didn't belong, and not understanding why. Now he knew why, but that didn't ease the pain of the past.

He looked over at Becca and saw her huddled in her chair, concentrating on her soup bowl. Under the table he touched her thigh. She whipped him a startled glance. Before he could soothe her, his mother said, "I'm so glad you decided to joined Becca and the rest of us for lunch, Steele. I wouldn't want you to miss our discussion, since it does involve you."

He set his spoon down on his soup plate. *Here it comes.*

When his mother glanced at Becca's left hand sparkling with the new diamond addition, Becca whipped her hands under the table, clutching them in her lap. His mother caught his gaze and managed a stiff smile. "I see you've decided to grace Becca with an engagement ring. I applaud your selection. How magnanimous of you to purchase it on your brother's behalf."

"I don't want him picking out a friggin' ring!" Conn challenged. His mother raised a hand just slightly from the table. Conn snapped his mouth shut and glared down at his untouched soup bowl. Steele dared a look at The Ogre to his left and saw him training his beady eyes on him as if he were aiming to take a shot at him.

Steele turned to his mother and smiled, refusing to dignify her goad with a reply. He watched her sip her tea, then gauge Conn and The Ogre. Seeming satisfied they were under control for the moment, she set her glass down and sampled a spoonful of soup. With that formality completed, she laid her spoon aside and folded her hands, resting them on the edge of the table. "Now that you've had your fun besmirching our family reputation, it's time you stepped back and let your brother take the limelight. After all, it's *his* wedding scheduled for next Saturday."

"Too bad he doesn't have anyone to marry," Steele retorted, dabbing his mouth with his napkin.

Conn gave a little yelp, and Lila stared him to silence. Hunkering down, he focused on the table, daring only a flitting glare at Steele.

161

"All the arrangements have been made, and I see no reason to change any of the details, despite your interference. The wedding *will* take place as planned, and Becca will become Conn's wife." Lila glared at Becca. "Isn't that right, dear?"

Becca looked to Steele for reassurance, and he smiled.

"While there's no question in my mind about what you two did last night," Lila continued, "I can't say that I'm pleased. I only hope you had the good sense to use *precautions*."

Conn locked his eyes on Steele with murderous intensity, but didn't say anything. His mother had given him 'the look,' meaning he wasn't to speak. Despite his surliness, he obeyed. His mother's demanding table training was deeply ingrained.

"Mrs. Morse, I don't want to listen to any of this," Becca blurted.

"But you will, if you know what's good for you."

When Becca started to scoot her chair away from the table, Steele placed a hand on her arm to still her. He wanted to leave as much as she did, but he sensed his mother was working up to something. He knew he needed to endure her veiled insults long enough to find out what she intended to spring on him. "Get to the point, will you? What Becca and I have done and continue to do is none of your business."

"On the contrary, it is my business. Everything you've done for the last several years has become my business." From her lap, Lila produced a thick nine-by-twelve manila clasp envelope and set it on the table beside her plate. Steele glanced at it, then eyed his mother. She almost smiled as she rested a palm on the envelope and explained, "A little *insurance* to keep you from interfering further with your brother's wedding."

James Morse slammed his napkin down on the table, glowering at Lila as he snarled, "You pulled that underhanded trick on me, but you're not going to do it to Conn. He's *not* going to raise somebody else's bastard and pretend it's his own!"

Lila turned on him, an unspoken exchange flaring between them. James's pocked, craggy face turned red, and he seemed about to lurch to his feet, but Lila stared him down until he eased back in his chair. He shot Steele an enraged scowl, then dropped his gaze to the table.

Now Steele wanted to leave more than Becca did. The old memories of The Ogre came flooding back and almost choked him with fear until he realized he had nothing to be afraid of. James Morse could no longer hurt him. It was his mother he needed to worry about. He wasn't sure what she had in the envelope, but he doubted it was the false evidence against Becca's father. If she claimed to have 'insurance' to keep him from fouling up her plans to marry off Conn to Becca, the envelope had to contain something incriminating. He couldn't imagine what it might be. Finally he forced a smile. "You can't blackmail me."

"Oh, really?" Lila perked her thin black brows and continued to rest her hand on the envelope.

Steele's mouth went dry, and his self-confidence shriveled. Either his mother was bluffing, or she believed she had the goods on him. What could it be? He shot Becca a quick glance, then took a gulp of water. After clearing his throat, he sat back and crossed his arms over his chest, forcing himself to stay calm. "I don't care what you think you have on me, I'm not backing down. Becca's marrying *me*, not Conn."

His mother gave a chilling smile and motioned at the maid who stood waiting just outside the arched doorway. Steele turned in surprise as Patricia reached beside him to remove his soup bowl and replace it with a plate of Chicken Kiev and steamed broccoli spears. No one moved as Patricia completed her serving tasks and again left the dining room. Steele glanced over his shoulder to make sure she was out of earshot, then eyed his mother. "I am curious, though. What have you got?"

His mother smoothed her hand over the bulky envelope, then picked up her silverware. As she eyed her plate and made a formal production of slicing three bite-size pieces from her Chicken Kiev, she said in a blasé tone reserved for discussing the weather, "Just a few snapshots of you enjoying after-hours leisure time with a business acquaintance. You are quite photogenic, even in less than optimum lighting." She flicked him a quick smile and looked back at her plate. "I'm surprised at you, Steele. Didn't law school teach you anything about business ethics? I thought you had better sense than to *entertain* the wives of your own clients."

Steele scowled at her but dared not say anything. How could she have come up with pictures? With telephoto lenses and the right angles through windows, perhaps it was possible. But he'd always been careful, discreet. Anytime he was seen with a client's wife, he was in the client's presence or with a group of people. And he allowed no hint of funny business. The only other explanation was hidden cameras. But that would require advanced planning, and most of his 'dates' had been impromptu, rarely at the same place. For photos or videos to have been made, there had to have been some colluding somewhere. Could one or more of his 'partners' have been planning to blackmail him? And how would his mother have become involved in the scheme? He couldn't come up with a connection.

Lila took a bite of chicken and chewed with appreciative slowness. Chasing it down with a swallow of tea, she said, "What will the senior partners of Hastings, Fehrnman & Reinhold say when you're subpoenaed to appear in court as a material witness in the divorce suits that are sure to result when I distribute this information to your clients?" She clicked her tongue in mock admonishment. "Those poor cuckolded fellows might even go so far as to sue your firm for your unprofessional behavior." She speared another bite of chicken with her fork. "You could face disbarment."

Holding his water goblet, poised to drink, Steele felt his face lose color. He set his glass down. How could the situation have deteriorated to this seamy and embarrassing scenario? As he lifted a hand and skated his fingertips across his brow, he sensed Becca staring at him. He couldn't face her.

He never meant to hurt anyone. It had all started so innocently and unexpectedly – even in good faith. At a client's party, the hostess, the wife whose husband was called away on a

164

pressing business errand, came looking for an escort for the rest of the evening. As the husband's trusted corporate attorney, Steele, romantically unattached, was the obvious choice. How could he say no? Later, when all the other guests and the caterers were gone, and he was the last to leave, that invitation for a nightcap led to another kind of invitation, and eventually to his moral downfall.

His after-hours reputation grew, and other clients' wives began inviting him to business entertainment forays, then keeping him late, hoping something more would develop in the wee hours. Nothing permanent. Nothing harmful. No love lost. Just a bit of casual sex. Their husbands did it all the time with mistresses, prostitutes, whatever. Why would anyone care if they partook as well?

After a few drinks and a few interludes, it didn't seem to be such a bad thing. He had fun, they enjoyed themselves, and all was well with his clients. But his conscience never stopped nagging him. He was an attorney who had somehow managed to pervert his clients' trust. He'd become nothing more than a convenient gigolo, and he didn't like what it did to his soul.

Steele eyed his mother and fought to calm his rapid, shallow breathing. Apparently his mother had hired a private investigator to follow him and keep tabs on his activities. What had she been planning to do with the information she gathered? It had been more than six months since he'd indulged in any indiscretions. The last two women, Sheila Breckenstern and Vera Mills, had been persistent, but he'd vowed not to continue. Sheila was the only one who threatened retaliation if he didn't keep seeing her, but she backed off when he pointed out her position was just as vulnerable as his. The phone calls eventually ceased, and he was glad of it. He just couldn't do it anymore. The companionship and the sex were okay, but they weren't worth the damage to his long-term self-esteem. And something had always been *missing*. He hadn't realized what it was until he met Becca.

"Mrs. Breckenstern was under the peculiar perception that you and she could have a future together – once she unloaded Mr.

Breckenstern and relieved him of a healthy portion of his assets."
Lila smiled. "But she changed her tune once I showed her what
Mr. Breckenstern would receive as ammunition from me if you
don't do exactly what I want."

Good Lord! His mother had contacted Sheila. Steele
wanted to see the envelope, wanted to confront the evidence, to
know what he was up against. But not here, not now, not in front
of Becca.

He glanced at Becca sitting silent next to him. She stared at
her hands clasped in her lap as tears ran down her cheeks. He
wanted to take her in his arms and remove her from this affront,
but he didn't feel he deserved to touch her and had no idea how to
repair the rift developing between them. Why had he been so
stupid? He knew better than to get mixed up in the mess he'd
made of his personal life, but still he'd done it. And there was no
undoing it now, or getting around it. At that moment he loathed
himself more than at any other time he could remember.

"You said you were hungry, Steele, but you've barely
touched your meal." Steele turned on his mother as she added,
"And look how you've upset Becca. Perhaps it would be best if
you left now. Conn can take her back to her parents' house. I'll
give you until the end of the day to leave town. After that..." She
patted the despicable envelope and smiled at him.

Steele threw his napkin on the table and shot up from his
chair, making it totter behind him. "Come on, Becca. We're
getting out of here." He held out his hand to her, but she seemed
frozen with indecision. She couldn't even manage to look up at
him.

"She's not going anywhere with you. She has enough sense
to know what needs to be done, and to accept her responsibility.
Do her a favor and just go – now."

Steele glared at his mother standing with her fingertips
braced against the tabletop. Anger lunged out of his throat like a
wolf leaping for attack. "If you think I'm going to walk out of
here and leave her to–"

"Get the hell out of my house, you trouble-making selfish

bastard!" Surprised, Steele turned on The Ogre as he barged up from his chair. "You've done nothing but make me miserable from the moment you were born, and I've had enough. Now get out!"

Steele met his full frontal assault and push him away. The big oaf lost his balance and staggered backward, falling across the table. The table, unaccustomed to bearing such weight, cracked and gave way. The entire mess – the table, the fancy linens and dishes, and the chef-prepared meal – came crashing down in the middle of the floor. Steele stared in disbelief as his regent father writhed amongst the wreckage, trying to right himself. If not for the grimness of the situation, the scene would have been laughable. In one horrendous instant, Lila Morse's distinguished environment was destroyed, all because of James Morse's unruly temper – the same temper that had driven Steele away and made him believe he deserved the loathing leveled against him.

Steele glared at his mother in hollow triumph. She lurched at him with the enraged look of a banshee, trembling and sputtering with clenched fists, but she couldn't speak. Conn, covered with the remains of his own lunch, was too dumbfounded to move. Steele grabbed Becca cowering by the doorway and pulled her from the house.

CHAPTER 16

"*I* can't." Becca sat on the foot of her bed, struggling to hold back the sobs forming a knot in her throat. "I can't go with him."

"Why the hell not?" her mother asked. She sat down beside her and put an arm around her shoulders.

Becca glanced at her mother, wondering why she wasn't hollering like usual. Swallowing hard as a tear escaped down her cheek, she shook her head. "I have to go to work Monday. I just can't."

"Now, listen to me. Steele is out there is pacing around in our itty-bitty living room like a caged tiger, wondering why he didn't just kidnap you and take you away from all this mess when he had you in the car, instead of driving you back here because you said you had to pack some things. Maybe I haven't been the greatest mother in the world, but I'm smart enough to recognize he's the best thing that could have ever happened to you. So get busy stuffing your suitcase as fast as you can!"

Sucking in a deep breath, Becca tried to keep the tremor from her voice. "Mom, you don't understand. It's not that simple. There are *complications*."

"The only complication I see is that you're holed up in your room, sniveling like a stupid ninny, instead of doing what you know is best for you. This may be your one and only chance for real happiness. Steele is a great-looking guy, he has a high-paying job, and he cares about you. He seems like a good, decent man, despite the bitch that spawned him. And a good man's hard to find, let me tell you."

She stroked Becca's hair and continued in a coaxing tone, "Anyway, you don't have anything to do at that darn bank that's so all-fired important you can't afford to take off a week or two. I'll call Helen Martincek at home right now and tell her you're taking next week off, and the week after that, too. I mean, you're supposed to be getting married next Saturday – to Steele, I hope."

Becca tried to face her mother but couldn't. "Work's not the problem. I–"

"Oh, for Heaven's sake, Becca! Stop with the excuses and straighten yourself up. Throw some clothes together and *go with him*. The man is crazy about you. Even I can see that, and you know I'm no romantic."

Becca swiped at her teary face and almost laughed at the irony of that overstatement. No one would ever accuse her mother of being a softie, yet here she was, giving sage advice like she never had before. Still, that didn't erase the fact that Lila Morse had the goods not only on her father, but on Steele, and would do her damnedest to ruin both of them if Becca refused to marry Conn next Saturday. Running off with Steele to his aunt and uncle's farm in Edgarsville for a few days wouldn't solve anything, but could end up making things worse.

Becca couldn't allow Steele to endanger his career by defying his mother. She had to do what his mother said, and she had to make Steele agree to it, no matter how much it hurt him. She crinkled wads of her skirt in her clenched hands and tried to keep her voice even as she said, "Mom, I can't go with him. If I could, I would. But I *can't*. And I can't explain why." She shot up from her bed and raked her fingers through her hair as she paced away.

Her mother stood up from the bed. "Obviously Steele's mother has the two of you tied up in knots about something. I don't know what's going on, and I know you think you can't tell me. I suspect you're trying very hard to protect your father and me from something, and I sure wish you'd tell us what it is. Nobody can help you if you don't let anyone know what's wrong!"

"No one can help me, so it doesn't matter." Becca looked out her bedroom window and shivered as a chill wash through her, as if her body and mind were shutting down in anticipation of the fate she had accepted. "Please ... please tell Steele to go." She gulped back a new flood of tears and took a deep breath. "I can't see him anymore."

Her mother stood behind her for some time and then said, "You're going to have to tell him that yourself."

Becca heard her mother open the door and walk out without closing it. With a shaky sigh she put a hand over her eyes as more tears streamed down her face.

A minute later the door creaked, and she jerked with a start but refused to turn around. "Mom, I told you to tell him to go away! Please, just–"

"'Mom' told me to come in here and talk to you myself."

Becca whirled toward the sound of Steele's voice and froze in shame when she saw him standing in her doorway. His presence dwarfed her tiny room and invaded her last retreat. She shuddered at the sight of him, wanting him to hold her in his arms and promise he would make everything all better. But she knew he couldn't keep that promise. She turned her back on him. "Please go. Please."

"I'm not going anywhere without you, Becca. Now, are you going to pack some things, or do you plan on running around in your birthday suit while we're at the farm?" She felt him move close behind her. When he whispered, "Personally, I prefer you naked, but it's your choice," she wilted and turned to face him.

She tried to be strong, but one look at his smiling face laced with concern made her lose her resolve. "You know we can't do this." She choked back a new onslaught of tears.

He grabbed her by the shoulders. "Yes we can, and we are. Don't give me any arguments about what my mother might do. I've already explained everything to your father, and he knows what's going on."

Becca moaned with dread, and Steele tightened his grip on her shoulders. "He knows I'm working to set things right before the inquest, and there's liable to be some trouble if I'm not successful. But he's hoping, like we all are, that things will turn out all right. In the meantime–"

"Damn it, Steele" She pushed her hands against his unyielding arms. "Why do you think I've been trying all this time to keep the truth from him? He'll march right over to your mother's house and–"

"Becca, your father knows better than to confront my mother on his own."

Becca lurched away from Steele, and he released her. "But I didn't want him to worry about any of this! I knew there was nothing he could do to help."

"Don't you understand? He has worried more *not* knowing than he ever would have if you'd just told him the truth in the beginning. At least now he knows what's going on, and he can deal with it."

Becca turned to face Steele, realizing what he said was true. In her almighty quest to take on the burden of all things, she had ignored reality. Believing that she was doing the right thing by protecting her father from the truth, she had made him more miserable. On top of everything else that had happened, she felt even worse for having subjected her father to needless stress by trying to handle things all by herself. Why did she always think she had to support the weight of the whole world on her own narrow shoulders? She put a hand to her head, feeling confused and overwhelmed.

"Come on," Steele urged, grabbing her arm. "Get your suitcase, and I'll help you pack."

* * * * *

Around two o'clock that afternoon, Becca and Steele reached the Krueger homestead outside Edgarsville. As Steele's tires crunched over the white gravel drive, Becca saw a green John Deere tractor exiting the property. Steele lowered his window and waved at the tractor operator, a man who looked to be in his early sixties. The farmer pulled to a halt and shut off his roaring diesel machine.

Steele parked the car near the rambling old farmhouse and grinned at Becca. "I want you to meet Harold Watkins. He and his wife Louise live down the road and keep an eye on the place for me. He farms some nearby fields, including mine, for a share of the proceeds. He must be checking the soybeans." Steele opened his door.

Becca hesitated. She didn't expect to socialize with any locals during their short stay at his late aunt and uncle's home. What would Mr. Watkins think of Steele bringing some woman he'd just met, to shack up and play house for a couple days?

"Come on, Becca," Steele coaxed. "Harry and Louise are nice people, almost family. I've known them ever since I left Fenton and came here to live."

Becca bucked up her courage and forced a smile. Steele seemed almost giddy to be back in his old stomping grounds, and she didn't want to spoil things for him. He beamed and circled around the car to help her out. A moment later she found herself shaking hands with wiry, weathered Mr. Watkins. He wore dusty leather lace-up boots, gray cotton work pants and long-sleeved shirt, and a faded blue cap that advertised the Edgarsville Farmer's Co-op.

"So pleased to meet you, Becca," Mr. Watkins said with a warm craggy smile. "When Steele called and told me and the missus about you two getting married next weekend, a feather could've knocked us over. I just wish he'd given a little more notice. But don't you worry. We'll be there. Wouldn't miss it for the world. Finally we're gonna see this ornery critter tie the knot and settle down!" He gave Steele a good-natured slap on the shoulder.

Becca managed a smile and flicked Steele a secret glance, wondering why he had boldly announced *their* wedding, when nothing was settled.

The sound of Steele's voice soothed her worries as he discussed farming techniques with Mr. Watkins. The two men joked and laughed as if they were friendly neighbors who saw each other daily.

172

As Steele praised Mr. Watkins' maintenance of the property, Becca glanced at the various pole barns, machine sheds, and other outbuildings completing the homestead. The house behind her, a well-kept two-story with a wraparound porch, boasted a recently applied coat of white paint on the clapboard siding. Bright patches of hothouse petunias in a bursting array of colors trimmed the porch between deep green yews and other bushes. Rather than the dilapidated, deserted shack she had envisioned, the house looked inviting, perched on a rolling hill with a freshly mowed lawn and mature shade trees. A slight breeze carried the scent of cut hay and raw dirt.

"Yep," Mr. Watkins assured Steele with a sun-drenched grin as he fingered his toothpick and moved it to the other side of his mouth, "Lou came over here to check on things and tidy up a bit – dust a little and so forth. Good thing she was home when you called. Otherwise she might not have had time to run to the grocery too, before you got here. I think she left you some eggs, milk, bread, and other staples – not sure what all. Anyway, it should do you till you can go into town and get whatever else you need."

"She didn't need to go to all that trouble."

"Trouble? No such thing where Lou's concerned. She thinks of you as one of our own. Oh, and she put fresh linens on the beds."

"I really appreciate it, Harry."

"No problem. When was the last time you were here, anyway? Been several months, I know."

Becca turned on Steele, wondering how many other women he'd brought to this fine old house. Just as the thought crossed her mind, Mr. Watkins added, "Course, this'll be the first time I ever seen you bring somebody *with* you. It's a nice change, I can tell you."

Steele looked at Becca and laughed as he put an arm around her shoulder and hugged her. Obviously he could read her jealousy like an open book, and the realization made her wilt with an apologetic smile.

173

Still grinning, Mr. Watkins offered a big, rough hand to
Steele. "Well, congratulations again, son. Looks like you got
yourself a mighty fine woman. Pretty as they come, and sweet
natured too. Now don't you worry," he added with a wink. "Me
and Lou won't let anyone else know you two are on the place. So
you'll have plenty of time to yourselves. Be sure to call the house
if you need anything."

Steele nodded as he let go of Mr. Watkins' hand. "Thanks
again for all your help."

"The way you've helped us out over the years, it's me
should be thanking you." He turned to Becca and smiled. "Once
you spend a little time here, missy, maybe you'll find a way to
convince this jackrabbit to leave the big city and come home
where he belongs. Good to meet you."

Mr. Watkins tipped his hat, then ambled toward his tractor
and climbed aboard. Becca watched the green machine rumble
down the driveway, belching out smoke from the side exhaust
pipe. Mr. Watkins turned onto the gravel-sprinkled oiled road and
looked back to give a hearty wave and a smile.

Becca raised her hand to wave back, then yelped when
Steele scooped her up into his arms as if she were a sack of
feathers. "What are you doing?" she demanded, craning her neck
back in embarrassment to see Mr. Watkins looking back over his
shoulder, slapping his knee and laughing.

"Carrying my bride over the threshold." Steele walked
effortlessly up the porch steps. She didn't want to spoil his
moment by reminding him they weren't married.

He grabbed the screen door handle and pushed the redwood
door open with his knee. Entering the living room bathed in soft
sunlight streaming through the big picture window, he whirled
her around, then planted a ferocious kiss on her mouth. When he
set her on her feet, she wavered. He grabbed her shoulders to
steady her until she got her balance back. Before she fully
recovered from that surprise, he sniffed the air. "I smell food!"

He charged out of the living room and headed for what she
assumed was the kitchen. She scrambled after him and found him

examining two covered glass casserole dishes on the gold-flecked kitchen counter. "Still warm," he announced, touching the sides of one of the dishes. Then he spied a tin canister and pried off the lid. "Cookies!"

Becca picked up a nearby hand-scrawled note which read, 'Steele, congratulations! I knew the right gal would find you, no matter how hard you tried to hide. Since you eat like a horse, I figured your better half could use some help till she gets used to feeding you herself. I'll pick up the dishes after you leave. See you in Fenton next Saturday for the big day. Lou.'

Becca set the note aside and caught Steele's arm before he could stuff a third chocolate-chip cookie into his gaping mouth. "Mrs. Watkins obviously went to a lot of trouble to make all this food. Don't spoil your dinner by gorging on *our* desert."

Grinning, he dropped the cookie back in the tin and shoved the lid down over the top. Reaching up, he opened one of the wood cabinet doors, thick with layers of white paint, and pulled out two speckled stoneware plates. "Let's eat. I'm starved. Then I'll take you on a tour."

* * * * *

After that late but tasty home-cooked lunch, Becca let Steele twirl her around and propel her through successive rooms of the surprisingly large house, as if she were on a carnival ride. His greased-tongued spiel, glossing over the shortcomings of the dated furnishings, was worthy of a practiced real-estate salesman. He assured her the worn tweed living room couch and chair, the faded gold brocade curtains, the aged television, the yellowed wallpaper – everything but the house itself – could immediately be swept away and replaced with new items of her choice. "So, what do you think of the place?" he demanded with pride as he looked around the living room basking in afternoon sunlight.

Still reeling from the whirlwind tour, Becca glanced from the wagon-wheel light fixture overhead to the homemade wooden bookshelves on either side of the stone fireplace. The sagging shelves overflowed with tattered and worn volumes ranging from an ancient encyclopedia set to classic fiction titles in hardback. She eyed Steele curiously. "The house is wonderful. Everything's fine the way it is. This place has sentimental value for you. I wouldn't change a thing."

"But, if we're going to live here and–"

"Steele!" She glared at him. "Your job is in Chicago. You have a condo there, an investment portfolio, friends, business contacts, a *life*. You're a successful corporate attorney. What would you do way out here in the middle of rural nowhereland? We barely know each other and we aren't married – and there's a good chance we won't ever be, considering what your mother's got hanging over our heads. You have obligations, and so do I. How can you talk about all this nonsense of living happily ever after, as if nothing else in the world mattered?"

"Our future's not nonsense, Becca, and right now nothing else does matter." He took her by the arm and guided her to the couch, urging her to sit down beside him. "We are getting married one week from today, no matter what my mother has planned. So we'd better get busy and start planning our life together because, whether you want to admit it or not, it's already begun."

Becca sighed. "We can daydream and suppose all we want, but you know there are too many problems still up in the air for us to be sure about anything. Maybe ... maybe we ought to wait to see how things turn out before we–"

"I *am* going to marry you next Saturday, Becca. There's no question about that, and there's no reason to wait for anything."

She took his hands in hers. "Listen to me, please. I am not going to let you trash your career over some misguided idea that you have to marry me to save me from your mother and your brother. You don't. Okay? Just try to be reasonable about this."

"I am being reasonable. You're going to be my wife."

Scowling, Becca let go of his hands and turned away. No matter what he tried to tell himself, he wasn't being rational or realistic. "You can't just skip along like nothing's wrong and expect all our troubles to magically disappear."

He sat in silence for a long while. She looked back at him when he said, "I'm sorry. I guess I've been so busy making plans and doing things the way I thought they ought to be done, I haven't bothered to ask you what you want. After dealing with my mother's highhandedness, I ought to know better."

She placed a hand on his knee. He looked hurt as he said, "It never occurred to me that you might not want to marry me. I guess you're right. I'm not being very reasonable or fair." He shot up from the couch and strolled to the large picture window.

Sighing, Becca got up from the couch and walked up behind him. Her thoughts drifted as she looked out the window, across the road at the rolling fields of growing corn and thick hay. The farther fields, small against the horizon, joined to form a lush green patchwork quilt glowing under the sun. The light blazing in through the window, warm and golden with the hint of oncoming evening, imbued her with a sense of longing.

"I didn't say I didn't want to marry you, Steele. I said I didn't want you to think you *had* to marry me out of some misguided sense of obligation."

He turned on her. "Don't worry about what I want, Becca. Tell me what *you* want. What would you do if none of this mess had ever come up, and you'd just met me? Would you still want to be with me, or would you walk away?"

She frowned. "How can I answer that? If you hadn't come along when you did and picked me up the other night, things might have turned out a lot different. I probably wouldn't have met you until after–" She gulped and stopped herself from completing that sentence, *until after I'd married your brother.* She turned away and hugged her shoulders. She didn't want to think about what might have happened. All that mattered was what had happened. She and Steele had fallen in love, and in the process had stirred up a hornet's nest in the form of his mother's wrath. Now everything was in such a complicated mess, she couldn't sort it out.

Steele grabbed her by the shoulders and spun her around to

177

face him. "Becca, do you love me?"

She lowered her head and blushed. "Yes."

"Do you want to be my wife?"

She nodded her head. "Yes."

"Do you want to live with me – wherever that might be – and make a family with me?"

She looked up at him and dared to smile. "Yes."

He stroked her hair with restrained intensity. "Then let's get on with it, and to hell with the consequences." He kissed her with deep reverence until her body tingled and her knees trembled. Taking her by the hand, he led her down the hall.

CHAPTER 17

*T*he corner bedroom wasn't large but seemed warm and inviting with late afternoon sunlight streaming in between the wide slats of Venetian blinds shading the two tall windows. Stripes of light caressed the antique oak veneer dresser and glinted playfully across its lyre-shaped mirror. The patterns of light stretched across the tall, wide bed with its ornate white iron headboard and subtly colored double wedding ring quilt. The room glowed with nostalgia, making Becca feel comfortable and at peace. The mood was a welcome change from the tearful stress she'd suffered for the last several weeks.

When she sat down, the bed springs creaked, lending a sense of reality to her quiet, dreamy surroundings. Running a hand over the faded cotton quilt, she smiled as she looked up at Steele standing nearby, watching her. "Did your Aunt Sybil make this?"

Seeming to have lost his voice, he nodded. She eyed him a moment longer, then tilted her head. "Is something wrong?"

He sucked in a deep breath and smiled. "No, nothing's wrong. I was just ... you look so beautiful, sitting there. I can't believe you're really here with me. I feel like I was sleepwalking through life until I met you." He sat down beside her and took her hands in his. "Becca, I know this is all so sudden, and I've made a lot of changes – demands – in your life in the last few days. I know this is what I want, but I need to be sure it's what you want too."

Becca touched a palm to his dark, angular face. "If I didn't want this, Steele, I wouldn't be here right now."

He sighed with obvious relief and pushed her back on the bed. She put her hand on his chest to stop him. "Before we get too involved, you'd better get our luggage from the car."

He smirked and got up from the bed. "That chore will create only a short delay."

"And then?"

He bowed toward her, took her face in his hands, and planted a deep, lingering kiss on her parted lips. She tingled with pleasure, anticipating 'and then.'

* * * * *

"You might as well use the closet and the drawers. We're going to be here for a couple days until I get a call from the firm's investigator, or until Judge Forrester returns to town."

Becca set her small blue nylon suitcase on the bed and unzipped it. "What about your mother?" She turned toward the dresser with a handful of clothing – underwear, shorts and tee shirts, and so forth. "She's going to get suspicious when my parents tell her I'm holed up in my bedroom at home and won't see anyone. And, although your hotel room is still checked out under your name, your unanswered phone messages are going to pile up. It won't take her long to realize you're not there."

"She'll be suspicious, but she won't know for sure what's going on. I'll deal with that when we get back."

Becca sighed and carried her garment bag and empty suitcase to the small closet concealed by wooden sliding doors. She pulled back one of the doors and hung up the one dress she'd brought along. When she bent down to set her suitcase on the floor, she spied a small, very old and tattered hardboard suitcase covered with an imitation tweed pattern. She looked over her shoulder at Steele, then pulled the suitcase out of the closet. "What's in here? Anything?"

The moment Steele saw the suitcase, he got a startled look on his face. His slow smile seemed more sad than happy. "I haven't seen that since I moved to Chicago. I forgot it was in there."

He took the suitcase from her and set it on the foot of the

bed, staring at it for a moment before unlatching it. When he lifted the lid and Becca saw the ragged bundles of envelopes, she thought the worst – that they were love letters from an old sweetheart.

In silence Steele unbanded one of the bundles and removed a letter at random. Becca was surprised to see a photocopy of a check enclosed. He handed her both pieces of paper. The two-hundred-dollar check was dated seventeen years ago, made out to Steele in care of his adoptive aunt and uncle. It was signed by Norman Fields, a trust officer of Southern Illinois Bank & Trust, the same bank where Becca now worked.

Setting the copy aside, Becca read the typewritten, unsigned letter. Addressed to Steele, it contained personalized encouragement from the unidentified author. Very uplifting in tone, the letter urged Steele to keep a positive outlook and make the best of his new living arrangement with his great aunt and uncle. The author appeared to be familiar with Steele's adolescent angst and anger resulting from his unhappy life in the Morse household.

Becca looked up to find Steele's eyes clouding as he read another of the letters. "They're all pretty much the same," he said. "Asking for details of my day-to-day activities, or reassuring me about some minor setback, or praising me for an accomplishment."

Becca glanced again at the letter in her hand. "The person who wrote this obviously cared a lot about you. Who was it – your real father?"

"Damned if I know." He tossed the letter aside, and it fluttered to the bed. When she gave him a questioning look, he forced a smile. "They were all unsigned. I wrote back to the box number on the return address, and I know that my letters were received, but I was never told to whom I was writing, even when I demanded to know. I'm sure my aunt and uncle didn't know who wrote all these letters. They may have suspected, but they never would say. And I was at a loss to guess.

"I used to get so angry and frustrated, sometimes I'd whip

off a nasty reply, or refuse to write back for a month or two. But no matter what I did, I always got a letter every month, on schedule. And it was always pleasant and encouraging like the others."

Becca refolded the letter and photocopy he'd given her and returned them to the envelope. She understood why he ached to know the author of those letters – no doubt it was his biological father. What a loss he must have felt, being unable to meet and talk with this man who apparently regarded him with esteem and genuine caring.

"A couple years after I moved here and started getting the checks and letters, there was lull of about six months when I'd get a check straight from the bank, with no letter. By the time I got my driver's license, I had the bright idea that I'd go to the bank or courthouse in Fenton and track down whoever was sending the money through the trust fund.

"All the bank would tell me was that a blind trust had been set up, separate from the profit-generated trust my mother was forced to establish on my behalf when she adopted me out. The stipulation with the other trust was that the donor would remain anonymous, so the bank wouldn't reveal the person who set it up. Ever. Not even after the trust terminated on my twenty-fifth birthday. The letters stopped coming a couple years before that, and I figured something had happened to whoever was writing them. I'd pretty much given up hope of every finding out the identity of my real father."

Becca placed a hand on his nearest arm. "I'm sorry."

He frowned and shrugged. "It's his loss, not mine. For whatever reason, he chose not to come forward, but decided instead to pay off his guilt by sending me secret money every month. Still, I'd like to know who he was."

"Your mother's very cruel to keep that information from you. You have a right to know."

He reached over and tweaked her chin with his thumb and forefinger. "Don't worry about it. If my guess is right, she needs money. With a little dough to grease the wheel, I just might be able to convince her to tell me, after all these years."

Becca shook her head. "Don't get caught up in her games, Steele. You could get hurt."

He bent over and kissed her, then whispered, "The only way she'll be able to hurt me is if I care. And I don't. I've had years to get over the notion of knowing my real father. If he didn't want me then, it's much too late now to make amends. The potential for hurt is dead." He tossed the remaining letters back into the suitcase, snapped it shut with finality, and set it aside on the floor.

Becca looked up into his cool gray eyes and remembered how soft and cloudy they'd been when he'd seen those long-neglected letters. She wasn't convinced by his nonchalance. He still had an emotional emptiness that needed to be filled, and only the closure of learning who his father was would do that. She vowed to support him in his quest for the truth.

In the fading glow of afternoon light, she smoothed her palms over the front of his shirt, feeling his hard muscled chest underneath. She tried to soothe the tension and anger vibrating just under the surface. When she looked into his eyes, she saw his pain and frustration easing away. He reached for her and pressed her back on the bed, then maneuvered himself on top of her, to the groaning protest of the bedsprings.

"I don't think this bed's going to hold both of us," she objected, halfheartedly pushing at him.

"Then we'll have a good time breaking it."

He devoured her lips, inflaming her body with the memories of their lovemaking the night before. He coaxed her blouse open and eased her bra down over her taut nipples. Her breasts bounced free, perked with anticipation, and he covered them with the wet warmth of his mouth.

Pulling at his polo shirt, she tried without success to slide it over his head. He reached down and pulled it off with one swift motion and flung it at the dresser. Breathing hard, he paused for a moment to survey her with lust-darkened eyes. "I don't want to screw up again. This time I won't forget to—"

She pressed a finger to his lips and silenced him. It didn't matter now. After all her gut-wrenching worry and agony over the past several weeks, the idea of finally being with someone who wanted to share her life gave her meaning and purpose. She was committed to this course, no holding back. If that 'little slip' their first time together didn't make a baby, she was hoping this time would. "No excuses, no apologies," she whispered. "The second time's not an accident. It's planned."

He grinned and kissed her with renewed enthusiasm. Embracing him, she trusted everything would work out right.

* * * * *

By late afternoon Wednesday, Steele decided it was time to head back to Fenton. They couldn't hide from their troubles forever, he said, and time was running out for them to come to Becca's father's defense at the inquest scheduled for Monday.

As Steele trudged out to the car with their bags, Becca looked with a sense of foreboding at the rain front moving in to block the formerly blue horizon. The dark clouds gathered like the trouble she knew was brewing back in Fenton for her family, for her, and for Steele. A breeze kicked up a whirl of dust in the gravel driveway, and she looked longingly at the rambling old white house they had to leave behind. In the dim light of the graying sky, the house seemed as depressed about their imminent departure as she was. She felt she'd lived and loved a lifetime in only a few days in that house. Sighing, she reassured herself that she and Steele would soon return. Then she faced the car.

With a hug of encouragement, Steele opened the door for her and then got behind the wheel. As they cruised down the driveway, Becca turned around to watch the house receding in the rear window. A jumble of memories flooded her, and she felt her one chance for happiness disappearing behind her. Gripped by unreasoning fear, she wanted to cry out for Steele to stop the car and turn around and go back. Something told her if she left now, she would never again go hand in hand with him to walk the fields and admire the fruits of his land. He would never again make love with her on a dusty haystack, with afternoon light peeking through gaps in the barn's siding. She would never again feel the sense of calm and satisfaction, hearing his deep voice murmuring their future plans while they swayed on the porch swing and enjoyed the soft evening breeze. She would never again snuggle in his arms while they lay in bed and listened to the distant chirping and croaking of the creatures of the night outside their bedroom window.

Those tranquil images were replaced with visions of Lila Morse's cold, calculating face and Conn's fists of rage. Becca's feeling of loss and impending danger was so strong, she trembled with fear. They must not leave this place, this one spot on Earth where they could be happy. Before she could voice her objections, the farm vanished from sight beyond a bend in the road. She turned around and sank down in her seat.

"Everything will be okay," Steele assured. He shimmied his hand up the skirt of her cotton summer dress and ran his palm over her bare thigh. "I love you, we've got a home to come to when we get married next weekend, and..." He slipped his hand out from under her skirt and rubbed her tummy. "We've already got a good start on making our first baby."

She tried to smile, but tears threatened to gush from her eyes like rain from the cloud-laden sky looming overhead.

"Chuck Lapinski, my firm's investigator has dug up some interesting information on the doctor with the evidence against your father. Seems good Dr. Farnsworth resigned from his last job when he was accused of falsifying medical records. As a member of the Fenton Hospital board of directors, my mother was instrumental in getting him hired. If we can somehow introduce that information at the inquest, the case my mother's trying to build against your father will weaken."

Becca blinked back her tears and swallowed down the shakiness in her voice. "The investigator called you today?"

Steele shot her a reassuring smile. "Yeah. On my cell, while you were taking a bath. And Chuck also said Judge

Forrester just got back in town. I'm going to try to talk with him about this whole mess."

"And about the anonymous letters and the trust fund?"

Steele shrugged and eyed the road. "Couldn't hurt. If I can convince him to give me even the slightest hint about who set up that trust, I'll be closer to finding out my father's identity than I was a week ago."

He drove in silence for a moment, then said, "Do you mind if we make a little detour before heading back to face the lions?"

* * * * *

By the time they reached the small country cemetery nestled in a grove of trees at the crest of the hill, the sun had dipped below the blanket of thunderclouds dissipating in the distance. The sky, ablaze with color, bathed the remote home of those who'd passed with a warm enthralling pink glow that seemed to breathe new life into everything it touched.

Becca watched Steele stroke the gleaming rose marble double headstone marking the side-by-side graves of his Aunt Sybil and Uncle Charlie. A stand at the front and center of the headstone contained a lush bouquet of silk flowers that almost looked real.

With a small laugh that was more a sigh, Steele said, "I don't like fake flowers, but they've got staying power. Nothing looks worse on a grave than wilted flowers. If I could get down here more often, I'd set out fresh bouquets." He fingered the flowers and frowned. "I guess I could arrange for someone to tend their graves, but it just doesn't seem right to impose on or pay someone else to do it for me."

When Becca touched a hand to his arm, he forced a smile and shrugged. "Guess it doesn't matter. Flowers are for show anyway, for the sake of the living, not the dead."

Trying to search for something appropriate to say, Becca recalled her grandmother's funeral last year. Her father's mother had been ill for some time, confined in a nursing home in Marion.

Becca had never been able to get to know her paternal grandmother well. In the waning years of her life, Melva Sedder should have been able to enjoy her grandchildren with a sense of wisdom and love, but couldn't because she was too far gone both physically and mentally. Her passing had been a blessing in disguise for everyone. But the few times Becca's father spoke of his mother, he did so with a wistful tone and a look of fondness in his eyes. The fact that he cared was enough to convince Becca that she should care too.

She hooked her arm around Steele's and stroked his hand. "All that matters is that you still think about your aunt and uncle and keep them close to your heart. It shouldn't make any difference to them – or anyone else – whether the flowers on their grave are real or not. At least you care enough to remember them and honor their memory by coming here to visit when you can. They're the only real parents you ever had, and they did a good job raising you, as far as I'm concerned. That's testament their lives were well spent. Whenever anyone meets you, they get the benefit of your aunt and uncle's love and patience and wisdom."

Steele squeezed her hand resting on his arm. "I never was able to call them 'Mom' and 'Dad,' even after they adopted me. I always knew them as my aunt and uncle, and it seemed a little weird to suddenly call them something else that, at the time, I didn't feel they were. I guess I was still too rebellious and angry at my real mother about everything – so angry, I couldn't think of anyone as a parent."

Becca ran a hand over his back. "That's understandable. You were a child who felt betrayed and abandoned. Opening up to anyone after what you suffered must have been very hard."

He shrugged. "After I got older and had grown accustomed to living with Sybil and Charlie, I understood what it meant to have people who cared about me. But I still called them what I'd always called them – aunt and uncle – and never bothered to address the issue again. Now I'm sorry I didn't."

"I'm sure they knew you cared about them and had grown to love them with a fondness you would have showed your own

187

mother, if she'd deserved it."

He remained silent. She looked up at his face washed in the waning evening light and was amazed at the hurt she saw. He still grieved for a childhood badly spent, never to be redeemed. Or was it some other yearning that carved sadness into his face? Perhaps regret over the father his mother denied him. By not revealing the man's identity, his mother might actually have done him a favor. But knowing Lila Morse, Becca found it hard to believe the woman would withhold such important information with the sole intention of protecting her son's feelings. She suspected quite the opposite was true. "Come on," she encouraged. "Let's get on the road. We've got people to see and plans to make."

Finally able to smile again, Steele turned to her, his eyes gleaming with love.

* * * * *

As Becca walked with Steele into his room at the Standish Inn, she felt a little weird and self-conscious returning to the site of her introduction to love. Had it been just five days ago? She felt as if she'd known Steele forever, that they were soul mates. Somehow it seemed her life had begun five days ago, and everything before that was just a distant memory.

"Hungry?"

Becca turned with a start to find Steele surveying her. Feeling herself blushing, she shook her head in answer to his inquiry and looked away, pretending to admire the room. Her gaze landed on the bed, and she heated with the memory of Steele making love with her. She knew she had acted every bit the frightened virgin that she was, yet he had been patient and gentle. She still marveled at the idea of a practiced lover like Steele being interested in her in the first place. He had been with plenty of experienced women before he came to her. What had he seen in her that had attracted him, that he hadn't seen in any of the others?

188

She turned to find him still staring at her. His look bordered on lustful admiration. The situation made her feel odd, out of place, as if she were in a too-perfect dream that was about to end. She managed a weak smile and picked up on his earlier attempt to make small talk. "If you're hungry, we can go somewhere and–"

"I'd rather stay here to satisfy my hunger," he murmured as he walked over to her.

She felt her face redden. "Steele, I need to get home and unpack. And you have a lot of things to take care of."

"You're right." He gave her a lopsided sexy grin, then eyed the bed. "I have something very important to take care of. *You.*"

Laughing breathlessly, Becca let him fold her into his muscular arms. Just as he was about to kiss her, she put her hands on his chest and looked up into his eyes. "Do you really love me? I mean, if things hadn't turned out quite the way they did between us, would you still–"

"Yes, I'd still be chasing you around with shameless abandon." After touching his lips to hers, he looked her straight in the eyes and confessed, "I finally feel alive, Becca. And I'm not going to give up that feeling for anything. We belong together. Nothing will keep us apart."

Despite her misgivings about their situation and his mother's interference, she let out a shaky sigh of relief. Steele scooped her up in his arms and carried her to the bed. Depositing her among the pillows, he grabbed the bottom hem of his shirt and jerked it up over his shoulders and off over his head. Tossing the shirt to the floor, he reached for the button of his jeans.

Becca felt her heart pounding in her stomach as she looked at his magnificent naked torso. He was he really hers – all hers. When he peeled off his jeans and revealed the absence of underwear and the prominence of his desire, she writhed on the bed. *Yes, every glorious inch of him, all hers.*

CHAPTER 18

"*I* figured you'd want to see this for yourself," Chuck Lapinski said.

Sitting in the wingback chair nearest the open French doors of his hotel room, Steele eyed the tenacious investigator perched on the chair opposite the round table. Under the soft light of the lamp, the short and stocky man with his Marine buzz cut and drooping bulldog mouth was not pretty, but he was good at what he did and earned every penny of his hefty retainer from Hastings, Fehrnman & Reinhold.

Steele looked back at the bulky packet Chuck handed him. He dreaded seeing the contents, but after dropping Becca off at her parents' house, he knew he had to address the filth his mother had amassed against him.

"You have no idea how this got in your hotel room," Chuck cautioned. "In case the subject ever comes up."

"Of course." Steele flicked Chuck a knowing look. Breaking and entering was still a crime, even if it was perpetrated against Lila Morse in an attempt to defuse her blackmail scheme against her own son.

"It's not as bad as you thought," Chuck said in his naturally gruff tone.

Steele grimaced and pinched the metal clasp on the envelope flap. Reaching inside, he pulled out a bundle of eight-by-ten black-and-white photos. The images were dark and grainy, shot with a telescopic zoom lens on high-speed, low-light film. He barely recognized himself.

Once he recognized the setting as Sheila Breckenstern's living room in her ostentatious multi-million-dollar home, he shuffled through the photos quickly, hoping nothing salacious would catch his eye. Most of the pictures showed them standing close to each other, conversing, arguing. A few shots showed Sheila touching him, embracing him. He was amazed to see the lack of physical response on his part, reported by the objective eye of the camera. He looked bored or uninterested in most of these shots – even when Sheila was trying unsuccessfully to remove his clothes.

Whoever had taken these photos in hopes of catching him in the arms of another man's wife, had chosen an unlucky evening to spy. That was the night he'd broken things off with Sheila. She had tried to coax him into the bedroom, but he was having none of it. As his last paramour, she had turned out to be the most stubborn and difficult to convince that there was no hope of maintaining a long-term relationship.

He wondered if she had arranged the surreptitious photo session herself, believing she could blackmail him into continuing their affair. She hinted as much the last time she'd called him. Maybe she'd contacted his mother and provided the photos, instead of the other way around.

Despite what his mother had claimed, Steele didn't want to believe she'd been keeping tabs on him all this time. She'd stretched the truth about the nature of these photos. Maybe she'd been lying about other things as well. And Sheila's compulsion to find out personal details about him would explain how his mother had come to be in possession of these photos. Perhaps Sheila had managed to track down his mother, and the two kindred spirits decided to pool resources to get what they both wanted – Sheila, his attention, and his mother, his money.

He stuffed the photos back into the envelope. Scowling, he faced Chuck. "Do you know who was responsible for this?"

The investigator shook his head. "I made some discreet inquiries, but nobody owned up to doing the job. From the looks of it, my guess is Mrs. Breckenstern paid to catch more on film than she got." Chuck perked his low-slung, wooly-worm brows for emphasis.

Steele nodded, then handed the packet back to Chuck.

191

"Dispose of these, would you?"

Chuck took the packet and slid it into his tan, soft-sided briefcase.

"What about the doctor?" Steele asked.

"We came to a quick understanding." Chuck's grin was downright mean. "After our little talk, Dr. Farnsworth realized how close he was to losing his medical license. I don't think that fake blood-alcohol test is going to surface at the inquest after all."

Steele nodded again and glanced toward the open French doors beside his chair. The night breeze outside was strong, intermittently blowing the heavy drapes against his right leg. He turned back to Chuck. "Any luck finding the missing safety report Becca's father filed?"

Chuck shook his head. "No sign of it in the dairy records left behind after the district attorney's office took what they wanted. Didn't find it at your mother's house either, but I wasn't there very long. My guess is, she destroyed it. No sense keeping something like that around. It would be incriminating for management if it ever surfaced."

Steele frowned. "Well, we still have several of Mr. Sedder's coworkers who will vouch for the fact that he mentioned, right before the accident, that the scaffolding was a safety hazard and advised against using it." Steele rubbed his smooth-shaven chin, noticing Chuck's grayish five o'clock shadow. "I guess it boils down to the word of the dairy's management against Becca's father. The decision will rest with Judge Forrester and which story he chooses to believe."

"Maybe you should go talk to him about that and let him know one story's full of holes."

"I intend to."

"There's something else."

Steele met Chuck's small, knowing eyes. The man didn't mince words, and Steele could tell by the set of his thick jaw that what he was about to say wouldn't be pleasant.

"You were right about your mother's corporate finances. I did some snooping around at the dealership too. I'm no CPA, but what I saw didn't look good. Seems like your mother's been stealing from Peter to pay Paul."

Steele nodded and stood up. "I figured as much. My mother was in an awful damned hurry to get her hands on my trust fund. If she's so desperate to bail herself out that she would turn to me for help, she must be in a real pinch."

Chuck opened his mouth as if to give some more sage advice, then clammed up. Standing, he offered his hand to Steele. "Good luck. I'll stick around till after the inquest, in case you need anything else. Just call."

Smiling, Steele gripped Chuck's beefy hand. "I appreciate everything you've done."

"No problem. Glad to be of service."

Steele showed Chuck out of his room, then turned to face the phone. He didn't want to make that call. The angry child inside him told him to forget it; let her drown in her own greed and malice. But despite all the hurt she'd caused him from the time he was growing up to the present, he had to try one last time to make peace with his mother before he lowered the boom on her. It was the right thing to do.

* * * * *

"Considering what happened the last time you were at the house, I don't think your coming over would be a good idea. I'd like to keep what's left of my household furnishings."

Steele frowned. His mother's voice sounded colder than usual. She was still pissed about the dining room. Why did material things matter so much to her, when other more important personal things didn't? He wanted to shout at her, *You can buy new dishes, new furniture, but you can't replace your son's love!* But he said nothing. It was no use. She had long ago substituted money and social standing for the love of her family – his love. Public prestige in this little one-horse town was all she had left, and she was hanging onto it with every underhanded trick she could think of, even going so far as to force Becca to marry Conn

193

in hopes the union would elevate her remaining son to the ranks of respectability. But Conn would never measure up. Never. He was too much like his father and had been spoiled for too long to ever become a responsible adult.

Steele sighed. "We need to talk. What I have to say is better said in private, just between you and me."

After a long pause, his mother said coolly, "What makes you think I want to hear anything you have to say?"

He sighed again. "It concerns money. When have you not been interested in hearing about that?"

After another long pause, she said, "All right. I'll have a light lunch served in the sunroom while you tell me what's on your mind. Come around to the back at noon tomorrow."

* * * * *

Steele was anxious about making this last call. It was late, almost eight o'clock, and Judge Daniel Forrester was the last and most remote bastion of his past he was daring to challenge. Would the judge hear his plea on behalf of Becca and her father, or would he refuse to listen because Steele was related to the opposition? It didn't matter. He had to try. He had to speak up for Becca and expose his mother's machinations. The questions about his father's identity could wait.

Sucking up a deep breath, Steele grabbed the phone receiver.

He remembered Judge Forrester as a big stately man with thick graying hair and steely blue-gray eyes, who never seemed to look straight at him unless he caught him by surprise. The judge had probably been in his late forties the last time Steele had seen him. Nearly eighteen years had passed since then, and Steele was sure Daniel Forrester had changed physically. He'd be older now, probably in his early to mid sixties. Steele hoped that was the only thing different about Judge Forrester.

Steele needed him to still be the fair and compassionate man he was eighteen years ago. A man who'd ignored the rules and removed Steele from a detrimental home life at the Morse household. A man who'd taken enough of a personal interest in Steele's situation to investigate the possibilities before placing him in the care of relatives, rather than abandon him to the state's foster care system. The judge had bent the rules and had exerted considerable personal force to make everyone involved agree to the arrangement that put Steele with his great aunt and uncle. Why Judge Forrester had gone to those lengths to ensure Steele received a proper upbringing was the real puzzle. Did he take a personal interest in all the cases he oversaw? Or was Steele's situation different in some respect? That was one of the things Steele ached to ask him. But his hand remained frozen to the phone. What could he possibly say to this man who had single-handedly changed his life? 'Thank you' didn't seem adequate.

Gripping the notepad hard enough to keep his hand from shaking, Steele read the scribbled number, then punched it on the phone before he could second-guess himself. The phone rang one, two, three times. Steele was just about to hang up when a soft, deep, male voice said, "Hello?"

Steele tried to speak, but found his throat constricted as Judge Forrester repeated, "Hello? Is anybody there?"

Swallowing hard, Steele blew out the air he'd imprisoned in his lungs. "Uh, yes. Sorry to bother you, Judge Forrester. This is Steeleman Krueger. I don't know if you remember me, but—"

"Yes," the judge answered quickly. "Yes, of course, I remember you, Steele." His voice seemed to bubble with excitement, anticipation, or maybe Steele just imagined it. "What a pleasant surprise to hear from you."

Steele licked his lips that had gone dry. There was so much he wanted to say, but he didn't know where to start. "I apologize for calling so late."

"It's all right. I was just sitting in the study, reading."

"I was afraid you'd already gone to bed"

"I hear you've been with Hastings, Fehrnman & Reinhold for several years now. That's a fine firm. Solid, good reputation. Congratulations, son."

Steele sat down on the edge of the bed. Judge Forrester still called him 'son' after eighteen years. He wanted to believe the bestowed title was especially intended for him, but suspected the old fellow addressed every younger male as 'son.' And how did he know where he was working? "I ... well, thank you." He bit his lip and grimaced, realizing he sounded like a tongue-tied idiot. "I hate to bother you, Sir, but I was wondering if I could set up an appointment to talk with you."

"You don't need an appointment," the judge answered. "I'd very much like to see you."

Steele let out a big gust of relief. "I was afraid you'd say no."

"I wouldn't pass up the opportunity to talk with you."

Swiping a clammy palm over his mouth, Steele hedged, "I was concerned about the inquest next week. You know my mother is–"

"The inquest. Of course, that's why you're calling. I assumed you wanted to catch me up on what you've been doing. It's been a long time."

Steele paused, not sure what to think. The judge sounded disappointed. "Yes, it has been a long time, and I have a few personal things I'd like to discuss. But right now there is a pressing situation I need to bring to your attention."

The judge started to interrupt, but Steele charged ahead before he could make any objections. "I know you can't discuss any details concerning the inquest, and can't allow yourself to be swayed prematurely regarding your ruling. But there are some other things I need to tell you that have a bearing on the situation with Becca's father."

"Becca ... Rebecca. Ray Sedder's daughter." The judge went quiet for a moment, then asked, "You're familiar with her?"

Steele raked a hand through his hair. How much gossip had Judge Forrester heard? Fenton was a small town where news of an intimate nature traveled fast. He had to know about the situation with Becca and the arranged marriage to Conn. Steele took a deep breath, then exhaled. "Yes, I know her. Quite well, in fact." He felt his face redden when he realized how that sounded, but he bumbled on. "The problem is ... well, I'm sure you've heard by now that Becca is scheduled to marry my brother this Saturday, right before the dairy inquest scheduled for the following Monday morning."

The judge remained silent for a moment, then said, "I'm aware of the wedding arrangements. Are you suggesting there's a connection between the timing of the wedding and the inquest?"

Steele breathed a sigh of relief. At least he wouldn't have to spell things out. "Yes. That's one of the things I need to discuss with you. I want you to understand what's really going on. Becca doesn't want to marry my brother, but my mother's doing her very best to convince her to go through with it. I'm trying to help Becca avoid that situation, but there are some ... *complications* with the inquest that are influencing her decision regarding the wedding."

"Complications. I see."

"It's important that I speak with you as soon as possible. Tomorrow – Thursday – if that's convenient."

Over the phone, Steele heard the judge sigh heavily. "There are a few things I need to discuss with you too, Steele. I have a full day in court tomorrow. Let's meet tomorrow evening."

Steele tried to swallow down his excitement. Judge Forrester sounded as if he understood the situation and might be willing to help. "Tomorrow evening would be great. Just tell me when and where. I'll be there."

Judge Forrester took a long time to answer. "Considering the subject matter we'll be discussing, I think it might be best if you came to my house. Around six o'clock. I'll have a light meal prepared, if that's all right with you."

"Yes, that would be great. Six o'clock. Thank you, Judge Forrester."

"I look forward to seeing you again, Steele."

Steele hung up the phone with renewed confidence. Things were finally starting to come together. His mother wasn't going to win after all. He phoned Becca to tell her the good news.

* * * * *

Steele ignored the other diners in the Standish Inn restaurant and smiled at Becca across the intimately small table. "I missed you last night. It's a good thing we only have two more days to stay single." He winked.

Becca gave him a shy smile and returned her attention to the leather-bound menu in her hands. Ignoring the rumbling in his stomach, Steele stared at her, trying to think of some way to convince her to skip breakfast and let him whisk her up to his room, to his bed. But he knew he would be meeting his mother at noon, and he wanted to have a clear head. Plus, he wanted Becca to feel comfortable around him and not assume that every time he looked at her, it was with the intent to bed her – although that was true. Smiling to himself, he focused on his menu.

By the time the waitress refilled their coffee and left with their orders, Steele felt a little more at ease. He reached across the linen tablecloth and took hold of Becca's hands. "I'm glad you decided to take off work this week and next. I want to take you for a real honeymoon, once we get this situation with my mother straightened out. After Saturday, everything will be smooth sailing."

Becca shrugged noncommittally and withdrew her hands, hiding them in her lap. Steele could tell by her tentative nature that she still didn't believe their problems were behind them, even after he told her about the progress Chuck Lapinski had made with Dr. Farnsworth, and explained that the pictures his mother had weren't incriminating. Even his confidence about the upcoming meeting with Judge Forrester this evening didn't seem to alleviate her doubts. "Think positive," he murmured. "Everything will work out fine."

She winced. "I have this awful feeling that your mother's holding back on us, that she's still got some tricks up her sleeve."

"Has she tried to contact you, leave any messages?"

"No, but that's my point. It's like she's lying in wait,

knowing we think everything's over and that we've beaten her. And all the while she's sitting back, smirking, because she's got the element of surprise."

"Sweetheart, that's part of her plan – to try and psych us out, make us think she's got the upper hand when she knows she doesn't. In any game that doesn't depend solely on skill or chance, half the ability to win depends on how well you can bluff. I'm a lawyer and see it everyday. How do you think my mother got where she is now? Not by giving others the benefit of the doubt, or by doing the right thing. She's going to bluff her way to the very end. And even when she knows she's beaten, she won't admit defeat. Believe me, she has nothing left to manipulate us."

Becca sighed. "Still..."

"Trust me. We're on the home stretch. All we have to do is stay calm and wait her out. I've taken care of everything – got the license and explained everything to the minister. When Saturday rolls around, you'll walk down the aisle just like my mother planned. Only it'll be me standing there at the altar with you instead of Conn. And neither he nor my mother will dare show up or try to cause trouble. Everything will be fine – great, in fact. Because we love each other, and day after tomorrow we'll be husband and wife."

He reached over and touched a finger to her chin to lift her face. She smiled as if she believed what he said. Having her trust him bolstered his confidence. Everything would go without a hitch.

He withdrew his hand as the waitress arrived, bearing plates of food. After she left, Becca fiddled with her fork and said, "I don't know how you've put up with her all these years."

"My mother?"

"I can understand her motivation to set up my father to take the blame for Larry Carter's death. She has the dairy to think about, and a lawsuit for malicious negligence and wrongful death could make real trouble for her company. I can even understand her attempt to make Conn settle down by forcing him to marry. But she's been awful to you. And trying to blackmail you..."

199

Becca sighed and put her fork down beside her untouched scrambled eggs. "I just don't see why she would treat you so bad. You haven't done anything to deserve that. Doesn't it bother you?"

Steele forced a smile. He wasn't going to let the subject of his mother spoil his time with Becca. "I refuse to let it."

"But..."

"Don't give my mother a second thought. It's not important, and I don't want you stressing about it."

Becca reached over and placed a hand atop his. "It *is* important if it makes you unhappy. I want her to stop being so awful to you."

Steele squeezed Becca's hand. "She will, soon. And then we won't have to worry about her anymore. Trust me. Everything will be all right as long as we're together."

She gave him one more sympathetic look, then picked up her fork again.

"After breakfast, I'll drop you off at your parents' house," he said, changing the subject. "I've got one more thing to take care of before I talk with Judge Forrester this evening, and I'm not sure how long I'll be tied up. So I probably won't see you until later tonight."

Becca nodded and began to eat her breakfast. Steele was glad she didn't ask what he had planned. He didn't have the heart to tell her he was going to talk with his mother at noon. Telling Becca that would only upset her, and he wanted to keep her as calm and collected as possible. She'd suffered enough over the past few weeks because of his family, and he wasn't going to let that happen anymore.

* * * * *

As soon as Steele waved goodbye and pulled his car away from the curb, Becca shut the front door and peeked into the hallway, looking for her father and mother. At this late hour of the morning, she expected at least one of them to be up, but apparently they'd slept in or gone back to bed. With no one else in the house, they must have decided it was the perfect opportunity to catch up on their rest.

Satisfied she wouldn't be disturbed, Becca headed for the olive wall phone in the kitchen. Its faded color somehow managed to coordinate with the garishly bright sunflower motif her mother had doused on the kitchen like gasoline on a brush fire. Becca eyed the yellow and black design bursting from the tablecloth and the curtains and the dishtowels hanging from the cabinet handles, wondering if her sister and her mother had been drinking when they'd chosen this decorating scheme. The chipped and peeling white paint covering the kitchen cabinets added to the unsettling feel of the room, and Becca caught herself thinking some gas and a lit match might be the best way to improve the kitchen's appearance. Shaking her head, she dismissed the idea and punched in Mrs. Morse's home number.

Lila answered on the first ring, with a tone of anticipation mixed with irritation. "Mrs. Morse," Becca blurted, before she lost her courage, "I want you to be aware that our agreement concerning Conn is canceled. I want you to stop taunting Steele and leave my family alone." She knew she should hang up, but she was anxious to see how Lila would respond.

After a moment of silence, Lila said, "I'm very sorry to hear you say that, Becca. I was hoping you and Conn would have a long and happy future together."

Becca almost choked on her own indignation. "How could you expect anyone to have a happy future with *him*?"

Lila sighed. "Becca, you poor, ignorant child. Under my care, you would have flourished. Now..." She clicked her tongue in admonishment.

"Look. All I want is for you to leave me and my family alone. And to stop torturing Steele. He's your son too. I can't understand why you treat him so bad. I want you to quit hurting him."

"I take it you care for him – so much the worse. You'll suffer dearly when he drops you."

"He is not going to drop me. We're getting married Saturday."

Lila's sudden harsh laughter startled Becca. "You believe the lies he's been telling you, don't you?"

"He hasn't been lying to me, Mrs. Morse. He loves me."

"Oh, yes, just like he 'loved' all those other women."

Becca felt her face heat. Calling Mrs. Morse had been a huge mistake. What had made her think the woman would respond to simple reason? It hadn't worked before.

"Actually," Lila taunted, "Steele's coming over here to talk with me in a few hours. I can ask him then how he feels about you."

Becca frowned. Steele claimed to have something to take care of, but hadn't said anything about seeing his mother. Why hadn't he told her?

"I think he's ready to make a deal," Mrs. Morse continued. "Obviously he does care about you and your family enough to make a small sacrifice on your behalf."

"What are you saying?"

"He offered to sign over his trust fund, along with some other assets, if I agreed to let you and your father off the hook. I'm considering it. All I have to do is find a way to get his money before Saturday. Then I'll have it all – the cash flow I want, plus a wife for Conn."

Becca gripped the receiver hard enough to turn her knuckles white. That couldn't be true! Why would Steele do that when he'd assured her everything was going well? He said Dr. Farnsworth had been convinced not to produce the falsified blood-alcohol test on her father at the inquest. And that private investigator, Mr. Lapinski, had obtained the non-incriminating pictures Steele's mother was using in her blackmail bluff. What would possess Steele to go to his mother now?

"I take it he didn't want you to know he was coming to see me," Lila deduced during Becca's long silence.

"He ... I'm sure didn't want me to worry or be upset."

"Yes, yes, that has to be it."

202

Becca could hear her quick breaths huffing into the phone speaker. She put her hand over the mouthpiece and closed her eyes, trying to make her scrambled brain function. Steele wasn't trying to keep things from her for surreptitious reasons. She took her hand off the mouthpiece. "Steele wouldn't hand over any of his financial assets to you."

"You're right. He wouldn't. Not voluntarily."

Becca took a deep, calming breath. Steele had warned her that his mother would try to rattle her confidence. She bit her lip, then spouted, "He's got the pictures you were holding over him. They weren't what you claimed. And the blood test Dr. Farnsworth falsified won't be showing up in court either."

In the short silence that followed, Becca couldn't tell whether Lila Morse was angry or surprised. Finally she said, "Tell me you're not gullible enough to believe everything Steele tells you. Of course he's going to say whatever he thinks you want to hear. The pictures? I've still got them, and they're as incriminating as ever. I suggest you come over and have a look, to set yourself straight once and for all about my wayward son. And the blood test? Dr. Farnsworth is still comfortably in my pocket. In fact, I just spoke with him before you called. What's more, I've got Judge Forrester in my corner too. I have a tidy bit of information about his past that he'll do anything to keep secret – even if that means compromising his professional integrity on the bench. His ruling at the inquest will go just the way I want. Rest assured, if you're not Mrs. Conner Morse on Saturday, your father will be jailbait on Monday."

Becca shook her head, trying to clear the foggy uncertainty from her mind. "I don't believe you. Why would Steele lie to me about all that? He has nothing to gain."

"Oh, doesn't he? Stop and think about it. All Steele cares about is getting you for himself and keeping you away from Conn. Nothing else matters to him right now. Not your father, not his reputation. Nothing. His true objective should be clear to you. I'm surprised you haven't figured it out. He doesn't want you because he *wants* you. He wants you just to get even with *me*.

Once he's spoiled Conn's wedding, I'll be made to look the fool, and his job here will be done. Then he'll rush back to Chicago so fast, you'll be left coughing in his dust."

Becca gripped the phone receiver harder to keep her arm from trembling. "You're lying. He wouldn't go to all that trouble just to ruin your plans. He doesn't care that much about you. In fact, he doesn't care about you at all!" She slammed the phone down on the hook and whirled away, crossing her arms over her stomach. Why would Lila Morse say such hateful things about Steele? How could she despise her own son that much? Surely there wasn't a thread of truth in what she said.

Haunted by doubt, Becca wandered down the hall to her bedroom and collapsed face down on her bed.

CHAPTER 19

*S*teele strolled along the flagstone path around the side of his mother's house, noting the rose bushes with rich deep red buds just beginning to open. He reached the white arbor entrance signaling the transition from the stately front yard to the secluded privacy of the back. The heady scent of honeysuckle wafted through the air with overpowering enchantment, flooding him with old memories and mixed feelings.

He glanced overhead at the wisteria entwining the arbor. Its woody trunk and ferny leaves created a canopy refuge that, in spring, sported cascading grapelike clusters of blossoms, their fallen petals carpeting the ground like lavender snow. The memory triggered a childhood flashback of him crouching under the arbor, hiding like a frightened animal to escape The Ogre's wrath. After eighteen years, the fear had passed, but he still felt uneasy as he pulled back the white picket gate.

The gate creaked open to allow him entry to his mother's religiously cultivated sanctuary. Overhanging willows and oaks shaded her voluptuous meandering flowerbeds showcasing benches and diminutive statuary – cupids, Greek mythical figures, and the like. Hybrid Asian lilies offered an array of spotted showy hues - soft and dusky pinks and peaches, white, purple, orange, yellow, and bronze. He'd come too late to catch the spring blooming of dogwoods, crabapples, and cherry trees, but could still vividly recall the image of a soft, eerie fairyland of pink and white blossoms. His mother's lush and dignified retreat would have been awe-inspiring, had he not known she paid a landscaping service and a professional horticulturalist to tend the beauty of her realm.

Steele turned to face the massive glassed-in porch spanning

the rear of the house. The windows were open to allow the yard's delightful scents to permeate the screens. But, like his mother's heart, the screens let light and fragrance in while giving nothing in return. Unable to see inside, he knew she was enthroned there, watching him with regal authority. Sighing, he walked up the brick steps and tapped on the door.

"Come in. It's open."

He closed the door behind him and saw her sitting in an oversized white wicker peacock chair, sipping coffee from a china cup – not the same pattern as the set he had helped destroy in his scuffle with his stepfather days earlier.

His mother looked calm and collected in her royal blue silk blouse, white slacks, and white leather sandals. Of course, it was Friday – casual day. Steele checked the smirk threatening to spread over his face.

"Would you like a sandwich?" she asked, leaning forward to touch a plate on the wicker table in front of her. "A glass of iced tea? Coffee?"

He shook his head and managed a polite smile. "Nothing for me, right now, but you go ahead." He sat down on the wicker couch nearby. The bold flowered cushion sank with forgiving ease under his weight, inviting him to lean back and take a load off, but he remained sitting upright. He didn't feel at ease, even though he knew he had the advantage now.

When his mother crossed her arms and sat back in her chair with its high fan back, Steel realized just how much it looked like a throne. Her pretentiousness galled him. He wanted to laugh out loud, but held back the urge, deciding to leave that sort of nastiness to her, the undisputed queen of belittlement.

"What did you want to discuss?" she prodded.

He sucked in a deep breath and exhaled. "I came to see if I could somehow convince you to retire the campaign you've been waging against Becca and her father."

His mother screwed up her mouth in obvious distaste. "I haven't been waging anything against anyone. Ray Sedder's ruin is not my doing. He brought it on himself with his drinking. After the accident at the dairy, Becca came to me and asked for my help. I promised to do what I could to protect him, in exchange for her help with Conn. Becca and I had an agreement until you took it upon yourself to interfere. If she backs out, her father will have to face his personal demons and handle the consequences on his own."

Steele struggled against the urge to yell obscenities at his mother. The way she twisted everything around to support her view, and her insane cruelty in thinking she could glibly destroy other people's lives to suit her whims, disgusted him. But he knew leveling insults and accusations wouldn't solve anything. He took a deep, calming breath. "You and I both know Becca's father isn't to blame for the accident. And I don't think Dr. Farnsworth is going to back you up at the inquest with that false blood-alcohol test you've been holding over Becca. Farnsworth left his last job under similar accusations involving falsified medical records."

"The rumor was never proven."

"Nevertheless, I believe he prizes his physician's license too much to risk another scandal, no matter what kind of personal favors he may owe."

His mother huffed. "Again you've managed to create an inconvenience. Farnsworth called me after that snoop you hired paid him a visit and threatened to expose him. That was a truly mean and underhanded tactic, hinting that you'd ruin a man's professional reputation just to further your own schemes."

"Well," Steele said with a breathless laugh, "now isn't this the pot calling the kettle black?"

"Farnsworth's testimony doesn't matter," she said, ignoring his jab as she folded her hands in her lap. "As long as the death of that unfortunate man—"

"That unfortunate man worked for you for twelve years and left behind a wife and three children who are still grieving for him. His name was Larry Carter."

She sighed. "Mr. Carter's death was regrettable, but I still have my business to worry about. The dairy employs too many people for me to let this go without trying to work it for the best possible advantage. If the dairy is fined for willful negligence – or worse, shut down – a lot of workers would lose their jobs. But as long as the death is ruled an accident, the dairy's liability insurance will help cover the court expenses and any settlements that might result. I don't like leaving it that way, but you've given me no other choice."

She skewered Steele with a hard look, then reached for her silver coffee server to top off her cup. "I don't need the blood test to point a finger at Ray Sedder. Enough people already blame him for Carter's death, without my saying anything to bolster that perception."

"There you go," Steele said with a smirk, "indulging your wishful thinking again."

She frowned at his comment and set the server down on the table. "What happens to Becca's father as a result of the inquest depends entirely on what she decides to do this weekend. Supporting testimony for her father could go either way."

"You'd stick with your lies about Becca's father and the accident out of mere spite, if Becca crosses you?"

Sitting back in her chair, she took a sip of coffee, then cradled the cup in her lap. "Despite your annoying attempts to interfere, I won't give up seeing Conn married and settled."

Steele looked at his mother in amazement. She still sounded sure of herself, even though she had to know she possessed no solid evidence with which to sway Judge Forrester's ruling. She was truly a consummate player – he had to give her credit for that. He wanted to end things now and tell her she'd lost both her bid to marry off Conn and to pin the blame for the dairy accident on Becca's father, but caution and a miniscule vestige of parental respect urged him to give her one more chance to make things right on her own. "I'm appealing to your sense of fairness. Stop torturing Becca with this crazy arranged marriage. She agreed to it in the first place only because she believed you had the power to influence her father's future. Now she knows better, and she's not going through with the screwed-up fantasy you've cooked up for her and Conn."

Leaning forward, his mother set her cup down in its saucer with a clatter, then sat back again. "Becca can provide the stability and family responsibility your brother needs. And she'll do that, no matter what you want, if it's the only way her father can be vindicated of wrongdoing."

Glancing down at her white slacks, she picked at an imaginary thread. When she glared back at him, she sighed with seeming exasperation. "I know how the girl thinks. Her track record so far will bear me out. If she has to make a choice between her family and her own happiness, she'll choose her family without hesitation. So, you might as well pack up and leave now, because you and she are never going to be together." She perked her thin black brows to drive home the point.

Damn, she was bold! But he wouldn't let her get to him. He leaned back, crossed his legs, and rested his hands in his lap. "Eventually Mr. Sedder will receive the medical benefits to which he's entitled. You can try to delay that, or expedite the process by showing your support at the inquest. Whatever you decide, your time for making Becca's life hell is over. I'm not going to let you cause her any more emotional anguish."

His mother snorted. "You make it sound as if you've got this all neatly packaged up." She reached for her coffee cup, took a leisurely drink, then rested her elbows on the arms of her peacock chair. "You're forgetting the pictures I have of you and your lady friend back in Chicago. I'd hate to think what would become of your law career if those photos happened to fall into the wrong hands."

"I've seen the pictures. Unless you've got other more revealing shots stashed away somewhere, I don't think I have anything to worry about."

When his mother failed to respond, he uncrossed his legs and sat forward. "Come on, Mother! End this foolishness now, and leave Becca alone. Let Conn live his life his way – good or bad – and quit trying to force him to be something he's not."

She brought her hands together and gave him a cool, even

stare. "Conn needs direction. He needs purpose. Becca will help give him that."

"No. Becca won't be manipulated by you anymore, and she's not going to give Conn anything – especially not a sense of pride and responsibility. No one can do that for him. Not you, not Becca, not anybody. It has to come from within him, and nothing will change that. Living in the same house with The Ogre for so many years should have taught you that lesson already."

He sat back and folded his arms across his chest. "You know what? I don't give a damn. Do what you want at the inquest. The facts will come out about the dairy accident, and things will work out for Becca's father in spite of your scheming."

His mother said nothing as she glared at him. He frowned. Was there no way to get through to her? "For once, be honest with yourself and face the truth. Conn doesn't want to marry Becca any more than she wants to marry him. This harebrained arrangement of yours isn't going to work. I know it, and you know it. Hell, everyone in Fenton knows it."

"Conn has his faults," she snipped, "but unlike you, he usually does what he's told."

Steele chuckled breathlessly as shook his head. "Mother, you're smarter than that. You have to realize that even if you did manage to marry Conn off, your battle would only just begin. He'd go along with your dictates under duress, but he'd resist you every step of the way and take out his displeasure on everyone around him – mostly on his unfortunate bride."

"Yes, Conn will take it out on everyone around him, just like you did when you were living at home." His mother leaned forward and took a white-bread triangle sandwich from the platter sitting on the table between them. "You have no idea what kind of hell you put me through with your antics." Sitting back with regal authority, she took a mincing bite, chewed, swallowed, and pointed the dulled tip of her sandwich at him. "You nearly destroyed my family."

Family? More like a pack of hyenas. Steele lunged forward

210

in his seat. "And you had no concern for what you put me through, forcing me to stay under the same roof with a man who literally wanted me dead."

His mother stared at him in prickling silence, then said, "Believe me, there were times I wanted the same thing. Everyone would have been better off if you'd never been born."

He felt the blood drain from his face and swallowed hard as his gaze fell away from her. He tried to focus on the abstract pattern in the gray tile floor, but his eyes skittered as his mind reeled from what he'd just heard. His mother had never before dared voice that truth aloud. Now that she'd said it, there was no taking it back – not that she would want to.

So, she regretted the very day he'd been born. She wished he'd never existed. After more than thirty years, she was still trying to negate him, devalue him, reduce him to nothing, and rid herself of him.

A tiny part of him wanted to curl up and whine bitterly over the affection she denied him. Another part wanted to make her see he wasn't a mistake, that he was a viable human being who deserved her respect and love. But as he dragged his gaze from the floor and made himself look at the stonehearted woman who had brought him into the world, he realized there was no hope of reconciliation. She simply had no feelings for him other than contempt. "Why the hell didn't you just get rid of me *before* I was born?"

"I still regret not making that choice." Her gaze darted erratically over him. "But at the time I was only nineteen, young and in love. I believed – foolishly, it turns out – that your father was going to take responsibility for you. By the time I realized he wasn't, it was too late to consider abortion."

Steele sat in silence, stunned by her brutal candor until he reminded himself he didn't care what she thought. He didn't need her love or approval, or anything else from her. "I don't give a damn how you feel about me. I came here for Becca. I'm asking you one last time to stop what you're doing and leave her alone. Surely somewhere, deep down inside, you have some shred of decency and compassion left in your heart." He searched her face for softness, capitulation, but saw only rancor.

Her smile appeared with chilling serpentine inevitability. "It bothers the hell out of you to think you come from such cold-blooded stock, doesn't it? Afraid you'll turn out the same? Well, take perverse comfort in the fact that your father was as cold-blooded as I am. He chose his career over you." She leaned forward for emphasis. "You were his only child, yet he *rejected* you, and left me facing the uncertain future of raising you on my own, alone, with no prospects of making it on my own."

Again Steele got the feeling his mother was twisting the truth to suit her needs, which right now involved making him lose his confidence. "It was *you* he rejected," he said finally. "Not me. I wasn't born yet. Did he even know about me when you married The Ogre?"

She set the uneaten portion of her sandwich aside on her plate, alongside her neglectedcoffee cup. "He knew, but didn't give a damn." After dabbing a sea foam green linen napkin to the sides of her mouth and dusting her fingertips together, she brushed imagined crumbs from her lap and sighed. "He had his precious *reputation* to think about. Never mind me. He decided he couldn't afford the scandal of a divorce, and that left me – you – out of his life permanently."

"So, he was married," Steele confirmed, trying to hide his excitement mixed with disappointment. At last he'd learned a detail about his mysterious father, but it wasn't the kind of information he could be proud of. His father was an adulterer who'd sired a child with a teenage mistress. Not a glowing revelation.

"Obviously my father wasn't the only one concerned with his reputation. Is that why you lied and tried to pass me off as The Ogre's son to get him to marry you?" Steele stared at his mother as if he were seeing her for the first time. "I don't understand how you could have ever wanted to marry that monster, much less stay married to him. Surely you had to know what he was like. How many other women did he have to sleep with, before you got the point that he didn't love you?"

He watched with perverse satisfaction as his mother's face darkened with indignation. "You have no right to pass judgment on me! You don't know what it was like then for an unwed mother. My mother wouldn't allow her reputation to be sullied by a bastard grandchild. And she wouldn't hear of adoption – it simply wasn't an option in her mind. I married Jim because he was willing and available, and his father needed a cash-flow partner for the dealership. Blame me if you must, but I did what I had to."

"I guess I shouldn't blame you, but I do. Why did you let it go on for so many years, putting up with a sham marriage and making me suffer the consequences?"

Her eyes flashed, and her face got even darker. Reaching for her coffee again, she took a moment to compose herself, then said in a sinister tone, "Of course, you'd have the selfish audacity to think it was all about you. But it wasn't, and never was. It was *my* life I was trying to salvage *because* of you. My marriage to Jim was necessary, not only to cover up the truth of your paternity, but to forge a new future for myself."

"And to hell with what happened to me along the way."

Sipping her coffee with deliberation, she glared at him in silence. If she'd been a cat, she would have been twitching her tail with wild agitation. "You're so much like your father, and you don't even realize it. Your build, your coloring, your voice, even some of your mannerisms. And your damned self-centered confidence. You even pursued the same career path. Every time I see you, I'm reminded of *him*."

Steele tried to stay calm, but this stuff his mother was laying on him after all these years was almost too much. His father was a lawyer too? "Is that why you hate me so much – because I remind you of him?"

He thought he saw a flicker of vulnerability just before she turned her attention to the half-eaten sandwich sitting before her. She took a bite and then another, making him agonize in the silence. After she'd polished off the last bite and emptied her cup,

213

she trained her eyes on him. "I'm angry with you for coming back to Fenton and making my life difficult, Steele. But I don't hate you. I never did." Leaning forward, she refilled her cup and added, "And I don't hate your father, even though he hurt and disappointed me to an extent I can't expect you to understand. I harbor bad feelings toward him, but I blame myself for what happened, for getting pregnant. I was naïve, idealistic." She sat back and furrowed her brow. "And don't give me that look. I was nineteen, still an innocent girl, for God's sake!"

Steele blinked in surprise. His mother's perpetually sharp edge seemed to soften – or she was playing him. Having never seen this side of her, he couldn't be sure.

"I thought I could make a difference. Me, a poor little rich girl from a small rural community. And he, your father, was determined to make some changes in his life, having recently left a position as a trial lawyer in St. Louis to accept a position here with Cress and Bartlett."

Steele eyed his mother carefully. Was she going to open up to him about a subject that had been so personal to her, it had been off-limits for discussion all his life? In this rare moment of emotional exposure, he dared hope she might tell him what he'd been aching to know. Why was she dangling this carrot in front of him now? What was the catch? "Cress and Bartlett?" he echoed. "I don't recall–"

"That was over thirty years ago. They're not in business anymore."

She looked out the windows and sighed, as if her mind were traveling back to some long-forgotten place she hadn't visited in years. "He was older," she mused, "and handsome, full of enthusiasm. We were both working as campaign volunteers – it was a presidential election year, with the Viet Nam mess still a bad memory. There was so much to be done, and for the first time in my life I wanted to be a part of something important, larger than myself. Your father was so..."

She paused and took another sip of coffee. Steele studied her face openly. In the tree-filtered light of early afternoon, she looked troubled, unsettled by her recollection of her time with his father. With her face turned aside, he could see deeply etched lines of sorrow and regret. Yet even with those traces of emotion, she remained closed, forever the enigma he couldn't reach. Just when he thought it was safe to write her off as an unfit mother and hate her without reservation, he saw a gentler, vulnerable side that reminded him she was still human after all.

"Your father," she said again, sitting back and assuming an almost wistful air, "was soliciting for campaign volunteers. He was so charismatic, and I was romantically unattached, thinking I was too mature for boys my age. For the most part, I was.

"After suffering my share of secret crushes on college instructors, I was home for the summer, looking for something to occupy my time and keep me out of the house and away from my mother's watchful eyes. I wanted to be independent."

Looking off in pleasant distraction, she genuinely smiled in retrospect. "At the time I had no idea what it truly meant to be independent. My parents were footing the bill for my college expenses, and I didn't hurt for any extravagance. I lived in the sorority house rather than those awful dorms – worse than army barracks. Cramped little hovels with God knows who for roommates. Community showers..." She shook her shoulders in disgust.

"I was ready for a diversion, some excitement, something different." She gave Steele a quick glance, then leaned forward to set her cup down. "And along came your father, with his black hair and smoky gray eyes, and a smile that turned me inside-out."

Steele blinked again in amazement. He just couldn't fathom his mother unwinding enough to be enamored by anyone.

"He was ten years older than me, about the age you are now. He seemed so polished, sophisticated. He said he had come to Fenton for a quieter lifestyle, but I knew better. He had big aspirations for his career, which he hoped to accomplish in a rural area with less competition."

"Big aspirations?" Steele prodded, hoping to extract more clues about his father's identity.

"He ran into me one day at the grocery store," his mother said, ignoring his prod, "and asked if I'd be interested in doing volunteer work at the local presidential campaign headquarters. He'd set up an old storefront downtown, on the square, next to what used to be Dr. Amersol's dentist office. I hadn't really thought of myself as a political activist, but your father talked to me into it. More importantly, he paid attention to me and treated me like an adult. I was instantly taken by him, of course."

"Of course," Steele accorded.

His mother shot him a look, then continued, "When I found out he had Native American ancestry too, I–"

"Too?"

She smiled, not pleasantly. "Your Grandmother Delbridge was one-eighth Cherokee, and she'd turn over in her grave if she knew I told anyone."

Steele rolled his eyes. The rich bigot that she was, Bianca Steeleman Delbridge probably thought mixed heritage tainted her Daughters of the American Revolution standing.

"I agreed to join the campaign. Stuff envelopes, make phone calls. Mother didn't like it, said it was 'unseemly' for a girl of my upbringing. But I didn't care. I wanted to spend every moment I could with your father. And then one evening, about two weeks before I had to go back to school, he asked me to stay late and help him with a mailing he wanted to get out the next day. It was just the two of us there, alone, in a back room of the campaign office. One thing led to another and ... well, the mailing didn't get finished. That was the beginning of your existence and the end of my college career."

She reached for the cellophane-covered plate of tiny sandwiches. "Have something to eat."

Jolted out of her narrative, Steele accepted a sandwich and the glass she filled with ice from a silver decanter and topped off with tea from a glass pitcher. He gobbled the sandwich, just then realizing he was actually hungry. After finishing a second sandwich, he let his mother eat another and refill her coffee cup, then sat back and waited for her to pick up the story where she'd left off.

She dabbed her mouth with her napkin and sighed. "I shouldn't be telling you this..."

"Please," he urged, "I want to know."

She sighed again and looked away. Just when he thought she wasn't going to tell him any more, she murmured, "I was inexperienced and assumed, after your father and I had been together, that he loved me and would leave his wife so we could get married. But he said his wife was ill – something she would never completely recover from. He used her as an excuse to break things off, saying he loved her and couldn't afford to have her find out about us. But I think it was the possibility of a scandal that worried him more. He couldn't have the rumors of an affair and an illegitimate child coming back to haunt him when he got his career in full swing."

"Career?" Steele prodded. "I thought you said he was a lawyer."

"He was," his mother confirmed, "but he had bigger plans for himself. He knew it would take a couple years, with plenty of experience under his belt, before he could move up to be a ... to move up in the ranks."

Bigger and better things, move up in the ranks in the local legal system. Steele accepted this information, tucking it away for further study. He knew better than to push his mother for details. The fact that she was telling him anything at all about his father was an incredible breakthrough he hadn't expected.

"It took me a while to get the message," she continued, "but I finally realized he would never divorce his wife. By then, I needed to do something fast, since I was almost three months pregnant with you. So I made the only choice available to me at the time, and started dating Jim. He was a little rough around the edges," she admitted with a smirk, "but I naïvely I thought I could change him. I dangled the promise of money in front of him, and he didn't object when I told him I thought I was pregnant. We got married, and he naturally assumed you were his son, even after you were born 'early.' There was some gossip, of course, but I don't think he ever suspected my story about your being premature. It wasn't until Conn came along later that things got out of hand."

Steele nodded with a frown. Everything went downhill the moment Conn entered the picture.

"You know how sickly Conn was as a baby. He got every childhood illness there was, and then some. And he was a demanding child, always needing attention." She offered an apologetic sidelong glance as she admitted, "I know I neglected you, but I had my hands full with Conn. And Mother was never available to help out. She never did want the responsibility of childrearing. I guess that's why she allowed herself only one pregnancy."

Reaching for her coffee cup, she said, "It was some silly blood test the pediatrician insisted on, that let the cat out of the bag. The doctor wanted to rule out a specific genetic abnormality, so we were all tested. Around that time I'd caught Jim with another woman – just one of a long string of meaningless flings littering our marriage. I was so angry, I ignored my better judgment and showed him the test results confirming he couldn't possibly have fathered a son with type O-negative blood – you."

Leaning back in her chair, she sipped her coffee calmly. "I was surprised he was smart enough to understand the evidence." She shrugged. "In any case, I wasn't about to let him sully my life with his philandering. I told him he'd better keep a low profile, or I'd ruin him financially with a divorce. He has hated me, and you, ever since."

She eyed Steele critically as she ended, "You may think you're the only one who suffered for my mistake, but I've paid for it in ways you can't begin to imagine. I've wasted my life trying to create the illusion of a happy home – an illusion that has no basis in truth."

"Then why bother?" Steele demanded. "Why put everyone through all the hoop-jumping just for the sake of appearances?"

"Because appearances are all that I have left. Without some kind of reputation, I have nothing."

Steele shook his head. Material things and the veil of pretense ... that was her only justification for the life she led? She truly did have nothing left that mattered. He felt sorry for her.

"You know," she said softly, "I never set out to make your life miserable, and I never intended to keep information about your father from you. But I just couldn't bring myself to talk about him. And the reason I haven't told you who he is – and still can't – has nothing to do with spite. It's a matter of principle. I promised myself a long time ago, after I realized things weren't going to work between us, that I wouldn't do or say anything to anyone that might reveal the fact that he was your father. I especially couldn't tell you. I didn't know how you'd take it or what you'd do with the information. And I didn't want your father blaming me for forcing the issue."

Steele nodded. He was beginning to understand now.

"I wasn't trying to hurt you or to protect him," she clarified. "I simply decided that *he* should be the one to tell you he was your father. And if he never got the courage ... well, I wasn't going to make him own up to it." She looked Steele in the eyes and said, "I'm sorry for whatever loss and pain this has caused you, but I hope you understand why I did what I felt I had to do."

Steele nodded again, more slowly, with the dawning realization that his mother was not just an obstacle to be hated for the pain she had caused him. She had feelings too. It had always been convenient to forget that fact when he needed someone to blame for the unhappiness of his childhood. But when he put her confession into proper perspective, he could almost relate to her predicament. The only missing piece to the puzzle was his father's side of the story. He supposed he would never know it, but at least he was getting a better understanding of the situation his mother faced. And he could look at her with a new, objective sense of respect. She did what she had to do. And, although he was a burden she had never wanted, she had still tried to make the best of it. Things just hadn't turned out as well as she'd hoped.

Was she selfish, naïve, foolish? Yes. But that was an intrinsic drawback of being human. All this time he had been demanding perfection from her. How could she not resent him? He scowled at the floor. "I'm sorry. I wish things had turned out differently ... for everyone."

"But they didn't. Now here we are, in this fine mess."

He sighed and looked at her, seeing the grim lines anger and disappointment had etched in her face. She had been beautiful once, and still was in a mature way. But her youth had been spent trying to control an impossible situation full of emotional upheaval. Who was to blame? How could it have been made better? Steele didn't know. The only thing of certainty was the awful jumble of conflicting personalities and conditions combining to create the very worst situation possible for everyone involved. As his mother pointed out, here they all were, in this fine mess.

At that moment he saw a glimmer of the real mother Lila Delbridge Morse could have been, the kind of mother he should have had. Caring, compassionate, understanding ... and forgiving. Sadness washed over him ... sadness for the loss of what could have been but never was. "Please," he whispered, "won't you tell me who my father is?"

"I'm sorry, Steele. I won't break my promise, no matter how much I wish I could for your sake. Your father has to be the one to come forward. I hope someday he does, before it's too late."

Steele nodded, respecting her decision. "Can you at least tell me if he's still here in Fenton?"

She shook her head. "I've already told you too much. Please, don't ask any more about him."

With a sigh he got up from the wicker couch. He'd already gotten more than he'd hoped for. But there was still an issue to be resolved. "I came here to fight with you over Becca. I appreciate what you've told me about my father, but I still have to settle this predicament with the wedding you've planned. I'm going to marry Becca, and I'm prepared to make you a generous financial offer to ensure you'll stop harassing her."

When his mother looked at him, Steele saw defeat in her

face for the first time. It startled him. "You don't have to worry about Becca. I'm not going to push her to marry Conn. You're absolutely right. It won't work in the long run, and I know it. I've been deluding myself, just like I have been for years about everything else in my life." She folded her hands in her lap. "If I hadn't been so controlling and insisted on having everything my way, Jim and Conn – and you – might not have revolted so violently."

Waving her hand, she looked away and rested her head against the back of her chair. "I am so tired of all the struggling. And for what? I don't have a marriage, I don't have a family. And judging by the gossip flying around town, I don't even have a salvageable reputation. All I can look forward to is being the laughingstock of a dirty little backwater village that doesn't deserve what I can offer."

She looked at Steele and sighed with obvious exhaustion. "If you're intent on marrying Becca, feel free to use the church, the wedding dress, the caterer, the flowers, all of it, with my compliments. It will go to waste otherwise. And I hope you and Becca will be happy. Just be sure it's what you really want, Steele. Don't make a foolish, impulsive mistake like I did. It can ruin more than your own life."

"I'm sure, Mother." Steele walked over to her, and she looked at him in surprise as he knelt down before her. "I know you are in financial trouble," he whispered, daring to take her hands in his. He felt strangely elated when she didn't withdraw from him. "I'm willing to help. A loan, for as long as you need it. It comes with the caveat that you set Becca free. But even if you've already decided to leave her alone, I still want to help you."

She shook her head. "I don't want your money, Steele. At first I thought I'd try to trick you out of it, but ... it's not worth the trouble, and I can't do that to you. No matter what's happened between us, you are still, and always will be, my son. I..." She swallowed. "The money problems at the dairy and the dealership will just have to take care of themselves. I can't fix everything anymore. Apparently, I never could."

Steele held onto his mother's hands, stroking her soft, aged skin with his fingers. When he looked into her pale gray eyes, he saw the moistness of tears. Was her reaction genuine? He wanted to believe so. What had changed her in the last hour to make her someone he could reach? Or had *he* been the one to change, enough to see the real person behind the façade of her emotionless inflexibility?

Impulsively he reached out and encircled her with his arms to pull her to him. He felt her shocked resistance fade as she lifted her arms to complete the hug. It was the first real intimacy he had shared with her since well before he'd been shipped off to live with Aunt Sybil and Uncle Charlie.

The sensation of holding this woman, this stranger, his mother, felt oddly satisfying. It had been something he'd craved for so long that the craving had become an invisibly accepted part of his life he denied with subconscious anger. Now the need was satisfied, the anger released.

His mother's hand moved up to the back of his head. As she stroked his hair, she whispered hoarsely, "I wish I could have loved you more, as a real mother should. You deserved that, and I'm sorry."

Her words made his heart clench. The admission was negative, but as positive as he knew he would get from her. He accepted it for what it was and told himself it was almost as good as hearing "I love you." Almost. That phrase he'd never heard his mother say to anyone, and he knew he would not hear her say it to him. Not today.

She released him, and he took that as his cue. Standing up, he managed a smile. She looked up into his eyes brimming with tears and returned his smile. "I wish you and Becca a lifetime of real happiness."

He nodded and turned to the door.

CHAPTER 20

"*S*o, what's up, Dad?" Conn asked, once he reached his father at the graveled back lot where trade-ins awaited judgment on their fate. "Why'd you want me to meet you back here?"

Breathing hard after trudging from the showroom to the back lot, he leaned against his father's black Navigator and watched him pull a gray duffle bag from the rear cargo compartment. "You going someplace?"

"No, you are. Take this." His father handed him the bag.

"Huh?" The gray, soft-sided bag was full and heavy. Conn eyed his father suspiciously. "What's going on?"

"Just do what I tell you and don't ask questions. I'm giving you a chance I never got."

Conn squinted, unable to imagine what his old man was up to.

"I booked you a room at the Woodson House Bed and Breakfast in Marion for the weekend."

Conn perked his brows. The Woodson was that pricey place his mother mentioned now and then. "What – I'm going on an early honeymoon? Wedding's not till tomorrow."

"It's not a honeymoon," his father said with a deadpan glare.

"So I'm supposed to stay in that fancy hotel room all by myself?"

"I don't care if you take somebody with you, just so long as it's not Rebecca Sedder."

Finally the purpose of all this sneaking around made sense. Conn eyed his father with dawning admiration. The old man had finally grown a backbone. No more 'yes, dear' from him. Conn grinned. "Okay, but my car's parked up front, and Mom'll see me when–"

"You're taking that blue Buick over there."

Conn looked at the 1994 vehicle they'd bid on and purchased for almost nothing at old lady Gandy's estate sale. The car was in mint condition – low mileage, kept in the garage, and the oil changed every three thousand miles like clockwork. "But, Dad, it's a geezer car! I can't–"

"Here are the keys and some extra money." His father extended his hand, and Conn gawked at the tidy wad of cash.

"I already gassed up the car and put a set of dealer plates on it. Now get the hell out of here, and don't call anybody or let anyone know where you are until you hear from me. And whatever you do, stay out of town until Sunday."

Conn knew his father was up to some kind of no-good involving Becca, but at this point he didn't care – just so long as he didn't have to go through with that damned wedding. "Thanks, Dad."

* * * * *

She had always made him feel stupid, and she got a charge out of it. She'd played him for a fool over thirty years ago, and she was still doing it. But today it would end, and Lila Delbridge would never control him again.

Jim Morse downed his second shot of Seagram's and slammed the thick, yellowed glass on the counter with a loud thump. He glanced over his shoulder to make sure he was being noticed. Yep. There was ol' Shelby Hathelwaite staring at him as he sat at a table along the wall and nursed a warm beer. With his faded overalls and gray hair sticking up in an oily mess on top of his bloated head, he was a regular fixture at the Four Corners Bar.

And over yonder, seated at a table close to the bathrooms, was Nolan Mackey. Skinny old fart, should have died and gone to hell years ago. He drank away his farm and lost his wife to cancer. Now he lived in a ramshackle rental with the government paying his keep. How could he do that and never pay a dime of Social Security and Medicaid? It wasn't fair to folks who had regular jobs where they had to show up all the time. Well, okay, maybe Mackey did pay in some. He'd been self-employed all those years, riding around on his rusty tractor, pretending to grow corn and soybeans and tend his little herd of hogs. When it came time to buy a new truck, though, he was so tight, his farts squealed. Jim snickered.

When Lonnie the bartender ambled over to give him a refill, he put up a hand, then pushed himself off the barstool. He'd drunk just enough to establish his presence here, and just enough to bolster his confidence without becoming so sloppy that he'd muck things up. He couldn't afford to make any mistakes.

He looked over his shoulder again, then headed for the pay phone by the bathroom, rummaging for change and the wadded up piece of paper in his pants pockets. Once he made the call, he'd slip out the back, unnoticed, and nobody would be the wiser. Then when he was finished, he'd come right back. All the while, his Lincoln Navigator would be sitting out front as his alibi.

If he could manage to pull this off without a hitch, Lila's highfalutin plans would be ruined, and Conn would be saved from a loveless marriage where he'd be forced to raise his bastard brother's bastard child. But most important, the bastard himself would be left empty-handed. For once he wouldn't get his way. It was a lose-win situation ... everybody else would lose, while Jim himself would win.

But his success depended entirely on how convincing he sounded – assuming he even got to talk to her. He smoothed the crumpled piece of paper and squinted in the dim light to make out the phone number scrawled in his own illegible handwriting. He inserted the coins in the pay phone and punched the number. *Come on, little Becky. Pick up!*

* * * * *

As Steele started his car and pulled out of his mother's

drive, he reached for his cell phone. He couldn't describe the way he felt. There were no adequate words. He wasn't elated or relieved or sad or even happy. He just felt ... different. Finally he'd had the heart-to-heart talk with his mother he'd wanted for years. And now it was over. He knew about his father but still didn't know who he was. He'd made peace with his mother, but she hadn't told him she loved him. He knew "I'm sorry" was as good as he'd ever get, and she'd promised to leave Becca alone. He'd achieved mixed success, yet it was better than the outcome he'd expected.

Holding his phone in one hand, he punched in the number for Becca's parents. When her mother answered on the third ring, he asked for Becca. Her mother paused, then said, "I thought she was with you."

He frowned as he drove down Main Street toward Becca's house. "With me?"

"She answered the phone a little while ago, then left. I just figured she was going to see you."

Steele felt his heart pounding. "How long ago?"

"About a half an hour."

"Where did she say she was going, Mrs. Sedder?"

"She didn't say." Mrs. Sedder's voice trembled noticeably. "You don't think there's something wrong, do you?"

Steele felt his stomach trying to crawl up his throat. He swallowed down his manic fear. "Maybe she went to my hotel room to wait for me. I'll let you know as soon as I find out."

* * * * *

Still in the ragged jeans, tee shirt, and tennis shoes she'd worn to clean house, Becca sat in her car parked beneath a huge elm shading the Fenton Elementary School parking lot. She remembered jumping rope under that very same tree when she was a little girl, before the parking lot had been extended. She figured the tree had to be at least seventy-five years old.

With the car door open, she felt an occasional breeze and

226

relished the rustling sound of the leaves overhead. The respite from the heat of early afternoon broke the tension of waiting for James Morse to show up in his big black SUV.

Daring to take her eyes off the street, she glanced at the one-story school, small and dated, with its turquoise metal-frame windows doing nothing to enhance the plain brick façade. Mature trees and a rusty chain-link fence lined with overgrown bushes blocked the view from neighboring modest homes. Alone, with no witnesses close by, she began to doubt the prudence of coming here by herself without telling anyone what she was up to. But that's what Mr. Morse had requested.

A pang of suspicion shot through her chest, but she ignored it, reassuring herself she was doing the right thing. He sounded sincere when he called to say he wanted to do the right thing. He'd stumbled across her father's missing safety report at the house and wanted to hand it over to her. But he didn't want to chance anyone leaking that fact to Lila, so he insisted on secrecy. She couldn't argue with that. He suggested meeting at the schoolyard, a semi-private public place. The arrangement seemed reasonable.

Seeing no cars on the street, Becca glanced at the updated playground equipment deserted by kids on summer break. A treated-wood jungle gym built like a fortress with colorful flags replaced the old metal bars she'd played on. Plastic seats mounted on giant pogo springs glistened in the dappled sunlight, taunting her with childhood memories free of worries that plagued her now.

She sighed, telling herself everything would work out. She had to do what she could to help fix this mess she'd gotten herself into. She couldn't let Steele do it alone. It wasn't fair to expect him to take full responsibility. And right now she wasn't sure what kind of deal he was trying to make with his mother to protect her. She knew he wouldn't do anything that would put her in harm's way, but she wasn't so sure he'd take the same care with her father. His mother had claimed he'd agreed to a trade-off. She didn't want to believe that, but she was in no position to refute it. For now, she had to do what she could on her own to ensure her father's position was as well protected as possible.

* * * * *

As soon as the Standish Inn desk clerk confirmed that no one fitting Becca's description had come to the hotel, Steele called Chuck Lapinski. Chuck didn't seem overly worried, since Steele couldn't give him any specifics about Becca's presumed disappearance. He suggested she might have gone to the grocery store, and the phone call she received just before leaving was just a coincidence. But Steele wasn't convinced. He had a bad feeling about all this, especially considering all that had gone on in the last week. Right away he suspected his mother had a hand in this latest complication. But she had seemed so sincere in her capitulation earlier, he didn't have the heart to accuse her. Could she have fooled him that well?

Standing alone in his hotel room, he raked his fingers through his hair, then decided to pay his mother another visit, just to make sure.

* * * * *

Becca jerked with a start when she heard the backfire of the old truck coming toward her. That was not the vehicle she had expected Jim Morse to arrive in. When the rusted aqua pickup pulled alongside her car, she got out of the driver's seat and stood beside her open door. Mr. Morse lumbered out of the truck and swaggered toward her. Becca sucked up her courage and said, "Thank you for coming forward with the evidence to clear my father. That safety report will prove the management at Greenvalley Dairy, not my father, was responsible for the accident."

Jim looked over one shoulder and then the other, as if he were checking out the situation before proceeding. "I don't want to waste a lot of time. Let's get this over with."

"Fine. Give me my father's report, and I'll be on my way."

"Not so fast," he growled with a scowl. "How do I know you won't show up at the church Saturday to go through with the wedding with Conn?"

"Believe me, Mr. Morse. I'm not interested in marrying your son. The only reason I agreed to in the first place was because Mrs. Morse gave me no choice. It was that or see my father blamed for something he didn't do."

Jim grunted in obvious dissatisfaction. "Yeah, but I bet you'd like to get your hands on Conn's assets. He'll be pretty well off when he takes over things from his mother and me."

Becca wanted to add, *if he doesn't run it all into the ground first*, but she said nothing. Jim moved closer, and she backed away from him. "Where's the report?"

"In the truck."

Becca frowned at the old pickup. "Isn't that Mr. Gallard's truck? I've seen him drive up in it when he comes to town to do his banking."

"Yeah, well, old Gallard brought it in for some brake work. I figured I'd kill two birds with one stone and test drive it for the boys in the shop when I came to see you."

Becca didn't like Mr. Morse's ominous reference to killing birds, and his explanation sounded like an off-the-cuff lie if ever she'd heard one. "Look, Mr. Morse, I appreciate your coming forward, but I really do have to get back. Could you please just give me the report so I can go?"

He looked at her with a vacant expression, as if he were thinking of something else. "Sure, sure. It's in the truck, like I said. On the front seat."

He headed back toward the pickup, as if he expected Becca to follow him. When she didn't, he snarled, "If you want it, come and get it. If you don't, that's fine too. Just make sure you don't cross me and try to go ahead with Lila's screwed up scheme to marry off my boy."

Becca huffed and trudged toward the truck. "I wouldn't dream of going through with that 'screwed up scheme.'"

She stood back as Mr. Morse swung open the passenger door and announced, "There it is."

She moved around him and leaned into the truck to retrieve the document but saw nothing on the worn vinyl bench seat. Before she could react, he shoved her forward, and she lost her balance, falling against the end of the seat. She yelped in surprise "What are you doing? Let me go!" She almost wrested free of him, but he put a rough hand over her mouth and forced her up into the cab of the truck. She tried to kick and push him away, but he slammed the door shut. Fear paralyzed her as she fumbled around with the metal door panel, looking for the inside door latch. Dismayed, she realized the armrest and the door latch were missing. All that remained was a set of recessed holes.

Just as she started to scoot over to jump out the driver's door, Jim Morse hurried around the front of the truck and climbed into the driver's side. He slammed his door shut, then turned on her and growled, "Keep quiet and quit rousting around, if you want to stay healthy."

Frozen in shock, Becca sucked in hysterical gasps, smelling alcohol on him. She didn't want to think what he had in mind. "Please, Mr. Morse, just let me out of here."

He started the truck and waved a flat-head screwdriver in front of her. "The latch is broken and you can't get that door open from the inside without this. And the window crank is stripped, so don't get any bright ideas about trying to roll down the window and bail out or scream for help. Understand?"

Becca gulped hard. "What are you planning to do?"

"Don't you worry about it. All you have to do is sit still and don't cause any trouble, and you won't get hurt."

"What are you going to do to me?" Becca demanded shrilly.

"Calm down. I'm not going to do anything to you. I just want to make sure you stay out of the way until after Saturday." He almost smiled. "You behave yourself, and everything will be just fine."

"This is kidnapping," Becca warned feebly as he backed

230

the truck up. The engine revved with a grating sound as he put it in gear. "You know you'll go to jail!"

"Yeah, probably I will. But as long as nothing happens to you, I don't think they'll punish me too awful bad. And I'm thinking, even if they do, it just might be worth it to see the look on Lila's and Steele's faces when you don't show up at the church Saturday."

He maneuvered the rattling old pickup along the quiet back streets of town. "Lila's not going to have her way this time, and Conn's not going to go through life the way I did, forced to raise somebody else's bastard and pretend it's his."

"Mr. Morse," Becca offered in the calmest, most sincere tone she could manage, "I told you I had no intention of going through with the wedding your wife had arranged. *Steele* and I are getting married."

"Maybe you are, but not this weekend. I don't want Lila's plans to go through in any way, shape, or form. I want her to sit in that damn church full of people – the preacher, the caterer, the photographer, the whole town – all waiting for something to happen that never happens. I want to get all embarrassed and walk out of there, knowing that everything she's been scheming for has fallen through. I want her to look like a damned fool, just like I have most of my life. And I want her to know exactly how that feels. But more than anything, I want that son-of-a-bitch Steele to slink away empty-handed, with his tail tucked between his legs. I want him to know what it's like to get royally screwed-over."

Becca gripped the dash to keep from sliding sideways as Mr. Morse turned a corner. She glanced frantically around the vehicle interior, trying to figure out how she might overpower him or somehow get the door open without his handy-dandy screwdriver. She finally resorted to ramming her shoulder against the door, without success. Tears of fear and frustration ran down her face as Jim Morse steered the truck onto an old narrow blacktop leading away from Fenton.

* * * * *

When Lila answered the front door, Steele barged in and pushed passed her. "Where is she?" He turned on his mother, ignoring the surprised look on her face.

"Who?"

"You know who – Becca!" He darted into the dining room on the right and saw the room devoid of furniture. Obviously his mother hadn't yet gotten around to repairing or replacing the table and chairs he and The Ogre had destroyed earlier in the week.

"Steele, what are you doing here? What's going on? There's no one here but me."

"You won't mind if I see for myself," he snarled as he charged into the formal living room and then to the kitchen. His heart raced. He couldn't imagine his mother would be foolish enough to have Becca kidnapped and then brought here to her house. But someone had taken her. The police had found her car with the driver's door standing open, and her purse lying untouched on the passenger seat. There were fresh skid marks in the gravel beside Becca's car. Obviously another vehicle was involved. The question was, what in the hell was Becca doing, meeting someone at the schoolyard? The bigger question was, what had that someone done with her? His whole body revolted violently every time he dared consider the possibilities.

After checking the downstairs master bedroom – his mother's room – and finding no evidence that Becca had ever been there, he surveyed the guest bath nestled beneath the winding staircase and also found it devoid of clues. He rushed back into the foyer where his mother was still standing with her mouth open in a very convincing expression of shock as she asked, "Has something happened to Becca?"

He snorted, then whirled around and leapt up the stairs leading to the four bedrooms and bath on the second floor. When he opened his former bedroom, he didn't even recognize it from eighteen years before. His mother had completely refurbished it with an antique cherry bedroom set and accessorized it with vintage lace curtains and an old handmade quilt in remarkable condition. He was sure she'd paid a pretty penny for it at some highfalutin antique shop.

The neighboring bedroom was in the same pristine museum condition, but The Ogre's room was furnished with generic modern furniture and tastefully plain store-bought bedclothes. The room was tidy, everything in its place. But Conn's room, similarly outfitted, looked recently disheveled, as if he'd hurriedly pulled clothes out of his drawers and closet. The bi-fold louvered closet doors stood open, and some drawers in his dresser were open as well, with a stray sock draped over one drawer front. Immediately Steele's stomach sank. "Good Lord, he has Becca!"

He thundered down the stairs and grabbed his mother by the shoulders, shaking her. "Where'd he take her?"

"Who? What are you talking about?"

"You know damn well what I'm talking about! Becca's missing, and Conn's got her! Where'd he take her? Tell me, or I swear I'll–"

"Steele, let me go! You're hurting me!"

He gripped her shoulders harder and shook her violently. "If touches her–" He released her and she veered off balance. Raking a hand down his face, he glared at her. "Damn you. Damn you to hell! All the while you were pretending to come clean with me about my father, you knew Conn was luring Becca to the schoolyard. What did you dangle at her for bait? More trumped-up evidence against her father? How could you–"

"Steele," his mother implored, finally regaining her composure, "please believe me. I don't know what you're talking about. Conn's at the dealership right now with his father – at least he's supposed to be."

"Then why does his room look like it's been ransacked?"

His mother frowned and moved hesitantly toward the steps. "I don't know." She gave him another astonished look over her shoulder and added, "Don't go. Please. I want to take a look for myself." She hurried up the steps, and a moment later returned.

"You're right. It does look as if..." She glanced away, scowling with obvious dread, then turned to him. "I'm sorry, Steele. I don't know what's going on. Let me go with you to the dealership so we can straighten this out right now."

Steele tried to swallow down the sick feeling in his stomach as he escorted his mother out the door. Either she truly didn't know what had happened, or she'd polished her acting ability tremendously. Whether or not she was privy to Conn's activities was beside the point right now. The only thing he cared about was getting Becca back safe and sound.

* * * * *

Becca eyed the two-story ramshackle Greenvalley farmhouse. At the end of a gravel lane about a quarter mile from the blacktop and surrounded by huge old gangling trees, the house was impossible to see from the road. Once white, its clapboard siding had long ago been repainted forest green. Now the faded and blistered green paint had peeled back down to the original white layer. The shingles were curled, in need of replacement, and the brick chimney had crumbled, ready to topple at any moment. The place appeared to have once been a fine homestead that had outlived its natural usefulness.

Jim Morse left the truck engine running. The gears groaned as he put it in neutral. Stomping on the parking brake pedal, he turned and reached for Becca. She shied from him, making him grip her arm with unnecessary roughness when he did manage to grab hold of her. "Come on. This is where you'll be staying for the next couple days. It's not much, but it's out of the way, and I doubt anybody would think of looking for you here." He dragged her across the bench seat and out the driver's door. She knew she was no match for his strength, and she had no desire to make him angrier by continuing to resist him.

"I don't know why Lila insists on keeping her family's old homestead," he growled as he pulled Becca along with him toward the back of the pickup. "It can't be for sentimental

234

reasons." With his free hand he reached over the pickup's rusty bed and hoisted up a small red cooler and a plastic grocery bag. Becca could hear ice and cans slushing around as he brought the cooler to his side. "There's a couple sodas and some bottled water in here, plus some sandwiches. I got some other stuff, like toilet paper, too. It ought to be enough to last you till Sunday." He headed for the front porch. When Becca tried to dig her heels into the dirt path leading to the house, he gave her arm a hard, painful jerk. She came along.

Jim Morse looked up at the old house, then lumbered up the creaking warped steps. "Lila's daddy had this place fixed up a little, several years ago," he said, making idle conversation as if kidnapping were a normal and acceptable thing for him to be doing. "He was going to use it for the office for Greenvalley Trucking, back when he was just starting to expand it. He still had several herds of dairy cows then. But the old blacktop couldn't handle the semi weight, so he had to move the trucking operation closer to the state highway on the other side of Fenton."

He opened the wooden screen door, and it cocked sideways, the top hinge having rusted apart. "When Lila's daddy died, her mother sold off all the milk cows. I always thought it was stupid for Lila to hold onto this dump after her mother was gone, but now I'm kind of glad she did." He shot Becca a yellow-toothed grin.

Giving the swollen, splintery wood door a hard shove, he pushed it open to reveal a musty-smelling front room. With her arm still firmly in his grip, Becca stood just inside the doorway, warily surveying her surroundings. The dried and cracked wallpaper was torn off in several places, revealing crumbling, moldy plaster and bare lath. An old beat-up wooden desk sat abandoned in one corner, and a wooden chair with a broken leg lay overturned in another corner, near a burnt place in the stained and wavy hardwood floor. Discarded food, cigarette wrappers, and broken bottles littered the area. It appeared some kids had been using the place as a party house.

Becca jumped when a mouse darted out and scurried

underneath a scattered pile of rags and papers. "You're not going to leave me here," she pleaded, looking at her captor's pocked and craggy face for some trace of reason and compassion.

Huffing, Morse jerked her toward the narrow hallway to face a set of steep, narrow stairs. "You'll be fine. It's not the greatest digs, but it'll do."

Becca tripped several times, nearly falling as her captor trudged ahead, dragging her along behind him. When he reached the top of the stairs, he turned right and set the cooler and bag down in front of a closed door. Taking a skeleton key from his pocket, he unlocked the door, then shoved Becca into the room. He put the cooler and bag just inside the doorway, then darted out and slammed the door behind him.

When Becca heard the key turn in the lock, she grabbed the doorknob and turned it, yanking on it. Banging on the door, she yelled, "Mr. Morse, don't leave me here! Please!" When she heard Jim Morse's lumbering footsteps recede, she raced to the tall, dusty window in the room overlooking the front porch. A moment later he got in the aqua pickup and drove away. Tears streamed down her face.

CHAPTER 21

"*J*ohn, have you seen my husband and my son lately?"

Standing in the dealership main building, Steele eyed his mother purified by the late afternoon sunlight streaming through the showroom windows. Towering over the short salesman who wore a sporty green dress shirt and a tie with bright tropical colors, she seemed to be sincere in her desire to get to the bottom of Becca's disappearance.

"No, Ma'am," the salesman answered. "Haven't seen either one of them for a couple hours."

"Conn's Mustang is parked out front. Do you know if somebody came and picked him up, or if he might be using another car from the lot for some reason?"

"Not to my knowledge, Ma'am. Like I said, I haven't seen him for quite a while. But I can check the log for you to see if anyone's signed out a license plate for a test drive."

Steele knew enough about Illinois dealer licensing to realize all the plates issued to a specific dealership had the same basic number, with subordinate letters differentiating individual pairs of plates. The 'A' plates stayed on his mother's Towncar while the 'B' plates were issued to the black Navigator his stepfather drove. Conn kept the 'C' plates for whatever car he happened to be driving. The rest of the plates were used for salesmen to set up test drives for new and used vehicles on the lot. Since Conn was gone and his Mustang was still out front with the 'C' plates attached, Steele guessed he had put another set of plates on a different car.

John the salesman came back a moment later. "Nobody

signed out any plates, but I couldn't find the 'D' set in the cabinet."

Steele's mother turned and frowned. "Conn probably took them. He always forgets to sign the log sheet. If he didn't sign out the keys either, we won't know what car he took."

She eyed John. "Where's Mr. Morse?"

John looked a little sheepish as he mumbled, "I think I heard him say something about Four Corners."

"That figures," she snarled. "Thanks, John."

"Yes, Ma'am."

Steele escorted his mother to his car. Four Corners Bar was within walking distance from the dealership's back lot, but from the main showroom it would be a hike. Steele opted to drive his mother. She was steamed, and he didn't want the walk to overtax her patience.

When he pulled into the gravel lot of Four Corners, he saw the black Lincoln Navigator with 'B' dealer plates parked prominently out front.

"I don't know why he insists on frequenting this seedy dive," his mother grumbled.

"It's close by," Steele said with a shrug.

"Yes, a little too close."

About six people were inside, but Steele spotted Jim Morse's hulking form the moment they walked into the hazy dark drinking hole. Bellied up to the bar, hunched over his glass, he was hard to miss. When Steele's mother marched up beside him, Jim turned and growled, "What the hell do *you* want?"

Steele could tell by the slur of his words that his stepfather had downed more than a few.

"You've been here all afternoon?" Lila demanded.

"What's it to you? Nobody's buying cars today, so I figured I'd take a break."

Lila huffed. "Do you know where Conn is, or what car he's driving?"

Jim turned back to his heavy tumbler and downed the rest of the golden elixir swirling with melting ice. "Conn's a big boy.

He can do what he wants without you keeping tabs on him." With a flick of his hand he summoned the bartender for another.

"I think you've had quite enough," Lila said.

Slowly Jim turned half way on his bar stool to consider her. "That's the trouble with you. You think too damn much."

Lila shot the bartender a nasty glare, then spun on her heels and headed for the door. Steele hurried after her, glancing over his shoulder to catch Jim grinning at him.

* * * * *

At five-fifteen, they still hadn't come close to figuring out where Becca was. She'd been gone for over three hours, and Steele couldn't bear to let himself think of what might have happened to her in that time. He refused to believe that a stranger had abducted her. The signs all pointed to Conn. What he might do to her in the three hours he'd been alone with her–

"I was supposed to meet Judge Forrester at his house at six," Steele said to distract his raging doubts. He glanced at his mother in the passenger seat and caught her look of surprise.

"Judge Forrester? Why?"

Steele grimaced. "I was going to try to convince him that you were attempting to unfairly influence testimony at the inquest Monday."

"Oh." She sat in silence as he pulled up in the circular drive of her house. When he put the car in park, she said, "Perhaps you should cancel that meeting, since we've come to an agreement, and you've got other things on your mind right now."

He nodded. "I was curious to see him again. He seemed eager to talk to me, to catch up on what I'd been doing since I went to Chicago."

Steele saw his mother turn away, as if the conversation had made her uncomfortable. But she seemed to recover fast as she offered, "Why don't you come in and use my phone to call him?"

"Thanks, but I'll just call him on my cell phone while I drive to Becca's house. I need to see her parents."

Steele's mother put a hand on his shoulder and managed a reassuring smile. "Don't worry. I'm sure everything's fine."

Although he had a hard time being positive in the face of seeming disaster, he forced a smile and nodded as his mother got out of the car.

* * * * *

"Forgive me," Judge Forrester apologized before Steele could explain why he'd called. "I just got home and haven't had time to prepare the meal I promised. The docket was overflowing, and I had a difficult time getting out–"

"Then I don't feel so bad," Steele interrupted as he navigated his car through town. "I'd hate for you to go to a lot of trouble when I have to cancel on you."

"Cancel? I'm sorry to hear that. I was looking forward to talking with you. Perhaps we could reschedule, before you go back to Chicago."

"Actually, Sir, I'm not going anywhere until I find out what's happened to Becca Sedder."

"What do you mean, son?"

Steele cringed at the strain of worry in Judge Forrester's voice, reminding him of Becca's potentially dire situation. "Becca's missing," he explained with quick efficiency to keep his voice from cracking with emotion. "She appears to have been kidnapped. The police and my firm's investigator are following every lead, but so far we haven't uncovered any clues to her whereabouts. I'm going to her parents' house now, to talk with them and see how they're holding up."

"Steele, I'm very sorry. I take it you've grown quite fond of Miss Sedder, and I hope for your sake as well as hers that nothing unpleasant has happened."

Steele swallowed hard. "Thank you."

"Do you think her disappearance has anything to do with the wedding your mother had planned for Conner?"

"Actually, yes. Conn seems to be missing too." Steele felt

240

his face heat with rage as he pulled up in front of Becca's parents' house. The idea of Conn putting his hands on Becca made him want to tear his little brother apart. He sighed, knowing he couldn't let himself think about that now. He had to find Becca as fast as possible. That was all that mattered. "I'm sorry we won't be able to visit this evening, Sir, but thank you for understanding the situation. I'll—"

"Wait, Steele. I'd like to help if I can."

Steele frowned. "Thank you for offering, but I don't know what you can do that we haven't already."

"I suspect you could use some company. This must be very difficult for you to face alone. If nothing else, I'd like to offer moral support. Give me a few minutes to make some arrangements, and I'll meet you. Where did you say you'd be?"

Steele sat stunned to silence. Judge Forrester was the only person who seemed the least bit concerned about his emotional well-being. Of course everyone was worried about Becca, and he was going to try to offer moral support to her parents, but even his own mother hadn't presumed to stick by him in this trying ordeal. "That's very kind of you, but it's not necessary."

"I don't mean to intrude. If you'd prefer not to have me around, I'll understand. I just thought..."

"Thank you," Steele said with a sudden tinge of relief. "I could use some company." Anyone who could help keep his mind off his fears while he waited for news of Becca would be a welcome distraction.

He could hear the sigh of satisfaction as the judge asked for Becca's address and ended, "I'll meet you there in fifteen minutes."

* * * * *

Becca paced out of the narrow bathroom adjoining another room identical to the one Jim Morse had locked her in. That room was locked too, and the only difference between the two was a scruffy little wooden chair in the other room and a stained mattress lying on the floor in this room. Bugs – roaches and other critics she wasn't keen on identifying – scampered busily near the tall baseboard around the floor. She was sure the mattress lying in the corner was home to so many insects it could be declared an arthropod township.

Squirming uncomfortably, she recalled the condition of the smelly bathroom she'd just inspected. The sink on crusty chrome legs sported well water rust spots that long ago oozed from the faucet. The stool lid and water tank lid were missing. Black and brown stains enameled the toilet bowl. With no water or electricity, the decline of the old house had accelerated, and the bathroom was no exception. She had no intention of using those facilities, no matter how bad she had to go.

She shuddered and swiped at the veil of perspiration on her forehead, then glanced up at the nine-foot ceiling. The water-stained, cracked plaster hung down in big swags that looked ready to break free and fall at any moment. She could hear, in the unseen area above the rafters, scurrying noises most likely made by rats – big ones.

Shivering despite the musty stillness of the room, she gave the door another challenging glare. She had tried ramming it with her shoulder, but the solid wood door, although weathered and warped, refused to yield under her barrage. She found nothing suitable in her search for tools to try and pick the lock or dislodge the hinges. But she wasn't going to resign herself to sleeping in this filthy hole, only to have Jim Morse come back to find her waiting like a meek little victim at his mercy. Somehow, some way, she'd get out of here, back to Steele.

She wiped her sweaty hands on her jeans, then gripped the yellowed porcelain doorknob one last time. Grunting and growling, she pulled on it as hard as she could then – *bop* – the knob popped off in her hand, sending her sprawling backward on the dirty floor. She got up and dusted herself off. Loosing around, she she saw the light waning in the window and realized her situation was hopeless. Not only was evening approaching, so was a storm. As clouds obscured the sky outside, tears flooded her eyes. Angry, she wiped them away and swallowed down her frustration. She wasn't going to give up.

She looked back at the window, recalling the one in the next room was broken. Edging over, she looked out and surveyed the roof over the porch. The shingles had nearly disintegrated, exposing rotted rafters. She didn't know if the roof would support her weight. But even if it did, and she managed not to slip down the steep slope, what would she accomplish? She craned her neck to look aside and saw a large tree limb glancing the porch. She'd never been much of a tree climber, but she didn't have any other options. This was her one chance to escape before Jim Morse returned – if she didn't break her neck first.

* * * * *

Steele felt awkward making introductions under such stressful conditions. Becca's mother looked like she'd been crying, and Becca's father didn't look any better off with his stooped posture and dark circles under his eyes. Meg was there, without her four kids, but she wasn't much help with moral support, since she was just as upset as her parents. Steele was still trying to calm her down when Judge Forrester showed up.

None of it seemed to bother the judge as he appraised the situation and went straight to Becca's parents, offering comfort and quiet strength. His presence seemed to calm rather than complicate things, and for that Steele was thankful.

"Would anyone like coffee?" Judge Forrester asked.

Becca's mother awoke from her stupor of grief and stumbled up from the couch where she sat huddled next to Becca's dad. "I'm sorry. I'll–"

"I didn't mean to disturb you," the judge apologized in a gentle tone. "If you could show me around your kitchen, I'll be glad to make the coffee." He turned to Steele and gave him a look that implied he should help.

As Steele followed Judge Forrester into the kitchen, he compared the older man's appearance now to his memory of him eighteen years ago. The judge looked different, of course. Instead of a black judicial robe, he wore khaki trousers, a casual short-sleeve polo shirt, and wire-rim bifocals. His formerly dark hair was still full, now peppered with gray. He was big and tall like Steele remembered, but now Steele was slightly taller. The judge had adopted some extra pounds, and the brawn of his lost youth had shifted down to thicken his middle. But he was a man whose presence demanded attention and respect. Steele stood in quiet awe of him, all the while realizing it was his own childish recollections that fostered the reaction. Nevertheless, he was glad the man had the fortitude to offer emotional support during this situation.

As the judge allowed Mrs. Sedder to make coffee – which seemed to be his intention all along, to keep her distracted from her fear over Becca's situation – he turned to Steele. Putting a hand on his shoulder, he whispered, "You look worried sick. I'm confident everything will turn out fine, but I wish there was some way I could make things better right now."

Steele tried to smile but couldn't. He felt flushed, and his heart raced. He wanted to puke or run his fist through a wall. He wanted to find Conn and–

Just as he was about to break under his impulses, his cell phone rang. He plucked it from his belt, answering on the first ring. "Yes?"

"The Marion Police were doing a routine patrol," Chuck Lapinski said, "and spotted a car with dealer plates parked at the Woodson Inn. The number matched the APB, so they checked the hotel registry. They're holding Conn in one of the suites. He registered under another name. He's not alone."

"Becca?" Steele blurted with strangling pain.

"No. Some blonde waitress from a nearby restaurant."

Steele felt both relieved and more afraid. "Did they question him about Becca?"

"Yes, but he claims he hasn't seen her in days. Says his father reserved the room, gave him the car and some cash, and told him to get out of town for the weekend."

244

His father, Jim Morse. "Thanks, Chuck." Steele clipped his phone onto his belt, then turned to Judge Forrester. "The Marion Police are holding Conn at a hotel, with some waitress. I'm going to pay my stepfather another visit. Seems he wasn't entirely truthful the last time I spoke with him about Conn's whereabouts."

"Let me go with you," the judge insisted.

"What about Becca?" Mrs. Sedder cried, grabbing Steele's nearest arm.

Steele put a hand on hers to calm her. "She's not with Conn, Mrs. Sedder. That's all I know right now. But don't worry, I'll find her."

"*We'll* find her," Judge Forrester emphasized as he patted Mrs. Sedder's hand and extracted Steele from her grasp. "Come on, son. We'd better get moving. Where'd you last see Jim Morse?"

Steele gripped his keys and gave Meg and her father a reassuring smile as he followed the judge to the front door. "My mother and I tracked him down at Four Corners Bar. That was over an hour ago."

The judge held the door open and asked, "How is your mother?" He closed the door and followed Steele to his car parked at the curb.

"She's doing okay. Good, in fact."

The judge touched his glasses as if to adjust them. "Sounds as if you and she have come to an understanding."

Steele unlocked the car and circled around to the driver's side. "I guess we have, sort of."

The judge folded himself into the passenger seat and shut his door, then reached for his seatbelt. "I hoped one day you would find a way to make peace with her."

Steele frowned as he turned the key in the ignition. "I wanted to hate her the rest of my life for making me so miserable, for not being the mother I thought I deserved. But when she finally talked to me and told me a few things about my real father, I began to understand her situation a little better. I can almost sympathize with her now – and believe me, I never thought I'd be saying anything like that."

Judge Forrester looked down at his lap, seeming to consider all that Steele had confessed. Somehow it made Steele feel good to have this man he respected know that he had reached the point of moving past the dark hatred that had seethed in his heart for so many years. "After spending time with Becca, I realized how much I'd been missing, how easy it would be for me to be truly happy, or alone and unloved if I didn't change my ways. And I didn't want to hate my mother. The things I was so angry about when I was younger didn't seem as important anymore." He put the car in gear and kept his foot on the brake as he eyed Judge Forrester. "I guess it's true that time heals all wounds."

"I hope so," the judge murmured, looking almost pensive as he glanced out his side window.

Steele studied the man for a second, wondering about his cryptic comment. But his quest to save Becca quickly overtook his curiosity about Judge Forrester. A bolt of lightning grazed the distant sky, and he visualized himself beating The Ogre to a bloody pulp to get the truth about Becca's disappearance. Time might heal all wounds, but Jim Morse was one person he would never forgive. *Never.* He stepped on the gas pedal and the tires squawked as he pulled his car away from the curb.

CHAPTER 22

*B*ecca looked through the dirty window glass at the storm-darkened sky. Below, she saw the tree limb scraping the edge of the porch roof and wondered if her plan to climb down and escape would work, or end up killing her.

She eyed the gathering thunderclouds, then hurried into the other room. Returning with the chair, she hoisted it in the air and made a valiant swing at the window. The glass shattered, and she jumped back as big shards hit the floor. Using the chair's three remaining legs, she knocked out the pointed fragments left in the window frame and tossed the chair aside.

Taking a deep breath, she swiped at her face clammy with sweat, dirt, and humidity. Rain droplets pelted the roof. If what remained of the shingles got too wet and slippery, she could lose her footing and fall. It was now or never.

She lifted her right leg and hoisted it through the window opening. Pressing on the roof with the toe of her tennis shoe, she tried to reassure herself it wouldn't cave in. With a grip on the windowsill, she eased outside, hunkering down to keep from sliding off the steep incline.

The wind picked up, and the tree limb she'd considered as a possible escape route wagged back and forth with menacing force as its leaves fluttered in the wild breeze. Lightning struck in the distance, followed with a time-delayed rumble of thunder. Gulping back her fear, she inched across the creaking, groaning roof and avoided threadbare shingles sagging around open holes.

Another splinter of light blistered the darkened sky, this time much closer, and sent garish crackles in all directions. With her concentration jolted, Becca nearly lost her balance and pitched forward. She caught her breath and tried to calm herself, but it was no use. Her heart pounded like a jackhammer, and she trembled as waves of wind-beaten rain pelted her face and arms. *Move! Just move!*

She finally reached the edge of the roof and leaned forward to take a look below. Her current vantage didn't allow her to see where the porch support posts were, and she couldn't visualize how she would launch herself over without falling to the ground.

She looked again at the tree on her left. It was big and sturdy, and its many limbs offered graduated perches to reach lower branches. Although the tree swayed precariously in the wind, it seemed to be the best course.

She sidled toward the nearest limb as it moved to and fro, scraping brittle pieces of shingles off the roof. When she reached for it, thunder shook the roof beneath her, and the wind pushed the limb away with surprising violence. Another flurry of raindrops pelted her damp clothes. She knew she'd better get off the roof before the lightning moved closer.

With a burst of bravado, she lunged for the limb. In the process, her foot slipped and plunged through a flimsy rotted spot in the roof. Gripping the limb, she froze, fearing the entire roof was about to give way and let her fall through. After the initial shock, she assessed the damage. Her leg was buried knee-high. She didn't feel any pain and wasn't sure that was a good sign.

Still holding onto the tree limb with one arm, she tried to lift her trapped leg, but the toe of her tennis shoe caught under a rafter. With ballet precision, she turned her ankle to free her foot, then pulled her thigh up with her other hand. If she hadn't been wearing jeans, she was sure her leg would have looked like a cat-scratching post.

Maneuvering onto her knees, she turned backward to straddle the tree limb. As she hugged the limb and inched toward the trunk, she felt bark and broken twigs digging into her jeans. It was slow going to reach the juncture at the trunk.

Trying to judge the distance to the next limb below, she pointed her foot and felt around, then eased herself down. As she was about to descend, a flash of light – not lightning, but a steady beam – caught her attention. Frozen still, she stared at the lights of a car barreling down the lane toward the house.

* * * * *

Scanning the dark parking lot in front of the Four Corners Bar, Steele didn't see the SUV parked anywhere, but went inside just to make sure The Ogre wasn't still there. Seeming out of his element, Judge Forrester tagged along.

The bartender, a burly fellow whose acne-scarred face made him look like he'd lost a fight with a junkyard dog, identified himself as Lonnie. He busied himself by chewing on a toothpick as he wiped down the bar counter with a sour rag. He begrudgingly confirmed that Jim Morse had left a short time ago.

"And you're positive he was here all afternoon?" Steele asked. "You saw him?"

The bartender plopped his rag on the counter and glared at Steele. "Look. I don't know what your beef is with ol' Jim, and I don't care. Nobody likes him all that much, but in here his money's as good as anybody else's. If he wants to sit down and have a few drinks, I'm not gonna complain. And I'm not gonna snitch on a paying customer."

"I'm not asking you to snitch. I'm asking you to confirm his whereabouts."

"You mean, for an alibi or something?"

"Yes, something like that."

"Okay, sure, he was here all afternoon, from about two o'clock on. And he was sitting right in front of me the whole time, except for when he went to the john."

Steele glanced around to small beer joint, unimpressed by what he saw. "How many times did he visit the restroom?"

"How the hell should I know? I don't monitor everybody's pit stops."

"More than once?" Steele prodded.

The bartender scowled at him.

"More than once?" Steele persisted.

249

"No. He went just one time."

"How long was he gone?"

The bartender took the toothpick from his mouth and glared at Steele. "What's it to you? You with the Potty Patrol or something?"

"Answer the question, please."

Shaking his big bulldog head, the bartender let out a half laugh. "I don't believe this crap."

"Answer the question."

"Or what? You'll subpoena me to testify in court?"

"That's a strong possibility," Judge Forrester said, stepping forward. "Why don't you save yourself some grief and answer the question?"

The bartender's scowl transformed his face into an angry thundercloud, and Steele could almost see the gears turning in the man's head as he thought about Judge Forrester's suggestion. Finally he turned to Steele and said, "It was a long time. Half an hour. Maybe more. Happy?"

Steele glanced toward the rear of the bar. "Is there back door out of here?"

"Yeah. By the bathroom." With his toothpick back in his mouth, the bartender resumed wiping the bar counter. "Trial's over. No more questions."

Steele smiled. "Thanks. You've been a big help."

When he stepped outside, he felt the steady sprinkling of rain. He got in the car with Judge Forrester, then called his mother's house, not surprised to learn that The Ogre wasn't home. "I think Ol' Jim skipped out on us."

The judge frowned as he cleaned raindrops off his glasses with a handkerchief. "Maybe you should call the police. I'd say there's enough suspicion to bring him in for questioning."

Steele scowled. Jim Morse was a bully and a drunk, but would he stoop to hurting Becca out of sheer meanness? Steele didn't want to consider the possibility.

The judge put his glasses back on. "Don't worry, son. We'll find her. I'm sure she's fine."

"I hope to hell you're right."

After calling the sheriff's office and reporting his suspicions about his stepfather, Steele suggested, "Maybe we should go to my mother's house and talk to her again. She might have some idea where he's headed."

The judge didn't say anything as Steele started the car and pulled out of the parking lot. Steele eyed him and asked, "You don't mind, do you?"

"No. No, of course not."

* * * * *

Cringing in the tree to keep out of sight, Becca heard slamming car doors and the boisterous hooting and hollering of young men having fun. She didn't think Jim Morse was with them, but that didn't make her eager to give away her location. Those boys seemed too wild to be relied on for help in her desperate situation. Amid horseplay, they stumbled into the house. Soon loud country music vibrated from inside.

After scouting the area to make sure no one was outside, Becca fumbled her way down the tree and hit the ground butt-first. The impact almost knocked the wind from her, but she was quick to get up as she heard the front door scrape across the floor inside the house. A couple of the boys had gone out to the car with a flashlight. She scrambled around the back of the house, hoping they hadn't spotted her.

Ducking low behind some overgrown bushes, she squinted in the steady rain. Having no idea how long they intended to stay, she tried to decide where she could hide until they left. Behind her, the back yard sloped down toward an overgrown field. Amid receding lighting, she could make out the nearby silhouettes of various barns and outbuildings in the rainy darkness. She headed for the main barn that was closest and looked the sturdiest, slipping on the wet grass several times and almost going down. When she reached the parted doors constructed of jagged weathered boards nailed to rough-hewn timbers, she slipped

251

inside the darkness like a mouse. Wondering how long she'd have to hide out, she worried about the other creatures she'd have to share this space with.

* * * * *

Steele's mother smiled when she saw him at the door for a third time that day, but she assumed a quick look of dismay when Judge Forrester walked up behind him. He figured she still harbored strong negative feelings for the judge, due to his interference in their lives eighteen years ago.

His mother didn't bother to invite them in, so Steele took it upon himself to enter the foyer. He closed the door behind Judge Forrester, noting the silence between his mother and the judge seemed more than just awkward. The two of them appeared unable to look at each other. He was curious about it but didn't waste time wondering. His concern was to find Becca. "I take it The Ogre still hasn't showed up."

Lila turned on him, her face strained. "I'm here *alone*, and have been since you left earlier this afternoon."

Judge Forrester seemed to cringe at the way she stressed the word 'alone.' Steele frowned, wondering if she was referring to a time span much longer than an afternoon. He couldn't imagine what the undercurrents of her reference meant, but he was too preoccupied to puzzle it out right then. "Mother, I think The Ogre took Becca somewhere, and I hope you can come up with some suggestions as to where."

His mother looked at him as if he'd begun babbling nonsense. "Jim wouldn't dare do something insane like that."

"Why? Because that's not how you taught him to behave?"

"He has many faults, but he wouldn't hurt someone he has no grudge against."

Steele felt his face twisting with sudden pent-up anger. "He has every reason to hold a grudge against Becca, because you set her up. Now he thinks she's about to put Conn in the same position you put him in over thirty years ago."

252

His mother glanced at the judge, then back at him. She said nothing.

"I think he's a lot more desperate and close to the breaking point than you or anyone else imagines. Somebody called Becca at home just before she disappeared. My guess is, it was him, luring her with false evidence about her father."

His mother shook her head. "Why would he do that?"

"To get Becca out of the way and keep her from marrying Conn."

"But after you and I talked, I'd decided not to go ahead with that plan. Surely–"

"You told me, but you didn't bother to tell anyone else, did you? When the police in Marion tracked down Conn at a hotel, he said the old man had arranged for him to get out of town for the weekend. Obviously he knew they'd question Conn about Becca first, and that would give him extra time."

Lila paced away. "That idiot!" She turned on Steele as if he were somehow to blame.

Steele gave his mother a hard look and felt his face tighten as the memories of living in her house swirled in his mind. The constant bickering, the battle for power, his mother's relentless stranglehold on everyone – it all flooded him with renewed rage. And in that dark moment, he understood what drove Jim Morse, a man who'd been duped and controlled and emasculated all his married life. "I think he'd do anything to keep you from winning."

His mother looked stunned. Had it never occurred to her that she might someday lose control of the serfs in her little fiefdom? She should have seen the signs eighteen years ago when Steele staged his own teenage rebellion. Steele dismissed the issue with a wave of his hand. "Right now I'm not concerned about his motives. I just want to find Becca. Do you have any idea where he would have taken her?"

When she raised her hands in helpless confusion, he thought about the logistics of The Ogre sneaking out of the bar to get a car off the dealership lot, driving to the schoolyard to meet

253

Becca, then coercing her into his car. If what the Four Corners bartender had said was true, The Ogre had little more than thirty or forty minutes to accomplish that. "Someplace within fifteen minutes driving time," he clarified.

His mother shrugged. "He could have taken her to any of the motels near the interstate."

"No. It would have to be someplace secluded, if he was keeping her against her will."

His mother's eyes lit up. "The old home place would be a perfect hideout."

Steele scowled. *Not that disgusting farmhouse!* His mother had taken him there a couple times when he was a kid, and it was a dump then. He hated to think what condition it might be in now, with no utilities turned on. "I hope he'd have better sense than to leave Becca confined in a hole like that."

"Not if he'd planned this in a hurry," Lila said. "That might be the only place he'd think of on short notice. And he'd want a key if he planned to keep her locked up."

The more Steele thought about it, the surer he was that his mother was right. Without explanation, she left the foyer and headed down the hall toward her bedroom. She returned a moment later, wearing a concerned look. "I keep the skeleton key to the house in my jewelry box. It's not there."

Steele grabbed his cell phone. "I need to call the sheriff to send somebody to meet me out there."

Lila darted into the living room to fetch her purse. "I'll lead the way." She pulled her car keys out of her purse as she headed for the door.

"My car's out front. You can ride with us."

She gave Judge Forrester a searing glance, then said, "I'll drive myself. You might need to go elsewhere at a moment's notice."

* * * * *

As Jim Morse drove down the interstate toward St. Louis,

he glanced at the rain-laden evening sky and realized his life had taken a peculiar dark turn. He'd done a lot of stupid, senseless things over the years, but kidnapping Rebecca Sedder was really insane. What had he been thinking?

Maybe that was the problem – he hadn't been thinking. He'd let his anger and frustration for the last thirty years push him into action. At the time, keeping Becca from marrying anyone had seemed like the perfect way to let Lila know he wasn't going to take her crap anymore – and to let Steele know he couldn't breeze into town like a big-time celebrity and get whatever he wanted. But the more he thought about it, the more he realized getting the best of Lila and her damned self-righteous bastard wasn't worth going to jail.

Thank goodness he'd had the forethought to grab the rat-hole money he'd been stashing away for the last couple years. Lila might think she knew all his secrets, but she didn't know about that. He had squirreled away enough to vacation in the Caribbean for quite a while. And all this time she'd been beating herself up, wondering why they were losing money.

It wasn't the dealership dragging them down, and it wasn't Conn's fault. When she finally figured out who was really to blame, he'd be long gone, and she'd be left high and dry. That would teach her. Suddenly he wondered why it had taken him so long to get up the gumption to leave.

He passed a slow-going semi and, for a fleeting second, thought of Becca Sedder back at the farmhouse. How long would it take them to figure out where she was? The false trail with Conn would buy him some time. Once her disappearance was established, the cops would look to Conn for explanations first. But maybe they'd take too long to figure things out. Maybe they'd never piece together what had happened to Becca. If they never thought to look for her out at the old farm, she could end up stuck there for weeks or longer. And he'd left her only enough food and drink to last a couple days.

On the other hand, if they did realize where she was, they'd have one heck of a time getting her out. Those old doors on the second floor were solid wood. Nobody made them like that anymore. And he had taken Lila's skeleton key out of her jewelry cabinet. It was the only one, as far as he knew. They'd have to find a skeleton key from somebody else, or batter the doors down, or hoist Becca out through a second-story window.

Rearranging his weight in the gray leather seat of his Navigator, Jim gunned the engine to whiz around a rusty piece-of-crap compact driven by a skinny old guy with a dead cigarette hanging from his mouth. Lord, he hated small cars. They were deathtraps on wheels. As he glanced in the rearview mirror and pulled in front of the old beater with powerful ease, he caressed his leather-clad steering wheel. He was going to miss this big, bad beast.

Sighing, he recalled his earlier train of thought – Becca Sedder's plight. It didn't bother him so much that he'd left her in a world of trouble. After all, she was going to do the same to his boy that Lila had done to him some thirty-odd years ago. For that, the little bitch didn't deserve any more consideration than Lila did, even though the whole wedding thing was Lila's doing. Maybe he'd call Becca's parents and let them know where she was – if he remembered when he got to the airport.

* * * * *

Steele followed close behind the taillights of his mother's car, wishing she'd step on it and go faster. All he could think about was finding Becca, and his fear about the condition he'd find her in increased as they continued rambling down the blacktop.

"I know this isn't a good time to bring up the subject," Judge Forrester said after remaining silent for so long that Steele nearly forgot he'd come along. "But I don't know when I'll have another chance to say this."

"Say what?" Steele glanced at the judge, then trained his eyes back on his mother's Towncar. He needed to pay attention to his driving. He didn't want to miss the turn or ram her bumper.

"To say how sorry I am for everything, for all the trouble and hurt you've gone through. A child shouldn't have to grow up that way. I should have done better by you."

Steele glanced at him again, this time in surprise. The judge sounded as if he held himself responsible for the lifestyle Steele had been forced to endure in the Morse household. But Steele knew no one was responsible for that except his mother and her husband. "You did the best you could, considering the circumstances. You did what you thought you had to do, what you thought was right."

"I did what I thought I had to do," the judge agreed softly, "but it wasn't what I thought was right."

"Taking me away from my mother *was* right. Sending me to live with my great aunt and uncle was the best thing that could have happened to me."

Out of the corner of his eye, Steele saw the judge remove his glasses to clean them again. With his attention focused on the task, the older man mumbled, "Yes, I suppose that was the best alternative, after all."

"What other alternative could there have been besides putting me in a foster home with people who couldn't love and care for me the way my aunt and uncle did?"

The judge replaced his glasses and sighed. "I suppose you're right."

"*Was* there another alternative?" Steele demanded as he shot Judge Forrester a sharp glare. Before the judge could answer, Steele noticed the flashing lights in his rearview mirror, indicating the sheriff's escort had caught up with them. He looked ahead just in time to see his mother's turn signal blinking, and guided his car down the gravel lane after her.

Concentrating on the situation at hand made him lose interest in pursuing the peculiar conversation with Judge Forrester. He fell silent as the garish old farmhouse loomed in his mother's headlights. In front of the house sat the faded carcass of an older Chevy that looked beat to hell.

Steele bolted out of his car and leapt up the wet porch steps.

He rammed past the partially open front door, determined to catch whoever was holding Becca hostage. He saw a weak beam of light flickering around and assumed it was a flashlight. When he heard several young male excited voices shouting about finding a way out the back, he thundered after them, stumbling over debris and bumping against odd doorways in the darkness.

Zeroing in on the closest silhouette, he flew outside the back door of the house and made a desperate grab. Getting a handful of tee shirt, he grappled for a better hold and caught the boy's flailing arm. His captive shrieked with the froggy hoarseness of a voice still coping with the recent changes of puberty. Steele whipped the kid around to face him, guessing he was barely fifteen.

"Where is she?" Steele yelled. In the cloudy darkness he could just make out the terror of the pimple-faced kid, who smelled of beer and pot and body odor. He shook him and repeated, "Where is she?"

"I don't know what you're talking about," the kid wailed. "Me and my friends, we just came out here to do a little partying. There ain't no girls."

Steele turned as a flashlight shined on the boy's face. "How many more of them did you see?" Sheriff Rayborn asked.

"I don't know. At least two more. It was dark, hard to tell." Steele looked away from the portly middle-aged man in his tan uniform and studied the boy who'd wilted in his clutches.

"Look, we didn't do nothin' wrong," the boy pleaded.

"We're not really concerned about what you and your friends were doing," Sheriff Rayborn reassured as he took hold of the boy's shoulder and eased him from Steele's grasp. "We're looking for a missing woman we believe was brought to this house. Have you seen her?"

"No, we were just partyin', havin' some fun. That's all. We ain't seen anybody else."

"You didn't hear any noises, didn't go into any of the other rooms?"

The boy trembled and looked almost ready to cry. "My

258

dad's gonna kill me. I'm supposed to be staying over at Charlie Winfree's house. When he finds out I lied, he's gonna kill me!"

"What's your name, son?"

"Josh. Josh Cranston."

"Well, Josh," the sheriff said in an even tone, "Don't worry about the trouble you're in just now. If you can help us find the young lady we're looking for, I'm sure things will go better for you. Now, are you certain you didn't hear someone else in the house?"

"I'm sure. We were playing music and stuff. We didn't hear anybody."

"She could be tied up, gagged," Steele said as he turned back toward the house.

"Wait, Mr. Krueger," the sheriff said. "I'll go with you." He eyed the boy. "Go around front and wait with my deputy, Josh. Everything will be all right."

The boy did as he was told. Armed with his flashlight, Sheriff Rayborn followed Steele back into the house. By that time, Judge Forrester and Steele's mother were standing just inside the front doorway, joined by Chuck Lapinski who'd just arrived. "We've looked through every room downstairs and have been calling for Becca," Steele's mother said, "but haven't heard anything. I'm sorry, but I don't think she's here."

"I'm not giving up until I've searched every room to make sure." Steele glanced at Chuck who, without a word, handed him his flashlight. The sheriff followed Steele as he headed for the steep, narrow stairs. Behind, him, Chuck and Judge Forrester brought up the rear. With each step up, Steele's fear grew. If Becca couldn't answer, what had been done to her?

At the top of the stairs, Steele saw several doors and tried them one by one. All were unlocked except two. He knew those two locked doors represented his last hope of finding Becca this evening. And, without a key, he'd have to break them down. He handed Chuck his flashlight, then tested the strength of the nearest door, while Chuck went to the other. The door seemed sturdy and solid, but he wasn't about to let that deter him.

Backing off a few feet, he rushed forward and plowed his shoulder against it. The doorframe splintered, and he rammed it again. Shards of wood flew off as the door swung open. He stumbled forward into the room, with the sheriff and the judge rushing in right behind him. The sheriff shined his flashlight around as Steele called for Becca. He heard no answer, and his heart sank when Chuck emerged from the adjoining bathroom to report that he'd found no sign of her. Then the sheriff said, "Looks like somebody left some supplies for an overnight stay."

Steele and Chuck and Judge Forrester hurried over to the small red cooler and the plastic grocery sack lying on the floor. The presence of food and drinks, wet towelettes, paper towels, and toilet paper seemed to confirm the sheriff's suspicion.

Steele looked toward the window, then shined Chuck's flashlight in that direction, catching the glitter of shards of broken glass on the floor. He walked over to the window to investigate, and the others followed. He shined the flashlight over the window frame and saw more shards. His heart seized as he wondered if there'd been some kind of scuffle, and someone had fallen out the window. He leaned out the window, looked around, then pulled back and straightened. "I think Becca was locked in here, and she climbed out this window."

The sheriff and Chuck looked out the window. Both nodded in agreement. "She could be on foot, trying to make her way back to town," Sheriff Rayborn suggested.

"Or, she could still be here on the grounds, hiding," Chuck countered. "Especially if those kids arrived before she could make a getaway."

Steele turned and headed for the broken door. "We should check the outbuildings."

* * * * *

With her damp hair and clothes chilling in the breeze, Becca stayed ensconced in the barn, trying not to shiver. She had chosen a hiding place inside a stall partition roughed in with

260

warped wood slats. Directly in front of the stall sat a pile of discarded farm implements forming a chest-high rusty briar patch. Her eyes had adjusted to the darkness, and she was able to maneuver past the implements safely. She just hoped the barrier would discourage anyone else wandering around.

After being trapped inside the house, then the exertion of breaking out, she was thirsty and hungry. But her urge to urinate overwhelmed her. In desperation she finally peeled down her jeans and underwear and squatted in a corner of the barn stall, letting herself air-dry before zipping up. With the moldy hay and the population of rats and possums she was sure had overtaken the barn, she figured her leavings would do little harm.

Not wearing a watch, she had no idea how long it had been since she'd made her daring escape off the roof. Her only hope was that the boys partying in the house would leave soon or pass out and sleep there all night. Somehow she needed to get past them, out to the main road, so she could start her long hike home. She wasn't too keen on hitchhiking or having a run-in with a bunch of wild boys who were obviously up to no good.

When she heard the furtive voices coming close to the barn, she froze, wondering if the boys had realized she'd been in the house and had decided to search her out. Were they hoping to rescue her, or planning something else?

As the barn doors groaned in protest, she knew they were inside. She put her hand over her mouth, but when she heard their verbal exchange, her perception of the situation became even more confused. "Maybe they won't bother coming to look for us," one boy said. "They don't know how many of us are here."

"Yeah, but they will if Josh talks," another objected. "And if they take my car, how are we gonna get back home?"

The first boy swore. By this time she guessed there were only two boys in the barn, and their companion Josh was still at the house. But who was the 'they' the boys were afraid would come looking for them – another group of boys, bad enough to instill fear in these amateur miscreants? Considering the possibilities made her stomach roll.

"Man, I told you we should've went to my brother's place," one of the boys said. "At least he's got running water and electricity."

"Oh, yeah, and he's cool with us toking?" the second jibed.

"Hey, he used to do it all the time. He wouldn't care."

"Right. As long as we share, to keep him quiet."

"No, man, you got it wrong. My bro's all right."

"Shh! I see a flashlight. Hell, they *are* looking for us! That damn Josh snitched on us. I told you not to bring him along. He's just a snot-nose kid."

Becca could hear the boys scrambling and stumbling in the dark. Her worst fear was that they would run across her hiding place, but they were in such a frantic hurry, they didn't take time to move into the careful concealment she had found for herself. A moment later, the barn doors creaked again, and she saw the beams of two flashlights bouncing off various piles of junk inside the barn.

"Becca!"

Instantly Becca recognized Steele's voice, strained with worry. "I'm over hear," she croaked, rising stiffly from her hiding place. Relief washed over her, and the tears she'd been holding back gushed forth. Steele followed the sound of her voice and met her as she climbed out from behind the tangle of discarded implements.

"Good God, are you all right?"

"Yes," she squeaked, plowing into his open arms. She knew she must look a sight, but she didn't care. He hugged her as she wailed, "I was so scared! I didn't know what was ... I–" She let the admission drop. She didn't want to think about what could have happened, only that things had turned out all right.

"Come on. Let's get you home." As Steele stroked her hair and kissed her all over her face, she sucked up ragged breaths and tried to calm her wild emotion. She'd managed to keep it in check, knowing she had to maintain her senses if she expected to get away. But now that she was safe and sound in Steele's arms, she knew everything was okay.

* * * * *

The sheriff and his deputies rounded up the remaining boys, the two in the barn and one who had run for cover in a smaller outbuilding and surrendered after his buddies ratted on him. As Steele escorted Becca to his car, his mother, Judge Forrester, and Chuck Lapinski all gathered around. With curt reassurances, he informed them he was taking her back to her parents' house where she could clean up and rest.

Getting Becca settled in the passenger seat, he circled around to the driver's side and was met by Judge Forrester wearing an intense expression. "Once you get Becca settled, come and see me at my house. We need to talk."

Steele frowned. He didn't want to spend another moment away from Becca, but he knew she needed rest and some time to herself. Her parents would dote over her and scold her, but after that she would be on her own. He wanted to be with her, to lie next to her, to hold her, to reassure her and himself. But he was mature enough to let her parents spend the night with her, if for no other reason than to ease their terror over the near loss of their youngest daughter. "It could be late."

"I don't care," the judge insisted. "Just call me when you've got Becca home safe and sound. I'll be waiting."

Steele nodded, then got in the car, refusing to clutter his mind with the judge's seeming urgency. He turned to Becca and smiled. She tried to smile back, but her face, smudged with dirt and streaked with tears, looked like that of a frightened child. When he leaned over and hugged her, she wrapped her arms around his neck and held on as if she never wanted to let go. Finally he lifted his hands to ease her back into her seat. "Everything's okay now. I need to get you home."

She swiped at new tears sliding down her face and nodded, managing to smile.

CHAPTER 23

*B*y the time Steele walked out of Becca's parents' house, it was well past ten. That had been the most harrowing several hours he'd ever suffered, fearing the worst about the one he loved. He hadn't wanted to leave Becca's side, but he could tell by the anxiousness of her parents that his presence would be an awkward intrusion. It would have been easier for him to whisk Becca with him to his hotel room, but he wouldn't presume to take the Sedders' daughter from them after such an ordeal. He left, remembering to call the judge as promised.

He'd already memorized the number, just as he had memorized the number to Becca's house. It was something he did – committing numbers and facts to memory and storing them away for future use. He still recalled his mother's phone number, from eighteen years ago. Retaining that useless bit of information made no sense. Still, he did it.

When he called, the judge answered on the first ring, as if he'd stayed up waiting by the phone. Again Steele wondered what the judge felt was so important to discuss that it couldn't wait until morning. By the time Steele arrived at the judge's large two-story brick house, it was almost eleven. The landscaping spotlights and the entry light were on to offer an impressive welcome in the dark. Before he could ring the bell, the door opened to reveal Judge Forrester, still dressed and looking somewhat haggard from a long day. "Come in, son."

When Steele walked past the leaded glass door into the tiled entryway, he felt a strong sense of déjà vu. He'd been in this house many times, but never at eleven at night. The furnishings seemed familiar but somehow different – nighttime lighting and eighteen years of absence changed his recollection. He shrugged it off and turned to the judge. "It's really late, sir, so I won't stay long. I appreciate your agreeing to talk with me about Becca's situation, but since my mother and I have come to an understanding, I doubt it's still an issue of contention."

The judge's perfunctory smile came and went in a flash. "That's not what I wanted to discuss with you."

Steele eyed him, unsure how to respond. Alarms were going off in his head, telling him something of great importance was about to be revealed by Judge Forrester. Maybe he planned to tell him, after all these years of deliberate silence, the identity of his real father. No. It was too much to hope for. Anyway, after talking with his mother, Steele wasn't sure he wanted to know. Perhaps his mother and the judge had done him a favor by refusing to give him that information. What would he have done with it anyway? His father obviously didn't want to be part of his life. Knowing who his father was while knowing he didn't want him would have made things all the more awkward. Born of wounded youth and still trying to erase the meaningless violence in his past, Steele decided more awkwardness was not a good thing to add to his life. Yes. It was better this way, not knowing.

"Please, come into the study. Would you like some coffee, or a sandwich perhaps?"

Steele shook his head. He hadn't eaten since his talk with his mother at noon, but with everything that had happened after that, he couldn't handle solid food at this late hour. Sighing, he sat down in a leather wingback chair separated from an identical chair by an antique round table sporting an old brass lamp polished to perfection. Beside the lamp sat a photo in an ornate brass frame, a picture of the judge's late wife Miriam.

The judge eased himself down into the other chair. The soft light from the lamp cascaded over the weathered planes of his face as he removed his glasses and cleaned them with habitual care. Steele wondered if such frequent attentiveness marred the lenses.

"Your mother and I had a little talk after you left with Becca," Judge Forrester said, replacing his glasses on his face. He turned to Steele and tried to smile. "She explained to me why she had refused all these years to tell you who your father was. I hope you understand it wasn't her intention to keep the information from you out of maliciousness."

Steele smirked at the judge's lame attempt to defend his mother. "Yes, I know. She said she was leaving it to my father to own up to his responsibility and tell me himself. I'm still waiting, thirty-one years later."

The judge glanced down at the oriental rug accenting the rich hardwood floor at his feet, and Steele fidgeted with impatience. He didn't like the direction this conversation was taking. As far as he was concerned, it was a dead issue.

Eyeing the nine-foot ceiling in distraction, he glanced at the walls packed with law books and leather-bound literary classics. Judge Forrester's study was actually a library. A sliding wooden ladder attached to a track along the perimeter of the tray ceiling allowed access to the uppermost shelves. Where the shelves ended, tall windows dressed in opulent jacquard draperies filled the rest of the space. The effect was stately and overwhelming.

He spotted the crystal decanter sitting atop the polished wood buffet in front of the window across the room. "Do you happen to have some whiskey?"

The judge got to his feet and mumbled, "Yes. I think I could use a drink, too."

Steele watched with mild curiosity as the older man bent down to fetch two tumblers and some ice from the cabinet, obviously equipped with its own icemaker. Was he such a heavy drinker that he had a wet bar installed in his library?

Judge Forrester placed the two glasses on sandstone coasters, then sat down again. "When I had this house built," he explained as if he'd read Steele's mind, "I anticipated heavy social entertaining. But things changed when Miriam's health deteriorated soon after we moved here."

Steele nodded, dismissing the suspicions of alcoholism as he raised his glass to his lips. The elixir warmed his throat, easing the tension he'd felt ever since entering the judge's home. It seemed strange for him to have a friendly drink with the all-powerful man who had dictated his fate from the high seat of a judge's bench eighteen years ago. But after all those years, he realized the judge was a mere human being like everyone else – it was the office that garnered him prestige and respect. Still, Steele felt intimidated, awed, in the older man's presence. There was something about him...

"When Miriam became ill, I was wrapped up in running the democratic campaign headquarters for the upcoming presidential election. I had no idea the hell she was going through. I was too busy with the campaign to notice or care. And I regret that shortcoming, which turned out to be only one of many in my life for which I can never make amends."

Raising his glass to his lips, Steele froze. Ever since his heart-to-heart with his mother, his mind had been trying to process the clues she'd offered regarding his father's identity. But with everything that had gone on afterward, he'd been too torn about Becca's disappearance to concentrate on anything. Now that all the worry and heartache was over, he could relax, and his mind began to function again. At that moment, the judge's various comments over the past several hours clicked into place. The correlation of the election campaign was the clincher. His breath quickened, and he swallowed hard, unable to move his arm to set his glass aside.

Judge Forrester continued talking, seeming unaware of his reaction. "By summer I was bogged down with my new position as a junior partner with Cress and Bartlett. My objective to become district attorney, then circuit court judge, took all my remaining energy. I had it all planned out and didn't let anything get in my way. Not my wife's illness, and certainly not an unexpected affair with a college girl home on summer break. I was thirty-two years old, an ambitious, self-serving idiot."

The judge finally looked Steele in the eyes, but he couldn't move, couldn't speak. His mind was numb from the overload of this revelation.

Sighing as if relieved Steele's damnation hadn't yet spewed

forth, the judge said, "I never meant to hurt anyone. Truly I didn't. Having an affair was the last thing on my mind. I loved Miriam more than I can ever say. She was a special human being, and the world lost a grand individual when she passed away." He sucked in a huge breath, then turned his attention to his lap to clean his glasses again. In the stiff silence, Steele thought he saw tears moistening the judge's eyes.

As the judge replaced his spectacles once more, Steele finally managed to set his drink down on the table. His body felt as numb as his brain. He just couldn't process this – not here, not now, not yet. Maybe not ever.

"I never meant to mislead your mother," Judge Forrester confessed, facing him. "I never meant to encourage her. But I was so busy and stressed out, and Miriam wasn't ... she couldn't be there for me as she had been before. And one night ... one night of weakness..."

The judge shook his head and looked away. "Your mother assumed we would marry, but I couldn't forsake my wife to join the unrealistic fantasy life she had planned. She was too young, immature, and arrogant to understand that what had happened between us was a mistake."

I was a mistake. My mother had always told me that. I wasn't meant to be. Steele let the negativity of his thoughts wash over him like a cold shower drenching him with stinging hopelessness. He didn't try to fight it, but let it take control of his heart and chill it to a hard frozen block. It hurt much more than the aimless fiery anger he'd suffered as a youth. His breathing became shallow and irregular, and his head buzzed with resentment.

"Miriam and I had always talked about having children," the judge said, eyeing the floor. "She wanted to start right away when we got married, but I was convinced we should put that plan on hold until my career was in full swing. Then, when she got sick, having children was out of the question. She would have made a terrific mother. If I hadn't been so damned concerned about my future, we could have had the family she wanted. I don't know how she put up with me."

He eyed Steele. "When your mother told me she was pregnant, all I could think about was what the scandal would do to my career, my marriage. By then I'd had time to think about things. I knew I loved my wife. I knew I didn't want to lose her over an affair that meant nothing to me, that I hadn't even been looking for. I hadn't wanted any of it to happen. I just wanted it all to go away. But I knew it wouldn't.

"Your mother wouldn't get an abortion, she wouldn't consider adoption, and she wouldn't let me have you. When she found out I wasn't going to divorce Miriam and marry her, she took up with Jim Morse and immediately married him. It killed me to think she would pass off my only son as someone else's. But I was too much of a coward to fight for you."

Steele's eyes and ears seemed to go blank. He knew Judge Forrester was sitting beside him, talking to him, looking at him, but he couldn't register the sensory information.

"In my arrogance, I thought I'd fooled Miriam. But she knew. She knew all about it from the very beginning. It must have been my own guilt that gave me away. I finally confessed everything. She never blamed me, never got angry with me." He laughed with breathless misery. "I think she believed I deserved to have an affair, because she'd let me down as a wife. That wasn't true. That was never true. I had vowed to love her and honor her in sickness and in health, and I had no intention of forfeiting those vows for the sake of one night of sex. Still, the more she tried to ease my guilt, the more awful I felt."

Steele didn't want to hear any more, but he couldn't make his mouth move to form the words to tell Judge Forrester to stop his confession. He sat in helpless paralyzed silence as the judge continued with every hurtful detail. "Miriam knew you were mine. And it didn't make any difference to her that I'd fathered you with some other woman. She wanted you just the same as if she'd given birth to you herself. I felt it was best to let you go, to let Lila have you and not torture myself with possibilities I knew could never be. But Miriam wouldn't let me do that – not because she wanted to punish me, but because she wanted me to know my son."

"To know *me*," Steele managed to croak finally.

"Yes. *You.* My son."

Steele turned aside. His heart pounded, and his head felt light and feverish as he sucked shallow breaths into his beleaguered lungs. He wanted to yell and smash things, but he couldn't decide what to do first, and so he did nothing. "How ... how could you keep quiet about the truth, all the while knowing the hell I was going through with that son-of-a–"

"I didn't know, I didn't realize for several years that Jim Morse had found out you weren't his son and was taking out his anger on you. Your mother did a very good job of disguising things in public. But as you got older, you changed that. You let everyone know something was wrong. With your defiance, you told me you needed help. And I did what I could to help you."

Steele swallowed hard, feeling like a kid again, too mad and too stubborn to cry and let anyone know how bad he was hurting inside. He wanted to get up and march out the door and never set eyes on Judge Forrester – his father – again. But his body wouldn't move. "So, you shipped me off to my Aunt Sybil," he snarled, refusing to meet the judge's earnest gaze. "And sent me a nice letter every month with a guilt check to ease your conscience."

The judge lowered his head. "I didn't write those letters. Miriam did."

That revelation stunned Steele even more. Not only did his father not have the courage to stand up for him and claim him as his own, he hadn't even had the common decency to communicate with him. Instead, he let his wife do it, which explained the unceasing praise and encouragement flooding each missive. Miriam had always been a positive, uplifting person, even as she faced her own failing health and premature death. All the while she had been the one trying to make amends, trying to give him hope that someday he would be united with his father – and Steele assumed it *was* his father. But now he knew the truth.

His father was too busy building a career, too busy to give his name to his son. Steele chuckled breathlessly. The realization cut him to the core. He glared at Daniel Forrester, wanting to hate him with every ounce of emotion he had left. But his heart felt cold and lifeless like a block of steel. No feeling left at all.

Judge Forrester seemed to know he'd hit a brick wall. As he took off his glasses to clean them once more, he murmured, "I'm sorry, Steele, for everything. For letting your childhood go to hell, for not being there for you when you needed me, for not being a father to you. But most of all, I'm sorry I missed out on knowing you, raising you, enjoying you as my son. I'd give anything to get back those lost years, those precious moments we never had but should have. And I'm so very, very sorry that it took me this long to tell you the truth." He sighed and put his glasses back on. "I know it's too much to expect you to forgive me. Perhaps someday you'll understand my faults and accept me for what I am – a man who doesn't deserve your respect or friendship or kinship, but hopes you can, out of the goodness of your heart, freely give it."

As the shock dissipated, leaving him weak and bereft, Steele regained control of his body and his mind. Rising to his feet, he towered over the man he'd always looked up to until now. "You provided the genes that make up half of who and what I am," he rasped, "but you gave up your right to call yourself my father when you failed to claim me as your son. You had plenty of opportunities over the years to speak up, and you can't spend decades achieving all the other goals that took precedence in your life, then, after all that time, make one heartfelt speech and expect me to embrace you. I am not an afterthought, and I don't need or want a fair-weather father. A true parent does the job through adversity as well as triumph. You've done neither. Charles Krueger is the only man I will ever acknowledge as my father. You're nothing to me. I don't know if I'll ever find what it takes to forgive you, but I'm pretty damned sure you won't live long enough to see it happen."

Steele stared into Daniel Forrester's pale blue-gray eyes

until the older man lowered his head, saying nothing. Steele turned and left the house.

_____

CHAPTER 24

"*I*t's very late, Mrs. Morse. I appreciate you telling me about Mr. Morse, but I was just on my way to bed." Having just showered, Becca stood in the kitchen, barefoot in her nightgown. Holding onto the faded green phone receiver in one hand, she swiped her other hand down her face, then glanced at the kitchen clock over the sink with its garishly happy sunflower face. It was close to one in the morning.

"I wanted to apologize," Mrs. Morse said over the phone. "For everything."

Becca huffed. She didn't have patience for this – not after her harrowing ordeal, then trying to calm her parents. She'd just gotten them to bed after Steele left, and thought she could finally relax. But right after she'd finished showering, the phone rang. Lila Morse was the last person she wanted to talk to. "This really isn't a good time."

"I know you've had a distressing evening, but–"

"That's putting it mildly."

"There's something you should know. About Steele."

Becca bristled, fearing Steele's mother was still trying to negatively influence her about him. Why she'd stoop to that again now, after everything that had happened, Becca couldn't imagine. "Look, Mrs. Morse. I don't want to hear any more details about his past or–"

"He just talked to his father."

"His *father*?"

Lila cleared her throat. "Evidently things didn't go well."

"And how would you know?"

"His father called me after Steele left his house."

Exhausted, Becca glanced at the Formica table draped in a

vinyl sunflower cloth, then stretched the extra long phone cord to sit down. She rubbed her face again. Steele had talked with his father? He knew who the man was? When had he found out – or had he? Maybe Mrs. Morse was lying, deliberately trying to confuse her. "Look. I happen to know Steele left here just over an hour ago to see Judge Forrester." Oh. Oh my. *Judge Forrester!*

"Yes. Daniel was very upset after he and Steele talked – so upset, he called me for the first time in years."

Becca licked her lips. Her mouth had suddenly gone dry. "Judge Forrester is ... is Steele's father?"

"Daniel wants to make amends, but Steele has made it clear he doesn't want any part of it."

"Well, really, Mrs. Morse, I can't say I blame him."

"Yes, I agree. Of course Steele holds the same hard feelings toward his father that he does toward me, and I understand why. Nevertheless, I think it's important for him to come to terms with his father – if for no other reason than to ease his own resentment. That's a terrible burden to carry around all one's life." She sighed. "I know. I've been there."

Resting an elbow on the table, Becca scrunched up her face. This confession was untimely and unexpected. "I can see your point, Mrs. Morse, but what do you expect me to do about it? Steele has to decide for himself how he wants to handle it."

"True. But he cares for you, and I think he'll listen to you. Help him see the wisdom of making peace with his father. He and I..." She paused for a second, then continued, "He and I have already come to our own agreement, and I don't want him to start a new life with resentment still hanging over him. Talk to him. Make him see reason. Daniel wants to repair the rift between them, and he would like to attend your wedding."

Becca thought for a moment about what Mrs. Morse said. She made sense. It wasn't good for Steele to carry resentment around like a weight on his back. That darkness in his heart might eat away at his soul until there was nothing left. One way or another, he had to come to terms with the revelation of his father's identity. He had to deal with the hurt and loss and neglect

274

and rejection. Maybe he'd never feel right about it, but he had to face it and accept it. She just didn't know if that would include welcoming into his life a man who had wanted no responsibility for fathering him.

She knew this wasn't about making Judge Forrester feel better about himself, it was about helping Steele feel comfortable with the direction his life had taken. How he chose to deal with his father was up to him, but, as his mother pointed out, it would be best if he made peace. Becca wasn't sure there was time for him to make that emotional adjustment before the wedding. She sighed. "I can't promise anything."

"Do your best. I know Steele is very upset, and I don't want your wedding marred by this turn of events."

Becca blinked in astonishment. Mrs. Morse actually sounded concerned about Steele's welfare. Maybe they *had* come to an understanding. And if Steele could forgive his mother for years of unhappy childhood, then maybe Becca herself could consider forgiving her for the hell she'd put her and her father through. She shook her head. This was all too much to think about right now. "I really need to get some sleep."

"Goodnight, Becca. Rest well. And I'm truly sorry. For everything."

* * * * *

Steele awoke groggy, feeling the weight of someone moving on top of him. The instant his hands made contact with a scantily clad female bottom, his eyes flew open to find Becca grinning as she straddled him.

"Come on, sleepyhead," she taunted, wiggling back and forth to jostle him. "You told me you get up every morning at the crack of dawn to go jogging. I want to see you in action."

He groaned and tried to roll over underneath her. "Becca ... what time is it? How did you get in here?"

"It's seven-fifteen, and I bribed the clerk to let me in."

He flopped on his back and glowered at her through half-open eyes. "Bribed? With what?"

"A front-row seat at the church this evening." Still straddling him, she wiggled her hips again. "Now come on. Let's get our aerobic exercise for today."

He gave her a wry half-smile and closed his eyes. "Let me sleep just fifteen more minutes."

She smacked him on the shoulder. "Get your lazy butt out of bed right now, Steeleman Krueger. I'm all dressed and ready to go, and I want you to introduce me to the finer points of–"

He lunged up, and she yelped as he whirled her down on the bed and pinned her underneath him. "Maybe I'll show you the finer points of ravishing my bride-to-be before my morning jog." He ran his hand up her skimpy shorts and underwear, squeezing her naked rump.

She giggled and squirmed away from him. "I guess that would qualify as aerobic exercise."

Grinning, he weaseled his other hand under her sleeveless tee shirt and did his best to dislodge her bra.

* * * * *

Becca gasped for air and bent over, gripping her knees. "I can't take another step. Please, can we just rest a minute?"

Steele placed a hand on her hot, sweaty back and bent down to face her. "I warned you to pace yourself. What happened to the chipper little jogger who started out laughing and running circles around me?" His hand moved further down her back, and for a second she thought he was going to try to feel her up until he offered, "Want me to go back to the hotel and get the car?"

She huffed and puffed, finally managing, "Would you?"

He laughed and smacked her on the butt as he straightened up. "I doubt you're as bad off as you're letting on. Sit down and catch your breath, then we'll walk back at an easier pace."

Becca sank down and perched on the curb. When she saw Steele look around and then scowl, she knew he realized where she had led him with her teasing, backward-dancing jogging routine. The circuitous route brought them three blocks from downtown, to the cul-de-sac of Judge Forrester's home. The manicured lawn, big circle drive, and massive blue spruces careening upward on either side of the huge house made it a truly impressive display.

Steele glared down at her. "What are you up to, Becca?"

She cringed under his scrutiny, then sighed, suddenly recovered from her shortness of breath. "Our rehearsal luncheon is at noon. I thought it might be nice if you invited some of your family. You could start by asking your father."

"He *told* you? I can't believe he would admit it after thirty-one years of trying to keep it a secret!"

"No, Judge Forrester didn't tell me. You're mother did. She called last night and said the state police had picked up Jim Morse on the way to the airport. Evidently he was planning to leave the country with a lot of money he'd embezzled from the dairy and the dealership. Your mother and I had a little chat, and she apologized for all the trouble she's caused. She's really sorry, Steele. For everything. I invited her to the luncheon and the wedding."

"After everything she's put you and your family through?" He laughed breathlessly. "She was planning to let your father take the blame for something he didn't do, just to save her business from a scandal and fines. And you want her at our wedding? How can you be so quick to forgive?"

Becca ignored the incredulous look on his face. "I'll be the first to admit the last several weeks have been pure hell. The things your mother did were inexcusable. But I believe, deep down, that your mother and father are not bad people. They're just ... mixed up. They've made mistakes – some serious ones – but they're still your family, whether you like it or not."

"Well, I *don't* like it. My mother kept me in a dangerous situation for the sake of appearances, and Judge Forrester ignored the fact that I existed so he could build his career. They may be my biological parents, but in my mind they'll never fill the job as my mother and father. My Aunt Sybil and Uncle Charlie were there for me when I needed someone, unlike my real parents." He reached for her hand to help her up. "Come on. We're going back to the hotel."

"Steele, please. If you'd just think about it, you'd see it's the right thing to do."

He whirled away, then turned on her. "No."

She met his glare bravely. She had discussed things with her parents, and they agreed that holding grudges wouldn't make things any better for anyone. There were bad feelings between Steele and his mother, and him and his father too, now that his identity had been revealed. She didn't want the man she loved to go through life regretting the source of his very existence.

Jim Morse had given her a scare she wouldn't ever forget, and a lot of people had suffered great emotional upset, thinking the worst had happened to her. But Jim hadn't tried to harm her, and nothing terrible had resulted from the ordeal. What good did it do her to dwell on it? And what good would it do Steele to dwell on the pain and anger of his past? Everyone would be a lot better off if they all moved beyond their emotional torment and got on with enjoying life.

She couldn't help laughing when she considered the irony of Steele's mother. "Well, you have to admit, your mother is indirectly responsible for arranging our wedding. Without her interference, we would never have ended up together. Who knows how our lives would have turned out? If anyone deserves to be there to celebrate our marriage, she does."

"Becca, have you lost your mind?"

"It's the right thing to do. Years down the road, you're going to regret not–"

Steele grabbed her by the arm and hoisted her up like a sack of feathers. His grip almost hurt. She winced and he hugged her, whispering, "Sorry. I didn't mean to be so rough, but don't think for a minute that I'm going to agree to your scheme. I know you love me and you're doing what you believe is best for me, but don't try to maneuver me into something I'm not ready for. Neither of them is coming to the rehearsal or the wedding."

"Steele..."

"I mean it."

She hung her head and swiped a hand across her sweaty face. "A wedding is a family event and I want you to—"

"If Lila Morse and Daniel Forrester are all the family I have, I'd rather stand alone." He let go of her and started trotting toward the hotel, then stopped a short distance away. Turning to face her, he prodded, "You coming?"

"Yeah," she grumbled. "Good grief, you are one rock-headed stubborn man, Steeleman Krueger!"

Smiling, he walked back and slid an arm around her shoulders to urge her along. "Yes, and you're crazy about me."

She shrugged. "Maybe. I'm not so sure anymore."

He stopped short and spun her around to plant an urgent roving kiss on her mouth. "Maybe you need to hurry up and come back to the hotel with me so I can make you sure."

She slapped his arm, then took off running. "You have to catch me first."

"That'll be easy." He raced up behind her and scooped her up in his arms. When she yelped, he laughed and lowered her to her feet.

As they headed for the hotel, Becca glanced backward at the lonely bastion of Judge Forrester's mansion. She felt sorry for the man. It looked as if he'd never get the chance to make amends and know his son. And she was sure Steele would someday regret turning his back on this one chance to know his father. She didn't want him going through the rest of his life harboring the same kind of overwhelming resentment that had tormented him as a teen. She didn't want that hatred looming between them. Nothing would be quite right for anyone until he came to terms with the bitterness she knew seethed just under the surface of his steely, smiling exterior.

She wasn't going to give up until he made peace with his family, but she needed more time to make that happen. She had until noon to change his mind, and she feared that wasn't nearly long enough. She needed to enlist some help.

* * * * *

"This is something Becca feels very strongly about," Ray Sedder said over the phone at eleven, an hour before the rehearsal luncheon.

Tightening the knot in his tie, Steele cradled the phone at his shoulder. "I feel just as strongly about it, in the opposite way, Mr. Sedder."

"Don't disappoint my little girl, Steele. Please. She cares about you and wants this for you, for your own sake."

Steele ran a hand down his face and sighed.

"Marriage is all about compromises," Becca's father pointed out. "The sooner you accept that, the better off you'll be."

Steele chuckled. His future father-in-law was right. It didn't matter how he felt about his mother and father at the moment. To please the woman he loved, he'd walk through fire. It was a small gesture to let his parents share in the most important event in his life, and he was man enough to overlook childish resentment and make peace, for Becca's sake. He hoped this would be the last time he'd have to deal with those two. "When you put it that way, Mr. Sedder, how can I refuse? Tell Becca she can invite whomever she wishes to the luncheon and our wedding. I want her to be happy."

"Good decision, son."

Steele grimaced at the term 'son,' thrown around so casually by everyone. It meant almost nothing to him after hearing Judge Forrester call him that so often and finding out how little the term really meant to the man. "I'll see you in a little while, sir."

"Looking forward to it. And, Steele, welcome to our family."

As he hung up the phone, Steele warmed to the idea of joining a new family with Becca as his core, his mast, his true north. He knew she wouldn't steer him wrong. She'd already proved that by making him behave as a better man than he was.

She was right. Inviting his parents to the most important event in his life was a biggie he couldn't afford to deny them. To deny them would be to deny himself. And he couldn't ignore the plus side when she pointed it out. In the past week, he'd managed to gain a mother, a father, and a wife. What did he have to be upset about?

Weeks ago Steele's mother had reserved the private dining room at the Standish Inn for the noon rehearsal luncheon. The only difference was, now instead of being a pre-celebration of Conn and Becca's wedding, it was for *his* and Becca's wedding.

Just a short ride down the elevator would bring him to the party, but at 11:55 he was still holed up in his room, having trouble making the journey to the first floor.

How could he face Judge Daniel Forrester, his father? *His father!* For years he'd wondered how his life would change if only he could know his true father. He'd even entertained the fantasy that Judge Forrester would adopt him and rescue him from the unending stress in the Morse house. But that never happened. Judge Forrester had kept silent until Steele had grown old enough to make real trouble. And even then he looked for someone else to assume his parental duties, letting it fall to Steele's great aunt and uncle.

How could Steele look that man in the eyes and smile and be pleasant, knowing he had deliberately covered up his paternity out of selfishness and cowardice? He, one of the most respected members of the community, had engaged in an adulterous affair and fathered an illegitimate child, then allowed the unwed mother to pass that child off as someone else's son. And he didn't even have to common decency to tell Steele, his own son, the truth when he came of legal age. Now he had the gall to want to be part of his life.

Steele shook his head. If not for Becca, he'd turn his back on the jerk. The thought of Daniel Forrester sitting on his bench in his judicial robe, meting out justice to others while he escaped it himself, made Steele want to...

Want to what? There really wasn't anything he could do to

the man. Anyway, it wasn't worth worrying about. *He* wasn't worth worrying about. Steele would simply ignore him. He'd be polite for Becca's sake, but that didn't mean he had to carry on a conversation with the old weasel. With that decision made, he went downstairs to the restaurant.

* * * * *

Becca sat next to Steele and listened to him describe his most recent sailing excursion to her father. Her father's love of fishing put him near the water, so at least they had that in common. Her father seemed intrigued by the idea of sailing on the Lake Michigan, more like an ocean than the small lakes and ponds he was used to.

To Becca's chagrin, Steele casually snubbed his own mother and father. He seemed determined not to let the revelation of paternity ruffle him in public, but the reality of it still floored her. She still couldn't get over the fact that Judge Forrester, the very man who'd placed Steele for adoption, had turned out to be his father. At least she had the good sense to seat them at opposite ends of the table.

The judge made no attempt to engage Steele in conversation, but watched him intently. Steele's mother focused her attention on her impeccable table manners and let others converse around her. Becca wasn't pleased by the situation, but was thankful it didn't resemble the last Morse family lunch she'd attended – complete with yelling and shoving and breaking dishes and furniture.

She sighed and looked at Steele sitting next to her. He smiled down at her and squeezed her hand. Maybe someday he'd get over his resentment toward his parents, but she knew it wouldn't be today, their wedding day.

* * * * *

At 1:30, Steele drove to the stately chiseled stone building of the First United Methodist Church and parked his car in the asphalt lot near the other cars he recognized. In the afternoon sunlight, his mother's silver Towncar gleamed beside Judge Forrester's – his father's – light blue Cadillac. He just couldn't get used to the fact that he finally could refer to someone as 'his father.' Not that it made any difference now.

Nearby sat Becca's brown Toyota and a small white sedan Steele assumed belonged to the pastor. Three other cars also sat in the parking lot, but he had no idea whose they were.

As he walked up the wide, sweeping stone steps of the church and reached for the handle of one of the gleaming wooden double doors, the import of what he was about to do began to sink in. In a few minutes he'd participate in the practice run for the ceremony that would change his life in ways he couldn't begin to imagine. He was taking active responsibility for the life of a woman who might already be carrying their unborn child. He would promise to care for her and love her and keep her with him for the rest of his life. A month ago that prospect would have frightened the hell out of him. But now it made him feel excited ... queasy but excited.

For the first time in his life he had family responsibilities of his own to look forward to. For the first time he would be the captain of a ship with passengers of his own choosing, his own making. His decisions, good or bad, would affect all of them. He couldn't ignore the importance of what he was about to undertake, and there was no sidestepping it. He had set himself on this path the moment he admitted he loved Becca and wanted her with him always. Nothing would turn him away now.

With Conn out of the picture and The Ogre sitting in jail, he told himself he should feel some small sense of satisfaction. Belated justice had finally been served. As a bonus, he'd learned the identity of his real father, the objective that had initially lured him back to Fenton. But he didn't feel whole and healed like he expected. He felt ... wrong, empty. Something was missing, and he couldn't put his finger on it.

Yes, yes, he could. It was the pain in Daniel Forrester's

283

eyes last night and earlier at lunch. Stolen glances across the table confirmed that his father was bereft at being shut out. But at least he'd allowed Becca to invite him. The old man should be grateful for that much, considering all that he'd let slide in the past.

Exhaling, Steele forced out the lingering doubts clouding his confidence. In a few more hours, he'd be exchanging vows with Becca, and that's what he'd focus on. He couldn't let anything distract him from that moment. He grabbed the door handle and pulled the heavy door open, letting the afternoon sunlight stream inside with him as he entered the church.

* * * * *

Standing near the altar in jeans and a tee shirt, Becca half listened to Reverend Faulk explain the usual wedding proceedings as she watched the florist people set up the rented candelabras and strategically place the elaborate floral baskets and sprays. With early afternoon light streaming through the stained glass windows, the church took on a heady fairyland quality, intoxicating in its implications.

She glanced at her mother and father seated in the front pew to her right and saw their eyes misting. This was not the first time they'd married off a daughter. Meg had been in front of a justice of the peace twice. But this would be their first full-frills church wedding. Although the circumstances that had brought it about were less than desirable, the end result was better than any of them could have hoped for.

Behind them Meg and Pete battled for control of their four wild coyotes. Meg had expressed doubt about involving her boys in the wedding ceremony, especially if the roles included fire to light candles. But Becca insisted that Michael and Sean could handle the lighting of the candles. And the twins would be double ring-bearers. Jeremy would carry her ring pillow, and Joshua would carry Steele's. Really, it didn't matter to her what they did, as long as they were part of the proceedings – and didn't burn the church down.

Kessa Stranberg   *Heart of* STEELE

The one thing Steele had made Becca promise was to keep her family from trashing his BMW with traditional cheesy wedding decorations – balloons, noisemakers, shoe polish, and shaving cream proclaiming "Just Married" all over his pristine car. She knew only Meg and Pete would dare go that route, and made it clear the BMW was off-limits. The way Meg snickered, she feared her warning had been interpreted as an invitation.

Meg didn't want to stand up as her maid of honor because of her awkward appearance. But Becca had found a beautiful dress that actually complemented the bridal gown and fit nicely over Meg's very pregnant belly. Steele didn't name a best man, but that didn't matter to Becca. She wanted her sister up there with her, and her father to give her away. At first her father didn't want to do it because he was afraid his injury would prevent him from walking her down the aisle in a manner befitting the ceremony. But she had insisted that even if he needed to ride down the aisle in a wheelchair, he'd be the one to give her away. That eased his worry about marring her wedding.

Becca glanced at Steele's parents in the other front pew. His mother Lila, the former bane of her life, sat some distance from Steele's father. Neither spoke to the other, nor even glanced in the other's direction. But at least they had agreed to attend out of respect for Steele.

Becca wasn't sure how Steele's mother really felt about him. She seemed to have softened toward him in the last day or so, but Becca couldn't believe she'd turned over a new leaf, after years of resenting his very existence. Judge Forrester, however, wanted to build a rapport with Steele. He'd thanked Becca several times for making the necessary arrangements for him to be present. She just wondered what he'd do when news of his past discretion hit Fenton's gossip machine. That was his worry, not hers. Her only concern was whether Steele could manage somehow to get past his anger and resentment and see the potential for love and companionship from his newly proclaimed father. She hadn't had a chance to talk to him about it since this morning, and at lunch he didn't seem any more receptive to the

285

idea than he had been earlier.

Only time would tell. She eyed the church double doors at the back and wondered where he was. For a fleeting second she feared he'd changed his mind. But that thought vanished when the right door swung open and she saw him standing there, surrounded by the haze of outside sunlight. She smiled at him, and he returned her smile as he moved toward her. Everything else faded into background noise as she focused on him.

* * * * *

At 5:50, Steele wiped his sweaty palms on his tux trousers and peeked out the side entrance to the altar area. The church was filled to capacity with townsfolk and a few guests he was startled to see. As expected, Harry and Louise Watkins, his neighbors from Edgarsville, were seated among the crowd. He spotted his executive assistant Irene and her husband. Chuck Lapinski was there, along with Nate Fehrnman, one of the senior partners at his firm. Nate's six-foot-plus frame and shock of thick white hair made him a standout.

Of course Steele's mother and father were right up there in front, on the opposite side of Becca's parents. *His father and mother.* How odd to think of them in those terms. This had all hit him like a tornado – fast and furious, without warning. He just didn't have the time to make the necessary transition to accept it. He had come to Fenton, prepared to continue hating his mother and leave his father unknown for the rest of his life. But now ... who knew? While he never expected to have a close relationship with his mother, the possibility now existed for something between them. And his father? He still couldn't make up his mind about him. But he was sure Becca would continue sticking her pretty little nose into the middle of it things to ensure he had plenty of chances to get to know him.

He straightened and breathed easier, realizing his thoughts of Becca relieved his nervousness. He was eager to see her, to reassure himself that in these last few minutes, the event he'd

286

worked toward would finally happen. He was getting married to Rebecca Jean Sedder, whom he'd known for just under two weeks. The awe and fear of that life-altering event shook him once again, until he tried to imagine his life without her. What would he have done the rest of his life if he hadn't met her when he did? It was almost as if their meeting and falling in love was meant to be, like some force was at work to maneuver them together. As Becca pointed out, his own mother's diabolical plan had put it all in motion, despite the fact that the end result was the direct opposite of what she had intended. Funny how things worked out.

Looking down at his watch, he confirmed that the wedding would begin in less than five minutes. Butterflies fluttered in his stomach, and he swiped at the bloom of perspiration on his forehead.

"No need to be nervous, Steele," Reverend Faulk reassured with a whisper.

Steele straightened and smiled. "Who's nervous? Not me." He chuckled and added, "Well, maybe I am, just a little." He froze when he heard the organ music begin. With a gulp of anticipation, he watched the pastor stroll toward the altar. A moment later he stepped out from his hiding place and walked to his designated spot.

Turning, he watched Meg, maid of honor, walk up the aisle without incident. He shot her a smile of encouragement when she took her place on the other side. Subdued giggles and coos erupted from the crowd as Meg's twins, Josh and Jeremy, ambled up the aisle, each bearing a ring on a pillow. It might not be tradition for the groom's ring to ride on a pillow, but Becca had insisted on the symmetry so that both twins would have an equal part in the ceremony.

When the organist played the traditional wedding march, Steele felt his mouth go dry. With his palms sweating, his stomach turning flip-flops, and his heart racing, he wondered if he was having a heart attack – until he saw Becca. Lord, she was beautiful, draped in luscious white with the veil over her face.

She and her father walked so slowly, he wanted to rush down and take Mr. Sedder by the elbow and help him – hurry him. After what seemed like an eon, they stopped at the base of the altar. When her father lifted her veil and kissed her in a tearful farewell, Steele felt his eyes mist. When he took Becca's hand to help her toward the altar, he saw her eyes sparkling with moisture too.

The words of the minister droned in a blur, and Steele felt punch-drunk until the man turned to him and asked the all-important question. With all the feeling his heart could hold, he looked into Becca's soft amber eyes and murmured, "I will."

Becca's vow made his heart speed up, and when the minister gave permission to kiss the bride, Steele felt a flare of warmth and love he never thought possible. His lips touched Becca's, and time stopped for that instant. When he pulled away, and the minister announced them to the audience as husband and wife, they turned to a standing ovation. A sense of relief and joy washed over Steele. He wanted to grab Becca and run down the aisle, but he held the urge in check as he walked arm-in-arm with her toward the entrance. "I love you, Rebecca Krueger," he whispered in her ear.

The church emptied like a time-delayed parade. He shook hands and smiled and accepted kisses on the cheek and congratulations from so many people, he wasn't sure if he was really experiencing it all or just dreaming. Many of the people he barely recognized. With a few reminders, he placed faces with events in his life eighteen years ago – a past he'd thought he could forget. But every renewed acquaintance reminded him of moments slipped by, moments that defined his life in ways he was just now beginning to realize.

The sun glowed warm on his head and shoulders, giving him a sense of joy and peace and belonging. And then he found himself facing the image of himself in years to come – his father. They eyed each other for a moment, and he was unsure what to say or do. Suddenly Judge Forrester reached out and gave him a bear hug, patting him heartily on the back. "Congratulations, son.

I'm glad I got to share this day with you."

When the judge pulled away, Steele felt his eyes clouding. "Thanks. I ... I'm glad too."

His father took that as encouragement and hugged him again. Steele hugged him back, feeling suddenly as if a great weight had been lifted off his shoulders.

Pulling away again, his father pumped his hand with vigor and smiled, then stepped aside to allow his mother to greet him. Steele looked into her cool gray eyes, wondering what she felt, and knew the instant she reached out and hugged him. They'd made their peace. He held her tight for a moment, then released her. When she stepped back, she had tears in her eyes. So did he.

Becca squeezed his arm and moved close to him. He guided her to his car waiting at the curb, amid a gauntlet of red rose petals tossed from both edges of the sidewalk. Once he got her stowed comfortably in the passenger seat and slid into the driver's seat, he breathed a sigh of relief. "Thank God that's over with!"

She laughed. "Ditto!"

He leaned over and kissed her. "Thank you."

As he drove them away, the balloons fluttering from his side mirrors and the tin cans rattling from his bumper didn't faze him a bit.

EPILOGUE

*B*ecca opened the oven door and basted the roast, then recovered it and closed the door. When she straightened, she surveyed the sunny kitchen with its chipped white cabinets, not regretting at all that she hadn't had time to do a lot of remodeling. The back hallway got some updated wallpaper, and the living room got a bit of a makeover, but basically everything was the same as the first time she'd stepped foot in the house Steele had inherited from his late aunt and uncle.

Making her way to the kitchen screen door, she wiped her hands on the apron barely spanning her basketball-sized stomach. "Emily, Miriam," she called. "You girls better not be digging in my flower bed!"

She heard giggles and stepped outside. Looking around the back porch, she found her raven-haired twins covered with dirt from head to toe. "Look at you two!" she admonished, stepping off the porch. "Your grandpa's going to be here any minute. Get yourselves in here right now so I can change your clothes. And where is your father? He's supposed to be taking a shower."

She looked aside and saw Steele in grubby jeans and a dirty tee shirt sneaking around the side of the house. As he scooped up his daughters, one in each arm, they squealed like piglets off to market. She laughed. "While you get yourself cleaned up, you might as well hose them down too. Careful, or they'll turn into mud pies. But make it quick. Your dad's going to be here any minute."

Having come straight from cultivating, Steele gave her a dusty kiss on the cheek. "Yes, my love."

As Becca followed the shrieking, giggling entourage through the kitchen, Emily asked, "Is Pawpaw bringing us a widdle brother?"

Steele chuckled. "No, Pawpaw's bringing his new wife to meet us, so we have to get cleaned up. Your mother is holding onto your little brother for a while longer." He shot a look at Becca's stomach and winked, then whirled toward the bathroom with the girls.

Becca sighed and slumped down in the nearest kitchen chair. Twin three-year-olds and a rowdy husband were too much sometimes. She didn't want to think how it would be with a newborn son in the house.

The timer went off, and she rose to check the casserole in the microwave. Just then she heard a car in the gravel drive and hollered, "Forget your shower, Steele. They're here. Dust yourself off and bring your dirty children back in here."

Steele herded Emmy and Mirry back into the kitchen. All three were just as dirty as before. Becca frowned disapprovingly, then motioned everyone toward the living room. "Come on. Let's meet your new grandma. Maybe she won't notice all the dirt."

As soon as Daniel Forrester opened the front door and boomed, "Anybody home?" Em and Mirry tackled him.

Amid his laughing, he scooped up one and then the other. "Don't pick them up," Becca admonished. "They've been playing in my flower bed. They were clean earlier."

He chuckled. "I'm washable."

Déjà vu warmed Becca as she recalled Steele saying the very same thing when her nephews first set eyes – and dirty paws – on him in her parents' back yard. "Well, come on in. Dinner's just about ready."

Daniel put his granddaughters down, then straightened. "Everyone, I'd like to introduce Jannelle, the new Mrs. Forrester. Jannelle, this is my son Steele and his wife Becca. And this little Munchkin on my right is Emily, and the one on my left is Miriam."

The tall slender woman grinned. "How can you tell which one's which?"

"I don't. I just decide who's who, and they answer to

291

whatever I call them."

As everyone laughed, Becca took Jannelle's hand, sizing up her fifties face and dyed brown hair. She was an attractive, well-dressed woman with a friendly twinkle in her eyes. "So pleased to meet you, Jannelle. Did you enjoy St. Thomas?"

"Oh, yes. The weather was fabulous." She beamed at Daniel. "As was the company."

Steele held out his hand, then pulled back with a sheepish grin. "I'm sorry. I just got out of the field and didn't have time to clean up."

She held out her hand anyway. "A farmer's bound to get a dusty every now and then. Like Daniel said, a little dirt never hurt anyone."

Smiling, Steele shook her hand, then faced his father. "You're looking good, old man."

"You would too, son, if you'd take a shower."

They embraced and patted each other on the back. Becca warmed at the sight, happy and relieved that Steele had fully reconciled with his father. Now he even called him 'Dad,' saying he didn't think Charlie Krueger would mind. His uncle had always known Steele loved him like a father.

Steele's heart was big enough to love many people, and Becca was glad he shared that love without reservation or resentment over the past. The past was gone, just a distant memory. The son had found his father, and the son had become a father. He'd traveled full circle – the circle of love – and his heart was finally whole.

~ABOUT THE AUTHOR~

KESSA STRANBERG is a native of Illinois. She holds a regular day job and otherwise entertains herself writing emotionally charged romances.

Characters in her stories usually have a secret past that threatens their lives and keeps them in turmoil. She likes heroes with a dangerous edge, and heroines who are not afraid to tackle any problem.

Kessa is busy working on her next novel and enjoys hearing from readers. Please visit her publisher web site for more information.

www.penumbrapublishing.com